Au

Dear

Diolch yn fawr/ thank you very much for picking up my book, which I'm so excited to be sharing with you. *Is This It?* is the story of Ivy Edwards, our frank, funny and often filthy heroine. It is a novel about big dreams and big love and refusing to settle for a half-lived life.

At the beginning of the novel, Ivy feels like something's missing. She dreams of a better job, a better life, a better Ivy. The story touches upon themes of loneliness and the never ending pressure on women to self-improve, which have never felt more timely.

The novel also explores the power of family and is a celebration of the humour and romance of Welsh people, as well as the importance of making a pros and cons list when it comes to life's biggest decisions. You can find a translation of all the Welsh words and phrases used in *Is This It?* by flipping to the **Glossary** at the end of the book.

This novel means the world to me, and I really hope you enjoy it. I can't wait to hear what you think. If you want to get in touch, you can find me on Instagram @hannahclaretovey.

Cofion gorau/ Best wishes,

Hannah

x

Praise for Hannah Tovey

'Hannah is a **truly gifted comic writer**. Extremely funny, so perceptive and REAL'
Daisy Buchanan, author of *Insatiable*

'I wolfed it down in two days because **I was totally hooked**. Ivy [is] my personal hero and new fictional BFF.'
Helly Acton, author of *The Shelf*

'**I LOVED IT**. It's incredibly relatable, so horribly funny and clever, and just so good in all kinds of ways.'
Lucy Vine, author of *Hot Mess*

'Honest, gritty, surprising and confronting . . . **there's an Ivy in all of us!**'
Laura Jane Williams, author of *Our Stop*

'Tovey hits that sweet spot of **sharp dialogue and authentic characters** that are well-rounded, real, and messy.'
Abigail Mann, author of *The Lonely Fajita*

'**Bloody brilliant**. Grab a copy and some vodka.'
Melanie Blake, author of *The Thunder Girls*

'Raw, unapologetic and **pretty damn relatable**.'
Heat

'Funny, very frank, filthy . . . **will delight fans of Fleabag**'
Yorkshire Times

Working-ish.
Dating-ish.
Adult-ish.

IS THIS IT?

HANNAH TOVEY

PIATKUS

First published in Great Britain in 2021 by Piatkus

1 3 5 7 9 10 8 6 4 2

A CIP catalogue record for this book
is available from the British Library.

ISBN 978-0-349-42471-2

Typeset in Bembo by M Rules
Printed and bound in Great Britain by
Clays Ltd, Elcograf S.p.A.

Papers used by Piatkus are from well-managed forests
and other responsible sources.

Piatkus
An imprint of
Little, Brown Book Group
Carmelite House
50 Victoria Embankment
London EC4Y 0DZ

An Hachette UK Company
www.hachette.co.uk

www.littlebrown.co.uk

To Mami, for everything.

I drank my hot lemon water and sank back into the sofa. There were fireworks going off in my head, and my stomach was hurling abuse at me.

I can't possibly look for a job today, I think. *I should ring a doctor. I might have a severe underlying health condition that requires urgent medical attention. Maybe it's hereditary? Some class of rare genetic disorder?*

Or, maybe, and much more plausibly, I drank too much last night to escape the fact that I have absolutely no idea what I want to do with my life.

I looked over to the kitchen and saw the boxes of Domino's – a cold, stark reminder that I drunk-bought £45 worth of pizza last night. When I woke up this morning, I had stacked the boxes in a neat pile, hoping the art of organisation would make me feel better. Spoiler alert: it didn't. Over my breakfast of pizza, I looked at the receipt. It seems I was swayed by the 3-for-2 offer, which included extra garlic bread and BBQ Big Dip, which was now turned on its side, oozing brown goo onto the kitchen table.

'That's it,' I said, leaping up from the sofa. 'I can't do this any more.'

'You've said this before,' Dilys said.

Dilys was a new acquaintance of mine. The sort of acquaintance that makes you loathe yourself.

'This time is different, Dilys.'

'How?'

'I want a better life. A better job. A better Ivy.' I looked over at the pizza boxes. 'Or at least I want to live like an adult.'

'You don't even have a job, so . . . '

I raised my hand in defiance.

'I'm not listening to you today, Dilys.'

When you're in sixth form, and your guidance counsellor asks you where you see yourself at thirty-two, you wouldn't say unemployed, recently dumped by your fiancé, living in your brother-in-law's sexist uncle's one-bed flat. I try to forget that Mark's uncle is a misogynist, because the rent is cheap and he's never in the country to check up on me, but Dilys likes to remind me that at my age most women wouldn't be living alone – they'd be with their partner, have a stable income, and use fabric softener. Dilys likes to tell me a lot of things, most of which I try to ignore. She is blunt and unsympathetic.

She's also not a real person.

Last week, as I waited to see the hygienist – the true hallmark of being an adult – I read an article in a glossy women's magazine about the importance of naming the voice in your head – the voice that creeps up on you in the middle of the night and tells you that your worst nightmare is about to become reality. According to the article, if we recognise that the voice exists, we can acknowledge that it isn't us, and learn to rise above it. By the colourful language I display every time I speak to Dilys, it's evident that I haven't yet mastered how to rise above her niggling, incessant criticism. But then again, I am my mother's daughter, which means I can be childish, oversensitive, and like to bear a grudge.

I got showered and dressed, checked outside my front door to make sure the coast was clear, and ran downstairs to the communal rubbish bin to get rid of the pizza boxes. Then I went back upstairs and decided to make a pros and cons list.

REASONS WHY I AM A DREAM EMPLOYEE
Creative
Good with people
Have a lot of patience

REASONS WHY THINGS ARE A BIT SHIT
I don't know what I want to be

'This is useless,' said Dilys. 'You're directionless and you've put on at least five pounds. It's not even Christmas yet and look at your back fat.'

'I'm off to Spain soon. At least I'll be tanned.'

'Fuck tanned, you're unemployed.'

Over several cigarettes and a multipack of salt and vinegar McCoy's, it dawned on me that the last time I felt fulfilled at work was over a decade ago, at a summer job at a local school in Bristol, during my university years. The children loved me – we were all fond of penny sweets and toilet humour – and I think I even loved myself.

I saw a slice of salami from the pizza embedded into the carpet and I knew: the time was now. Was I swayed by the long summer holidays? Yes, I like a European jaunt just as much as the next person. But more than that, I wanted to be valued. I wanted to make a difference. I wanted meaning in my life. I wasn't going to win a Nobel Prize, or an Oscar – I'd never fit into a size-zero red-carpet dress anyway – but I was going to do something significant with my life. No, not something significant . . . something out-of-this-world explosive-knock-your-socks-off phenomenal.

I threw my dressing gown on the floor and channelled those gifs you see of Mariah Carey draped in diamonds the size of her face. I got up onto my footstool, fell off my footstool, got up again and threw my hands in the air. I was at Wembley Stadium, playing to a crowd of thousands. I grabbed my microphone (a personalised reusable water bottle) and shouted, 'I am Ivy Edwards, and I have arrived!'

'You're pathetic.'

'Pipe down, Dilys.'

I had to sit down before doing anything else, as prancing around after smoking had made me feel light-headed. Once I recovered from my over-zealous dancing, I googled the school and called the number listed on the website.

'Hi, my name's Ivy. I wonder if you can point me in the right direction? I used to help run your arts workshops. Do you think anyone might be able to speak to me about teaching?'

'Teaching?'

'Yes. I want to become a teacher.'

'I'm afraid we don't have anyone available to speak right now. Can I take your number and ask someone to call you back?'

Nobody called me back. So instead I called every school in London I could get hold of and asked if I could come in and meet with someone – anyone – to pick their brains about routes into teaching. Mr Reid was the first to say yes.

'This is never going to work,' Dilys said.

I put on my best Mariah Carey face and told her to fuck off.

1

Twenty-four wide-eyed children stared at me. It would have been twenty-five, but Nora had put her hand in the toaster and had to be taken to A&E.

Mr Reid clapped his hands.

'Everybody, eyes and ears to me, please. I'd like to introduce you to Miss Edwards. She'll be supporting us in class this week.'

Nobody spoke. I started to chip at my nail polish.

'Come on, everyone!' Mr Reid said. 'That's not the warm welcome we give our visitors.'

'Good morning, Miss Edwards,' they said, in unison.

'Good morning,' I said, 'I'm so excited to be here.'

A hand shot up from the back of the room. It belonged to a small, rotund boy with curly jet-black hair.

'Yes, Max?'

'Why is she here?'

Good question, I thought.

'Well, Max,' Mr Reid said, 'Miss Edwards wants to become a primary school teacher, so she's come here this week to listen and learn from us. I want you all to be on your best behaviour, OK?'

Mr Reid resembled the older brother of my school friend Glyn, who used to sneak me cigarettes and let me listen to

Alanis Morissette on his MP3 player. I thought this boded well for us. I put him at mid-forties, but his outfit made him look much older. He was wearing navy trousers with a matching waistcoat, and a navy and red striped tie. He also wore a waistcoat when he'd taken me on a tour of the school a couple of weeks ago, so waistcoats must be his thing. I made a mental note to get myself a thing.

'Why don't you take a seat?' Mr Reid said.

'Beside the children?'

'Yes, this is an immersive experience. Observe, listen, ask questions.'

I nodded my head, hoping the enthusiasm would conceal my mounting anxiety.

'Don't be afraid to jump right in,' he said.

Mr Reid directed me to the spare seat beside Max. I didn't want to sit next to him – he clearly had it in for me with his aggressive line of questioning at the start of the class – but I was determined to show them that I was flexible, easy-going and approachable. As I found on most recent encounters with members of the opposite sex, I knew Max could sense my fear and desperation for him to love me. I put on a smile and took up the seat next to him. They all giggled as I struggled to fit my adult derrière in the world's smallest chair.

They had a practice sheet in front of them where they had to link the fish to the penguin to equal the number ten. I looked at the paper, baffled. I looked down at my black jeans and saw a small stain from this morning's cereal spillage. Maybe that's why I could smell sour milk. I licked my finger and rubbed it off. I looked up and saw that they were all staring at me.

'Does anyone want any help?' I asked.

'Can you count?' Max said.

I hated Max.

'You sound funny,' another child said.

'What's your name?' I asked him.

'Bum Head.'

'Is that your real name?'

'No, it's Joey.'

I hated Joey.

'I'm from Wales,' I said.

'Whales are fish.'

'They're actually marine mammals.'

'You're a mammal!'

They found this hysterical. I did not.

'No, Wales is a country,' I said. 'Within Great Britain.'

'My daddy says Wales isn't a real country.'

'Your daddy is gravely mistaken.'

'You said gravy!'

Another child pointed to the pin on my dress.

'What's that?'

'It's the national flower of Wales. It was St David's Day recently, and we like to wear this flower to mark the day.'

'Why are you always talking about whales?'

I took a deep breath and focused my attention on the only girl who hadn't laughed at me. She had a perfectly symmetrical bob and neatly cut fringe; she looked like Uma Thurman from *Pulp Fiction*, only without the class A drug habit. She was wearing a colourful beaded bracelet, and I asked her where she got such a pretty piece of jewellery from.

'My boyfriend,' she said.

'Who's your boyfriend?'

'Joey.'

'Wow, that's kind of Joey,' I said, looking at Bum Head.

Unbelievable that a four-year-old gets jewellery when the last thing I got off a man was a failed engagement. Oh no, wait, there was also the UTI.

'Do you have a boyfriend?' she asked.

'No, I don't,' I said.

'Do you have a girlfriend?'

I looked at Mr Reid, who was at the opposite end of the room, helping another child.

'I'm alone right now,' I said. 'It comes down to a variety of factors. I'm using this time to figure out what I want.'

She stared at me and scrunched her nose up.

'How old are you?'

I paused. 'I'm twenty-one.'

'That's old.'

Everyone laughed.

Thank God I didn't tell them my real age.

'Society might tell you that someone of my age should be in a romantic relationship, but we shouldn't listen to such patriarchal expectations. It's toxic.'

I looked up and saw Mr Reid standing by the table next to us. He gave me a curious look and I changed the subject.

'So, does anyone have any pets? A puppy, rabbit, perhaps a small bird?'

One of the boys started crying. He had dinosaur stickers stuck to his jumper, shoes and glasses. His hands were trembling. I reached over to touch them, but he snatched them away.

'What's the matter?' I asked him.

'My hamster died.'

'Oh, I'm so sorry.'

'He was small and old and had hair on his face and was my best friend.'

The hamster sounded very familiar.

'I lost my best friend, too,' I said.

'What was his name?'

'Ivan, Ivan Thomas.'

Again, with the laughter.

'OK then, we can call him Gramps, or Grandad,' I said.
'Why's your best friend old?'
'I have friends my own age – Mia and Dan.'
'I'm bored.'
Brilliant, that's just brilliant.
'Why don't we get back to our numbers?' Mr Reid said.
I didn't realise he was standing behind me. I smiled at him and he turned around and walked to another table. It might have been my overwhelming self-doubt, but he looked at me like I was wasting his time.
I took another deep breath and looked down at the worksheet. I started to give myself a little internal pep talk, but in the time it took me to tell myself to get a grip, a child had drawn all over my new white trainers with a permanent marker. It wasn't the best start to the day, but, as D:Ream taught me, things can only get better.

Despite the shaky start, the next hour was rather enjoyable. I remembered basic arithmetic, and the girls warmed to me when I told them that *Frozen II* was one of the best films I'd ever seen. I'd never seen *Frozen II*, but I was in desperate need of some allies.
Things took a rapid downward turn just before lunch, when Mr Reid left the classroom for an emergency phone call. He asked me three times if I could handle the room for a couple of minutes. I said yes, of course I could.
The speed of it was extraordinary. Within sixty seconds, someone had got out a pair of scissors and was stabbing the desk like Chucky, but with better-conditioned hair. Another child had pulled out the stationery drawer and was hurling the contents across the room – I caught the ruler seconds before it hit a girl in the eye. In the corner of the room was Max, sitting on someone's head. The same child who drew on my

shoe was now drawing on the wall. I begged her to hand the marker over to me. She looked at me with sheer disdain and hurled it across the room in protest. I wanted to hurl her across the room in protest, but we can't always get what we want.

I knew it was important to put on a cheery face and keep the positivity flowing, so that's what I did, but that was before I realised that I had snot all over my hand – and it wasn't my own. I contemplated getting my bag and running out the room. This was my chance to prove I could do this. I was supposed to be a grown up, or at least do a good impression of one. It had to work.

'How did you find your first day?' Mr Reid asked, after the last child had left.

'I'm so sorry about the mess when you came back in. It all happened so fast—'

'The day's not been without its challenges. But the children seemed to enjoy having you here.'

Ah, so that was why they turned into psychopathic killers. It was because they liked me.

'I want to go through your feedback. But first, I must ask you, why do you want to become a primary school teacher?'

I was about to open my mouth when Joey ran back into the classroom; he'd left his hat on the table.

'Miss Edwards?' he said. 'Are you going to be our teacher?'

I looked to Mr Reid for reassurance. He was avoiding eye contact.

'Hopefully I can be someone's teacher one day,' I said. 'I need to go through some training first.'

'Why?'

'Because you can't become a teacher overnight,' I said. 'You need the right skills.'

'Like football skills?'

'No, like patience and listening and an understanding of the pedagogical approaches to early learning and development,' Mr Reid explained.

Joey looked as confused as I was.

'But what about football, Miss? Can you play?'

He really wasn't getting this.

'No, I can't play,' I said, woefully.

'That's a shame, I thought we could be friends.'

'I'd like to be your friend.'

He pondered this for a moment.

'OK,' he said. 'I like the noise you make when you laugh. And your hair is long and the same colour as chocolate, like Mummy's.'

I felt my heart break a little.

'That's very kind,' I said. 'Thank you.'

He ran towards me and hugged my leg.

'See ya, Miss,' he said, running out of the room.

I looked to Mr Reid.

'That question you asked me? That's why.'

2

I was late for dinner. I found Mia in the back of the restaurant wearing a crown. I rolled my eyes and sat down.

'Don't look at me like that,' she said, 'I stole it from the prop cupboard at the theatre. Along with this very chic scarf.'

She dove into her handbag and brought out a hideous fur shawl with a fox tail a mile long.

'It's a bit gauche,' I said.

'Ives, it's been dead for years. This is his moment to shine.'

She tossed the shawl over her shoulders and sat back in the seat. A few people in the restaurant were watching her now, which is generally what happens when we go out. It's not because she gets recognised as an actress; she's just so enigmatic – like some sort of mythical creature that none of us understand but want to be around all the time.

'I can't be late tonight,' I said, 'I'm going to my sister's for lunch tomorrow.'

'What's the big deal? It's only Anna.'

'She's being weird about it.'

'You look worn-out. Was this week that bad?'

'I found myself standing at the front of the classroom, looking out to the room as if I was watching someone set fire to a house.'

'You wanted to know what it was like to work in a real classroom. Well, now you know.'

'I don't know if I'm cut out for this.'

'Of course you are, Ivy. You can do anything.'

'There's a lot more to consider than I thought.'

'Like what?'

'It doesn't matter,' I said.

I didn't want to let on that I had just been told I didn't have the experience or skills to do the training scheme I wanted to do, and my vision of what next year might look like had been shattered by a man who seemed bored with my very existence.

'What was the teacher like?' Mia asked.

'He seemed to warm to me as the week went on, but—'

'Playing hard to get, was he?'

'Did I tell you he dressed like a seventeenth-century aristocrat?'

'He sounds hot.'

'He's not hot. He's, like, fifty.'

'Maybe you should broaden your horizons. You're not having much luck with people your own age, are you?'

'I'm having no more than three medium glasses of wine tonight,' I said.

'I thought we could go out with Dan.'

'No, I can't go "out out".'

'Nobody mentioned "out out".'

'This is you and Dan we're talking about; there's no other form of social occasion.'

Mia sat back in her chair and crossed her arms like a petulant child.

'Would you stop being so boring,' she said. 'You've not even started your teacher training yet.'

'I'm not boring. I'm refocusing. Besides, I need to start saving.'

'Are you back at the museum on Monday?'

'Yup, back to the gift shop.'

I'd applied for the job at the children's museum in the hope that I'd be able to engage with local young people, find out what's important to them. So far all I'd done is sell Jellycat toys and clean broken breadsticks off the floor.

She took my hand from across the table.

'It's a job, Ivy – a means to an end. Remember when I had to dress as a giant avocado to promote that new smoothie place?'

'And what a glorious avocado you were.'

'Come on, a little dance would perk us right up.'

'I don't need perking up. I need sleep.'

She clasped my hand tight. She was like my mother, so beautiful and manipulative – and exasperating.

'Fine, let's go out,' I said. 'But I want to be in bed by midnight.'

'In bed by midnight or in an Uber by midnight?'

'Mia!'

'Calm down. I'll call Dan.'

Dan's an enigma; one minute he's flush with cash, spending five grand on a week in a luxury villa in Ibiza, and the next he's flat-out broke, worrying how he'll make next month's rent. Officially, he works in 'restaurant PR' (which is ironic, because nobody has ever seen him eat), but we don't ask in case it's illegal and, knowing Dan, it probably is.

Later that evening, we met him at a cocktail bar near Angel Tube. He was propped up on a stool with a Martini in hand, wearing a black V-neck T-shirt with a glitter skull emblazoned on the front. He hadn't noticed us, so I walked over and gave him a hug from behind, accidentally spilling his drink.

'Ivy! You little shit. You've wasted eighteen pounds' worth of vodka.'

'Don't lie; I know you only come here because they're two-for-one.'

'I've missed you girls!'

'That T-shirt is loud,' Mia said.

'Mia, you look like you're auditioning for *RuPaul's Drag Race*,' Dan said. 'This is Alexander McQueen, thank you very much.'

'How posh.'

'It's a knock-off from Camden Market,' he said, erupting in his distinctive cackle. 'God, I'm glad to see you both. Alejandro is doing my head in.'

'Why are you still with him?' I asked.

'I've told you this, Ivy. He's very intelligent and has an immaculate penis.'

'Noah also has an immaculate penis,' Mia mused. 'It's so important to choose a life partner with attractive genitals.'

'New dress, Ivy?' Dan asked as we sat down.

'It's one of Anna's. I've stolen all her pre-pregnancy wardrobe.'

'Nice to see you're finally making an effort, even if it is all second-hand.'

'Fuck off. I'm trying.'

'How's the yoga going?' Mia asked me.

'I don't think I'm doing it right.'

'It's not about doing it right,' Mia said. 'It's about connecting with your inner self, achieving a peaceful body and mind – and, most importantly, getting impeccably toned arms like Jennifer Aniston.'

I splayed my arms out. 'What do we think?'

'Perfection.'

I laughed.

'Look at you, transforming your life,' Dan said. 'This time last year, you'd have been doing coke with some stranger in a bathroom, mascara running down your cheeks, lamenting that posh twat Jamie.'

'Shut up and order me a wine, please,' I said.

'Any preference on colour or size?'

'White. Large.'

The barman served me three tequila shots. I necked one before asking him for three double vodka sodas. Mia had dragged us to a karaoke bar, and I was flagging.

A man nudged in next to me. He looked down at the shots, then up at me.

'Long week?' he said.

He was wearing black jeans, but not the skinny sort that all the boys in East London wear. And his shirt didn't look like it came from a charity shop. He'd rolled the sleeves up to his elbows, revealing lovely toned forearms. I've said it before: you can tell a lot about a man from their forearms.

'They're not all for me,' I said. 'My friends are doing karaoke.'

'So are mine. I'm trying to escape.'

I liked his hair. Thick, soft, not too styled.

'Not a lover of karaoke?' I said.

'No, not at all. You?'

'No, especially considering I've just paid twenty pounds to sit in a darkened room and watch my friend sing power ballads for two hours.'

He laughed. A sniffly young man stumbled into us as he made his way to the toilet to do his next line.

'Why is this place full of nineteen-year-olds?' he said to me. 'And why aren't they wearing socks? If you're going to wear proper shoes, wear proper socks.'

'Wow, I've never heard someone be so passionate about socks before.'

He smiled.

'What's your name?'

'Ivy.'

'Hi, I'm Scott.'

He put his hand out to shake mine. Soft hands. Like his hair.

'Nice to meet you, Ivy.'

I liked the way he said my name.

'You have a very sing-song accent,' he said.

I tried to remain calm as I realised he might actually be flirting with me.

'*Diolch yn fawr iwan.*'

'Impressive.'

'That's the only Welsh I know,' I said. 'Well, that and tractor.'

'What's tractor in Welsh?'

'*Tractor.*'

His face creased up and I thought about what it would feel like to kiss him.

'Where are you from in Wales?'

'We live near the Gower. Do you know it?'

'No, but I was conceived in Wales.'

I laughed.

'Sorry,' he said. 'I don't know why I told you that.'

'No, thank you. I like to know where people were conceived.'

His face gave the impression that he was listening to every single word. It was unsettling.

The barman brought my drinks over and Scott ordered four pints.

'What do you do?' he asked.

'I'm a teacher.'

'Ah, my uncle's a teacher.'

'How about you?' I asked, before he had the chance to see right through me.

'I work in advertising.'

'That's cool. Anything I might have seen?'

'Last year's Christmas advert . . . It was with an international female singer who I can't name for legal reasons. There were mint chocolates involved.'

It took me a few seconds before I realised who he was referring to.

'Oh my God, yes! I loved that advert.'

'I'm glad someone did. It cost me my soul.'

'Was it that bad?'

'Yes, Ivy. It was that bad.'

We stood there for a moment. I couldn't think of anything else to say. He had such delicious dimples.

'Sorry, I should let you get back to your friends,' he said.

'Yes, she's probably halfway through the Celine Dion catalogue; I couldn't possibly miss out on the rest.'

He scanned my face.

'You've got a cracking smile, Ivy.'

'Cracking?'

'Yes. What's so funny?'

'Nothing, it's just . . . "cracking" is a very Welsh thing to say.'

'Is it? My gran used to say it all the time.'

'Yeah, my grandad did too.'

'Well, Ivy, it was nice to meet you.'

'You too.'

I walked away feeling better than I'd done in months, which says a lot about recent times.

'Where the fuck have you been?' Dan asked. He was sprawled out on the sofa with Mia beside him, singing along to Bonnie Tyler.

'I was at the bar. There was a man.'

'Oh, a man!'

'He looked a bit like Hugh Grant in the nineties.'

'Did you talk to him?'

'Yes.'

'Did you get his number?'

'No.'

'What the fuck is wrong with you? You haven't had sex since two thousand and one.'

'Take the bull by the china,' Mia said. She had finally stopped singing and was twirling the microphone lead in her hand.

'What?' I said.

'The bull by the china ... it's an expression.'

'Take the bull by the horn is the expression, Mia. Bull in a china shop is something entirely different.'

Mia looked like I'd asked her to explain quantum theory. Journey came on. Dan grabbed my arm and walked me out of the room and back to the bar, where I saw Scott, still waiting for his pints.

'Is that him?' Dan asked.

I nodded.

Dan touched him on the shoulder.

'Scott, is it?'

'Yes.'

'Hi.'

'Hi. You OK?' Scott asked.

'Yes, Ivy here would like to give you her number.'

'Is that right, Ivy?' Scott said.

'I figured it would be good to find out where the rest of your family members were conceived.'

His face broke out in an enormous grin. We locked eyes as he got his phone out and asked me to type my number in.

'Grand, Ivy. I'll text you.'

'Great. Have a good night.'

'You too.'

I was elated. Maybe I would be having sex this decade.

Dan and I sat in the corner of our private karaoke booth as Mia got started on the *Dreamgirls* soundtrack. We'd finished the vodkas and were now on to our second bottle of Prosecco, most of the contents of which were spilt all over the burgundy faux leather sofas.

Dan asked me to lay my head in his lap.

'I want to connect with you, Ivy. Tell me everything.'

'What do you want to know?'

'I want to know about you,' he said, prodding me with his finger. 'What's going on with you?'

I was drunk enough that all my insecurities were bubbling just under the surface, as they always are at 1 a.m. in a karaoke booth.

'What if this is a mistake?' I said.

'What is?'

'Me, trying to be a primary school teacher. What if Dilys is right?'

'Dilys?'

'You know, the voice in my head.'

'She's a fictional construct, you twat.'

'I named her after a girl I knew from school. Did you know Dilys means "genuine" in Welsh? Which is ironic, because the Dilys I knew was a two-faced backstabber who stole my boyfriend in Year Nine.'

I got up to get some more Prosecco, than lay back down in his lap.

'She speaks to me when nobody else is around. It's like she sees into my soul, Daniel.'

'Babe, you're talking about your brain in the third person. That's the fucking issue here, not you changing careers.'

I looked to Mia for consolation, but she was busy gearing herself up for the high note of 'And I Am Telling You I'm Not Going'.

'What if the children hate me,' I said.

'Some of them will.'

'What if the staff hate me.'

'Some of them will. You can be really annoying sometimes.'

Still feeling the high from my first successful flirt in months, I got up from Dan's lap, stood tall, and denounced Dilys.

'I will not let Dilys get to me.'

'Fuck Dilys.'

'I deserve to be happy.'

'You do.'

'Yes, it's taken me thirty-two years to figure out what I want to do with my life. Who fucking cares! I can reinvent myself every bloody year if I want to!'

'You're a warrior, Ivy!' Mia shouted into the microphone. 'Come on, get up here and say it with me.'

Dan and Mia helped me stand up on the sofa. We stood in a line, holding hands.

'Repeat after me,' Mia said, 'you are brave.'

'I am brave.'

'You are powerful.'

'I am powerful.'

'You are a lion.'

I guzzled the last of my Prosecco and put the glass down.

'I'm a fucking lion!'

We jumped up and down on the furnishings, then Dan went to get another round.

I looked at my phone: 1.47 a.m. There was a message from Anna at 11 p.m.: 'Don't be late tomorrow.' I got back up on the sofa with Mia and started singing 'Girls Just Want to Have Fun'.

3

I'd woken up after five hours' sleep to the driest mouth in existence and ketchup smeared all over my pyjamas. After scrambling to get ready, I paid £2 to hire a bike and cycled as fast as I could to Anna's. I almost fell off trying to take my jumper off mid-ride. It's my own fault; Mam always says you should never wear wool on a hangover.

I knocked on the front door. I could hear feet shuffling at the other side of the doorway, alongside some whispers. I knocked again, and someone said 'Shush!', a little too loudly.

'Anna?' I said, knocking even louder this time. 'It's me. Can you let me in, please?'

I waited. Still, no answer.

'Hello? It's hotter than the sun out here! Open the bloody door!'

Suddenly, the door flew open and there was Anna, in a figure-hugging black dress revealing her big, beautiful baby bump.

She dragged me into the hallway.

'You're late.'

'I'm sorry.'

'You're sweating.'

'It's unseasonably hot.'

'This was all Mam's idea, just go along with it.'

'What? Why is Mam here? Is Dad here, too?'

She pushed me through the hall and into the darkened living room.

As I stepped inside, the lights went on, various voices erupted in a bellowing 'SURPRISE!' and there, standing in front of me, was Mam, Dad, and my brother-in-law Mark.

'What's going on?' I asked.

'Darling! Congratulations,' Mam said, running towards me and almost knocking me over.

Mark was shaking his head at me in a manner that conveyed that he, too, had no idea why I was being thrown a surprise party. I looked to Dad for an answer, but he was too busy trying to reset the 'Congratulations' banner, which was falling off the wall.

'This is why I do these things myself, Tony,' Mam said, running over to Dad. 'You didn't put enough on the wall, did you? Why are you being so tight with the Blu Tack?'

Anna handed me a glass of champagne.

'Why are we having champagne?' I asked.

'Mam's idea. There was a special offer in Aldi.'

'Well, this is a genuine surprise,' I said, hugging Mam. 'I didn't know you were coming to stay.'

'We drove up this morning,' Mam said. 'Luckily, I had Graham Norton to keep me company; your father refused to speak to me the entire drive.'

'I didn't refuse to speak to you, Mags. I need a little bit of quiet when I'm driving, that's all.'

He held his arms out and I walked right into them. 'We've missed you girls.'

'I've missed you too but I'm a bit confused – can someone tell me why I'm being thrown a surprise party?'

Mam started to untie my ponytail. I stood stationary as she reached for her comb.

'I thought we could celebrate you getting on to your teacher training thing,' she said.

'I've not sent off my application yet.'

'So, what was this week for? Wasn't that your interview?'

She was tugging at the ponytail on my head.

'Mam, please, stop it. That hurts.'

'If you're going to have your hair up at least make it tidy, *mun*.'

'It wasn't an interview,' I said. 'It was a work experience week to see if I've got what it takes.'

'I'm sure my precious baby lamb was the most popular girl in school.'

'It's not about being popular. It's about being equipped to do the job.'

Mam let go of my hair and started to untangle the balloons. I gave Anna my glass of champagne.

'There's no way I can drink that today,' I said.

I patted her stomach, desperate to feel a kick. I'd been singing noughties pop to her bump for weeks now, and still had nothing in response. It was making me nervous we'd have nothing in common.

'You've really grown this week,' I said.

Her face turned to a scowl. 'Ivy, that's not an ideal thing to say to a pregnant woman.'

'How come Ivy's allowed to touch your belly like that?' Mark asked.

'I'm not going over this again,' Anna said.

'Over what?' I asked.

'Mark and I had a bit of a disagreement yesterday, but I don't want to go into it.'

'OK—'

'Fine, I'll go into it.'

I looked to Mark, whose facial expression had turned to exasperation.

'We were having a drink after work when his colleague started rubbing my belly.'

'She was trying to be nice, Anna,' Mark said.

'She'd already made a comment about me taking a sip – and it was the smallest sip – of Mark's wine,' she said to me.

'Anna, let's not sensationalise,' Mark said, touching her arm.

There was a new vein on her forehead and it was pulsating as she spoke.

'If I want a drink, I can have a drink.'

'It's a classic example of the male patriarchy,' Mam said, pointing at Mark. 'Anna is in control of her body and if she wants a one hundred and twenty-five millilitre glass of Picpoul de Pony, then that's on her.'

'It's Picpoul de Pinet,' Dad said.

'I give up,' Mark said, walking into the kitchen.

'So, I shouldn't have touched your belly?' I asked.

'You're allowed to touch my belly, because you're my sister. Susan from Leeds who I've met three times in the past decade isn't allowed to start rubbing my lower regions, all whilst telling me that I need to watch what I'm eating as I'm already a lot bigger than she was in her second trimester.'

Anna's face was now scarlet red.

'Why does it matter that she's from Leeds?' I asked.

'Ivy!'

'Sorry. Why don't you sit down?'

She sat on the sofa and hoisted her legs up on the armrest.

'Anna, when's the last time your cleaner came over?' Mam asked, picking a sock up from the floor.

'A couple of weeks ago.'

'You need someone to come more often when the baby is born; the house will be a state.'

I watched Anna's vein beat rapidly.

'Ivy,' Dad said, 'why don't you come sit in the garden with me for a minute?'

I did as I was told and followed him outside.

'You're hung-over, aren't you?' he said.

'How did you know?'

'You stink of booze and you're on the verge of tears.'

'I'm sorry.'

'What happened?'

I considered how to tell my father the reality of the situation without him thinking I was a complete failure.

'If you're like me, and you're going into teaching late, you can learn on the job. That's what I thought I could do – train full-time in a school, and earn a salary doing it. But Mr Reid said I don't have the experience.'

'But you're doing work experience now, and what about those summers at the school in Bristol?'

'It's not enough. He said I need to go back to university, for at least part of the course anyway.'

'What's the problem with that?'

'The tuition fees are nine grand. I can't keep working and do the course. I'd have to live off the money Gramps left me.'

'That should be plenty. Don't tell me you've been squandering it on nights out with Mia and Dan?'

'No, but—'

'Ivy, how much of Gramps' money do you have left?'

I told myself last year that I wouldn't be a disappointment to my parents any more. Yet, there we were.

'Just under seventeen thousand.'

'Seventeen! What happened to the rest? That money is for your future, Ivy.'

'Dad, I live in London. I was unemployed for two months.'

He shot daggers at me.

'I know Gramps left me the money to do something with

my life, and I'm sorry I dipped into it without telling you, but I didn't have a choice.'

'You're a grown up, Ivy. You should be able to manage your own finances.'

'I know, and I'm sorry. I want to use Gramps' money to do this teaching course. I know I've had a few second thoughts, but the more I think about it, the more I want to do this. I can make it work.'

'In that case, we're going to sit down and go through your spending. Don't you dare think you can hide anything from me, Ivy. If you're serious about this, then I need you to start taking responsibility.'

'I'm deadly serious about this. And I will, I promise.'

'Don't look so forlorn. Believe in yourself. Focus on the future, not the past. Be the driving force in your life. Stop making excuses.'

'What a splendid bunch of clichés.'

'Who you are is up for grabs, and if you don't decide who that person is soon enough, someone else will decide for you.'

'Who?'

'Your mother, probably.'

He lifted my chin with his fingers so that I was looking directly at him.

'Choosing to do something different with your life is never easy. It takes courage and guts and determination, and I know you've always had those in spades.'

'Stop it, you're going to set me off.'

'That's your own fault for being hung-over and emotional.'

4

I stared at the application form on my laptop – just as I'd done every day for the past seven days since finishing my work placement. There were two questions I could not find the adequate words to answer: why do you want to be a teacher, and why now?

I wanted to say that I was tenacious and imaginative and felt absolute joy at even the smallest connection with a child. But all I could think about was how scared I was – scared that this year would turn out to be another disaster, just like the last.

I looked under my bed to see if I had an emergency stash of cigarettes, but much to my disappointment, there was none. I messaged Anna: 'Are you home? I need to see your face.'

She replied immediately: 'Sitting on the sofa watching *Million Dollar Listings Los Angeles*. Come right over.'

I woke up on 11 March last year blissfully unaware of the new direction my life was going to take. Every day since, there's been this sinking feeling in the pit of my stomach – which isn't ideal, considering it was almost four hundred days ago. Whilst the whole 'working in a gift shop with no romantic prospects' thing doesn't look great for a thirty-two-year-old, outwardly I have the ability to come across as a person who is in control of their life. That afternoon walking to Anna's was no different. I was wearing Gramps' old cricket jumper, which Mia reliably informed me was on-trend, Anna's fancy skinny jeans that she's too pregnant to fit into, and Mia's designer trainers that a love-struck producer had gifted her. My posture had improved because of the yoga, so I looked taller, and leaner, and even though my hair was up, it had that unwashed, messy look that is considered fashionable in Hackney. I like the idea of people thinking I'm someone who has their life in order. Surely that's what adult life is – a series of pretences to make others think we're not totally inept.

We were sitting in Anna's garden and I was gaping at the monstrous courgette growing in the corner.

'He said he'd text,' I said. 'Why hasn't he texted me?'

'Who? The bloke from the bar? Men are very confusing, and often full of shit.'

'It's fine, I'm fine. That courgette is huge.'

'Mark wants to enter them into a competition. Fine is half-dead, darling.'

I handed Anna my phone and directed her to the spreadsheet I'd made.

'Dad and I spent all of last night on the phone trying to figure out how I'm going to get by next year,' I said. 'We did the maths, it's all there.'

She studied the spreadsheet for a few moments.

'A grand a month isn't a lot to live off, Ives – not in London. Most of that will go on rent and bills. You're going to have to be a bit more frugal.'

'I can apply for a bursary and I've got more shifts at the museum.'

'Do you really want to work there until September?'

'Well, no, but I'm helping to plan their summer children's

programme, so at least I won't be stuck behind the till all day, and I'll be around kids all the time.'

'I wish I could help, but with me going on maternity leave and Mark paying for his aunt's care home—'

'Please, it's OK. I need to do this myself.'

She passed my phone back to me. 'I know it seems like an impossible task right now, but all this will be worth it.'

'I hope so. This time last year I almost lost control of my bowels during a trip to Ikea, so this is definitely an improvement.'

Anna held her hand to her mouth but was unable to hide her smirk.

'Can I say something?' she said.

'When have you ever asked for permission to speak?'

'I don't think you would've done this if you were still with Jamie. If anything, he would've discouraged it.'

'And you know what the worst part is?'

'What?'

'I would've listened to him.'

Shortly before Jamie left, we'd been sitting on the bed while I'd moaned about how much I'd hated my job. I'd never cared for it; I'd been a PA at a private bank that nobody had ever heard of, and my boss had spent all day glaring at me whilst nibbling on a single cherry tomato.

'Once we're married, you won't need to worry about work,' Jamie had said. 'Dad's bound to give me a promotion to cover your salary, so you can focus on being a mum.'

'Wow, William Langdon has it all figured out, doesn't he?'

'Don't say it like that; he's doing this for us. Besides, you hate your job – this is win-win.'

There'd been a quiet but relentless whisper inside me that had got louder every time Jamie had recalled conversations with his parents about our future. But I'd been madly in love with him and, everything he'd wanted, I'd thought I wanted too.

Anna got up from her seat, stood behind my chair, and wrapped her arms around me.

'Stop beating yourself up about last year,' she said.

'I'm not.'

'You are. I can read your mind, darling.'

I kissed her cheek and rested my face against hers.

'Where's Mark?' I asked.

'I sent him out. He's so mopey on a hangover, it does my head in.'

'Remember what Gramps used to say about him?'

'He's not worth a sheep's fart on a hangover,' we said, in unison.

We both laughed, and Anna sat back down in her seat.

'And he never lets me watch reality TV,' she said. 'Why did I marry someone who doesn't like reality TV? What sort of life is that?'

'I'm glad he's out. I need to make the most of this before the baby comes along and I never see you again.'

'What's that supposed to mean?'

'I was joking, calm down.'

She brushed her hair away from her face and I saw the bulging vein glower at me.

'Nothing's going to change. I'm not going to become one of those mothers. I'll still be me.'

'OK, if you say so.'

'Ivy!'

'OK, OK. Nothing's going to change.'

The vein quietened down, and she asked if I wanted to stay for dinner.

'You're sure Mark won't mind me crashing again?' I said.

'Mark came home at three this morning and passed out on

the toilet with a bag of Doritos in his lap, so Mark has no say in the matter.'

'He's getting it all out before the baby comes.'

'I'm so jealous. I'd love to get pissed with you tonight.'

'Dad says I'm not allowed to go out boozing until I get accepted onto the course.'

She began to laugh.

'I'm so glad you find my situation amusing,' I said.

'I do love you, darling.'

'I know. I love you too.'

When I got home that night, I opened the drawer in my bedside table, to the box of photos, keepsakes and memories. I took out the letter and imagined him reading it to me in his distinctive baritone voice, a tone that almost every elderly Welshman possesses.

Babes,

I can't believe today's the day, and you're off to Bristol University. I couldn't be prouder of you, mun. *I'll put this in your sketch book because I knew if I said this to your face, you'd get all upset, then you'd get me all upset, and you know what I'm like when I get started.*

I thought I'd make you a bit of a list, to keep you in check, like. Here goes:

1. *Be kind to yourself – sometimes you can be a right* twmffat
2. *Keep drawing – even if it's only little doodles to send home to me*
3. *Don't spend all your money on fags (yes, I know you smoke)*
4. *Stop spending all your time watching* Friends. *It's gobshite*
5. *Ring your mother*

6. *Enunciate your words. You always lose your r's. It makes you sound dead* twp
7. *Say hello to everyone on your first day*
8. *Don't forget your roots. I asked Mammy to put my Welsh grammar book in your suitcase for you. I know everyone in Bristol is dead posh like, but for the love of Christ don't come back with an accent*
9. *Don't stay out till God knows what time in the morning*
10. *Never miss a deadline.*

Right, I've waffled on enough. Owen's at the door and I'm late for cricket. I'm umpiring the U18's again today. Little shits need to get their act together. Remind me to tell you about Owen's grandson – now there's a boy and a half!

What I wanted to say is: BE BRAVE, Ivy. I know this will be brilliant, because you're brilliant. Don't stop believing in yourself, OK? And don't forget about your old Gramps. I'll be counting down the days till you're next home and we can watch Sleepless in Seattle *together. Don't bring that popcorn over next time. You eat like a heathen and I keep finding sodding kernels everywhere.*

I love you with all my heart.

Gramps xxx

It was the first time since Gramps' death that I'd been able to finish reading the letter. Usually, I would get to the part where he said he was proud of me, and I'd be so overwhelmed that I'd have to stop.

I put the letter away, opened my laptop to the blank application form, and started typing. For the first time in a long time, my head was clear, and I knew what I had to say.

5

I rang Mam on the way to the interview, a decision I will regret until the day I die.

'Are you prepared?' she asked.

'No, I didn't think I'd need to prepare anything for a five-hour interview, so I went out clubbing last night.'

'Christ alive, *mun*.'

I smiled; she sounded just like Gramps.

'Of course I'm prepared,' I said. 'I've been planning this for weeks.'

'You've not been smoking today, have you?'

'No, I told you, I'm trying to give up.'

'What are you wearing?'

'I guess you'd call it a smock dress.'

'Your figure doesn't suit a smock.'

'What do you mean "figure"? I'm a size ten.'

'Did you moisturise this morning? You get dry skin in spring.'

'Yes, I moisturised.'

'What about your hair?'

'I blow-dried it last night.'

'And the poem?'

'I'm going to do an extract from *The Giraffe and the Pelly and Me*.'

'*Joio*. Everyone loves Roald Dahl – and he's Welsh. It's important to show your roots.'

'Anything else, Mam?'

'Why are you using that tone with me, darling?'

'Because I've got a potentially life-changing day ahead of me and you're focusing on my hair.'

'I asked you one question! Why do you have to jump down my throat all the time?'

'Me jump down your throat? You jump down my throat.'

'You're under a lot of pressure so I won't take that personally.'

'I need to go, I'm almost at the gates.'

'Hang on a minute, darling. Listen, they're not expecting you to be a fully formed teacher today. So just go in there and show them your passion, your drive and your sparkling personality, and they will love you. When you are yourself, truly yourself, you shine.'

'Thank you, Mam. Why couldn't you lead with that?'

'It's good to keep you on your toes.'

'I'll ring you later.'

'*Pob lwc*! Go forth and soar, darling.'

I had chosen to interview for the split course back at Clerkenwell Primary, with Mr Reid. There was a place for a first-year trainee in his Reception class and I was going to prove to everyone that I was deserving of it. Yes, I would often break down when a four-year-old made fun of me, and at times I could be scatty and disorganised, but I had developed exceptional asset control when it came to crayon usage. Not to mention having a clean driving licence. I was born to do this.

'You're wasting everyone's time,' Dilys said. 'You might as well go back home and eat boiled eggs for the rest of your life.'

'I only ate boiled eggs last week because I was waiting for pay day.'

'International summits take less time than it took you to decide what to wear this morning, and you still got it wrong.'

I looked down at my dress and wondered whether Mam – and Dilys – were right.

'I'm shutting you off now, Dilys,' I said, stamping my foot on the pavement. 'I can do this.'

'You can't.'

When someone tells you that you can't do something, you go out there and you do everything you can to prove them wrong. I held my head high and walked through the playground – past the snakes and ladders, hopscotch and noughts and crosses – towards the entrance of the school. Mary, the receptionist, was standing by the door, waving her arms high above her. She reminded me of my own primary school receptionist, although Mary's skin wasn't so leathery – probably because she didn't spend every weekend sunbathing starkers on Oxwich Bay.

'I can't believe it's been five weeks,' Mary said. 'How are you?'

'Raring to go. I've stocked up on snacks and I've got two litres of water to keep me hydrated.'

'What sort of snacks?'

'Mixed nuts, apple slices with peanut butter, carrot sticks—'

'Very healthy, Ivy. I'm impressed.'

'There's also a family-size pack of Haribo in there if things start to get ropey.'

She laughed. 'They're not going to get ropey.'

'I know, but I feel safe knowing they're there.'

'Try not to think of it as a day-long interview, but a series of activities.'

I visualised myself and Gramps on a beach, drawing together. Drawing and painting are the only activities I've ever done. I don't think clubbing counts.

'It's a good thing you already know Mr Reid,' she said. 'It'll be nice to have a familiar face in there.'

I wanted to respond but all I could think about was my increasingly sweaty under-boob. I put my hand behind my back and lifted my bra to let some air in.

'You've got to have a thick skin to be a teacher, you know,' Mary said.

'Don't you worry about me, Mary. I'm like a Rhino. Thickest skin in all the land.'

'I knew I liked you. Right then, let's get you into that interview room.'

She told me to walk down the corridor, past the assembly hall and into Room 103, where Mr Reid would be waiting for me.

I peeped into the assembly hall on my way to the interview room; it was my favourite room in the school. Every child had contributed to a piece of art on the walls. There were so many colours and textures, and right in the middle was a massive turtle made from plastic bottles, with 'TOGETHER, WE CAN SAVE THE PLANET' written in huge letters above. I've always admired turtles; I like the way that they can retreat into their shell to get away from the world. What a glorious skill to have.

I stood in the middle of the room and began to picture myself as a real teacher, addressing my class. I started to get heart palpitations as I heard someone call my name. I turned around and saw Mr Reid.

I walked towards him and he put his hand out to shake mine.

'Ivy,' he said.

He had greying stubble on his chin and dark circles under his eyes. He looked just like I felt. Luckily for me, however, Mia's new friend Patricia – a Professional Spell Caster and Experienced Spiritual Healer who she'd met at an actor's workshop – had made me a cleansing mask to bring good luck, prosperity and a dewy glow that you typically only find on pregnant people.

'We'll start with the interview first,' Mr Reid said, 'and then move on to the maths and English tests. After that we'll have a break before your presentation to the class, OK?'

'Excellent, I'm looking forward to it,' I said, doing my utmost to look like a person who knew what they were doing.

He led me into the interview room. There were four people sitting behind a long rectangular table at the back of the room, talking in hushed voices. As I entered the room, they turned towards me and smiled. I was expecting this number of panellists but seeing them there in front of me made my heart rate shoot up a notch. I looked to Mr Reid for assurance, but as usual he gave nothing away. As I approached the desk, I took a long deep breath through my nose, then exhaled all the air out through my mouth, just like Patricia had advised.

'Great to meet you, Ivy,' the one on the left said. I moved towards him, and, for reasons I'll never understand, I leant into his face, and kissed him on the cheek. Then I moved towards his other cheek, and planted a kiss on him there, too.

I didn't know where to look or what to do. I had another three people to greet. I moved to the woman beside him. She reached her hand out and I did the only thing I could do, and I went in for two kisses. I did the same to the third interviewer, and then the fourth. After I'd finished kissing everyone, I stood at the end of the desk and tried to smile. I felt my lips quiver and curl upwards, in a move that I can only imagine made me look like a complete sociopath. I'd fallen victim to this social tradition many times before, but never in an interview setting. I thought about the turtle and wished I had my own shell to retreat into.

'Well, how very European,' the woman said, after an awkward moment's silence.

'I've just come back from Spain,' I blurted out.

I went with Mam and Anna for two weeks back in December, so this wasn't strictly true.

'Where did you go?' the woman asked, as she motioned for me to sit down.

'We started off in Seville,' I said, taking my seat in front of the desk. 'I wanted to see the flamenco dancers and Gothic architecture. I thought it would inspire me.'

'Inspire you?'

'Yes – to paint. Sorry. I didn't make that clear. I like to paint. I used to do it all the time, mainly for my grandfather. I'm trying to pick it back up again.'

'Did you do much painting on your trip?' they asked.

'It's a funny story, actually. I envisioned myself walking around with my apron and sun umbrella, but my mother likes us to do everything together, so I didn't get much free time.'

Nobody spoke. I didn't know whether to finish the story, but I hadn't given myself any other choice, so I carried on.

'When we got to Cadiz, I took myself off to Playa de la Caleta, in the old town. Have you been?'

One of them nodded. 'We took our daughter there when she turned eighteen,' they said.

'It was so charming, sitting there on the water front, eating fried fish. I felt very Julia Roberts.'

Nobody seemed to get the reference.

'You know like in *Eat, Pray, Love*? It's a film, based on a book. Anyway ... I was hoping to paint, but after about an hour or so, my mother found me. She'd found out that this was where Halle Berry emerged from the sea in *Die Another Day* and insisted we re-enact it, film it, and send the video to my father.'

One of the interviewers snorted.

'She stripped down to her swimsuit and everything. The locals were perplexed . . . It was the highlight of the holiday.'

They were all smiling now, even Mr Reid, and for the first time in weeks – and without the aid of a vodka soda – I felt myself relax, if only a little. They were normal people and I was a normal person, trying to achieve something with her life.

I thought about what Mam had said about showing my creativity and confidence, and for the rest of the day that's what I did. That's all I could do: prepare, show up, be myself. If that wasn't good enough then so be it, but at least I would've given it my best shot.

6

After pricing endless boxes of knitted animals for eight hours, I finished at the gift shop and walked to Anna's. I'd asked for all the extra shifts at the museum, so I was practically living there at this point, and when I wasn't, I was at home, eating budget food, checking my phone every minute to see if Mr Reid had called, or emailed, to let me know the outcome of the interview. But five days had passed, and I hadn't heard a peep from him.

I handed Anna the prune juice I'd picked up for her and sat down beside her on the sofa.

'Thank God,' she said, swigging from the bottle. 'You wouldn't believe how constipated I am.'

Mark came out of the kitchen. 'As you can see, romance is alive and well.'

'Mark's not seen my vagina for weeks,' Anna said. 'To be fair, I've not seen my vagina in weeks. I look like a bleached whale.'

'You mean beached?'

'For fuck's sake, why doesn't my brain work any more.'

She looked me up and down. 'How come you look so good today?'

'Mam sent me twenty quid, so I bought this dress in the ASOS sale. I saw Gemma Arterton wear something similar.'

'You do have a Gemma Arterton vibe about you today.'

'That's the nicest thing you've ever said to me.'

She took her bra off under her T-shirt and flung it at me. 'Ah, that's better.'

'You look like you're in pain.'

'That would be the gas, the bloating, and the constant ache around my pelvis.'

'But everything's fine, isn't it? With the baby, I mean.'

'Yes, darling, don't worry. I just need work to ease up a bit.'

'You need to take a step back, Anna. This is more important than work.'

'You don't know what law firms are like. There's always some middle-aged posh white bloke eyeing up your job. I need to win this case.'

Anna is a chronic overachiever. Pregnancy has forced her to slow down, but not without a good fight. She must do everything herself, and it must be perfect. You can imagine how fun it was growing up with her. She was like Veruca Salt, but without the heiress bit.

'I long for the day when I can lie on the sofa in my pants and eat canned mackerel,' she said.

'Canned mackerel?'

'The ones in sunflower oil, with shedloads of hot sauce.' She licked her lips. 'I can't tell you how moreish it is.'

'I'll take your word for it.'

'I've got to see the next three months out, then the baby will be here, and I'll be relaxed.'

'Yeah, having a newborn in the house does sound relaxing.'

She lay down on the sofa and put her feet up on me. 'How are you? Any news?'

'No. It's been over a month and he hasn't messaged.'

'What are you on about?'

'The boy – Scott.'

'I meant your interview, you tit.'

'Oh, sorry. No news.'

'Don't look so panicked. It's only been a few days.'

She flicked through the channels until we saw *Desperate Housewives of Atlanta.*

'Quick, put it on before Mark comes in,' Anna said.

I watched her get comfortable on the sofa and felt an overwhelming surge of love towards her. I knew how hard it had been for Mark and her to get to this point, and it didn't matter how many times she told me not to worry, I always worried. I wanted to create a protective shield around her stomach and never let anyone other than the world's finest obstetrician go within an inch of her.

'Stop gawking at me,' she said.

'I was thinking about what to do with Mam and Dad this weekend.'

'Shit, I almost forgot about that. Is it too late to cancel?'

'Be nice. They're not even staying here.'

'Never again, Ivy. Never. Again.'

The day after my surprise party, Mam went to John Lewis unsupervised and bought six cushions for Anna and Mark's bedroom. She said she didn't understand how anyone could sleep without at least one decorative cushion on their bed. She rearranged all the artwork in the living room and put up several framed photos of herself around the house. She then sacked Anna's cleaner because she wasn't doing a good enough job and conducted several rounds of interviews for the replacement before calling the original cleaner to admit she acted a bit hastily. Mark almost had a nervous breakdown and so it was agreed that, next time, Mam and Dad would stay in a hotel.

'I'll take them out for lunch tomorrow, just the three of us.'

'Thank you, Ivy. I just need one moment's peace. Mam's been all over me like a rash.'

'Makes a change to being all over me like a rash.'

'Can your life go balls up again, please, so the attention can go back on you?'

'It will at some point, don't worry.'

'Don't be sarcastic.'

I wasn't.

The next day, I met Mam and Dad at a new tapas place in Highbury, not far from their hotel.

'How long do we have you for?' Mam asked, as we browsed the menu.

'We have ages. I'm not meeting Mia till much later.'

'How long is "ages"?'

I put my arm around her and kissed her cheek. 'You're being overbearing. Stop it.'

She picked up the drinks menu and winked at me. 'I want to be sure we have enough time for a little afternoon sesh.'

Mam made disgruntled noises like she often does in restaurants when one of the words on the menu isn't in English.

'Why don't you get out your phone and use the translator app?' I said. 'The one I downloaded for you to use in Spain?'

'Don't you need 3G for that?' she asked.

'No, we had to use Wi-Fi when we were in Spain, but that's only so the app wouldn't drain your data.'

'Drain my data? Speak English, *mun*?'

'Why don't you just order for us, eh, Ives?' Dad said.

The waiter came over and Mam argued with him over how many plates were acceptable for three people. Despite the endless tutorials we gave her on holiday, Mam can't grasp the concept of tapas.

'I had a long chat with Mia yesterday,' she said, once the waiter had taken our order. 'She's teaching me how to use Instagram and I'm teaching her how to clean diamonds. I told her she should use an old, soft bristled toothbrush. No need to pay for one of those fancy cleaning cloths.'

'What are you on about?'

'You and I both know that Noah is dragging his feet. Jamie proposed to you in no time at all.'

'And look how well that turned out.'

'It's been on her mind, that's all.'

'What has? Getting engaged?'

'I'm an excellent reader between the lines.'

'How long did it take you to propose?' I asked Dad.

'Your father took ages, *mun*,' Mam said.

'Margaret, that's rubbish and you know it,' he said. 'I knew your mother from when we were teenagers. But she was three years below me and you just didn't mix with people who weren't in your class.'

'Or school!' Mam said. 'Your father likes to forget that I went to the posh grammar school whilst he was stuck in the local comp.'

'You love bringing that up, don't you?' Dad said.

'Tell Ivy how long it took you to propose.'

'Six months and four days,' he said, without missing a beat.

They looked at each other and smiled. I saw Dad's hand move to take hers under the table. How is it that I have the perfect model of a relationship right in front of me, but I can't even get a man to send me a text?

'If I got engaged after six months, you'd have something to say about it,' I said.

'Please don't say you're engaged again?' Mam said. 'Is this why you wanted to take us for lunch? You're getting married?'

'I've never been further from getting married.'

'Just make sure he's Welsh next time,' Mam said.

'It's difficult to meet a Welshman in London.'

'Fine, but at least date a Celt.'

'I'd be very happy to, but the right person hasn't come along yet.'

'Maybe Ivy's not ready,' Dad said.

'Ready? Jamie left her over a year ago!'

'It was only last November that we almost got back together. I'm doing the best I can with what I've got.'

'I know you are, darling. I think you could try harder, that's all.'

The waiter came over and asked if we were ready for our wine.

'Yes!' I said, a little too loudly.

After enduring a tense discussion between Mam and the waiter over how to pronounce Rioja, Dad asked me how I was feeling about the interview.

'I keep flitting between fierce optimism and absolute dread,' I said.

'And today?'

'Absolute dread.'

'Ivy . . . '

'It was a joke, Dad. I just wish they'd ring me. I hate the not-knowing part.'

'You're taking a great big leap of faith with this teaching thing,' Mam said, stuffing a cheese croquette into her mouth.

Mam loved calling it a 'thing', like it was a phase I was going through. I had spent months trying to prove to her it was much more than this. She even found me in the garden once, standing in superwoman pose, shouting 'I AM TEACHER. I AM WARRIOR' into the night. It was Dad's idea; we'd had a few too many Tia Marias and he thought it would soothe my nerves.

'We want you to know that, whatever happens, we're proud of you,' she said.

'I'm going to give this everything I've got.'

'We know that. Focus on being the best you can be, Ivy. No distractions.'

'We want you to be happy,' Dad said.

'Me too,' I said.

A week later, I got accepted as a first-year teacher trainee at Clerkenwell Primary. I'd spend two-thirds of the year training on the job in Mr Reid's class, and the rest at university.

I rang Mam straight away to tell her. She put me on loud speaker, so that I could repeat the good news to Dad. We cried and cheered; Mam popped the champagne, Dad moaned that all Mam does is pop champagne and Mam argued that it was Asda's own brand, which doesn't count.

They told me how proud they were of me, and how proud I should be of myself.

I said I was, because for the first time in a long time, I truly, genuinely was.

7

I met Mia at a cocktail bar in Fitzrovia. She wanted to take me somewhere fancy to celebrate. I was told to dress up for the occasion, but I couldn't afford to buy anything new, so I raided Anna's wardrobe and borrowed an emerald green velvet trouser suit with a lace top. I wanted to be sexy, but not OTT. Mia on the other hand only does OTT. She arrived wearing a long dusty-pink satin slip, with very thin, delicate straps, over which she wore a full-length cape, covered in gold sequins. She said she woke up feeling like Ariel from *The Little Mermaid*, so naturally this was the outfit choice she went with.

'You're showing me right up,' I said. 'You look incredible.'

'I need to feel strong and empowered for this new role.'

'You know Ariel gave up her voice for a man?'

'Oh, shit, you're right. Forget Ariel. Give me Jennifer Aniston, or Chrissy Teigen.'

'Do you think you talk about Jennifer Aniston too much?'

She took a sip of her Negroni and stared at my chest.

'I'd love boobs like yours,' she said. 'They bounce a little whenever you move. I like watching them.'

I laughed. 'Thank you, Mia.'

'And for someone who doesn't care about their appearance, you always end up looking killer hot.'

'I care about my appearance; I just can't afford to do anything about it.'

'You don't need to do anything about it . . . you're perfect.'

I watched as she stirred the ice around the glass with her finger. When she got bored of this, she started to twirl large parts of her hair around her fingers, before putting thick strands in her mouth, like I saw the children do at school.

'Mia, can you stop eating your hair, please?'

She looked around the room before lowering her voice to a whisper.

'I have to tell you something, but you must promise not to judge.'

'I'll try.'

'Promise!'

'OK, OK, I promise.'

'Last week, I walked through Hatton Garden. You know, where all the diamonds are.'

I looked at her, baffled.

'Noah asked me how my day was, and I couldn't tell him I'd been looking at rings all afternoon, so I had to make something up.'

'Why were you shopping for rings? Does my mother have something to do with this?'

'I wasn't shopping for rings, I was looking at them. Haven't you ever gone into a jeweller's and tried on something outrageously expensive?'

'No.'

'You're judging, and you said you wouldn't judge.'

'Sorry, carry on.'

'I told Noah I'd gone there for research. I said that my agent had sent me a script for a new BBC drama, based on the heist.'

I shook my head, not knowing what on earth she was on about.

'You know, the one in two thousand and fifteen? They stole

all the diamonds. They're meant to be turning it into a film, or something.'

'And you're auditioning?'

'No. Well, yes. I told Noah I was, anyway. I said I was reading for the role of doting wife number two. I'm amazed he didn't clock on. Obviously, if this were happening for real, I'd be up for doting wife number one.'

'You do realise this is far worse than if you'd have just been honest with him about where you were that afternoon?'

'I know! And now I have to pretend I went to this sodding audition.'

'No! Say it was cancelled.'

'Yes, you're right. That's much better.'

'Honestly, Mia.'

'Stop it, I know what you're thinking.'

'You can't start obsessing about this. You've been together for five years, you're Mia and Noah. People should write sonnets about you.'

'I need a project.'

'You're about to start performing in the West End.'

'I know!'

She put her head to her knees. I moved closer and put my arm around her. She raised her head dramatically then shook her whole body, as if she were trying to get rid of every irrational bone in her.

'I'm over it,' she said.

'Are you?'

'I'll probably bring it up in five drinks' time, but for now, I'm over it.'

Mia started playing with the ice again. I moved her hand away from the glass.

'Sorry,' she said. 'Tonight's about you. Tell me everything, you angel goddess.'

'There's not much to tell. The most exciting thing in my life right now is that I get discounted sandwiches at the museum café.'

'It's going to be mad in there over summer with all the children off school.'

'I'm about to venture into a classroom of twenty-five four-year-olds. I need all the help I can get.'

We finished our cocktails and walked to a French bistro that an actor friend of Mia's had recommended. I was glad she was paying; whenever her actor friends recommend anything it always ends up costing me a fortune, and now more than ever I needed a cheap night out. Mia lives rent-free in Noah's dead auntie's house, but I don't know how the rest of them have so much disposable income. They spend most of their time in second-rate private members' clubs pretending to be on their laptops whilst secretly looking out the corner of their eye trying to spot actual celebrities.

Mia ordered in perfect French, flirting with the waiter the entire time.

'Stop making that face and get your phone out,' she said, when he'd taken our order. 'We need to get started on Serendipity.'

'What's "Serendipity"?'

'The dating app.'

'Is that its actual name?'

'Yes. Why's that funny?'

'It's idiotic. The whole purpose of the app is, by its very definition, the exact opposite of the meaning of serendipity.'

Mia looked mystified.

'This will be my new little project,' she said, beaming.

'I don't want to set up my profile now,' I said. 'Can we enjoy our dinner, please?'

'I've got to at least take some photos. This place has superb lighting.'

The waiter came over and poured us both a glass of wine. He helped Mia move the objects around the table as she tried to get the aesthetics right.

'Stop moving the cutlery about,' I said. 'I don't want to do a photo shoot in here.'

'It's hardly a photoshoot, Ives. Now, look to your left, out the window, and hold the wine glass in your right hand . . . '

I picked up the wine glass.

'A bit lower, so it's not covering your face. They need to see your face.'

I did as I was told and Mia took a few photos, directing me to lift my chin up a little, smile a bit more, then a bit less.

I took the phone off her to look at the photos – they weren't half as bad as I'd imagined. I'd spent the day in the park and the sun had brought out my freckles. Plus, I'd managed to get through my last period without a single spot. Life was on the up.

'Now . . . ' she said, taking the phone back off me, 'if it's OK with you, I want to use this one, with you by the sea.'

There was a photo of me in a swimsuit, in Spain. I was sitting by the waterfront, reading a book about teaching and neuroscience. I'd not told Anna or Mam at that point that I was thinking of applying to be a teacher, and whenever I could, I would sneak off and try to read bits of the book in secret. Then, I'd get so stressed about all the work ahead of me that I'd find the nearest bar and down a thousand Aperols. Maybe someday I won't self-medicate with alcohol. No, let's not get too carried away.

'Yes, I like this one,' I said, looking at the photo. 'I'm having a good hair day.'

'I knew I would project manage the shit out of this.'

'I'm not sure about going on an app, Mia.'

'Why not?'

I drank my drink in silence.

'You're still thinking about that boy, aren't you?' she said.

Considering I'd met Scott once, six weeks ago, I'm well aware of how pathetic this sounds, but the truth is that I'd thought about him a lot. I thought about what our first kiss would be like – would he be the sort of person to grab me by the waist and pull me in close to him, or would he take his time, ease into it? I thought about the glint in his eye and the way his chest moved when he spoke, but mainly I thought about whether I'd made the entire interaction up. What if I suffocated him with my tedious chat and he was just doing the courteous thing of staying at the bar with me because nobody else was there to keep me company? Maybe he was some sort of community key worker, or a Samaritan, patrolling North London bars, finding lonely thirty-something women to speak to, to make them feel better about their sorrowful, empty lives?

'I don't get it,' I said to Mia. 'You make a real connection with someone, they take your number and then they ghost you. What's the point?'

'Look, there's no logic when it comes to men. But luckily, there is logic when it comes to Serendipity.'

She showed me a photo of an excel spreadsheet on her phone. There were numbers beside words like 'athleisure' and 'on the razz'.

'What is this?' I asked.

'A girl in my theatre group devised an algorithm to track the success of your profile photos. She knows exactly which ones get the most likes.'

'Jesus Christ.'

'It works a treat for her. She's shagging blokes left right and centre.'

'I want something more meaningful.'

'According to this data, we'll need one of you in your

running gear – which we'll do tomorrow – and then one of you out on the piss – which we can do tonight.'

'Is this necessary?'

'Do you want to have sex or not?'

'Lower your voice, Mia.'

'Well?!'

'Yes, of course I do.'

'Then buck up your attitude.'

8

Mia was in one of her phases where she only watched content with Meryl Streep in it, so the next morning we *cwtched* up in bed with *The Bridges of Madison County*, lathered ourselves in a hydrating seaweed cleansing mask and wept for several hours, before getting ready for our photoshoot.

'We must act now,' she said, getting out of bed. 'I'm worried that in an hour or so your hangover will kick in and then your skin will start to sag.'

Her phone rang. It was Noah. She put him on FaceTime.

'Hi, darling,' she said, 'I'm about to do the photoshoot with Ives. Can I ring you later?'

'Why are you doing a photo shoot?' he asked.

'Do you think I had any say in this?' I said, from the bed.

Mia handed me the phone and started rummaging through my wardrobe.

'She's setting me up on a dating app. I need a snog, Noah.'

He laughed. 'You don't need a photoshoot, Ives. You're perfect as you are.'

'Have you two rehearsed this?' I said.

'Tell Mia she's got to be home by four; she promised to help me with my lines for tomorrow's audition.'

'I won't be back late,' Mia said.

'Yes, but will you be back sober?' Noah asked.

'We're not drinking today,' I told him.

'What?' Mia said. 'It's Sunday. Not even a cheeky Prosecco?'

'Good luck, Ives,' Noah said. 'You'll need it.'

I gave Mia the phone back.

'See you later, darling. Love you.'

I watched as Mia blew him kisses and he told her he loved her. I looked down at my shirt and realised it was Mark's. I was wearing my sister's husband's grotty T-shirt, I hadn't been on a first date in four years, and I was about to go pose for photos for my new dating profile. Dilys was about to say something, but luckily Mia's foghorn voice drowned her out.

'Where are all your workout clothes?' Mia asked.

'Those are my workout clothes,' I said, pointing to a pile of greying vests. 'I'm not spending money on stuff I'm only going to sweat in.'

'What about when you're transitioning from yoga to brunch?'

'When have you ever seen me transition from yoga to brunch?'

'Right, this will do,' she said, throwing me an Adidas vest. 'The white will serve the tan better.'

We walked along the canal to Hackney Marshes. I refused to have the photoshoot too close to home, to avoid the risk of bumping into people I know, and Mia thought the marshes would make me look like a 'proper' runner. I jogged past Mia several times as she clicked away on her iPhone, but after the third attempt I told her my soul was dying and it was time to go home. She tried to force me into doing a tree pose because she said it would elongate my waist, but I snatched the phone off her and told her I was leaving.

On the walk back to mine, she added filters, cropped some edges and adjusted the lighting, and, voila, we were ready to go.

Back home, I downloaded the app and created a profile. Mia said a bonus photo of me and my family would give me a 'softer edge', so I scrolled through my photos to see what others I could add. There was one of me and Anna, but Anna was really tanned, and Mia said that you should only include other people in your photos if they looked less attractive than you, so I went back to the drawing board. I decided on a photo of Mam and me, on the beach. It was just after the Halle Berry incident in Spain, and we were both bent over in hysterics. Mam had insisted Anna take all photographs of her from a lower angle, so that her legs appeared longer. As infuriating as it was having to retake every photo 120 times, she had a point – our legs looked sensational.

It was the 'say something about yourself' part of the profile that I found most difficult. It's terribly un-British to write complimentary things about oneself. I needed to come across as fun, but not someone whose only hobby is getting pissed. I wanted to appear cultural, but not too up myself. Also, what was I looking for, and what if I got bombarded with pictures of flaccid penises? In the end I went for: 'Welsh girl in London; teacher-trainee. Can draw a cracking stick figure.' It only took me four hours.

The next morning at the museum, as I was sorting through a pile of Julia Donaldson books, I noticed an elderly gentleman hovering outside the disabled toilets, holding a bright yellow children's rain jacket. When I was little, I had a Minnie Mouse poncho that I used to wear when I went down to the beach with Gramps. It had ears on the hood and deep pockets for all my Pick & Mix sweets. I don't buy anything without pockets any more. As Mia says, it's a feminist issue.

A little girl came out of the toilet.

'I'm done, Grandad,' she said, pulling on her cardigan. She had flame-red hair, with a red bow clip in it.

'Well done, Nancy,' he said, taking her hand and walking towards the gift shop.

'Good morning,' Nancy said, as she appeared beside the till.

'Good morning. I like your rain coat.'

'It's yellow.'

'Is yellow your favourite colour?'

'No, red is. But Mummy couldn't find a red one.'

Her grandad smiled at me and I felt an ache in my chest.

'Are you running storytime today?' he asked.

'Yes, I'll be doing it at twelve. Are you joining us?'

'I like the snail one,' Nancy said.

'Me too, it's one of my favourites,' I said.

'And I like bears and cats and penguins.'

'Have you read the one with the bear and the piano?'

She jumped up and down with excitement.

'I bought it for her last week,' her grandfather said. 'She requests it every bedtime.'

Nancy tugged at her grandad's hand and they walked off.

As I watched them go, I momentarily thought about calling Gramps, before going back to sorting the bookshelf.

At 11.45 a.m. I went into the story room. There's a whopping steel beam in the middle of the room that they've turned into a tree and hanging from all the branches are quotes from various children's books. There were a dozen or so children waiting patiently with their mums, dads, minders and grandparents sitting nearby.

I read enough Julia Donaldson to make my eyes sore before our time was up, and we had to call it a day. I thanked the children for being such good listeners, even though they lasted about seven minutes before they got bored and started fidgeting/crying/whinging or all three. This was the sort of time that Dilys likes to pop by to tell me I lack authority and confidence and I'm going to be an embarrassment in the classroom. This is when I tell Dilys to fuck off.

As I got up from my seat, I saw Anna standing at the back of the room. She was munching on a cucumber and smiling in my direction. I walked over to her.

'I didn't know you were coming,' I said, kissing her on the cheek.

'I brought you lunch.'

'You've never brought me lunch before. What a treat.'

'It's leftover BBQ from yesterday. The smell's putting me off.'

'Thanks for thinking of me.'

'I forgot the sauce, so the meat will be a little dry. And I forgot the salad.'

'So, it's just dry BBQ meat?'

'Yes, and half a charred pepper.'

'Well, it's the thought that counts.'

We walked arm in arm to the café and found a seat.

'Did you know that Mam sent me an article about air pollution and the damage it can do to pregnant women? According to the *Daily Mail*, my child could be born with severe disabilities.'

'You know you shouldn't read that—'

'I didn't choose to read it, did I?'

'I didn't say you—'

'It sent me into a tenebrous Google-shaped hole, and now I've convinced myself the baby will be stillborn.'

She took another bite of her extra-large cucumber. I saw the vein on her forehead vibrate.

'Anna, don't take this the wrong way, but, have you done any mindfulness recently?'

'I don't have the time! I told you, work's busier than ever.'

'You need to make time. You've got to take care of your mental health, especially with a baby on the way.'

She groaned. 'You're so preachy now that you're all zen and happy in yourself.'

'I am not—' I stopped myself before swearing. 'I am not preachy. I work in a gift shop, I can't get anyone to text me, let alone date me, and last night I ate a packet of microwavable rice for dinner that cost ninety-nine pence.'

'Why didn't you come over?'

'I need to fend for myself.'

'We've signed up for hypnobirthing.'

'What's that?'

'It's a course where I pay someone three hundred pounds to tell me how to breathe.'

'Sounds riveting.'

'Sorry, this is boring. How are you? Did you finish the dating profile?'

'Yes,' I said, getting my phone out to show her.

'These are great,' she said, flicking through the photos. 'You've got a bit of that morning-sickness glow going on. I miss that glow. Now it's just sweat.'

'I'm yet to find anyone decent on there.'

'You've only been looking a day, darling.'

'I can't be arsed,' I said, scraping charcoal off the pepper.

'It's modern dating, Ivy. You need to commit – Oh! What about this one?'

There was a very attractive man on the screen with luscious blond locks. He looked a bit like Rapunzel – if Rapunzel was sexy and male. He had piercing blue eyes and scrumptious pink lips. Anna read out his profile.

'He's thirty-five, a product manager – not sure what that means—'

'I think that means he's techy?'

'Likes the outdoors and *The Big Bang Theory*.'

'I could never get into that show.'

'Who cares about the show, he's hot.'

He was hot. He was hot with a ridgeback, hot with a guitar, hot with his arm around a teenager holding a laminated certificate, and hot on a canal boat with a woman I presumed was his mother.

Anna started typing.

'Hey,' I said, 'what are you doing?'

'Nothing.'

'Don't you dare message him.'

'I'm not messaging him.'

'Anna! Stop it!'

She gave me the phone back.

'You little shit, you swiped right.'

'I swiped right.'

'How do you even know how to do that?'

'Don't make that face. I'm forcing you to take the plunge!'

'I am plunging! I set up the profile, didn't I?'

'Yes, but, knowing you, you'll probably sit on the app doing nothing for three years before you actually get the guts to connect with someone.'

'It's been one day! I haven't been on a proper first date in over four years. I'm allowed to be nervous.'

She held out her hand for me to hold. 'Sorry, I'm being a dick. You're marvellous and I love you and you should go at whatever pace feels right.'

After a few minutes, my phone beeped. I looked down to see a notification from Serendipity telling me that Nick had 'liked' me back. I showed Anna the screen and she let out a little yelp.

'Christ, that was fast,' she said.

I opened the app and there was a message from Nick.

'Hey, Ivy. Great to connect! Fancy a drink on Thursday?'

'Ives! You've got yourself a date!'

'Do you think he sounds desperate?'

'No.'

'I'm not sure about the "great to connect" part.'

Anna snatched the phone off me and replied to say that yes, I would like a drink on Thursday. He wrote back suggesting Millie's in Soho at seven o'clock.

'You're going on a date!' she said, clapping her hands.

I tried to mask my anxiety by shovelling some charred pepper in my mouth.

9

I'd arranged to meet Mia at mine after work on Thursday. I asked her to bring over some appropriate date attire but stressed that it had to be my sort of appropriate, not hers. If it were up to her, I'd be covered in lace, or glitter, or both. Her original suggestion was to wear an ivory satin gown with lace trimming on the shoulders, paired with dark-brown cowboy boots. Both were Noah's dead aunt's. To amuse her, I tried them on.

'I look like a Texan bride,' I said. 'And I smell like a dead cow.'

'You've never looked better.'

'Have you ever asked yourself why you own so many prairie dresses?' I said, sifting through the pile of clothes she'd brought over.

'What's the vision for tonight?' she asked. 'Who are you channelling? Do you want him to see "fun, all-nighter Ivy", or "about to start teacher-training Ivy"?'

'Are they mutually exclusive?'

She put her hand to her forehead and let out an agonised sigh.

'What is this?' I said, pulling out a tie-dye velvet robe.

'That's for when I want to channel Jennifer Connelly from *Labyrinth*.'

I threw a pillow at her and told her she was from another planet.

We settled on something from my own wardrobe: a floral midi dress with buttons down the front. Mia said that because it fell to my calves, it made me look classy, but that the cut on my cleavage gave me a 'sensual edge', which was, according to her, the ideal combination. I put on some red lipstick and off I went.

'Be you, but not too you,' Mia said, as we parted ways. 'You're going to kill it.'

I'd painted my nails for the occasion, but by the time I arrived at Millie's, I had chipped most of the polish off, revealing a tinge of yellow that you usually only find on the deceased. I'd put too much hairspray on the right side of my head, so I spent most of the Tube journey into town trying to puff up the left side, which was rather flat in comparison. I was also a little bloated and could've easily passed as a woman nearing the end of her first trimester. If this wasn't adversity, I didn't know what was.

I spotted Nick at the bar right away. I never know what to do with my hands and, walking towards him, all I could think about was where to place them. I thought about Mam and how she says that I frown too much, which led me to think about the anti-wrinkle cream she said I needed to buy to counteract the frown lines. I then started thinking about the cost of anti-wrinkle cream, and whether it was all a con. Should I carry on with my usual moisturiser, or was it time to move on, as Mam had said?

He got up from his seat and, with the kissing incident from the interview still on my mind, I put my hand out to shake his. We said our hellos and smiled at each other in that awkward way you do when you're on your first, first date in four years. It felt like I was shaking his hand for hours. My hand was a bit sweaty. Everything was a bit sweaty.

'Ivy, how are you?'

'Good. How are you?'

'Good.'

'Good.'

More awkward smiles.

'Can I get you a drink?' he asked.

'Yes, please. I'll have a gin and tonic.'

He called the waiter's attention and ordered our drinks: gin and tonic for me, and a lemonade for him. I gave him a subtle look-over as he talked to the waiter. Why was he drinking lemonade? Was he training for some sort of ultra-marathon? Was he hung-over, and dehydrated? Perhaps he had recently undergone surgery and was on extra strong painkillers?

'So, how are you?' he asked again.

'I'm fine, thanks. And you?'

It felt like we'd had this exchange seventeen times in the past two minutes.

'Sorry,' he said, 'I must seem a bit out of it. I've been crazy busy this week.'

'Not at all,' I said, scanning his face. He really did look like Rapunzel. I started to think about all the other, attractive cartoon characters: Aladdin, Pocahontas . . . Mufasa.

'What do you do?' he asked.

'I start my teacher training in September, at a primary school in Clerkenwell.'

'That's amazing. You need a lot of patience to work with kids. I mentor a few teenagers at church. CV building, interview training, that sort of stuff.'

The talk of church should have sounded an alarm bell, but I was too impressed by the many strings to his hot, angelic bow to care.

'Ah, that would explain the young man in the photo,' I said.

'What photo?'

'On your profile. He's holding a certificate? I bet that gets a lot of likes. "Here I am out in the community, helping someone less fortunate than me".'

Nick looked wounded. 'Jack died of a knife stabbing earlier this year.'

'Shit. I'm so sorry. I was trying to make a joke. I'm sorry.'

There was silence as I tried to find something redeeming to say.

'Do you do a lot of work with the church?' I asked.

'Yeah, a fair bit. I started a band. We write our own material.'

'Cool. What sort of music is it?'

'Do you remember the band Creed?'

'Creed? As in the American Christian rock band from the nineties?'

'Yeah, I love those guys.'

There was no hope for us.

'Do you volunteer?' he asked.

'I started volunteering at a care home last year, but it's not so much volunteering any more. I go to see Maude, who's one of the residents. She likes to hold me accountable for things – the elderly are good at that, aren't they?'

Despite the initial awkwardness, the conversation flowed for the next half hour or so. He asked a bit more about my teacher training, and about Wales. He'd spent many summers in Tenby, so at least we had that in common, but talking about coastal paths can only get you so far.

'I'm going to order another drink,' I said. 'Do you want something a bit stronger?'

'I should have said, I'm a Methodist – I don't drink alcohol.'

'That must be hard.'

'Hard?'

'We're British; drinking is what we do.'

'I think that's a gross generalisation. Our drinking culture is an excuse for juvenile behaviour. Don't you agree?'

I decided not to order another drink.

'So, kayaking,' I said, changing the subject. 'What other sports are you into?'

I tried to focus on our conversation but his sanctimonious attitude towards alcohol had thrown me. There's nothing wrong with being sober, or being an active member of the Methodist Church, but save us all a bit of time and put it on your dating profile. Was I wrong to assume that our date would involve sharing an alcoholic beverage or two? Had I been out of the game this long?

I excused myself to go to the loo, where I called Anna.

'I'm pretty sure I saw a copy of the Bible in his bag,' I said. 'Am I being mean? Tell me if I'm being mean.'

'No, you're not being mean. He withheld key information, and I don't think you should go out with someone who carries biblical literature around with them. You don't have a good track record with people of faith.'

'He's a bit dull. But I think the hotness is masking that.'

'You could say I'm going into labour.'

'What? Now?'

'Pregnant people are the perfect escape goat. Go back to the bar and do exactly what I say.'

I went back to the bar and smiled at Nick. I know there's a direct correlation between how attractive people are and how many gins you've consumed, but he really was very attractive. If I'd have known there would be calibre like this at our local church, I'd have been much more enthusiastic about Sunday club.

I took my seat and, just like that, my phone went off. It was Anna: 'Ivy, I think I'm having contractions and I can't get hold of Mark. Come quick.'

'Fuck,' I said.

'What's wrong?'

'I think my sister's going into labour. Her husband's on a business trip. I've got to go.'

'Far out! I went through the same thing with my sister. Early labour! God's magnificent plan.'

I got up from my seat and collected my things.

'Goodbye then, Nick. This has been ... pleasant.'

I don't know why I chose that word. I don't think I've ever even used that word before.

'I'd like to see you again,' he said. 'I had fun tonight.'

Fun? He'd nursed a pint of lemonade for ninety minutes.

'You're great, but ... we're very different people.'

'That's cool, no worries,' he said, with his million-dollar Disney Prince smile.

'We lead different lives.'

'Don't worry, Ivy. I get it.'

'I'm sorry. I'm trying to be honest.'

He put one hand on my shoulder.

'Always be honest, Ivy. You can't go wrong if you're being honest.'

'You're very wise – and handsome. Has anyone ever told you that you look like Rapunzel?'

He laughed. 'We've got to be true to ourselves, Ivy. Good luck to you and your family, God speed.'

Strangely, his mature response to me running off made me fancy him a bit again, and for a minute there I thought, maybe I should stay. But I snapped out of it, hugged him, and ran off to tend to Anna's fake birth.

As soon as I turned the corner, I rang her.

'I'm not doing that again,' I said. 'I ended up telling him we weren't compatible, and he was so gracious about it.'

'I thought everyone lied on first dates? Maybe you should see him again?'

'I feel like such a tit. This is the last time I'm taking advice from you.'

'Do you want to come over? We've got that rosé you like, and Mark's cooking.'

'I'm already on my way.'

10

It was a blazing hot day in July, and Dan and I were at Teddies in Soho, well into the throes of their Independence Day-themed bottomless brunch. I had spent the entire morning telling Dan all the ways in which Serendipity was the most uneventful, tedious thing I'd ever gotten myself involved with. I'd swiped left so many times that I was convinced I'd given myself RSI. There were so many men. A ridiculous amount of men, in fact – and all of them looking for a supermodel fifteen years younger than them with a PhD.

'You connect with someone, have a little flirt, share a bit about yourself,' I said. 'They seem normal, you are normal. You're hopeful that this might not be a complete waste of your time. But then you bite the bullet and ask them out on a date, and either they disappear off the face of the earth or tell you they're not looking for anything serious.'

'Your standards are too high,' Dan said.

'You wouldn't be saying that if you'd seen the men I've asked out. It's been almost two months and I am yet to engage in a half-decent conversation with a member of the opposite sex. It's depressing.'

'You don't need men to have a conversation. You've got me and Mia.'

'You and I both know that's not the same.'

I drank the last of my mimosa.

'I'm putting myself out there, I'm swiping right for men I know I'm never going to like. I'm trying to be my quote unquote best self – and for what?'

'Try not to get disheartened, Ives.'

'Can we change the subject, please? How are things with Alejandro?'

'We had an almighty row last night.'

'What happened?'

'He used my Crème De La Mer on his ankles.'

I laughed.

'Ivy! It costs one hundred and twenty-five pounds for a small pot.'

'That's almost my weekly spending allowance.'

'Which is exactly why I'm treating you to brunch.'

'We should order, I'm tipsy already.'

Dan called the waiter over.

'Once we've ordered our food, do you think it would be possible for us to move on to straight Prosecco, please? The acid in the orange juice does nothing for my IBS.'

'Of course, say no more.'

'Also, how long do we have left of the bottomless element to our brunch?'

'Technically an hour, but—' the waiter lowered himself down to the table so that he was eye level to us both '—my boss is off today, so you can stay as long as you like.'

The waiter squeezed Dan's shoulder before he sashayed off.

'God, I love it in here,' Dan said.

'You're going to have sex with him, aren't you?'

'Maybe . . . if there's time.'

Three hours later, we stumbled out of Teddies. After a good five minutes trying to light our cigarettes, we realised we had them the wrong way around in our mouths and collapsed on the pavement in stitches.

'Stop making me laugh!' Dan cried. 'I can't breathe.'

'There are so many bubbles in my belly.'

'I think we need to call my dealer.'

'No, Dan!'

'Yes, Ivy! Let's get so fucked we can't remember our names.'

I was about to tell him that I was very nearly at that stage, when my phone rang. It was Anna. I showed Dan the screen.

'Oh lovely, lovely, Anna,' he said. 'I love Anna, don't you?'

I answered the phone and Dan and I both started shouting how much we loved her.

'Ivy—'

Dan grabbed the phone off me.

'You are such an amazing woman,' he said to her. 'I've always thought that. You're like a sister to me. Do you know that? A sister!'

I stood beside him, trying to grab the phone off him. His face suddenly turned to stone. I moved closer to hear what Anna was saying to him.

'I'll put her back on,' Dan said, shoving the phone in my face.

'What's wrong?' I asked her.

'My waters have broken.'

'Fuck!'

'Mark's visiting his aunt at the care home.'

'But that's in fucking Guernsey!'

'Ivy, please don't shout at me. I'm aware of its geographical location.'

'Is he coming back?'

'He's trying to.'

'Where are you?'

'I need you to meet me at Homerton Hospital.'

'How did this happen? You're not due for another five weeks.'

'Ivy, please stop telling me things I already know.'

'I'm—'

'You're drunk, aren't you?'

'No, I'm not drunk. I'm tipsy.'

'Fucking hell, Ivy. Get on the Tube, or in a taxi, whatever, and meet me there.'

'Fuck. OK.'

'Come right now.'

'I'm on my way.'

The calm of her voice couldn't mask her heavy breathing. She sounded like Darth Vader in a wind tunnel.

Remembering Anna's hypnobirthing advice, I took a few deep breaths myself, trying to compose myself, but the fresh air had sent the alcohol straight to my head and I was now more than tipsy – I was one hundred per cent drunk.

'What's the quickest way to Homerton?' I asked Dan.

'I don't know!'

'I'm going to get an Uber,' I said, pacing the pavement. 'Yes, I'll get an Uber. Or I could run to Oxford Circus and get the Victoria Line. No, then I'll have to change at Highbury onto the Overground to Hackney Central – no, I'd get off at Homerton. But then changing at Highbury is always dangerous . . .'

I was circling Dan in a frenzy.

'What do you think, Dan? Uber? Or Tube?'

'I don't know, Ivy!'

'I don't know either!'

'You're the one who lives in Hackney!'

'Stop shouting at me!'

'Book a fucking Uber!'

We stood in the middle of the pavement, chain-smoking, whilst I booked an Uber.

'Do you want me to come with you?' Dan asked.

'No, definitely not.'

'How pissed are you?'

'I'm not sober.'

Dan passed me another cigarette. I refused.

'I'll get some water and some Haribo and I'll be fine,' I said. 'I need sugar, that's all.'

A smirk grew on Dan's face. He put his hand to his mouth to try to shield it.

'Why are you looking at me like that?' I said.

'Nothing. It's just . . . funny.'

'How is this funny?'

'It's karma, isn't it?'

'What are you on about?'

'Well, Anna told you to lie to that churchgoer about her going into labour. And here we are . . . with her in labour.'

I felt a very strong urge to punch him in the face.

'Yup, this is karma,' he said. 'No doubt about it.'

'Dan?'

'Yup?'

'If you say one more word I might never speak to you again.'

With that, the Uber arrived, and I got in.

'Ivy, will you stop being so patronising?' Anna said.

We'd been waiting on the maternity ward for two hours. Anna was in a chair, gripping it with such force that I thought she was going to rip off the armrest.

'I'm not being patronising,' I said. 'I'm reminding you to breathe.'

'What do you think I'm trying to do!'

I went back to stroking her hair. My mouth was as dry as the desert, but God forbid I was going to ask for more water. Things were not going to plan; there were no beds available, so Anna was sitting on a chair, strapped up to a monitor, with only a flimsy curtain around her for privacy. The nurse had given her a paracetamol, and when I'd asked for one too, Anna had whacked me on the arm so hard I'd felt a bruise materialise.

'You're doing so well,' I told her.

'You stink of booze,' she said, through gritted teeth. 'And you've been smoking again.'

'I appreciate that I wasn't in the best of states upon arrival.'

'Why did you have to get so drunk?'

'I was tipsy.'

'You were wasted.'

'In my defence, you are five weeks early, and I wasn't fully up to speed with your birth plan.'

'Well, as you can imagine, this isn't in my fucking birth plan.'

She was sobbing now. We had been through a lot of tears in the past two hours and I was doing all I could to hold it together, but I was dehydrated, and the smell of breastmilk was making me want to vomit.

'Mark will be here soon,' I said, having no real idea where he was or how long he'd be.

'Why did I let him go to fucking Guernsey?'

'Because his aunt is sick and you're a good person.'

'I could kill British Airways.'

'That's good, focus on BA. They're bastards.'

The vein on her forehead was staring right at me.

'He should be here in a couple of hours,' I said.

'What if I don't have a couple of hours?'

'Try not to worry. All you need to do is breathe.'

'Is this paracetamol a fucking joke? I'm having a fucking baby!'

'Just try to focus on those visualisation techniques, darling.'

I was thinking of some mindfulness techniques myself as I crouched down on the floor beside Anna and tried to ignore the conversation about the colour of vaginal discharge that was going on beside me.

11

I heard Mark shout Anna's name from out on the ward. When he saw her on the chair he fell onto her lap and started cursing the island of Guernsey.

I left them to it and went to get more supplies from the café. I picked up a tuna sandwich, a couple of bananas that had seen better days, some crisps, bottles of coke and cereal bars. I regretted the tuna sandwich immediately, but it was either that or egg mayonnaise, and I cannot fathom why anyone would ever put egg in a sandwich.

When Gramps was in hospital after his stroke, he would ring me every day to complain about the food. He went on and on about the cold beans, lumpy custard, and brown-looking fruit. Mam never allowed him to eat biscuits, so he'd ask his friends to sneak them in for him. He'd have tens of packets of biscuits in the cupboard beside his bed, hidden behind his pristine polo shirts and boat shoes.

I stood at the counter in the café, looking at the biscuit selection, remembering the time we had polished off two packs of Rich Tea as we'd watched *West Side Story* back to back.

'Excuse me? Are you OK?'

It took me a moment to realise that the woman at the till was speaking to me. I wiped my eyes, cleared my throat and said, 'Yes, I'm fine.'

'Godforsaken places, hospitals. Aren't they?' I said, tapping my card on the machine. 'They're full of hope on one end, and full of—' I stopped myself, not being able to think of the word.

'I know what you mean, love,' she said, reaching out and squeezing my hand. 'I know exactly what you mean.'

I smiled at her and walked back to the maternity ward.

On the way there, my phone rang. It was Mam.

'How's my darling girl?'

'I'm OK, Mam. I wish you were here. Brunch got a bit out of hand, you know what Dan's like, the Uber took ages and—'

'Ives, not being funny, I meant Anna.'

'Oh, sure. She's with Mark now. Where are you?'

'We should be there in an hour or so. The sat nav is telling us to go through Kensington, but I don't think that's right. Saying that though, it would be nice to take a nose in some of the townhouses.'

'Now's not the time, Mam.'

'You sound like your father – who, by the way, won't let me listen to any of my calming playlist.'

'Of course you made a playlist.'

'I finalised it months ago. I knew I'd need something for the journey, to centre myself. It's not appropriate to drive with a gin and tonic, is it? Anyway, I have Lady Gaga. She's such an inspiration. Have you seen *A Star is Born* yet? Christ, Ivy, I don't know where to start – transformational, it was.'

'Get here as soon as you can, OK? Don't take any detours.'

'Yes, my darling. Tell Anna she's my superstar angel.'

I hung up the phone and made my way to the ward.

I drew the curtain back, expecting to see Anna and Mark, but there was nobody there.

'Excuse me, do you know where they've taken my sister?' I asked one of the nurses. 'Her name is Anna Booth.'

'They've taken her to the delivery room.'

'But she hasn't eaten anything,' I said, showing the woman the contents of my bag. 'What about her snacks?'

'She can eat them after, don't worry.'

'She said she was hungry. Her husband's rushed from the airport and he'll need his sandwich.'

My lower lip started to go. The nurse told me it was going to be all right.

'I'm sorry,' I said, knowing full well she had more important matters to be dealing with than me having just wasted twenty quid on snacks. 'I'm so tired, and I know you must be too, but my hangover has kicked in and I'm feeling a bit delicate.'

'Why don't you sit in the waiting room?'

I began to well up. She put her arm around me and led me to the waiting room, where I was pleased to see that they were showing *Harry Potter and the Prisoner of Azkaban*.

'Nothing like a good blockbuster to make you feel safe,' she said.

'Are you an angel?'

She laughed and told me she'd let Mark know where I was.

I found a seat and tried my best to focus on Hermione Granger, and not the half-naked woman sitting in the chair opposite me, itching her crotch. I held my bag to my chest and closed my eyes.

I was woken up by Dad, hovering over me, eating a pasty.

I grabbed him around the neck and wrapped my arms around him.

'I am so glad you're here,' I said.

'Everything's OK, don't worry.'

'What's the time?'

'It's almost ten.'

'Ten! How long is this meant to take?'

'Your mother was in labour with you for sixteen hours. You know what they say – difficult in labour, difficult in life.'

He gave me a coffee; it was lukewarm and bitter.

'This is both the best and worst coffee I've ever tasted.'

'Drink up, and eat some of your food, too.'

I got out a bag of crisps from my bag and shoved a handful into my mouth.

'Where's Mam?' I asked.

'In there with her.'

'In the room? With Anna? Did Anna say she could do that?'

'Yes.'

'Was she high?'

'Don't be mean, your mother always comes through in a crisis. It's with life's little things that she becomes a bit—'

'Unbearable?'

'Yes, you could say that.'

At 00:16 on the morning of Sunday 5 July, Eleanor Lowri Booth was born. Named after Mark's mother and my grandmother, and she was six pounds two ounces of pure perfection. I was fast asleep on Dad in the waiting room when Mam ran in crying, arms flailing like a wild dancer, shouting, 'SHE DID IT! SHE DID IT!'

There was a private room available, which Anna, Mark and Eleanor were taken into a couple of hours later, and that's when, finally, we were able to see them. I walked in to find Eleanor asleep on Anna's chest. Her head was a little bruised from the forceps, and her tiny body was red and wrinkly. She had an IV drip in one of her hands, and her thick black hair was matted to her head. She was the most beautiful thing I'd ever seen.

'This is Eleanor,' Anna said, her eyes glistening with tears.

Dad went over to hug Mark whilst I went right up to Eleanor and kissed her perfect little head.

'You're amazing,' I said to Anna. 'I love you so much.'

'Thank you for being here.'

'I'm sorry I was a bit tipsy,' I said in a low whisper, not wanting Dad to hear.

'Tipsy?' Dad asked. 'When were you tipsy?'

'She'd been to bottomless brunch with Dan,' Anna said. She was enjoying this.

'Ivy! Of all the days!'

'Hang on,' I said, 'I didn't know Anna was going to go into labour, did I?'

Mark stifled a laugh.

I was about to defend my case further when Mam came running in with two large shopping bags. She was soaked right through.

'Where have you been?' I asked her.

'I went to the car to get the rest of the stuff. *Mae hi'n bwrw hen wragedd a ffyn.*'

'What?'

'Well, seeing as you asked, darling, the literal translation is, "It's raining elderly ladies and sticks". Oh, Tony,' she said, turning to Dad, 'remind me to cancel my Welsh lessons next week; I can't possibly concentrate on irregular adjectives after all this.'

'Been in the sales?' Mark said, pointing to the bags Mam was carrying.

'Tell them how much you spent, Mags,' Dad said.

'Tony,' Mam said, with a tone we all knew so well, 'you're getting on my nerves now. Babies need bibs.'

I moved closer to Mam and peered in the bags.

'Bloody hell, Mam. There's a hundred bibs in there.'

'Your mother spent eighty quid on bibs,' Dad said.

'Would everyone stop going on about these bloody bibs!' Mam cried. 'I came prepared, which is more than I can say for the rest of you.'

'Difficult to be prepared when your baby comes five weeks early,' Anna said.

'Anna, I'm just saying, I had my hospital bag ready two months before you both arrived. No way was I going to let the bastards get me.'

Mam went on, but Anna wasn't listening; she was too busy smiling at Eleanor.

'Shall we say goodbye and leave them to it?' Dad said, interrupting Mam's monologue.

'But I brought champagne, Tony, from Lidl. They say it's as good as Veuve.'

'It's nearly three in the morning. I'm sure they want to get some rest now.'

'Oh, my little lambs!' Mam cried, hurling herself onto the bed. 'I will miss you both so much tonight.'

I went to hug Mark.

'Thank you for today, Ives,' he said.

'I didn't do anything.'

'You kept her calm, you were in control. Some might say it wasn't ideal that you turned up drunk—'

'Yes, some might say that.'

I hugged him again.

'It's so strange to think my parents will never meet her.'

He broke free from my embrace and I saw that he was crying. I dug around in my pocket to find a Prosecco-stained napkin I'd used at brunch and gave it to him.

'Sorry,' he said. 'Let's talk about you being drunk again.'

'Which time are we on about?'

He smiled. 'Thank you, Ives.'

We said our goodbyes and walked out of the ward. I saw the nurse who'd held my hand earlier. She was writing on the noticeboard.

'Excuse me?' I said.

'Hello! How are they doing?'

'They're doing great; Eleanor is perfect.'

I stood in front of her, unable to get the words out.

'Is everything OK?' she asked.

'I wanted to tell you that we think you're wonderful – all of you.'

She looked a bit taken aback.

'I can't thank you enough for what you've done for my sister.'

She smiled. 'That's kind of you to say, love.'

'I'm sorry, again, for being tipsy when I arrived.'

'I've seen far worse.'

'Really?'

'Well, maybe not much worse.'

'That makes me feel better, thank you.'

I walked away, feeling so happy my heart hurt.

12

People say it's important to honour your loved one's life; some chose to write poetry or send money to charity. But for me, the way to celebrate Gramps' one-year anniversary was to go down to the beach and paint. So, the first thing I did when I got home was get out my watercolours and set off down the cycle path.

'Where's my invite?' Mam said, shouting down the garden at me.

I turned around to see her standing by the back door. She had a glitter eye mask on and was wearing an ivory silk dressing gown that made her look like Miss Havisham, only less ruined.

'I thought you needed a lie-down?'

'I'm waiting for Linda to call. Guess who saw Beth Boston come out of the bathroom with a very young waiter last night?'

Beth Boston went to Boston once in 1982.

'Such gossip!' Mam said. 'I cannot wait to tell Linda!'

'So, you don't want to come to the beach?'

'No, darling. You go do your painting thing and I'll be waiting for you with a glass of wine when you come back.'

I waved and walked off.

'Wash your feet before you come back in the house – I don't want sand everywhere again!'

I hadn't been back to Wales for six months, the longest stint I can remember. It had begun to feel like Groundhog Day in London, but as soon as I stepped off the train in Swansea, something shifted. I closed my eyes and saw the sea, and I knew I was almost home. Swansea train station hums of urine and there's always a group of men hanging around by the entrance, off their faces on God knows what. It's not exactly the most romantic welcome home, but it's my welcome home, and I wouldn't change it for a thing.

As is custom, there were hordes of young boys on their bikes hanging around the beach café, with their arse cracks on show. I found a quiet spot away from them, sat down and looked out to the sea.

Sometimes when I think about last year – about Jamie and Gramps – it feels like a giant is standing on my chest. The only person I used to share this with was Maude; I'd visit her at the care home reeking of last night's bad decisions and she'd tell me it was going to be OK – but only if I started taking care of myself. She trusted that eventually I would start making good decisions again, which was astonishing, because most people had lost faith in my decision-making skills – and rightly so. But I hadn't seen Maude in a while, and once again I felt adrift. I kept thinking about Gramps, and whether he'd approve of what I was trying to do with my life. I knew deep down he would, but then Dilys would creep in, and I wouldn't be so sure.

I was sketching where the waves and shore would be when I heard someone call my name.

'*Prynhawn da*, Ivy!'

I turned around and saw Owen, holding his arms out to welcome me.

Owen was my grandfather's best friend. They are complete opposites; they'd argue over politics, sport, how to treat your neighbours. Gramps would always raise his voice and swear to get his point across, whilst Owen was the most softly spoken man you'd ever meet.

I got up and hugged him close. He smelt of sunscreen and I could taste the sea as I kissed his cheek.

'Funny I'm seeing you now, *bach*,' he said. 'I was going to pop by your mother's later; I've got something for her.'

He reached into his bag and got out a brown, tattered notebook.

'Your grandfather's Welsh vocabulary book,' he said.

Ivan Thomas was scribbled on the first page, alongside a date: 24 September 1942. Gramps would've been twelve.

'Where did you find this?' I asked.

'I must have picked it up when we were helping your mother clear out his house. I thought she could use it, now she's learning Welsh.'

I flicked through the pages, mesmerised. I remembered reading this for the first time years ago, seeing hundreds of scribbles of Welsh words I didn't recognise, alongside names: Rhian, Sioned, Megan.

'Girls he fancied,' Owen said, smiling.

'I thought we'd lost this. *Diolch yn fawr iawn*, Owen.'

'It belongs with you.'

We hugged again, this time for much longer. He looked me in the eye and smiled his warm toothy smile at me, and I laughed. He got out his hankie and patted my cheeks dry.

'No more tears today, OK, babes?'

'I was doing so well until you showed up,' I said. 'Do you want to come back up to the house with me? Have some lunch?'

'I'll come over later, love. Need to pick up Gaynor from the salon first.'

Owen's wife Gaynor is never seen looking anything other than immaculate. She gets her hair and nails done every week and is never without her signature bouffant.

'Good to see you're still painting, *bach*,' he said, looking down at my pad.

'I'm trying to get back into it. This is for Maude, the woman I see at the care home.'

'Your grandfather was jealous of her – said she was stealing you off him.'

'Nobody could do that, could they?'

Owen smiled. 'How's your sister doing? And the bab?'

'They're good. Anna's shattered, but that's to be expected.'

'And your mother?'

'She's having a debrief with Linda . . . some drama at last night's charity do.'

'She told me she was "over" charity.'

'She'll attend anything if there's free booze.'

He laughed. 'You remind me so much of your grandfather, Ivy.'

'Hopefully only the good bits.'

'He only had good bits.'

We said our goodbyes and I sat back down on the blanket and went back to my painting, feeling the giant's heavy foot pushing down on me again.

I got back from the beach to find Anna in the living room, wearing only her bra and joggers. There were two frozen cabbage leaves covering each breast.

'My boobs are in fucking agony,' she said.

'Can I do anything?'

'If you can't breastfeed, then no.'

I walked over to the Moses basket, where Eleanor was sleeping. She was wearing a pink cardigan that Mam's friend Linda had bought for her from Swansea Market. It looked like it belonged in the nineteenth century, and she was almost drowning in it, but she was so pretty, and peaceful. I couldn't believe she was ours. Anna came to stand over the basket with me, and we listened to Eleanor's sweet snore.

'I don't know how you get anything done,' I said.

'I don't. If she's not on my boob then I'm stood over her, like a dumbstruck stalker.'

I started to tidy the room. The carpet was littered with nappies, sanitary pads and creams I'd never heard of, and the last thing we needed was another lecture from Mam about us "spoiling" the house. Whilst I was enjoying having the attention deflected from me for a change, I was sure that if Mam made one more snide remark to Anna, we were going to have a real family drama on our hands. 'Angry, sleep-deprived daughter kills over-bearing mother in final act of defiance.' It has a nice ring to it.

Anna was making wincing noises from the sofa. I sat down beside her, and she rested her head on my shoulder.

'Do you know what I find remarkable?' she said. 'That my vagina is perfectly intact after delivering a six-pound baby, but here I am, nipples bleeding all over the shop, and a massive haemorrhoid in my arse.'

She took one of the cabbage leaves off her breast to reveal a bloody, scabby nipple.

'Do you remember me telling you that you don't need to share every single detail of your post-birth journey with me?' I said.

'Noted,' she said, putting the leaf back on. 'At least you know what to expect now.'

I had thought about children when Jamie and I broke up, but only because I was devastated that I wouldn't be having his children. Though to be fair, that was mainly because I realised that not having his children meant not having access to the family villa in Barbados. There was so much to grieve last year.

Anna read my face and asked me what was wrong.

'By the time I have a baby – if I ever have a baby – things will have moved on. It'll be different.'

'Different how?'

'I don't know ... It's not as if motherhood is in my near future.'

'It doesn't need to be in your near future – you're thirty-two.'

'Yes, but if you do the maths, having children means meeting someone now.'

'Don't buy into that shit, Ivy. It'll happen for you when it happens for you; I'm a great example of that.'

'I'm on the other side of thirty.'

'So was I! But countless fertility specialists and two rounds of IVF later, here we are.'

'I know what you mean, but—'

'Ivy, please don't get caught up on this. Babies are really hard work. You're much better off staying out till six in the morning with Mia and Dan.'

'You make it look easy.'

This wasn't entirely true, given my current view.

'That's a laugh. I need to master breastfeeding.'

'You don't need to master anything. Try being a bit kinder to yourself for once.'

'I couldn't even procreate without medical assistance, why did I ever think I'd be able to do everything normal mums do.'

'Anna, don't say that.'

'I've never had a problem doing anything in my life.'

'I know, you exceed at everything. It's infuriating.'

'I couldn't have a baby though, and my nipple literally falls off every time I breastfeed, but still I persist because I'm a fucking perfectionist.'

'Anna—'

'I don't want to talk about it any more. Can I nap on you?'

'Go right ahead.'

She lay across me, and we both closed our eyes.

We were woken by Mam standing in front of us in a patchwork shirt.

'I thought you weren't buying any more clothes,' I said.

'It's upcycled, darling. It's all the rage in Stockholm. This is one hundred per cent ecologically certified.'

'Do you even know what that means?'

'Something to do with silkworms?'

Anna smiled, her eyes still closed.

'What's with the box, in the garage?' I asked her. 'The one with all the cleaning products.'

Last year, when Mam turned my bedroom into a nursery for Anna's (not yet conceived) baby, she thoughtfully threw away most of my possessions, but said that if I looked in the garage, I might find one or two things she thought were worth keeping.

'When did you see that?' Mam asked. 'You didn't touch anything, did you?'

'Why do you look so concerned? What are they?'

'I am telling you this in the strictest confidence. One word to your father and that's it.'

Anna's eyes flicked open. We both sat up, intrigued.

'It was a couple of months ago. Linda had told me about this handsome salesman who'd come around her house. He was selling odd bits and bobs, you know, carpet cleaner, that sort of thing. Linda thought they were a bargain, so she bought a year's supply. But, you see, turns out, he wasn't a salesman . . . He was an ex-convict.'

Anna and I burst out laughing.

'Don't tease! He ruined the carpet in the hall!'

We ran to see. There was a new house plant in the corner, near the front door. I lifted it up and found a large moss green stain underneath. The carpet was singed, like there'd been a fire. We put the plant back in its place and headed back into the lounge.

'Your father hasn't noticed yet, thank God. I'm one of the lucky ones.'

'So, an ex-convict scammed everyone in your charity group?' I said.

'Just me, Linda, Weight-Watchers Wendy and Carol Cakes.'

Weight-Watchers Wendy has been on the programme since 1990 and is yet to lose a single pound, and Carol Cakes' great-great-grandfather was a baker, or at least worked in a bakery – nobody can remember.

'You wouldn't believe the drama it caused,' Mam said.

'Oh, we believe it all right,' Anna said.

'I can see you're making fun of me,' she said, sulking. 'You've got thirty minutes before we need to leave.'

She left the room and Anna and I collapsed in hysterics.

Later, upstairs, Mam asked Anna if she wanted some concealer to cover her bags.

'I've put some on already,' Anna said.

'You need more than that,' she said, squinting her eyes and inspecting Anna's face.

As Mam walked away, Anna took out an imaginary gun from her pocket and shot her in the back of the head.

'Stop it,' I said. 'You know she doesn't mean it.'

'Jesus,' she said, looking at herself in the mirror, 'I've aged a decade.'

She dabbed some concealer under her eyes then asked me to help her choose an outfit.

'Wear what you're wearing now, you look great.'

'I'm too fat. The zip is digging into my stomach.'

She collapsed onto the bed.

'Anna, we're about to pay tribute to our dead grandfather. Nobody cares what you wear.'

'It's easy for you to say when your orifices aren't leaking.'

She started pulling things out of one bag and putting them into another.

'You don't need all that,' I said. 'We're only going to the beach.'

'You have no idea, Ivy. There's so much stuff when you have a baby.'

'What can I do?'

'Nothing, just stay out of the way.'

I wanted to help, but she looked at me with such venom that I closed the door and left her to it. She'd never looked at me like that before.

I walked back towards her room, determined to show her that I could be useful. I opened the door and, before I'd even had the chance to open my mouth, she told me to get out.

13

I found Maude in the communal living room, watching *Come Dine With Me*. I was thrilled to see they'd finally moved on from *Pointless*. I don't know what it is with elderly people and Alexander Armstrong, but the man seems to have a hold on anyone over sixty. She was sitting in her wheelchair, wearing a red velvet eye patch, with her initials embroidered in sequins.

'Maude! Look at that eye patch, how fancy.'

'Don't,' she said, getting all shy. 'One of the care workers made it. It's not very me.'

'You look ever so glamorous.'

I crouched down to the wheelchair to hug her.

'It's so good to see you,' she said, cupping my face in her hands. 'And thank you for the flowers, there was no need.'

'I'm sorry I got you marigolds; I had no idea.'

Maude recently had cataract surgery. She'd been complaining about her eyesight for months, but had refused to go to hospital, for fear she'd never come out. It wasn't the brightest idea for me to send a giant bouquet of marigolds to her bedside, but how was I supposed to know they were associated with death?

There was an elderly couple by the TV, holding hands. The man leant over and kissed the woman on the forehead. I watched as she closed her eyes in a moment of sweet reverie. The man caught my eye and smiled at me, and just as he did, Sophie, the resident cat, started rubbing herself against my leg. She purred as I stroked her under the chin. How I longed for someone – anyone – to stroke me under the chin.

I heard Bill call my name from across the room. Bill is my second-favourite resident at the care home; he has dementia, is hugely unpredictable and always in fancy dress. Today, he was dressed as a ringmaster.

He walked towards us, panting. His shirt was undone, and he was soaked in sweat. He took out a handkerchief and wiped his brow.

'Good to see you, Bill,' I said. 'Great outfit today.'

'Never mind that, Ivy,' he said, itching his under arm. 'Did you bring the script?'

'Sorry, Bill, what do you mean?'

'For tonight's show. I'm Master of Ceremonies.'

'Bill, please. Ivy's just got here.'

'But I need to know the order of the acts, Maude. Are we finishing with Leona the Lion, or is Maureen the Meerkat doing her acrobatics?'

I looked to Maude to rescue me.

'This is typical of you, Ivy,' Bill said. 'Next time you need a hand getting on the unicycle, don't come rushing to me.'

He puffed away on his plastic cigar.

'Come now, Sophie,' he said, striking his whip to the floor. 'Your dinner awaits.'

Bill stormed off with Sophie sauntering behind him.

'Bless him,' Maude said. 'He's anxious this week. I'll write him up a little pretend script later.'

'Won't he have forgotten this whole conversation by then?'

'You never know with Bill. It'll give me something to pass the time, anyway.'

I pushed her out into the garden, and we sat overlooking the vegetable patch.

I reached into my bag and got out the painting I did for her.

'It's the beach by our house,' I said. 'Do you like it?'

'I love it. I'll hang it in pride of place in my room.'

'You don't have to, it's not exactly Monet.'

'But you did it, and that makes it special,' she said, holding it close to her chest.

'I thought of you when I was home,' I said, 'and about what you said to me – that you should give in to grief.'

'It's easy for me to say that, I'm well versed on the matter. But you – this is your first.'

'How much time are we supposed to allocate to it?'

She smiled at me. I loved Maude's smile; it was so expressive and open and overflowing with shiny gold fillings.

'You can't allocate time to it, Ivy. It's bigger than you. It's out of your control.'

'OK, but surely at some point you can be reminded of the person you lost and feel something other than this? It can't be like this for ever.'

'How do you feel?'

'Like someone's ripped a chunk out of me.'

She rested her warm, papery hands on top of mine. 'It'll come in waves,' she said. 'Some days will be agonising, and some days you'll feel accepting.'

'Accepting of what?'

'That every day is different, that everyone's recovery is different. Be patient.'

'It sounds like rehab.'

'It is, in a way.'

Maude looked at the painting again. 'How was it being home?' she asked.

'Nice. Stressful. Normal.'

'And now?'

'Dilys is doing my head in a bit.'

'I forgot about our friend Dilys.'

'I'm worried I'm going to fail my teacher-training, and then what?'

'Then you grow. Life is ever evolving. The most important adventures can come from times of confusion and uncertainty.'

'Anna said I need to stop getting caught up with my age.'

'Anna's right. People think if you're not achieving a certain life by thirty or forty then it's all over, but look at me – I sent my first voice note last week.'

I laughed. 'I would love to watch you send a voice note, Maude.'

'We're not bound by age. We're on our own adventure and our job is to learn how to enjoy the ride.'

'You're right. You're always right.'

'What's Dilys up to these days?'

'She says I'm going to waste Gramps' money and be on the dole for the rest of my life.'

'And you're listening to that drivel?'

'Gramps used to talk about the thing inside us that guides us,' I said. 'He said trusting it might not be the easy option, but it's the right one. What I didn't realise until after he died is that he was the thing inside me, and without him, there's just fear.'

'You've got to find a way to block out the negativity and go into school next month with an open mind. Gramps wanted you to be happy – nothing else matters.'

'Can I keep you in my pocket, so that every time I have a wobble, you can come out and fight Dilys for me?'

'Did I tell you that I'm calling my Dilys "Samantha"?'

'Why Samantha?'

'Because when my Martin was alive, every time he popped

to Iceland, he'd run into our neighbour Samantha. It was as if she timed her shopping trips just as he came out of the house.'

'Samantha sounds like a real piece of work.'

'She wasn't really. She was lonely, that's all. I appreciate that now.'

I wanted to tell her that I was lonely. I wondered if that would ever go away, or whether I'd have to get used to it, too.

A couple of hours later, I was sitting in a cocktail bar in Covent Garden with Wyatt, my date for the evening. I could have stayed at the care home – they were holding a fish and chip night and one of the care workers had brought in her copy of *Gone with the Wind* – but I was trying to be optimistic, to be open to love.

'A teacher? In London? Good luck.'

'It's a good school,' I said. 'The children are –'

'Chavvy?'

'No, they're not chavvy.'

'I wouldn't bother. Teachers get paid shit anyway.'

'What do you do?'

'I'm a fund manager.'

'What do you "fund"?'

'Global infrastructure projects.'

I had no idea what this meant.

'Do you enjoy it?'

'Not really.'

'How long have you been there for?'

'Six years.'

I waited for him to ask me a question. He didn't.

'Have you always wanted to be a fund manager?'

'No, but my dad's one and he makes a fortune, so it made sense.'

'Of course.'

'I was thinking about going on a sabbatical.'

'Where would you go?'

'Might go to Fiji, build a school or something. I'll need to show the company that I've done something worthwhile with my time off.'

'I wanted to go abroad this summer – there's an art school in the Loire Valley that people rave about – but I couldn't afford it in the end.'

He wasn't listening to me; he was too busy pretending not to stare at my chest. I downed what was left of my wine and ordered another.

Aside from lovely, albeit deeply religious Nick, my dating history since joining Serendipity consisted of a trip to an outdoor cinema with a man who got an erection the minute Margot Robbie appeared on screen; coffee with a fellow art-enthusiast, whose love of art turned out to be solely reserved for portraits of young men in ballet tights; and an evening with a man who looked about sixty years older than his profile picture suggested, who spent most of the date showing me pictures of his four grandchildren. (This one turned out quite well; he paid for dinner and gave me the number of a great sitter for Anna, i.e. his granddaughter.)

When Wyatt asked me out, I said yes in the hope that I might meet someone who was interested in what I did and what's important to me. Someone who didn't arrive forty minutes late and boast about how much they earn in the first five minutes. Maybe, if I was really lucky, I'd meet someone who looked me in the eye when they spoke to me, instead of salivating at my breasts. I wondered if he'd had a traumatic childhood.

He rattled on about his sister, an Instagram influencer who gets him into all the West London clubs.

'Do you know Lulu's?' he said. 'It's a private members' club.'

'On Frith Street? I know it well.'

He wasn't expecting that.

'Oh, are you a member?' he asked.

I've been dragged to Lulu's a handful of times. It's filled with vacuous people who fill their faces with Botox and their noses with white powder. You feel dirty when you come out; like you've had the best night of your life but need to be held by your mother.

'No, I'm not a member,' I said.

'My sister is, so I go all the time. Last week we went and got fucked up with Lucy Fenton.'

'Who?'

'She was almost on *Love Island*.'

'Right.'

I studied him from across the table. Anthropologically speaking, he was quite interesting. He had sharp, angular features and a small, uninviting mouth. I watched him as he talked and wondered how I'd gotten it so wrong.

He waffled on about his promotion and his new PA. He'd never had a PA before, you know, someone to get him coffee and shit.

We were out of wine.

'It's getting late,' I said. 'I should go.'

'Do you want to come back to mine?' he asked.

'What? Now?'

'Yes.'

He waited for me to answer.

'If you're not up for it, it's cool,' he said. 'I'll get the bill.'

I wanted someone to kiss me like they do in the movies. I wanted to be held, to be able to wrap my arms around a man and breathe them in. I knew Wyatt wasn't the most suitable candidate, but I wanted to feel something – anything – other than this current version of myself.

'OK, I'll go home with you,' I said, 'but you need to buy me another drink first. And you need to stop talking about work.'

'Sorry, I didn't think that was a problem.'

'It is, and I'll have another glass of wine, please.'

We went back to his, or rather, his sister's – his flat in Battersea was being renovated. There were framed family photos everywhere and horrible signs that read 'LIVE, LAUGH, LOVE' on the walls. I was half expecting to see a poster of a sunset beside some God-awful motivational quote. I was looking through her bookshelf when he took my hand and led me into the bathroom.

He turned the shower on and started to take his clothes off. I'd almost forgotten what it was like to see a man naked. His body was sinewy, like he cycled a hundred miles a day, and he had very little hair on him. I tried not to look directly at his sizable erection as I took my clothes off and stepped into the shower.

'You have excellent shoulder definition,' he said.

'Thank you, I've recently taken up yoga.'

'You can tell.'

'Thanks, you look great too.'

This was a half-truth; he had the body of an eighteen-year-old and his lack of pubic hair was deeply off-putting, but it's important to be complimentary when a man's standing in front of you with his penis out.

After some minor geographical issues, where he spent an uncomfortable amount of time poking around my vagina, Wyatt got the showerhead and angled it towards my clitoris, a gesture I appreciated immensely.

'Can I come inside you?' he asked.

It was the first time I'd ever been asked this.

He hurriedly put a condom on, hoisted me up on his waist

and pinned me against the wall. I gripped his shoulder as he kissed me like an angry schoolboy, and when I came he shouted, 'Do it again, Ivy, do it again,' right in my ear.

'I can't,' I said.

He was still inside me. Thrusting away.

'What's wrong? Is this OK?' he asked.

'Yes, but I've had a bottle of wine and the fact I came from the showerhead is somewhat of a miracle.'

'Can I keep going?'

'Yes, go right ahead.'

He continued for what seemed like thirty minutes but was probably only another three. I wanted to comment on the temperature of the water; it was far too tepid for my liking, but instead I used the time to consider what I would wear on my first day at school.

'You're really good at that,' he said, after he came.

I barely did anything, which boded well for future sexual relations.

He handed me a towel; it was much higher quality than my own. I made a mental note to add new towels to my list of 'Things to buy when I can afford stuff'. The list was quite extensive at this point.

'Are you hungry?' he asked.

'I need to head back to mine.'

'There's a bloody good Indian down the road, and I have more condoms.'

'Thank you, but I need to get going.'

I closed the bathroom door on him, got dressed and made a swift exit. On the bus home, I sat beside a young woman and wondered whether she could smell the sex on me. I concluded that she couldn't, because of the shower. I got a textbook out of my bag – *Get to Know the Curriculum* – and started reading. Just before my stop, my phone went off. It was Wyatt.

'Let's do that again soon,' he wrote.

I deleted Wyatt's number and turned my phone off.

My benchmark for whether I've made a good decision is if my sister would approve of it. I know she wouldn't approve of what happened that night. She'd tell me that sex with strangers isn't going to make me feel any less alone, and she'd be right. But I longed for someone to touch me like they wanted me, and I wasn't going to apologise for that.

14

I couldn't sleep, so at 4 a.m. I gave in and got up. I opened the curtains and saw the aftermath of the bank holiday weekend – young girls in crop tops and men in floral shirts roamed the streets, trying to cling on to the party.

I went into the kitchen and started eating the chocolate chip biscuits I'd made the night before. I had started baking – mainly out of boredom – but I was out of practice and they resembled sawdust. I'd also attempted a Victoria sponge, which was sitting on the kitchen counter, gradually sinking, with pink cream spewing from its side. I sat on the sofa and painted my toenails, then tried to do some gentle yoga, but had to stop after a few minutes because I'd smudged the polish and smeared it all over the mat. Then, as Mia suggested, I listened to Katy Perry's 'Roar' and stomped around the flat shouting, 'I am a woman, hear me roar', which is what she does before auditions, and apparently it has a 62 per cent success rate. At 6 a.m. my neighbour knocked on the door asking me to turn the music down. I'd used up my daily quota of energy, and I hadn't even got to school yet.

The night before, I'd spent three hours picking out an appropriate outfit for my first day. After a couple of meltdowns and several non-starters, I settled on a black dress with white polka dots and black flat sandals. My main concern was my armpits; I was on my period and my sweat glands had failed me once again. I'd already cried three times that morning. Once when looking at photos of Gramps; again when I opened a card from Eleanor – Anna had taken Eleanor's handprint and written, 'I love my clever auntie to the moon and back' beside it; and thirdly when I opened a present from Dan and Mia: a caramel-leather satchel with 'IVY EDWARDS' embossed on the front. Make-up was a complete no-go.

Anna called at 6.30 a.m.

'Sorry, I know it's early, but I'd seen you'd been online,' she said.

'I couldn't sleep. What's your excuse?'

'I have a two-month-old baby.'

'How was last night?'

'Brutal. She woke five times. She's been glaring at me for the past hour, refusing to go to sleep.'

'I miss her.'

'You saw her two days ago, darling. How are you feeling?'

'I've been reading online blogs about what to expect from your first day and I still have no idea what I'm getting myself into.'

'This first week was always going to be the hardest.'

'I had an email from my university tutor over the weekend. I've got to write an essay about the purpose of education and what I think its values should be.'

'If in doubt, be like a man and fake it until you make it. You don't see a man going into the workplace, worrying they won't be able to handle it. They talk over you in every meeting and ask you to do the Pret run and cup their balls as they walk around the office like they fucking own the place.'

'You OK, Anna?'

'You deserve to be there just as much as anyone else. Sorry,

I've got to go give my boobs a massage. Call me as soon as you can, OK?'

'Will do. Love you.'

'Love you more. You've got this, Ivy.'

I stood in front of the mirror, with my new satchel draped over my shoulder. I wanted more than anything for this to be it. I couldn't waste another decade watching others make something of themselves whilst I sat back avoiding anything of real substance. I checked my bag for the hundredth time, picked up the Victoria sponge, and set off to Clerkenwell Primary School.

I decided to walk so that I wouldn't get stressed out on the Tube, but of course this did nothing for my sweating, and I had to stop off at Tesco en route to buy myself some deodorant and wet wipes. By the time I arrived I looked like I'd come out of an aqua aerobics class.

I walked in the reception and said hello to Mary.

'Miss Edwards! Welcome back!'

'Thanks, Mary. It's so good to see you again. How are you?'

'I've been great. My broad beans and chard are thriving. Do you garden, Ivy?'

'No, I wish I did. People who garden are so optimistic, aren't they?'

'It's the great outdoors, Ivy. Come around mine one day and I'll show you how it's done.'

I smiled and a large bead of sweat fell from my forehead onto my upper lip.

'Why don't you go to the bathroom, freshen yourself up,' Mary said. 'Mr Reid will be here in a few minutes.'

After using an entire loo roll trying to soak up the waterfall on my face, I walked back to reception, and found Mr Reid leaning against the desk. He was wearing another waistcoat, and he'd grown a few grey hairs in the four months since we'd last seen each other. But he'd lost weight and looked much younger because of it.

He put his hand out to greet me.

'And so it begins,' he said.

I wanted him to say something like, 'Great to see you! Well done on your interview! We're excited to have you!'

'Thank you so much for the opportunity,' I said. 'I'm so excited to be here.'

He smiled and led us to his classroom. Our classroom.

The room was larger – and neater – than I remembered. Everything was labelled and laminated, and every item on a desk was positioned at a perpendicular angle. There were neat rows of rulers and notepads and worksheets, and by the window was a large basket with 'The Cleaning Bee' written on it. There was a box of wet wipes, hand sanitiser and several rolls of toilet paper under his desk. I wondered whether this was because children lose control of their bowels so easily, or because Mr Reid had a nuclear-grade personality disorder. Either option wasn't ideal.

There was a grand canvas on the back wall, splattered with various shapes, colours and patterns. I walked over to it and put my hand on a cardboard rainbow butterfly.

'I thought we could do a lot more painting this year, with you as our driving force,' he said.

'That would be great. The children must love it.'

'They do, yes. It gets very messy.'

I could see his eyebrow twitch at the very thought of this.

'It's so freeing, that's the beauty of it,' I said.

'I'm glad you think so, Ivy.'

I walked around the room, marvelling at it all. I couldn't believe I was in my own classroom, and that someday I might be in charge of all this.

There were deep shelves stacked with hundreds of books, a creative writing space, a painting and gluing area, a table for all things numbers. I spotted some practice sheets and remembered my first day back in March, looking at the numbers on the page and wanting to flee.

I felt Mr Reid watching me. I put the papers down.

'We were very impressed with your interview,' he said. 'You were a different person to the one I saw in your work experience week.'

'I'd like to take this opportunity to formally apologise for the kissing.'

'Don't worry. I had stomach flu in my interview; I was so disorientated that, when I got into the room, I walked right into a cupboard. Seconds later, I threw up and had to be escorted out.'

'Wow, that's quite the first impression.'

'It says a lot about you that you came back here to interview.'

'That I love a challenge?'

'It means you took a leap of faith. It means you believed you could do something, and you did everything you could to make it happen.'

'Thank you,' I said.

'I saw something in you, Ivy, but you needed a push. You let the little things get to you; you let the children's moods get to you. It's important to pick your battles, see the bigger picture.'

'I'm going to work my socks off for you.'

'We're going to have a cracking year together.'

I smiled. 'You say cracking too?'

'Yes,' he said, 'I think it's a Welsh thing?'

'It is, yes.'

He put his hand out again to shake mine. 'We're excited to have you with us, Ivy.'

'Me too, Mr Reid.'

'Please, call me Finn when the children aren't around.'

'OK, Finn.'

'Today's a lot of admin, I'm afraid. But you can familiarise yourself with the space, take a look at the expressive arts corner, see if it's up to scratch.'

'Great. Is there a fridge I can put this in? I baked a Victoria sponge for everyone.'

'Is it gluten-free?' he asked.

'Absolutely not.'

'It's my fault, I should've told you,' he said. He walked to the door and peered down the corridor, then came back inside and spoke in a whisper.

'One of the teachers – and I won't name names – is allergic to gluten. It's caused quite the furore in the staff room. She said people were deliberately leaving her out of the bake sales, but the truth is that nobody can master a gluten-free cake.'

I sympathised. I had tried for Mia and failed. Also, being gluten-free isn't a real thing.

'There was a disagreement about whether she was in fact allergic, or mildly intolerant,' he said. 'Because the two are very different, Ivy. White pasta doesn't agree with me, but you don't see me going around telling everyone that I'm allergic, do you?'

'No?'

'We've agreed that we should make all cakes gluten-free. I can't say I was on board with this decision. But this is a democracy.'

'I can try and make one for next time?'

'I'm sure everyone would be thrilled. There, first challenge of the day done!'

I spent the next hour organising the stationery, games and materials into various tubs, boxes and folders. Mr Reid gave me very specific instructions, and I could feel him watching my every move. I made sure the books in the literacy corner were organised in height order, just as he requested, which I thought was a pointless exercise, but I wasn't there to comment on his neurotic compulsions.

'The methodology helps to centre me,' he said. 'Are you an organised person, Ivy? Or do you enjoy mess?'

'I enjoy organised mess.'

He laughed. 'So you enjoy mess.'

'I am here to learn.'

'On a serious note, whenever you feel overwhelmed, or uncertain, please come to me. You can ask for my help anytime – it's what I'm here for.'

I was admiring the various colours in his beard – ginger, white, grey and black – when suddenly, and completely involuntarily, I found myself imagining him naked. I shook my head to try to get the thought out of my mind and put my attention back on the phonics sheets I'd been sorting through.

'It's important to keep things in perspective and learn to breathe,' he said. 'You'll be navigating a colossal amount of change this year. Things will go wrong. You must ask for help.'

'I will, I promise.'

'Have you eaten?'

'Not since five this morning.'

'No wonder your stomach's making such a racket. Why don't we take your cake to the staff room, and I can introduce you to everyone?'

After shaking several hands and failing to remember anyone's name, Mr Reid and I took a slice of cake and a cup of tea and went to sit out in the sunshine.

'Have you ever had a really challenging class?' I asked him, as we looked out to the playground.

'Yes, several. It's down to communication, Ivy. We've got to remember that they're only just learning how to communicate verbally. We've got to be clear, simple and direct.'

'I'm quite direct with my mother, so hopefully that'll put me in good stead.'

'We've got to learn to move at their pace, which is much slower than ours. Even learning to exhale around them is good practice.'

'That's great advice, thank you.'

'It's mostly the parents that you need to worry about. And the death of your social life.'

'I was getting bored of mine anyway.'

Mr Reid told me the lay of the land, as I sat beside him, eating my substandard cake.

For every hour-long lesson, I will spend three to four hours planning.

I will be stressed, emotional and I'll never be able to catch up with the lost sleep.

Lots will go wrong.

Some of the children will drain the very life out of me.

It will be the most rewarding thing I'll ever do.

'Oh, and you need to get used to National Curriculum as your bedtime reading.'

'I started reading it over summer. It's denser than the Bible.'

'Your university tutor will be a great support. All the ones I've met have been excellent. Strict, but excellent. Their goal this year is the same as mine: to develop your practice.'

'Got it.'

'So many people describe this first year as a juggling act of three hats: teacher, student and teaching assistant. You must keep on top of things from the start. Getting into a routine early will make it feel far less stressful later in the game.'

I ate the rest of my cake in silence, as I contemplated the immense amount of work ahead of me.

'Let's try to be as open and transparent with each other as we can,' he said.

'Yes. Thank you.'

'We'll get on like a house on fire. I'm sure of it.'

'Me too. Thank you.'

'Stop saying thank you, Ivy.'

We spent the next hour walking the length and breadth of the school, with me typing non-stop on my phone, trying to take note of everything.

At 2 p.m., he said we could call it a day. 'You need to preserve some energy for tomorrow.'

'I'd like to come in as early as possible, if that's OK?'

'How does seven thirty sound? That should give us plenty of time to get our heads together before the chaos commences.'

'That sounds great, thank you.'

'Well done for today. I know it's a lot to take in.'

'Thank you for talking me through everything, Mr Reid. It's been great. Thank you.'

He laughed. 'Mr Reid it is then.'

'Sorry, I'll get the hang of this at some point.'

'I think we're going to make a great team, Ivy.'

'Me too.'

We shook hands and I walked back down the hall, saying goodbye to Mary on my way out.

'How was it?' she asked.

'I loved every minute.'

15

After barely getting through ten pages of *The Evolution of the English Education System*, I closed the book and decided to make a gluten-free cake.

Three disappointing trial rounds later, and several hours wasted on baking sites clearly composed by three-year-olds, I gave in to a dry, dense, carrot cake. By the time I got to bed, it was after one, and I had stomach cramp from eating all the excess cream-cheese icing. I went into a deep slumber until about 5 a.m., when I woke mid-nightmare, having dreamt that I'd poisoned my entire class and was on trial for manslaughter. It was exactly how I'd hoped to start my official first day on the job.

I left the house just after six and rang Mam on the walk to school. She wouldn't usually be up at that time, but Olga, her cleaner/assistant/life coach, was coming over to look at mood boards for the spare room, which was, finally, to become my official bedroom.

'How's my precious baby lamb feeling?' she asked.

'Good, tired. I stayed up late baking. I'm trying to win this teacher over. She's intolerant—'

'Darling, you don't want to befriend racists.'

'She's gluten-free.'

'Maybe you should go GF, I heard it helps you lose weight.'

I was so used to comments like these that they barely even registered with me any more.

'I remember my first day of work,' she said. 'I told myself, I said Mags, you go in there and you show them who's boss. So, I put on some rouge and your grandmother's perfume, and off I went. And you know what? I bloody showed them.'

'What job was this?'

'At the post office, when I was sixteen. I was up against it all back then, Ivy. The pressure, the workload – God, those were the days.'

'I thought you only worked a couple of hours on a Saturday?'

'I had to be confident, command respect.'

'When are you ever lacking in confidence?'

'I taught myself to be resilient. It'll be the exact same with you now, and your teaching. Oh, before I forget! I've been looking at your grandfather's notebook and I've learnt what teacher is! It's *athrawes*. Isn't that great?'

'I'm sure that'll come in handy during this morning's carpet discussion.'

'Do you remember Linda's friend, Carys? She had a mental breakdown and fled to India for six months?'

'Isn't she in an institution?'

'She's out now. Anyway, we had an S and M about the importance of authenticity last night, and it made me think of you.'

'Do you mean D and M? As in deep and meaningful?'

'Ah, yes. That makes more sense.'

'Where are you going with this?'

'It's important to go in there today and be you. The real you. Not the you you think you should be. Be our Ivy Edwards. The one everyone loves.'

'Thanks, Mam. I'll do my best.'

'How's the sweating?'

'Better.'

'Trust you to time your period to your first week at work.'

'How did I time it?'

'And you've got your new satchel? I can't believe Mia and Dan trumped my gift.'

'You didn't get me a gift.'

'Well, exactly.'

'I've got to go; can I ring you later?'

'Not until after lunch. Olga and I need complete quiet so that our creativity can thrive.'

'I can't ring before lunch anyway, I'll be in class.'

'But you can send a little text, can't you? Tell me you're OK, that people are being nice to you.'

'We can't use our phones in class.'

'That's absurd. How are people supposed to check in with their mothers?'

'Mam, I'm hanging up now. Speak to you later.'

'*Pob lwc*, Ivy!'

I put my phone away and decided to keep it off for the whole day.

Mary was standing by the entrance of the school, staring out into the playground, holding a mug that read, 'I love gardening from my head tomatoes' across it.

'Good morning, Ivy! You're nice and early.'

'I couldn't sleep. I dreamt that I killed all the children.'

'Was it poisoning?'

'Sort of. It was a very slow, dramatic death.'

'We've all been there.'

As I walked past her, she patted me on the shoulder and reminded me to breathe. It would be the first of many times that day.

I walked to my classroom, where Mr Reid was waiting for

me. He handed me a tote bag with 'Be extraordinary' written across it. There was a reusable coffee cup and a hefty jar of jam inside.

'A little welcome to the school.'

'This is so kind,' I said, reading the label on the jam jar: Mel's Marvellous Marmalade.

'My wife Mel made the jam. That's not false advertising – it genuinely is marvellous.'

'Oh – I made a cake. It's gluten-free, and rather bland. Maybe the jam would help?'

'That's an interesting combination, but let's go for it. See, I told you we'd make a good team.'

We sat down and took one last look over the day's lesson plan. At some point I was going to have to teach my own lesson, but, for now, I was to shadow Mr Reid and soak up as much as I could. After introductions, we were going to do literacy, then have an assembly, followed by a break, then expressive arts, then lunch, and maths in the afternoon. This was far more stimulating than my own experience at school – all we ever did was sit in a circle and drink milk.

'This is it,' he said. 'This year will be the blueprint for their whole adult life.'

I felt a little faint all of a sudden.

'Right then, shall we meet our new friends?'

I repeated, 'You are a warrior, you can do this,' in my head as we walked to the playground.

At 8.35 a.m., the little people descended upon us. There were apprehensive parents, consoling their children as they refused to let go of their hands; fake smiles and nervous laughs; children high with excitement and parents overcome with emotion. New parents tried to find allies whilst old acquaintances hugged and air-kissed, content in the knowledge that their first day was a distant memory. There was so much anticipation and expectation, it reminded me of the drama and apprehension of my first day at university. Though, instead of sexually ambiguous teenagers, there were hordes of snotty children with watery eyes and tiny, whimpering mouths.

Mr Reid and I greeted various parents as they lined up with their children, ready to be taken into class. I recognised Nancy right away. Her ringlets were tied up in a pigtail and her yellow raincoat was hanging out of her backpack, which was almost causing her to topple over. I approached her and her mother and said hello.

'I remember you from the museum,' I said. 'You came in for storytime.'

Nancy ran between her mother's legs to shield her face.

'Isn't it nice that the lady remembered you, Nancy?' her mother said.

I crouched down so that I was at Nancy's level.

'You came in with your grandfather and we read *The Snail and the Whale.* You told me it was your second favourite book.'

'Grandad stayed with us this summer,' Nancy said.

'That must have been lots of fun,' I said.

'Mummy told Daddy that four weeks was too long for him to stay—'

'Nancy, don't be silly, I said nothing of the sort,' her mother said.

She picked Nancy up and kissed her. Nancy put her head to her mother's shoulder and refused to look at me.

'My name is Miss Edwards; I'll be assisting in Mr Reid's class this year.'

'Nancy! Isn't this exciting. This young woman is going to be in your classroom.'

Nancy lifted her head up and stared at me.

'Do you like cats?' she asked.

'I do like cats and I remember you telling me that you did too.'

'Ginger cats?'

'Yes, especially ginger cats.'

'I like ginger cats the best because they have the same hair colour as me.'

'How very observational of you, Nancy.'

Nancy smiled, and my shoulders relaxed. I had built this day up for so long and catastrophised every single situation, but there I was, winning pupils over with a shared affiliation for felines. The truth is, I've never liked cats; they're bossy and demanding, and I don't need that sort of negative energy in my life – I get enough of that from my mother.

After some more introductions and very tearful goodbyes, we followed Mr Reid into the classroom. Hakim screamed so much that his perfectly spherical face went flaming red. Amit banged his head on the floor and begged us to let him go home and Mabel refused to let go of my hand. It was 9.05 a.m.

After everyone calmed down, we finally got stuck into carpet time, where we talked about their summer holidays. Lots of children talked about their pets, their siblings, or their new toys. Then there was Kitty, who let us know that Mummy peed herself yesterday when they were shopping in Waitrose with her newborn sister.

I later told Anna this, and she said she probably had post-partum urinary incontinence. I was learning so much, not all of it useful.

'We're going to have fun with the Highgate set,' Mr Reid said, in a very rare moment of peace.

'Highgate?'

'Primrose, Ophelia, Kitty, Tarquin, Horatio and Leopold. These aren't your average working-class kids from Barking, are they?'

I looked out to the class. There were children whose parents were first-generation immigrants, children who lived with their grandparents, children who spent summers abroad and children who had never left London. It was a marvellous melting pot with one thing in common: Disney.

Just before lunch, we asked the children to draw a self-portrait. I went over to help Jamar, who was sitting in the corner of the room, tearing up pieces of A4 paper, which wasn't quite the objective of the exercise.

'How are things going, Jamar?'

'I want to play football. Can you play with me at lunch?'

'Of course I can. But, I must warn you, I'm not very good, I'm afraid.'

'That's OK, Miss. I can show you my football sticker book one time?'

'I'd love that.'

'Do you know Harry Kane?'

'No. Who is he?'

He looked at me like I was a complete idiot.

'He's my hero,' he said. 'Who's your hero, Miss?'

I tried to think of a public figure I admired but the only person who came to mind was Mel C. As I pondered this, Jamar got up from his seat, walked to the other side of the room and sat back down on his own again. I waved at him, but he ignored me and went back to tearing up pieces of paper. I thought about what Mr Reid had said about the importance of connecting with the children on a personal level. This was going to be a disaster.

Primrose wasn't interested in the task either. She was too busy rummaging through the costume box. I watched her take out a white wig and small handbag. Hakim ran over to her, wanting to get in on the action, but she pushed him out of the way. Unphased by her robust attitude to play, he left her to it.

Imagine someone being cruel to you like that, and you not caring about it? What an incredible skill to have.

At lunch in the staffroom, Mr Reid announced that I had made a gluten-free cake. Ten minutes later, the cake had been eaten, and I overheard someone say it was 'Clerkenwell Bake Off standard' – a blatant lie, but one I was very grateful for. The discussion moved on to charity bakes and who should organise what and why it's important to get newcomers like me involved in extracurricular activities.

I sat there, nodding as I agreed to everything everyone threw at me. As I left the staff room Mrs Lyons said how great it was to have someone with my enthusiasm and energy. Everyone in the room smiled in agreement. I was elated. Mam was right: it was all about praise and popularity.

Just before the bell went, Jamar tugged at my dress. There was butter grease smeared all over his brow. I tried not to laugh.

'Is everything OK, Jamar?'

'Thank you, Miss Edwards.'

'For what?'

'I was sad this morning, but you've made me not sad.'

He smiled the loveliest, gummy smile that made me want to hold him and never let go.

'I'm so glad. Today was a big day and you did really well.'

'Can you play football with me again tomorrow?'

'I'd love to.'

'You're not very good. But, we can practise together, if you like?'

'That would be great. Maybe someday, I'll be even better than you.'

'No, you'll never be better than me.'

He walked away, looking very pleased with himself and I

breathed a sigh of relief. It was the first real connection all day, and it meant the world.

'How do you feel?' Mr Reid asked me, when everyone had left for the day.

I almost told him about Dilys. How she came into my head throughout the day and told me I had no right to be there. But I didn't, because, as Dan has told me on countless occasions, referring to my brain in the third person makes me sound unhinged, and that wasn't the impression I wanted to make on my first day.

'Like I've been in a battle but won – marginally.'

'That sounds about right. The next step is to work on a naming system.'

'Was I that bad?'

'You called Horatio "Horis". Though, I think I prefer Horis.'

'I'm sorry. I'll get better.'

'I find it helps if you try to picture their doppelgänger. Take Kitty, she looks like James Corden's twin sister,' he said. 'And Horatio—'

'Boris! He's Boris Johnson!'

'And Amit?'

It only took a second to come to me. 'Al Capone.'

'Precisely!'

I began to tidy the rest of the desks.

'Before we go,' Mr Reid asked, 'do you like music?'

'Yes, I love music. I'm an ardent fan of the Backstreet Boys.'

'You're joking?'

'One Direction?'

'Please, stop. My wife Mel and I do a gig night once a month in Shadwell; we play folk music. Why don't you come along next weekend? It'll be a great opportunity for you to meet some of the other teachers, get to know them outside of school. It'll be good fun.'

'That sounds great, I'd love to come.'

'Sometimes, when Mel's had a few too many, she insists on singing "Mama".'

'The Spice Girls one?!'

'Yes.' There was a look of the utmost seriousness on his face. 'Please don't encourage her.'

16

During the first term, I'd be in the classroom with Mr Reid from Monday to Thursday, then at UCL most Fridays for lectures, training and study sessions. I was to immerse myself in the school as much as possible but be strict about setting clear boundaries. I was to plan carefully but try to be spontaneous. I was to talk through any challenges I was facing, but to appreciate that things will go wrong. Make lists. Don't burn out. Breathe. What could possibly go wrong?

I didn't have much to compare it to – as Anna so often reminded me, I'd never had a baby to keep me up all hours of the night, so how could I possibly know what real fatigue felt like. But I felt hung-over every day, without having had the joy of drinking. I don't mind being hung-over if the night before was worth it. In fact, I often think that I deserve to feel so rotten because I had so much fun. A tit-for-tat situation, if you like. But this wasn't like that. Things that had happened yesterday felt like they'd happened weeks ago. I found myself unable to hold conversations outside of the classroom. Mam couldn't comprehend why I wasn't able to message her every hour, on the hour. Mia said she'd lost her best friend. Dan said I might as well have moved countries. I spent most staring at the ceiling, worrying about the next day at school, whether I could keep up, let alone inspire the children and support Mr Reid. It had only been two weeks.

Sometimes at night, I logged on to Serendipity, just to get a little break from reading about educational theories. One night, I matched with Ian. He was an electrician, thirty-three years old, lived in Herne Hill. So far, so good. We spent the next few nights messaging back and forth. The conversation was always on the edge of flirty, but he'd not yet asked me out, which didn't bother me, because I had no time to sleep, let alone date. Also, Serendipity had crushed all optimism I had about ever meeting anyone normal ever again.

I was sitting at home reading about how to bring equity, expertise and empowerment into the classroom, when Ian messaged, asking for a picture. It was 10 p.m. and he was drunk. I gathered this not because he'd asked me for a nude, but because he'd misplaced two commas in the text: 'How, are you babe? Send me a, dirty pic :)'

I peered down at my chest. I was wearing an old sports bra and my breasts looked flat and deflated under the thick fabric.

After googling 'How to take the perfect selfie', I changed into a black lace bra that used to work wonders on Jamie. I took dozens of photos in various, unnatural poses but my boobs still resembled last week's Victoria sponge.

Fuck it, I thought, took one final photo, and pressed send.

Immediately, I regretted it. I deleted the message, then sat down on the bed in a state of wild panic. What if Ian knew a parent at the school and showed them the photo? What if that parent sent it to the principal and I was sacked for sending nudes? I was contemplating leaving the country, when Ian replied.

'Why the deleted message?' he wrote.

I almost chucked my phone out the window, but seeing as I couldn't afford a new one, I decided to block him instead.

Then I deleted Serendipity. I was going to meet a man the old-fashioned way. Or I was going to die alone. Either way, no more nudes.

The next day, I had my first session with my university tutor, Dawn Wilkins. She was a towering figure who vaped excessively and was partial to a slogan tee. On our first meeting, her T-shirt had a picture of a vagina on it with the words 'Anatomy of Freedom'. She inhaled on the vape as she spoke.

'This is about collaboration and creating, but you must develop your own teaching and leadership talent.'

I was typing feverishly on my keyboard, struggling to keep up.

'You will take things from our university sessions,' Dawn continued, 'and immediately implement them in the classroom.'

She stopped in the centre of the room, and everyone looked up at her.

'Does anyone have questions?'

I raised my hand high in the air.

'Ivy, over to you.'

'What do you think is the most demanding aspect of the study programme, and what's your advice on how we can overcome it?'

'Good question,' she said.

The woman beside me, Courtney, nudged my elbow and winked. I felt a surge of pride wash over me.

'The most demanding thing is time,' Dawn said. 'There's so much going on; it's imperative that you have the tools to maintain good mental health, so you can stay on top of it all.'

'And how do we stay on top of it all?' Courtney asked.

'You must get lots of rest, exercise both body and mind. If I can urge you to do one thing this term, it's to look after yourself.'

I couldn't remember the last time I'd gone for a run, or managed more than thirty seconds of mindfulness, but I told myself that afternoon that I was going to smash it. I was going to find inner zen and balance and thrive in my first year. Or, I was going to fail miserably and work in a gift shop for the rest of my life. I could sense Dilys was gearing herself up to say something, so I shook my head vigorously to block her out.

'Is everything OK, Ivy?' Dawn asked.

'Yes, of course,' I said, trying to look nonchalant.

She looked at me quizzically then carried on with the rest of the seminar. I wrote a note to myself on my laptop: STOP ACKNOWLEDGING DILYS IN PUBLIC YOU LOOK INSANE.

At the end of the session, Courtney suggested we go for bibimbap at a local Korean restaurant. I wanted Courtney to like me – she looked like a Scandinavian supermodel, wore head-to-toe Nike, and had personalised the entire contents of her pencil case – but I wanted to catch Eleanor before bedtime, so I said my goodbyes, and caught the bus to Anna's.

'Why didn't you go out with them?' Anna asked.

We were sitting in her living room later that night, eating a takeaway.

I yawned before I could even speak.

'Don't talk to me about being tired.'

'This isn't the Olympics of Fatigue, Anna. I need to knuckle down and focus; you know I'm easily led.'

'What about meeting a nice, like-minded man? Someone who also cares about supporting the learning and development of young children.'

'You've clearly not seen the men in my class.'

'You're being negative. You said last week you didn't know anyone single – now's your chance.'

'I know single people . . . They're either actors or don't like vaginas – or both.'

'I think you should say yes next time they ask you out. I'd like to see you finally meet someone.'

Anna had never made a comment like this to me before. She was like the self-help guru I never had; she was a straight-shooter, but she was never holier-than-thou about it – until now.

'I almost sent a man a nude last week.'

I thought this might annoy her. I was right.

'Ivy! What were you thinking? You can't do that – what if someone got hold of it?'

'It was a momentary lapse of judgement. Don't make me feel even worse about it.'

Anna glared at me. Mark came back into the room with a bar of chocolate and handed me a piece.

'I've come off Serendipity,' I said. 'I was drowning in a sea of wankers.'

Mark laughed. 'I thought you said there was an algorithm?'

'It doesn't work – clearly. The whole thing is humiliating. Let's just put on *Notting Hill*.'

'I thought you said you couldn't watch Richard Curtis films.'

'That's only when I'm heartbroken, Mark. I'm not heartbroken any more; I'm destitute.'

Nobody said anything. I got comfortable on the chair and devoured the chocolate.

'Anyway, the good news is that my tutor liked my essay. She said she saw courage in my writing. I don't know what it means, but it sounds promising.'

I didn't get a response. I turned my head to look at Mark and Anna. They were both asleep. As I got up from the chair, Mark stirred.

'I'll leave you guys to it,' I said, grabbing my stuff. 'Besides, you were right: it's too soon for Richard.'

Mark got up quietly, careful not to wake Anna, and walked me to the front door.

'Do you think Anna will still want to come to Shadwell tomorrow?' I asked him. 'I invited her to my teacher's gig.'

'What kind of music is it?'

'Folk, I think.'

'That'll be fine. If it was anything heavy she wouldn't come.'

'Do you think I'd be going if it was anything heavy?'

'Why are you going?'

'I want to get to know Mr Reid and the other teachers outside the classroom.'

'That's great, you'll need a strong support network this year.'

'That's what I thought.'

'You know Anna will only be able to come for a couple of hours anyway – Eleanor still won't take the bottle, so she can't leave her side for too long.'

'I'd be happy with any time with Anna – even if it's only a couple of hours.'

He smiled.

'I know you would, Ivy.'

17

I was already en route to Shadwell when Anna called to say that Eleanor had a temperature.

'You're sure this isn't an elaborate lie because you're too tired to leave the house?' I said.

'I resent that accusation.'

'I wanted to introduce you to everyone.'

'As if I would ever lie about my child like that.'

'Anna, can you lighten up a little, please?'

'I know this is important to you.'

'It doesn't matter. Is Eleanor OK?'

'I think she smelt my desperation and longing to go out and thought, you know what, fuck your plans, Mammy, I'm going to get sick.'

'Yeah, that sounds like something she would do.'

'At least Mia will be there with you.'

'She's not coming. She's too busy prepping herself for tonight's party.'

'Is this the infamous annual end-of-summer party?'

Mia likes to throw an annual end-of-summer rave, like they do in Ibiza. She gets her friends to DJ, and there's a lot of narcotics and topless snogging. Everyone leaves three days later, having lost their dignity – and their souls. It's an exceptional night out.

'Yeah, she's asked Noah to widen the net and invite some fresh meat,' I said.

'Does her pre-party routine still involve the *Cats* musical?'

'It's much more nuanced now. She likes to do power yoga in the garden – naked – followed by a bath of natural oils that smell like a vagina.'

'Whose vagina?'

'God knows, I stopped listening.'

'Right, well, enjoy. Try not to come home in such a state this time.'

'I resent that accusation.'

I walked into the pub and spotted Mr Reid at the bar. I looked around, wondering where the rest of the teachers were. There were meant to be at least ten of us.

'Didn't you hear?' Mr Reid said. 'Nobody else can make it. There's been an outbreak of diarrhoea in the staff room.'

'Oh, shit.'

'Literally.'

His wife Mel came up behind him and introduced herself. She had voluminous golden-brown crimped hair, a broad, welcoming smile, and she wore an acoustic guitar draped over her shoulder. I pictured her being this quiet old lady making jam all day, but she looked just like Shania Twain in the late nineties – I'd know, because Dad used to have a not-so-quiet obsession with her. He used to pick me up from art class after school – it was easy to spot him in the car park; I just had to follow the sound of him singing 'Man! I Feel Like a Woman!' at the top of his lungs.

I told Mel how much I loved her jam, and she said how much Mr Reid was enjoying working with me.

'That's very kind,' I said. 'I feel like a complete fraud most of the time.'

'We all do, trust me,' Mel said. 'I hear Nancy has taken a shine to you?'

'I know you're not supposed to have favourites, but she's this perfect little ginger doll. I'm in love.'

Mel was about to say something when she spotted a man across the room and started waving in his direction.

I turned around and couldn't believe who was standing there.

Scott.

It had been almost six months since I'd given him my number in that dark, sweaty, overpriced karaoke bar. He'd never called, or texted, but there he was, standing at the other side of the room, and all I could do was stare at the delightful curl flopping to the right side of his head.

As soon as he saw me, he stopped walking and smiled. He was so effortlessly attractive, it was impossible for me not to reciprocate. He was shorter than I remembered, no more than 5'10. He was wearing an army-green linen shirt that looked like it had been in a suitcase for months, and once again I was impressed by the fact that his jeans were not the tapered sort you find on every try-hard in East London. Part of his shirt was hanging loose, exposing a bit of his stomach. It was toned and olive in complexion. I started to feel a bit sick.

'Hello, Ivy,' he said, approaching us.

'Hello again.'

We stood there scanning each other.

'Do you two know each other?' Mr Reid asked.

'Yes, sort of,' Scott said.

'We'd better go get ready,' Mel said. 'Why don't you both grab a drink . . . catch up.' She turned to Scott. 'And try to sit in the front this time. I hate it when you heckle us from the back.'

'I've never heckled you,' Scott said. 'You know I think you have the voice of an angel.'

'Stop being such a smart arse,' she said, as she took Mr Reid's hand in hers and walked towards the stage.

'What are you doing here?' I asked him, when Mel and Mr Reid were out of earshot.

'Finn's my uncle. How do you know him and Mel?'

I suddenly remembered him mentioning his uncle was a teacher.

'I've just started my teacher training at Clerkenwell Primary. I'm in his class.'

'You told me you were a teacher?'

'That was a minor fabrication.'

He smiled. 'So, he's your boss?'

'Boss, mentor, teacher, guidance counsellor. He's a bit of everything.'

Scott was gaping at me, like he couldn't believe I was standing in front of him. I couldn't believe it either. I'd thought about those delectable dimples for so long, and then one day I'd told myself to stop being so deluded; he wasn't going to get in touch . . . that's not how life works.

'Do you want to grab a seat with me up front?' he asked.

'Yes, OK,' I said, gazing into his hazel-brown eyes.

'Great, I'll get us some drinks. What are you having?'

'I'll have a glass of white wine, please – anything but Chardonnay.'

'No tequila this time?'

I felt a smile itch at the corners of my mouth. He smiled back, and then I felt it: panic.

I found two tiny bar stools by the stage, sat myself down, and messaged Mia. 'SCOTT IS HERE. IN THE PUB. HE'S GONE TO GET US A DRINK. WHAT DO I DO?'

Mia wrote back instantly: 'Wow, I thought he was dead. Be cool. Tell him you're dating someone really hot and famous and mention that he has a massive penis.'

'That's terrible advice.'

'Has he apologised for ghosting you?'

'No, he's literally just walked through the door.'

'Can you leave your phone on, so I can hear what happens next?'

'No. Shit, he's coming back.'

'REMAIN CALM. I LOVE YOU.'

I put my phone away and Scott sat down beside me.

'Thank you for the drink,' I said.

He took a sip of his beer. We locked eyes. I took a sip of my wine. We locked eyes again.

'I owe you an explanation,' he said. 'I'm sorry I never got in touch. I wanted to.'

'Did you? Because it's fairly simple to compose a text message and press send. I can show you how to do it now, if you like?'

'OK . . . I deserved that,' he said.

I waited for him to speak again.

'I was seeing someone. I've known her for a while, we started dating, and then her mum passed away. We stayed together, but we weren't really together, if that makes sense?'

'But you took my number. Why did you do that if you had a girlfriend?'

'It's not what you think.'

'How is it then?'

'We both knew it was going to end at some point, but she needed me, and I couldn't let her down.'

I wanted to say something witty and condescending. I wanted to be pissed off with him. But all I could think about was his hair. I wanted to take him home and run my fingers through it for hours on end.

'I wanted to ask you for your number the minute I saw you standing at the bar,' he said. 'I knew I wouldn't be in a relationship for much longer, which might make me sound like a prime tosser, but it's the truth.'

'Are you with her now?'

'No, we broke up in May. I would have called – I should have called – but it had been two months since I'd met you, and I thought I must have missed the boat by then.'

I thought back to what I was doing in May. Ah yes, I lied about my sister going into labour to run from my first, first date in one hundred and twelve years. Exciting times.

'I thought about you a lot,' he said. 'I don't go out much.'

'Are you not allowed out or something? Is this you trying to reintegrate yourself back into society?'

'Were you this sassy when we first met?'

'Yes.'

He was so close to me that I was convinced he was going to kiss me, but he didn't, and the moment passed.

'I'd like to start again,' he said, taking his hand out to shake mine. 'I'm Scott.'

I'd never instantly connected with anyone like him before. I'd never met a man and felt comfortable enough to be my slightly odd, shameless self – not right away, at least. He spoke with such sincerity that I trusted every word that came out of his mouth. Maybe I was being foolish, and maybe I shouldn't have forgiven him so quickly, but I didn't have the energy to play games. I was done with being single and above all, I really, really, wanted to snog him.

I took hold of his hand.

'I'm Ivy. Nice to meet you.'

'I can't believe Mr Reid – sorry, Finn – is your uncle.'

'It's cute that you call him Mr Reid.'

I wanted to throw myself at him and snog his face off.

'How come you're here on your own tonight?' I asked him.

'Mel likes to make me feel guilty for never coming to hear them sing. I can't stay for long; I'm meant to be going to my mate's in Brixton later.'

'I'm meant to be going to a party in Highgate later.'

I said it too quickly – it reeked of desperation.

'It's sort of my birthday party,' I said.

'Is it today? You should've said!'

'It's next week.'

Someone sat down beside Scott, forcing him to move closer to me. I caught a glimpse of his chest as he shifted in his seat. It didn't look like it had been carved out of marble, but there was enough muscle there to make me feel a little clammy.

He ran his fingers through his hair and I watched the curl bounce on his head.

I excused myself to go to the loo, sat down on the toilet seat, and tried to recover some sanity through a short series of deep breathing techniques I'd seen Anna do in labour.

'How are you finding the school?' he asked, as I sat back down beside him.

'I love it. Everyone's been so welcoming – well, aside from Sammy, who likes to troll me for an hour at the start of the day.'

'I don't know how you do it – you must have a lot of patience.'

'Not really. I'm constantly seething with irritation.'

He smiled.

'They're amazing kids,' I said. 'They're adventurous and curious and wildly entertaining. I lucked out with your uncle's class.'

My hand was right by his, on the table. We both looked down at our hands, then to each other.

'Mr Reid – sorry, Finn – doesn't have children of his own, does he?'

'No.'

He looked at the floor, then to his pint glass, then to me.

'Do you have children?' he asked.

'No. Do you?'

'No.'

There was an awkward moment's silence.

'How old do you think I am?' I asked.

'Forty-seven.'

'You think you're real funny, don't you?'

'Yes, as a matter of a fact, I do.'

A massive grin swept across his face and I thought about what he would look like naked. Hopefully he'd have more hair on him than Wyatt.

'I'm so glad I got to see you again,' he said.

'Me too.'

He moved his arm around me and stroked the base of my spine. It was singlehandedly the sexiest thing anyone's ever done to me.

Mr Reid and Mel came on stage and we all clapped and cheered. The pub was filling up and we had to move our seats even closer together. His legs grazed mine. It was unbearable how close we were. Mel's guitar struck its first chord, and the room went quiet.

When she started to sing, Scott whispered in my ear that he loved her voice. I did too; it was deep and gravelly, full of guts, and heart. The chemistry between them was palpable; they were so at ease, as if being up on stage together was the most natural thing in the world to them.

At the end of the song, Scott and I stood up and cheered, and Mel winked in our direction.

I sat back down and got my phone out to check the time.

'Shit,' I said, a little too loudly.

'Is everything OK?'

'I didn't realise the time. I need to get going.'

'Oh, that's a shame.'

He held my gaze and I realised there was no way I could leave just yet.

'I'll stay if you stay.'

'I'll stay if you stay.'

He interlaced his fingers with mine. My entire body felt like it had been zapped by electricity.

We both made our way to the bar and stayed there.

18

After finishing their set, Mel and Mr Reid mingled with the crowd whilst Scott and I sat back down and talked endlessly, oblivious to everyone around us. I'm so used to being with people who don't stop for breath – my mother, Mia, the children at school. But Scott didn't speak over me or second-guess what I was going to say. He was considered and eager to listen. He was intoxicating.

Scott had been brought up in Crouch End but now shared a flat with his brother Oliver, in Pimlico. He spoke a lot about his mum, how she liked to send him home with meals for the freezer because she wasn't yet convinced that he could function as an adult. She called him a hopeless case, which I liked because it sounded like something Gramps would say.

When he went to the bathroom, I checked my phone and saw nine missed calls from Mia.

'Why are you stalking me?' I messaged her.

She was online. Two blue ticks immediately appeared on the screen.

'Are you still with Scott? TELL ME EVERYTHING.'

'I'm going to be late.'

'You're already late. Are you going to have sex with him?'

'No, we're watching a gig. Everyone else has diarrhoea.'

'What? Who's got diarrhoea?'

'I'll be there as soon as I can.'

I closed WhatsApp and put the phone back in my bag.

Scott came to sit back down, looking agitated.

'You know what pisses me off?' he said.

'What?' I asked.

'The Foo Fighters.'

I laughed.

'I'm being serious. Finn's at the bar arguing with some bloke over what their greatest album is.'

'So, people who don't wear socks, and the Foo Fighters. Good to know.'

'Did I mention the sock thing last time we met?'

'You did.'

'Wow, what a chat-up line.'

I didn't say anything. I was too busy thinking about his lips.

'What?' Scott said. 'Why are you looking at me like that? You're some sort of super fan, aren't you?'

'I think a lot of people say they like them because they think they should, like it makes them cool or something. But I'm perfectly content with how uncool I am.'

'You do seem terribly uncool.'

'Thank you, I appreciate that.'

His phone rang.

'Sorry,' he said, looking at his phone. 'The boys are hounding me. It's my mate's leaving do tonight; he flies to Australia tomorrow.'

'It's OK, I need to go to Highgate anyway.'

'We could stay for one more drink?'

'Come on, we should get going.'

Despite not wanting to play games, I was going to make him work for this. I wanted him to think I was extremely popular with a flourishing social life. In reality, if it hadn't been for Mia's party, I'd have been in bed with a hot chocolate and a bag of bacon rashers. But to him, I was Paris Hilton circa 2006, minus the criminal offences. Those were simpler times.

'I'm going to call you tonight,' he said. 'And tomorrow. And I'm taking you out for your birthday next week.'

I smiled. 'Let's go,' I said, getting up. 'I'll walk out with you.'

We got up from the table and went to find Mel and Mr Reid to say goodbye.

'Oh, don't go!' Mel protested. 'I've not had a chance to speak to you properly.'

'You guys were so good. I loved it.'

'Are you leaving together?' Mr Reid asked.

'You are such an old man, Finn,' Mel said.

We said goodbye and Scott grabbed my hand and walked me through the crowd. As soon as we were out the door, he kissed me, in the middle of the pavement, amongst all the smokers. I moved my hand to the back of his head to bring him in closer, and his hands went to my waist. I couldn't help but laugh.

'Well, that's great, isn't it,' he said. 'I kiss you, and you laugh.'

I held my hand up against my mouth to try to stop myself, but I couldn't.

'I'm sorry,' I said. 'I don't know why I'm laughing.'

But I did know why I was laughing. I was laughing because it was the best first kiss I've ever had. I was laughing because I'd felt something stir deep inside me. I was laughing because I just couldn't believe my luck.

The door to Mia's was open, and I could hear her singing. I walked through the cloud of smoke and down the hallway, stepping over scattered bodies, drinking from beer cans and bottles.

In the front room, Mia was lying on top of the piano, serenading the crowd. She was on her back, with one leg up in the air, and her head hanging off the edge of the piano. She was on the last verse of 'Memory'.

The whole room was transfixed on her. Nobody moved, or spoke, but when she sang the last note, everyone erupted in applause. She sat up, her legs dangling from the piano and motioned to Noah, who was playing. They both bowed to their audience, then he grabbed her face and kissed her in that inappropriate way lovers kiss when they're several glasses of alcohol down. I shook my head and laughed.

When they finally stopped snogging, she jumped off the piano, and caught my eye.

'Listen up, people!' she shouted into the microphone, announcing me like I was the final act in her warped musical. 'Our guest of honour has finally arrived!'

Everyone turned to look at me, and I acted out a fake apology.

'She's late because she was snogging some boy.'

'I wasn't snogging anybody,' I said.

'Snogging or not, this is your birthday, and we need to sing you a little song.'

She started to sing 'Happy Birthday', beckoning the whole room to join in. I was dragged to the centre of the room, paraded about like a show pony. Noah came over and kissed me on the cheek and they both put their arms around me. When the song stopped, I said thank you, and asked if someone could kindly get the birthday girl a drink.

'You are so embarrassing,' I said to Mia.

'You love me, Ivy.'

'I do love you. Thank you for this. And sorry I'm late.'

'Let's go into the garden for a debrief. I'm so excited I can hardly contain myself.'

'Fag?' Mia said, offering me a cigarette.

'No, I shouldn't. I haven't smoked in over a month.'

She lit her cigarette. I took it off her, held it to my lips and inhaled slowly.

'I really wish I didn't like smoking so much,' I said.

'So, do we believe him?' she asked.

'We believe him.'

'How fit is he?'

'He's so fit, Mia. He's got a bit of a tan, his hair's all bouncy, and his lips – Mia, his lips.'

'Why didn't you bring him over here?'

'Because that would be too easy. I want to be wooed.'

'This is the most exciting thing to happen since Sarah Jessica Parker started developing her own brand of wine,' she said, hugging me. 'I'll go get us another bottle, and in the meantime, don't talk to the man next to the BBQ.'

I lay in the hammock for all of thirty seconds before said man appeared beside me. My eyes were level to his stomach, where a bulge of fat was hanging over his jeans.

'Where do people go around here to make love?' he said.

I sat up.

'What?'

'I've been staring at you all night.'

'I've only been here half an hour.'

'I like the way you move.'

'Sorry, who are you?'

'Jake. I'm surprised Mia didn't tell you about me.'

He sat down beside me.

'I think I was meant to be at this party tonight,' he said.

'Were you?'

'You have such a great energy.'

'Thank you.'

'I know we've only just met, but I feel like we have this deep connection.'

'Is everything OK, Jake?'

'Everything's magical. You're magical.'

I inspected his face closer; there were little sweat beads coming out of every pore.

'Have you taken anything?' I asked.

'Do you want some?'

'What is it?'

'Mushrooms.'

'That's very kind but no, thank you.'

'I want to be with you, here in this moment.'

'I'd argue that mushrooms aren't the drug to help you stay in the moment.'

He leant in to kiss me, but I put my hand out to stop him.

'Why don't you stay here,' I said, getting out of the hammock. 'I'll go get you some squash.'

'Lay with me.'

'I'll be back soon,' I said, as he lay down in the hammock and rested his head on both hands. 'Try to rest.'

'Can I get your number?'

'I don't think so, no.'

He grabbed my hand and wouldn't let it go. I stood there for a moment before his eyes closed and his grip loosened.

I walked into the kitchen to find Mia hunched over the sink, helping someone with their nosebleed.

'There, there, love,' Mia said. 'Maybe don't inhale so much in one go next time?'

The girl held the tissue in place, thanked Mia and started to walk out to the garden.

'Before you go,' I said to the girl, 'can you take a pint of squash to Jake, please? He's lying in the hammock.'

She puffed her cheeks, poured some squash and off she went. I grabbed Mia by the arm and walked her to the hallway.

'Who was that girl?' I asked Mia.

'No clue.'

'Who the hell is Jake?'

'I told you not to speak to Jake.'

'How do you even know him?'

'Remember the voiceover I did for the fish finger advert a few years ago? Well, he was the sound engineer. He was going through a hard time; I think his wife had just left him. I don't know, I felt bad for the guy.'

'You need to stop doing this.'

'Doing what?'

'Trying to be everyone's friend.'

'Do you want to sit in the living room with me and talk shit about everyone?'

'Always,' I said.

We took a seat on the sofa, in full view of the dance floor. There was Leanne, a mediocre TV actress, being felt up in the middle of the room. Beside her was Luke, who we shared halls with in Bristol. Luke hates people and loves smoking weed. He shows up everywhere, despite the fact that neither me or Mia have had a proper conversation with him in over a decade. Then there was our old neighbour, a goth called Rowan. He used to be quite the talker but now he just stands in the corner of the room and glares at everyone like he's plotting a mass murder.

'Let's play Shag, Marry or Kill,' Mia said.

'OK. Luke, Leanne and Rowan.'

Mia threw her head back and laughed.

'Sometimes I think we should film the people in this room,' I said, 'so that, in years to come, we can have proof that they existed.'

'Fuck no, I'd get arrested.'

She looked at Luke, then to Leanne, then to Rowan.

'Right. I'd marry Luke.'

'Why?'

'Because he's so out of it all the time. I could do whatever I wanted.'

'Fair point.'

'I'd kill Leanne.'

'That's harsh.'

'Do you remember the time she broke my hair straighteners?'

'So, you'd shag Rowan? He's the sort of person who'd wank over your dead body.'

'Do you not think he's sexy? Imagine those dark, brooding eyes luring you into bed.'

'Are you well?'

'Shall we go upstairs to play dress-up and dance to Taylor Swift? I want to be *Folklore* Taylor, you can be *1989* Taylor.'

I laughed. 'I love you, Mia Bradley.'

She kissed me smack on the lips.

'You too, Ivy Edwards.'

As we were walking up the stairs I saw a message on my phone. It was Scott.

'I can't stop thinking about you. When am I taking you out? x'

I showed Mia and we did a little dance on the landing, before going into her bedroom and closing the door.

19

I spent the next few days in a state of dreamlike euphoria. We flirted several times over the phone, where we discussed what our mastermind round would be, where our favourite pub was, and what we would cook for Adele if she came over for dinner (this was more of a one-sided conversation on my part). I told him he could take me out on Thursday, the day after my birthday, because Anna had planned a little something at hers for the actual day. She'd bought Eleanor a new outfit for the occasion, and there'd be cake and wine – the fancy sort that I couldn't afford to buy myself.

I was telling Anna how much I liked Scott, and how uncomfortable that made me feel because I barely knew him.

'Do you think that's strange?' I asked her.

She mumbled something inaudible. It was obvious she wasn't listening.

I bounced Eleanor up and down as we stood in front of the mirror.

'I was thinking of wearing this jumper on the date tomorrow,' I said. 'It's one of Mam's. Cashmere always makes me feel classier than I actually am.'

I tickled Eleanor on her belly.

'Don't you look divine in your little dungarees,' I said to her.

They had a rainbow on the front with her name embroidered in gold letters.

She started to cry. Anna walked over and took her off me.

'She's like clingfilm with me these days, don't take it personally.'

'I can try and hold her in another position.'

'No, it's not worth it.'

I went back to looking at myself in the mirror. 'I thought I could borrow your miniskirt for tomorrow. The dark burgundy leather one?'

'Yup.'

'I never wear miniskirts, but Mia said I need to start appreciating my legs.'

Anna was making fart noises on Eleanor's belly now, and Eleanor was shrieking with laughter.

'Anna, can we have a proper conversation, please?'

She looked at me suspiciously.

'You look different? Have you changed your hair?'

'Yes. I had a trim yesterday.'

'And you've had your eyebrows done.'

'It's my birthday and I have a date, it's a very important week.'

Her attention was back on Eleanor again. I walked into the bedroom to get the skirt.

'I think I need to cut back on the cakes,' I said, walking back into the living room.

'Nice.'

'I've seen a sharp increase in back fat since I started my training.'

She didn't even look up at me.

'Anna?'

'What?'

'Have you been listening to anything I've said?'

'Sorry. I'll put Eleanor down, then you can have my full, undivided attention.'

'I don't want you to put Eleanor down; I want to have a proper conversation with you.'

Anna began setting the table for dinner, so I moved down on the floor and started singing 'Wind the Bobbin Up' to Eleanor.

'Have you talked to Mam today?' I asked.

'No. I swear to God, if she makes one more comment about how much she loved her post-partum body, I'm going to scream.'

'Does post-partum mean post-birth?'

'I'm thrilled that her breasts popped back into shape and her thighs weren't covered in stretch marks. I'm absolutely fucking ecstatic.'

'She's trying to find common ground, Anna.'

'I don't want to talk about it.'

I went back to Eleanor, but I could feel Anna's eyes on me.

'Why are you looking at me like that?' I said, turning around. 'What have I done now?'

'Have you told Scott that you want children?'

'We haven't been on a date yet, Anna.'

'I see the way you look at Eleanor.'

'I look at Eleanor like this because she is perfection—'

'You've got to at least consider this. You're thirty-three now.'

'You're the one always banging on that age is just a number.'

'It is, aside from when it comes to your ovaries. This is science, Ivy.'

'You've changed your tune.'

'What if you date him for three years and then find out he doesn't want children? What will you do then?'

'We've just met! How would I even approach the subject?

"Oh, by the way, my sister feels very strongly that I tell you that, sometime in the future, I'll probably want children. Not sure how I feel about it now, but I wanted to take this opportunity and scare you into never having sex with me".'

'I'm just saying . . .'

'You sound like Mam.'

'Don't say that!'

I started to argue with her but was interrupted by Mark. He walked into the room carrying a bouquet of blue hydrangeas.

'Happy birthday, Ivy,' he said, kissing me on both cheeks. 'These are for you.'

'Thank you, Mark. They're gorgeous.'

He might occasionally come home too late and he gets nervous if he has to drive over forty miles an hour, but I'd be lucky to find someone who had an ounce of Mark in them. He often catches me staring at him, which I know makes him feel uncomfortable, but then again, a lot of things I do make Mark feel uncomfortable. Number one on the list is how much time I spend at his house.

'You look different,' he said to me.

'Different?'

'Yeah, you look good.'

'I'm not sure how to take that.'

'She's put on weight,' Anna said, 'Too many cakes.'

I grabbed Sophie the Giraffe and threw it at her head.

'You almost hit Eleanor!'

'You are insufferable,' I said.

I looked out to the classroom feeling calm, optimistic and in control of my life. Here I was, with a new man and a new career. At last, I was a fully fledged adult. But as I was daydreaming about stroking Scott's stunningly smooth neck, Nancy ran in, screaming at me, and I was reminded that I was a teacher trainee, and any moment of solitude I ever experienced in the classroom would always be directly followed by complete mayhem.

'Miss,' she said, 'come quick!'

Her thick-rimmed glasses were covered in dirt and she was so worked up she could hardly breathe. She looked like one of those mad scientists, just without the extensive intellect that comes with a higher education.

'Nancy, please stop running in and out of class.'

'But Miss, Horatio is stuck.'

'Where is he stuck?'

'In the toilet, Miss.'

'Is he actually in the toilet?'

Nancy often erred on the theatrical side, so it was important to get the full story before I could assess how to proceed.

'Erm, I don't know, Miss. But the pea is stuck.'

Mr Reid wasn't in the classroom, and I couldn't leave a room full of four-year-olds unsupervised, so I asked Nancy if she would go and find Mrs Alan and tell her I needed to see her urgently. Nancy howled.

'I don't like Mrs Alan,' she said. 'She wouldn't let me sit next to Mabel in assembly.'

Her lip was quivering, and her little body started to shake. She closed her eyes and squeezed both fists into angry balls.

'Nancy, please. This is really important.'

'I don't want to!' she cried. She squatted on the floor and lifted her dress so that it was covering her entire face, revealing her knickers to everyone in the room. The blue elephant with the yellow tail reminded me it was Thursday.

Mr Reid walked back into the class. I grabbed Nancy, told Mr Reid I would explain later, and ran off with her to find Horatio. I found him standing outside the toilets, in fits of laughter, with one single garden pea stuck up his nostril.

Mrs Alan had heard the commotion from her classroom and came out to scold everyone, me included.

'How am I supposed to start my lesson when your voices are like foghorns! What on earth is going on?'

Horatio pointed to his nose, where the single pea from his cottage pie was wedged. Nancy was hiding between my legs. I had tried to tell her that Mrs Alan was a gentle woman at heart, but Nancy thought she was Miss Trunchbull reincarnated, and there was nothing I could say to change her mind. To be fair, I also thought Mrs Alan was Miss Trunchbull reincarnated, but part of my job was to fake confidence and cheeriness at every opportunity, so that's what I did.

'We need to take him to A&E,' I said.

'I can assure you, you do not need to take him to A&E, Miss Edwards. The most effective way to deal with a foreign object in the nasal passage is to place your mouth over the child's mouth to form a firm seal, hold the unaffected nostril with your finger, and blow.'

I looked at the layer of dried snot on Horatio's upper lip. I moved closer to Mrs Alan and lowered my voice to a whisper.

'I feel like you've done this before, so perhaps you should do it, and I'll watch and take note.'

'Absolutely not. You must learn, Ivy. I've been here a hundred times before, be it with raisins or marbles or peas. With a little bit of force, the pea will come out of the nasal passage and all will be well.'

'OK, but, can you at least supervise me? Please?'

'Ivy, my class is waiting for me.'

I wanted to give her the finger but swearing in front of children is inappropriate, so I thanked her for her recommendation, then walked to the nurse's office.

Turns out, there isn't a dignified way to give

mouth-to-mouth to a small child. After ringing Horatio's mother to confirm that she was on board with Mrs Alan's suggestion, I told Horatio he'd need to be a brave boy whilst the nurse tried to excavate the pea. Luckily for me, the nurse was new on the job too, and, eager to please, offered to perform the procedure herself. Horatio's floppy, white as white hair kept getting in the way, so it took the two of us to get him into a position where his mouth was clear. I held the other nostril shut as the nurse put her mouth over his and blew. After the sixth attempt, the garden pea shot out and Horatio laughed so much that he wet himself.

Back in the classroom, the children were getting ready for PE. Mr Reid said he was proud of me for handling the situation so calmly. I wondered how he'd forgotten that he'd walked back into class and was greeted by Nancy's bottom.

Horatio was parading around the classroom like he'd just won a heavyweight boxing match, whilst all the boys crowded around him, asking to see the infamous pea. When I told them that the pea had been disposed of, they turned into an angry mob, and Mr Reid had to quieten them down.

Nancy was standing next to me, surveying the room, with a bemused expression on her face that mirrored my own.

'I'm not sure about boys, Miss.'

'What do you mean, Nancy?'

'Sometimes I like them. But sometimes, like today, I don't.'

'We all have our quirks.'

'What's a quirk?'

'It means we all have our moments, when we play up and annoy others with our behaviour.'

'Sammy said I was annoying.'

'You, Nancy, are anything but annoying.'

'Do you want to play with me?'

'Just me and you, or the boys too?'

'I don't think I'm ready to play with boys.'

I looked at her and realised that maybe I wasn't either.

20

Scott had booked us a table at a wine bar in Soho. It had low, romantic lighting, the sort that creates a flattering ambient glow that makes you feel instantly more attractive. I sat down, ordered a glass of wine, and rang Mam. I thought she would help calm my nerves, but then I remembered that she was my mother, and this conversation was going to do nothing to level my blood pressure. It took all of sixty seconds before she went off on one of her notorious tangents.

'That reminds me,' she said, after I told her about Horatio and the pea, 'I saw Huw's mother last week.'

'Who?'

'You know Huw, from school? He liked to stick things up his nose? His mother sends her love. I was thinking, Huw's quite the looker now. I told her that you would get in touch with him next time you're home.'

'I wish you wouldn't do that. I've not seen him since school. He was weird then; God knows what he's like now.'

'He wasn't weird. He just liked to put things up places, that's all.'

'There's a line.'

'A line?'

'Yes, a line to determine when and where it's appropriate for you to pawn me off on your friends.'

'I wouldn't call Huw's mother a friend, darling. I hardly know the woman.'

'I can't think of Huw tonight, I've got a date.'

'Of course! I'm so proud of you – making your way out into the scary world of dating again. You must ring me first thing tomorrow morning. I want to know everything.'

'I'll do you a summary text.'

'When was the last time you got tested?'

'Tested?'

'For sexually transmitted diseases.'

'I'm not having this conversation with you, Mam.'

'Why didn't you go see Tanya when you were last home? She could've done you a little check-up.'

'I don't like the way Tanya looks at me.'

'Well, if you didn't waste all your holidays back from uni in her clinic, asking for free condoms, maybe things would be different.'

'She's so judgemental.'

'To you, yes. Because of all the condom requests.'

'Can you pass the phone to Dad, please?'

'Of course, darling. Now be good tonight. Don't drink too much. And don't do that thing where you get nervous and talk too fast.'

'I don't do that.'

'And for goodness' sakes, don't call him Jamie.'

'Why would I call him the name of my ex-fiancé?'

'I don't know. You do lots of things I don't understand.'

'Well, this has been stimulating, thank you.'

She passed Dad the phone. He sounded very distressed.

'What's the matter?' I asked.

'It's the margaritas. I didn't close the lid of the blender and the liquid's gone everywhere.'

'Why are you making margaritas at five thirty on a Thursday?'

'Your mother's got the girls coming over. Fundraising for some sort of rare facial paralysis thing.'

'I thought she wasn't doing that any more?'

'She says I need to try new things.'

'So, take up a hobby.'

'Your mother says margaritas are a hobby.'

'Well, good luck.'

'Good luck to you too, Ives. Don't drink too much.'

'Why does everyone keep saying that?'

'Darling, come on.'

He had a point.

I nursed my drink and waited for Scott's arrival. Mia said that having one drink before the date would give me some much-needed Dutch courage, but anything more would be reckless, which was rich coming from her.

Right on time, Scott walked into the bar wearing a white Oxford shirt, rolled up to his elbows, revealing those delicious forearms (I will stop going on about his forearms at some point). When he saw me, his face lit up and he began to bounce enthusiastically in my direction. I couldn't work out whether he was excited to see me or had some sort of nervous tick.

I stood up to greet him.

'Happy birthday, Ivy.'

His lips moved past my mouth as he kissed me softly on the cheek. He smelt heavenly, with just the right hint of aftershave.

As he put his bag down, a book fell out onto the floor. He hurried to put it back in his rucksack.

'What are you reading?' I asked.

He hesitated. 'Oh, it's . . . it's a history of the feminist revolution . . . in Central America.'

'Check you out.'

'Sorry, that's a lie. It's actually a book about . . . '

He looked nervous and I started to laugh.

'What? Tell me!' I said.

'It's about tidying up.'

'Tidying up?'

'Yes.'

'Interesting . . . '

'It's a masterclass in organisation, from a Japanese sorting guru. Japanese people are exceptional at decluttering. It's in their bones or something.'

'Why did you tell me it was about feminism in Central America?'

'I read something in the *Metro* earlier and thought it would make me sound intellectual.'

I laughed.

'You know you laugh with your whole face,' he said.

'Do I?'

'Yes, it's beautiful.'

It was the kindest thing anyone has said to me in about a year. I almost told him this, but stopped myself, in the knowledge it would make me sound tragic.

'I bought you something,' he said, handing me a small parcel. The wrapping paper was decorated with images of the Welsh flag.

'Where on earth did you get this from?' I said.

'I spent weeks tracking this down for you.'

'Weeks?'

'I found it in some weird card shop on Carnaby Street yesterday. The manager said I was the first person to ever purchase this paper from them. Shocking, isn't it?'

I opened the parcel to find a leather notebook, with my initials embossed on the front. On the first page he'd written, 'Happy birthday, Ivy. I hope this is one to remember x'. The leather was the same colour as the satchel that Mia and Dan had bought me, and the lettering was embossed in the same font. I picked my bag up from the floor and showed him.

'Yes, I know,' he said. 'I spotted it on Saturday. There's this boutique in Highgate Village where I assumed Mia got it from, so I went in there on Sunday to get it for you.'

'We hadn't organised our second date on Sunday.'

'I know, but I was being hopeful.'

'Thank you,' I said. 'I need a notebook for school; we've got to keep a reflective journal, to record our experiences in class.'

'I know, Finn mentioned.'

'Thank you, Scott. I love it.'

'You're so very welcome, Ivy.'

We ordered drinks and talked about our days. He spoke slowly, like he was trying to make every word count. I told him about the pea, and he laughed so much that he spluttered out some of his drink. He wasn't trying to be funny, but everything he said brought a smile to my face. After a couple of glasses of wine, I couldn't stop myself from telling him that I'd spent an embarrassing amount of time thinking about his hair.

'I'm using a new shampoo,' he said. 'I stole it from my friend's fancy gym. It's such a hit with the ladies.'

'The ladies?'

'Our company receptionist, who's about seventy, and now you.'

'What makes this gym so fancy?'

'Well, it's a hundred and forty quid a month.'

'That is fancy.'

'Don't worry, I'm not, like, gym-obsessed or anything.'

'I'm not worried.'

'Do you . . . work out?'

I made a face.

'Sorry, that was a shit question,' he said. 'Can we forget I said that?'

'That's the sort of thing a creepy personal trainer would say. Someone who pretends to run their own private practice but in fact kidnaps young vulnerable people and hides them in their basement.'

'Being a creepy personal trainer is my side hustle.'

'How entrepreneurial of you.'

He took a sip of his drink, and I could see him grinning behind the glass.

'What's your favourite roast, Ivy?'

'Roast?'

'Yes, roast dinners. It's important.'

I thought long and hard, which he seemed to appreciate.

'It would have to be pork belly. Then again, I do love a good Norfolk chicken.'

'Why does it need to be from Norfolk?'

'It doesn't, but they're generally bigger and juicier. They're looked after; it makes a difference.'

'You have passed.'

'Phew, I can rest easy.'

'Do you cook?'

'I do, yes. Though I'm not as imaginative as I'd like to be. It's difficult when you're cooking for one.'

'What kind of things do you make?'

'I'm trying to get back into baking.'

'I love *Bake Off*.'

'I'm not *Bake Off* level. But I do enjoy it. Especially now I can bake stuff for school. It's an excellent way to win people over.'

'How did you get into baking?'

'You want the truth?'

'Always.'

'In sixth form, everyone started smoking weed. It used to give me a nasty cough, but I didn't want to stop hanging out with them, because then I'd get massive FOMO. So, I started baking.'

He seemed confused.

'I'd rock up with my biscuits so that when everyone was high, they'd have delicious treats to gorge on and I could still be included in all the fun.'

'I thought you were going to say you started baking weed cookies.'

'That would've made me sound much cooler.'

'You're adorable.'

'Thank you.'

'Would you judge me if I said I couldn't boil an egg.'

'Yes.'

'Let's get this all out in the open, then . . . I don't know how to turn on an oven.'

'You're joking?'

'I eat microwavable food and/or takeaways.'

'I thought you lived with your brother? Why hasn't he ever taught you?'

'He's never at home.'

'How old are you?'

'I'm thirty-four.'

'Wow.'

'Don't look at me like that! I need guidance, that's all.'

'What do you eat when you're on your own?'

'Before you start judging me—'

'Don't worry, I'm already judging you.'

He laughed again, and I thought about dry humping him right there on the chair.

'I make a respectable stir fry.'

'Respectable because you buy a ready-made packet and throw it into a wok?'

'Yes. And then, without fail, I burn the wok.'

He excused himself to go to the loo, and I messaged Mia to tell her how well it was going. She sent numerous thumbs up before reminding me not to drink too much and to remember what my mother said about not calling him Jamie. I typed, 'STOP MESSAGING MY MOTHER', then put my phone away.

When he came back from the bathroom, he put his hand to the back of my neck and kissed me. I wondered how many more times he would need to do that before I dragged him to the downstairs loo.

He sat back down and put his hand across the table to hold mine. Neither of us spoke, we just sat there, grinning like two tipsy Cheshire cats. The waiter came over and asked us if we wanted another drink, and we both ordered without breaking eye contact.

A little while later, Scott asked me what made me want to train as a teacher.

'It's a courageous move,' he said. 'I hope that doesn't sound condescending.'

There was something about him that encouraged a certain level of honesty, but I wondered whether there was a danger of being too open, too soon. I decided I had nothing to lose.

'Last year was a difficult one,' I said. 'My fiancé left me. It was all very sudden and, well, awful. I was getting back on track but then my grandfather, who was my best friend in so many ways, got sick. He was in hospital, then he got better, then . . . he died.'

'Shit, I'm so sorry.'

'I woke up one day late last year, unemployed and broke, with no real future ahead of me—'

I paused, realising I wasn't exactly selling myself.

He smiled and told me to continue.

'I used to work in a school years ago, and I loved it: I laughed all the time; I could be creative; I was making an impact on people's lives. It inspired me.'

'I get that.'

'I lost my way a bit – a lot – last year. But with teaching, it's not about you. You're there to encourage them, to make them love learning. You can't afford to be selfish. You've got to lead.'

'You wanted to lead – I like that.'

'It's more than that. Have you ever felt like you wanted to reinvent yourself?'

He sat back in his seat as he pondered this.

'I turned myself into a punk when I was fifteen. Does that count?'

'Was it to impress a girl?'

'No, it was when my dad left us . . . The first time around.'

'Oh God, I'm sorry.'

'It's OK. It's funny, I've not spoken about this in years.'

The waiter came and asked us if we wanted another round. We said yes.

When the waiter left, Scott asked me what my favourite kind of potato was. I said roasted, with duck fat, and very crispy edges. I said that I liked to eat the burnt bits, and he said they were his favourite, too. Then he leant across the table and kissed me again.

'You're not laughing this time,' he said.

I didn't say anything; I just closed my eyes and drank him in.

21

We stayed in the wine bar until closing, then ran across Soho, holding hands and stealing kisses, until we found a bar that was open until late. We paid £5 for the courtesy to get in, only to find out that they were holding a bizarre auction where middle-aged men in tracksuits were trying to fob off second-hand Louis Vuitton Supreme trainers to swarms of seventeen-year-olds.

Despite the odd setting, we stood on the dance floor, hands all over each other, kissing like there was no tomorrow. I could feel his crotch vibrate and I thought my body was going to burst into flames. We moved to the back of the bar and he pinned me up against the wall. I desperately wanted to take him home, but then I thought about school the next day, and those poor, innocent children having to endure my alcohol-infused breath.

'I need to get home,' I said, shouting over the grime music.

His face fell.

'Really?'

'I'll be surrounded by screaming children in five hours. It doesn't bear thinking about.'

'You said you had lectures on Friday?'

'Oh, fuck! Tomorrow's Friday! I've got a workshop in the morning, then I'm in school for the afternoon.'

'Please stay, Ivy.'

'I can't. I have the fear.'

'Of what?'

'That I stink of booze.'

'I think you smell fantastic.'

'Stop it. You're going to make me stay and I need to go home.'

'Define "need", Ivy?'

'Scott!'

'I'm meant to be hosting a breakfast meeting for a client at eight a.m.'

'We're fucked.'

'Yes, but at least we're fucked together.'

When we said goodbye, he held my face in his hands and kissed me – a long, lingering kiss that I thought about every second of every day for the next week. There was a moment where I almost reconsidered my decision, but I didn't. At the grand old age of thirty-three, I had finally developed some willpower.

Anna rang me as I was walking to school the following afternoon.

'What time did you get home?'

'I don't know, around two a.m.'

'How come you were last seen at three forty?'

'Why do you ask me what time I got home when you already know because you were stalking me on WhatsApp?'

'I wasn't stalking you; I was up feeding Eleanor. How's the head?'

'Either I'm still drunk or drinking water really does work.'

'Good to see you're finally learning.'

'I treated myself to a bacon sandwich before class. I know I said I wasn't going to buy any food out, but this was an exception.'

'Ivy—'

'I was on top form this morning. Dawn said I contributed a great deal to the discussion.'

'Ivy—'

'I think we're going to do more social science stuff over the next few weeks, which sounds interesting. Anyway, I showered when I got home, and then again when I woke up, so I think the boozy aroma has left me.'

'Ivy! Tell me about the date!'

I didn't want to jinx it.

'We had a nice time,' I said.

'Nice? What do you mean by "nice"?'

'Fine, it was the best first date ever.'

'There we go! What's he like?'

'He's incredible.'

'What does he think of you?'

'The same, I think.'

'Why do you sound so sceptical?'

'I don't want to get my hopes up, that's all.'

'Ivy, come on. You deserve this. When are you seeing him again?'

'We've arranged to meet next Thursday. I would see him this weekend, but I have so much reading to do, and I need to prep for this presentation next week. Though now I think about it, I've got class all day next Friday and I can't be hungover for that because I've got to get up and talk about what I've learnt the past month. So now I'm thinking I should have just suggested that we meet on Friday, but if I message him asking to move the date then he'll think I'm some loser with unlimited free time. No, you know what, I'm going to move it to Saturday.'

'You're overthinking this.'

'I've lost the plot.'

'I can't believe you didn't have sex with him. You always have sex on the first date.'

'I've had sex with, like, four people on the first date.'

'Is that all? It feels like more.'

'It isn't. Anyway, how are you?'

'I feel much better than last week. I've come to terms with my fatness.'

'Would you stop this? You're not fat.'

'I need to lose the last of the baby weight.'

'You don't need to do anything.'

'I've not had more than one hour and forty minutes uninterrupted sleep since July and Eleanor refuses to play ball with my breasts, but other than that, I'm doing great.'

'Your tone indicates otherwise.'

'Did I tell you that my friend had a prolapse? It's a miracle I didn't have one, what with the shit show that's going on down there.'

'I don't even know what a prolapse is.'

'It's when one of your pelvic organs—'

'I'm going to stop you right there, Anna. I'm almost at school and I feel queasy enough as it is.'

Mr Reid gave me a knowing look when I got into the classroom. He said he hoped my evening was fun, but we didn't speak about Scott, which is exactly how I wanted it to be. What was I going to tell him, that his nephew was the best kiss I'd ever had? That I wanted to curl up in his dimples and never leave?

I kept thinking about his kissable lips, the faint hint of green in his eyes, his infectious smile. He looked right at me when we spoke. He listened to every word. It had been so long since I'd met someone that I liked, that I wondered whether my feelings were genuine. Was this real, or was I just excited to be getting attention from a seemingly normal man? One who was actually interested in things I had to say?

I was daydreaming about Scott's mouth when Mr Reid walked out of the classroom and, once again, the children went nuclear. It was as if they had orchestrated the delirium to erupt at the exact moment he left the room, just to make a point that I was clueless and lacking control.

It started when Primrose pushed Nancy off her beloved red chair. As I tried to explain the importance of sharing – for the hundredth time that week – I saw Amit take Leopold by the neck and smother glitter paint all over his face. In amongst them was Mabel, standing with her pants down to her ankles, shouting that she had a rash on her bum. She did have a rash on her bum, but I didn't have the mental capacity to deal with that specific issue at that time. Was it too much to ask them not to touch their genitals for all of ten seconds? Was that so hard?

I ran to pull Mabel's trousers up, took the chair off Primrose, and told Amit that if he didn't let go of Leopold right this second, he was going to spend the rest of the day in Mrs Alan's classroom.

I'd been reading about proactive approaches to discipline for weeks now, but no amount of literature could've prepared me for this.

'Would everyone please be quiet,' I said, as calmly and authoritatively as I could. 'This is not how we behave in this classroom.'

My heart was racing, my headache had gone from a three to a ten and my salivary glands appeared to have stopped working. I was ready to break all the rules and ring Mam right there and then and ask her how on earth I was going to survive, when Sammy called my name.

'What's this, Miss?'

He was holding a drawing I'd done of Gramps, shortly before he died. It was only a sketch, and Gramps had hated it; he'd said it made him look like a geriatric. But it was the last drawing I did of him before he died, and I carried it around in my bag wherever I went.

'That's my grandad,' I said.

'That doesn't look like a grandad,' Sammy said.

'It's not all about talent. It's got to come from your stomach.'

'I've got a banana in my stomach,' Amit said.

Everyone laughed, me included.

'I've got strawberry jam in mine!' said Mabel.

'I want to draw a picture for my grandad,' Nancy said.

'You know what,' I said, 'that's a brilliant idea.'

I laid out some wipe-clean mats to protect the floor, alongside paints in various colours, and asked the class to use their pieces of paper to tell us about something or someone they loved.

'Think of a thing or a person that means the world to you,' I said. 'That makes your heart sing.'

'Your heart can't sing!' said Jamar.

'My heart certainly isn't singing today,' I said, under my breath.

Horatio painted a gorilla, because he said his sister reminded him of one. Nancy painted cat ears in orange, to represent her beloved ginger beast, and Jamar painted a picture of Tottenham Hotspur Stadium. With them being four, none of the pictures looked anything like they were supposed to, but I'd come to realise how important it was to express encouragement and empathy at all times – especially when it came to the children's artistic pursuits.

'I loved today, Miss,' said Horatio.

Lots of tiny heads were nodding in agreement.

'Thank you, everyone, I loved today too.'

Mr Reid came back into the classroom, surprised to see the children so quiet and engaged in a task.

'This is such a positive way to end the week, Ivy.'

'I'm so proud of them.'

'Were you thinking of anyone in particular when you set out this exercise?'

I felt the colour rush to my cheeks.

I caught his eye. He was smiling.

'I know what you're doing,' I said.

He gave me a little nudge.

'It's good to be happy,' he said, as he walked back to his desk.

'I'M HAPPY!' Nancy said.

'Me too,' I said. 'Me too.'

22

Scott suggested we meet south of the river, but I desperately wanted him to stay the night at mine, so I did all I could to sell my side of town. Far from being the edgy, hip part of London it was lauded as, Shoreditch had recently become a playground for sixteen-year-olds from north-west London, who used their fake IDs to buy drinks with Daddy's bank card. This might not be a wholly accurate reflection of how the district had changed – I might have just aged a little – but either way, everyone looked like teenagers, which wasn't quite the second-date vibe I was going for. I asked Dan to get us a table at a new restaurant in Haggerston. I wanted Scott to think I was the sort of person who knew about trendy new restaurant openings, whereas in reality, I'd be happy eating Twiglets for dinner. Dating, as I had come to realise, is about making the other person think you're much more compelling than you are.

I spotted him at the bar. As I walked over to him, I tried to resist the urge to snog his face off.

He got up to hug me. I almost went in for a kiss but when he didn't, I changed my mind. I took my coat off and put it on the rack beside him. I had a sudden panic that maybe he didn't fancy me as much as I fancied him. Maybe I was reading too much into this? Maybe he was like this with everyone? I banished the thought to the back of my mind and sat down beside him. He was sporting a wide mischievous grin.

'What is it?' I asked.

'Would you mind if I kissed you?'

He was going to be the end of me.

'No, I wouldn't mind.'

His hands went to the back of my neck, and we stood up together and snogged like it was the last snog of our life.

A frustrated waiter pushed past us, a man on his way to the bathroom said, 'Go for it, mate,' and a small dog started to get a little over-zealous on my leg. But we didn't care. I was so happy my face hurt. Or maybe that was because of all the snogging.

'I'm sorry I made you come east,' I said as we sat back down. 'I went to see Maude at the care home today and it would've taken me ages to get down south.'

'You're a terrible liar,' he said, with a smile. 'I know full well you've brought me here to lure me back to your abode.'

I licked my thumb and rubbed my lipstick off his lips.

'I have not.'

'Shall we call a spade a spade and go back to yours now?'

'No. We're having a proper date.'

All I wanted was to take him back to mine and have uninhibited, electric sex for the foreseeable future. Or at least until we ran out of condoms.

'You're right,' he said. 'Let's be adults. Now, what are you drinking?'

He told me about his week at work. He was project managing the launch of a new whisky campaign that a 'famous artist' was fronting and they were scheduled to do some paid appearances in swanky bars across London. The artist had been hooked on a cocktail of whisky and dodgy back-alley pills since the breakdown of his marriage to a French supermodel, so Scott had spent most of the campaign being a shoulder to cry on, all while begging the artist to attend just one of the several appearances they were paying him a fortune to make.

'Who's the artist?' I asked.

'I can't tell you that. You'll tell everyone, and I'll get sued.'

'What's the point of working with celebrities if you're not even allowed to air their dirty secrets?'

'What about you?' he asked. 'How's your week been?'

'Um, let me see. The children like to play a little game with me, whereby every time your uncle leaves the room, they act like savage animals. I was fifteen minutes late for my lecture yesterday, and my tutor spent the whole session scowling at me. Oh, and she said in front of the entire class that I was distracted and must learn to focus better. I was so stressed that, when I got home, I drank a bottle of wine and cried into my copy of the school handbook for a couple of hours. So, yeah, similar type of week to yours.'

He laughed.

'I really like you,' he said.

'Good, because I really like you too.'

I sat across from him as he told me about his childhood summers in Wales. My mind raced forward to five years from now, and I pictured myself carrying his child. I hadn't pictured myself carrying someone's child since Jamie, and I felt a hot flush come over me. I escaped to the bathroom and tried to recover my senses.

'I'd be concerned, too,' Dilys said.

'I'm not concerned. I'm alluring.'

'It's only a matter of time before you say something wildly idiotic and humiliate yourself.'

'Dilys, I'm killing this. Fuck off, please.'

I rearranged my bra so that my breasts looked perkier, before giving myself a final look-over.

'Fabulous,' I said, forcing myself to believe it.

'Tell me about your family,' Scott said, when I was sitting back down at the table.

'Suffocating, incredibly loving – the kindest people you'll ever meet. What about you?'

His body language shifted.

'My parents are divorced, which complicates the family dynamics somewhat.'

'I'm sorry. Do you have many siblings?'

'Just my brother. He's not around much.'

'What does he do?'

He hesitated.

'He's a foreign diplomat.'

'What does that mean?'

'It means he works all over.'

'All over?'

'Yes. All over.'

I contemplated this for a moment.

'Is he a spy?' I asked.

He stirred in his seat.

'No.'

'He's a spy!' I said.

'No, he's a foreign diplomat.'

'You can't even say it with a straight face!'

'Yes, I can.'

He couldn't.

'He's so a spy,' I said.

He changed the subject.

'What about your sister?'

'She's my best friend but . . . she's just had a baby – my niece, Eleanor – she's almost three months. Things are a bit different now. I didn't think they would be, but maybe that was me being naïve.'

'I don't think you're being naïve.'

I grazed his lips with my fingers. They were so soft to touch.

'Do you want to go dancing tonight?' Scott asked.

'I would love to go dancing.'

'There's this working men's club in Stoke Newington; my grandad used to take me there.'

'You mean the one by Clissold House?'

'Yes.'

'I used to go there!'

'What? When?'

'When Mia and I lived in Stoke Newington, we went there all the time. Who was that woman who used to work on the front door?'

'Shelley! My grandad was secretly in love with her. Hang on – were you there for her sixtieth, when they had the stripper from Dallas?'

'Micky!' I cried.

'You know Micky?'

'My mate Dan got a lap dance from him, before we got kicked out. Dan got so drunk that he went into the DJ booth and started ranting that the songs were shit. He tried to steal the mic from the DJ but fell off the side of the stage instead.'

'I remember that guy!'

'Hard to forget, isn't he?'

'Isn't that weird? We must have met that night.'

'How did I miss you?'

'How did I miss you?'

He leant towards me and kissed me so fiercely that I almost fell off my seat.

'I want to go dancing with you,' I said.

'Then let's go dancing.'

I realised then that I was in big trouble. I was falling for him, and there was nothing I could do about it.

*

We arrived at the working men's club and, as expected, Shelley was on the front door, draped in diamanté jewellery with long stiletto nails and perfectly coiffed hair. She eyed me up and down as she tried to place me.

'This is Ivy, you've met before,' Scott said.

'It's been a long time,' she said.

'Your sixtieth.'

'I remember your friend – what's his name?'

'Dan. I apologise unreservedly for his behaviour.'

'He tore the curtains down when he fell off stage.'

'Yes, sorry . . .'

'And he broke the toilet seat. He stood on it and tried to get everyone to join in on a Queen medley.'

'Again, so sorry—'

'Then he wet himself on the sofa.'

'Christ, I didn't realise.'

'He isn't coming tonight, is he?'

'No, he isn't.'

'So, you two are together then, are you?' she asked.

Scott and I looked at each other and grinned. She told us to behave and let us inside. Thanks to Scott's charm, she even waived the entrance fee.

The clientele was exactly how I remembered it. Old East End cockney types who'd been coming there since they were boys, with their wives in tow, dressed up to the nines, cackling away in the corner. There was a patio outside for all the smokers, with rattan wicker furniture and fifty-year-old ash trays that had probably been used to batter someone to death. There were broken lampshades, stained velvet furnishings and sticky carpets throughout – it had the most electric atmosphere. Everyone in there made up part of a wonderfully eccentric community.

It made me think of Gramps' old club, where he used to take

me for a pint of lemonade and a bag of Skips. I'm not sure I was even allowed in there, but nobody dared question Gramps. We'd sit in the corner of the room, him with his paper, me with my colouring book. We'd always bump into my primary school teacher, or doctor, or father's second cousin once removed. I'd listen in as they came to sit next to Gramps and gossip about the locals. The last time I was there with him, we spoke to not one but six Dai's: Dai Milk (milkman); Dai Brains (brain surgeon); Dai Twice (his full name is David Davis); Dai Sinus (likes to get up people's noses); Dai FT ('fucking tight'); Dai Bulb ('big ugly lazy bastard'). We had some of our best days together in that club.

We ordered two shots of tequila and two double vodka sodas before making our way to the dance floor. There was Diana Ross, the Temptations, Jackson 5 – hit after hit played and Scott and I danced like there was nobody watching. When Four Tops' 'Baby I Need Your Loving' came on, Scott shouted, 'I fucking love this song!' and swung me around the dance floor, singing every word directly to me. When the song finished he lifted me off the floor.

'I want to go home with you,' he said, when he finally put me down.

I said nothing. I just took his hand and led him out the door.

23

In the back of the taxi, my hand rubbed his crotch as he felt my breasts under my shirt. I no longer cared about my Uber rating; I wanted to have above-average sex with a man I fancied the pants off. I was close to straddling him when the car stopped, and we were outside my flat.

When we got into the lift he pressed me up against the wall and I started unbuttoning his shirt. When we got to my floor, I sped down the corridor and he tried to catch me up, his shirt half open and the buckle of his jeans undone, revealing his grey boxers. I fumbled with the door keys as he came up behind me.

'I want you so much, Ivy,' he said, biting my ear.

He reached in front of me and put his hand to my crotch. I turned around to face him, kissing him so violently that the door flung open behind me and we stumbled into the hallway.

I couldn't believe that he was there, inside my flat. My only two sexual experiences over the past year were with Wyatt, a man with strangely long fingers – like Gru from *Despicable Me*, only with less of a belly – and Rob, who kissed me like a wet dog. I almost had sex with an Idris Elba lookalike, but I'd ruined my chances by getting blind drunk at his house party. Last year would not go down as my finest.

I went to lock the door behind us and struggled with the chain. By the time I'd turned back around again, Scott had taken off all his clothes, aside from his boxers.

I moved closer to him and put my hands on his chest. He was warm and strong, and his heart was beating as fast as mine.

'I'm usually much cooler than this,' he said.

'I don't believe you.'

His lips moved to my neck and I dropped my bag to the floor.

'You're lush, Miss Edwards,' he said.

I led him to my bedroom and turned on one of the lamps. When I turned back around to face him, I noticed his boxers again, and laughed.

'You're not allowed to laugh at a naked man like this!' he said.

'Your boxers, they're the wrong way around.'

'Oh, are they? Shit, actually, these aren't even my boxers.'

'Whose are they?'

'They're my brother's.'

'That's a coincidence, because I'm wearing my sister's knickers.'

'Are you?'

'No! Of course I'm not, you weirdo.'

We fell onto the bed as he unclipped my bra.

'You're so beautiful.'

'Stop it.'

He lay me down on the bed and took the rest of my clothes off. He grabbed the fleshy part of my thighs and took his time to kiss every part of me, from my forehead all the way down to my toes. He opened my legs and began to trace little circles on my clitoris with his tongue. I knew because of the alcohol that I wasn't going to come, and I didn't want to set a bad precedent and lie about it, so I grabbed his hair and moved him up towards me, so I could kiss his face again.

I asked him to get a condom.

He jumped off the bed and I heard his foot hit something.

'Fuck!' he shouted.

'What's wrong?'

'Fuck!'

He was doubled over on the floor, exhaling in a manner that reminded me of Anna during labour.

'Fuck fuck fuck. I've stubbed my pinkie,' he said.

I tried not to laugh.

'Are you going to be OK?' I asked him.

'You're mocking me.'

'I'm not.'

'I lost my toenail earlier this year when I ran the London Marathon. It's just growing back!'

'What does that have to do with you stubbing your toe?'

'It's extremely sensitive!'

He was still on the floor. I moved down to join him.

'Do you want me to kiss it better?' I asked.

'Don't speak to me like one of your four-year-olds.'

'I'm sorry. Are you coming back to bed?'

'Yes, give me a minute.'

I moved back onto the bed and waited.

A few moments later he crawled underneath the covers.

'Sorry, I've gone ... erm ... '

'You've gone soft.'

He grabbed the pillow and covered his face with it.

'This is a bit mortifying,' he said.

I moved under the covers and down to his crotch.

He got hard quickly, which was surprising considering the amount of tequila in him.

It wasn't how I expected the first blow job with Scott to

be; not that I'd given it much thought, but it hadn't involved me kissing his flaccid penis after he'd cried like a baby about stubbing his pinkie.

Life is so full of surprises.

I woke up an hour or so later with a crooked neck; we'd both fallen asleep and he'd not taken his condom off. A shrivelled condom on a flaccid penis is not something one wants to be faced with, especially not when one has an onset hangover. I didn't want to take it off for him, so I went into the bathroom and tried to make a lot of noise, in the hope that he'd wake up.

When I walked back into the bedroom, Scott was sitting up in bed, the condom now enfolded in tissue paper on the bedside table. We both looked at it and laughed.

I climbed on top of him.

'I want to do that again,' I said.

'Where did you come from?' he asked.

'Same place as you.'

In the morning, I lay beside him, studying his face as he slept. He had long eyelashes and dark stubble around his chin. My fingers were in his hair, admiring his few greys, when he stirred. I jumped, and pretended I was asleep, before I realised that he was actually asleep, so I decided to go and make some coffee.

Two more hours went by, and he still didn't wake. I went back into the bedroom three times, going right up to his face to check he was still breathing. I was so scared that he'd wake with my face pressed up against his and think I was some weird stalker, like the woman in *Misery*, only thinner, and Welsh.

By midday, I'd read over my latest essay, and reorganised the crockery cabinet in the kitchen. I made so much noise I was certain he was going to wake. But he didn't, so I put some highlighter on my cheeks, made another pot of coffee and went into the bedroom to wake him up.

I opened the curtains and sat down on the bed beside him. He opened his eyes and smiled right at me.

'I'm sorry to wake you, but I'm starving.'

He yawned and stretched his delectable arms above his head.

'I made coffee.'

'Thank you, Miss Edwards.'

He put his hand to my cheek.

'How come you look so bright this morning?'

I shrugged my shoulders and made a mental note to thank Mam for the new highlighter.

'I don't feel all that great,' I said. 'How about you?'

'I feel fantastic. Never better.'

'But we had so much to drink last night.'

He leant in to kiss me.

'The thing is, Ivy . . .'

'Yes?'

'You make my hangovers go away.'

I was eager to show Scott that I was a go-getter, someone who liked to get up early and do things on the weekend. Normally, I'd be so tired from the week at school that I'd happily lay in bed all day, surrounded by textbooks, instant coffee and crusts of toast. But after kissing him for a solid hour, I asked him if he wanted to go and get some brunch.

He hesitated, and I was worried that, despite him acting like he fancied the pants off me, he was going to tell me that this was all a scam; he didn't like me at all, he was just some sicko with a pregnant wife at home who was a translator at the UN and much prettier than me.

'I don't want you to judge me on this,' he said, 'but I don't do brunch.'

'What sort of person doesn't do brunch?'

'Me. Out of principle.'

'Why?'

'Because I've been brought up to believe that we are built to live on three meals a day.'

He sat himself up so that he was leaning against the headrest. His face took on a new, serious expression.

'I'm a regular person who likes breakfast, lunch and dinner. Why should I be forced to skip a meal?'

'Nobody's forcing you—'

'Plus, it's one o'clock. If this were midweek, I'd be allowed to have lunch. But somehow because it's the weekend, it becomes brunch. Why?'

'I don't know . . .'

'This is exactly what's wrong with the capital.'

'The capital of London?'

'Yes!'

'What else don't you like?'

'Quizzes.'

'Quizzes?'

'They bring out the very worst in people. People cheat, they lie, they lose all sense of manners.'

'Anything else?'

'No. It's just brunch and quizzes, oh, and the Foo Fighters and people who don't wear socks with shoes. I can assure you I'm into everything else. Well, most things.'

Lying in bed that day, I asked Scott about his previous relationship. He said they were still friends, which he was grateful for, because they'd started as friends in the first place. I've never understood how people can be friends with their exes. How are you able to renegotiate a friendship after seeing that person naked? I'm not mature enough to look a person in the eye, someone who's stood naked in front of me, and not think about their exposed genitals. Who are those people?

'What about you?' he asked.

'We don't speak, which is for the best. I often wish I hadn't been engaged.'

'Why does it matter?'

'I think there's a stigma attached. It's quite the failure, isn't it?'

'I don't agree. People change, they fall out of love. I admire you being brave enough to get through it.'

I wasn't ready to tell Scott the whole truth about Jamie, because if I did, it would become blatantly obvious that I was still reeling from it, and I wanted him to think I was the sort of person who moved on from heartache. But I hadn't; I'd simply developed an effective way of hiding it. Isn't that true for most of us?

'Can I ask you something?' Scott asked.

'Of course.'

'Are you seeing anyone? Aside from me, I mean?'

'No, I don't know where I'd find the time and—'

'I'm not seeing anyone else, either. I wasn't before, and I'm definitely not now.'

'I was hoping you'd say that.'

I wanted to play it cool, but I couldn't. I blamed it on his hair.

'Sorry, I'm being way too keen,' I said. 'We've been on two dates—'

'I've deleted all the apps.'

'Really?'

'The thing is, Ivy . . . I've been swiping left trying to find you ever since I started online dating.'

I was unable to find the right words to tell him how I felt. So I kissed him, and got lost in his embrace.

'I want to go down on you, then have sex with you again,' he said.

I had to stop myself from thinking about how he would propose to me.

By the time we left the house, I had four missed calls from Mia and three from Mam. It felt like they were competing, because when I got back home that night, there were a further nine from Mia, and six from Mam. Anna had also messaged.

'You're probably having sex, which is fine, although my vagina hasn't seen the light of day since June 2008. But please ring Mam. She is stalking me. Eleanor is being a right brat today and I can't cope with two children.'

I messaged Anna and said that I'd ring Mam asap. She replied with a voice note. I couldn't hear anything, so I called her.

'Did you mean to send me that?' I asked.

'Yes! It's Eleanor. She smiled! Couldn't you hear?'

'No. Can you send me a proper video of her, please?'

'I can't get her to do it on demand.'

I wanted to tell her all about Scott, but, before I could, she'd put the phone down.

As I was getting ready for bed, Mia called.

'Where have you been? I've rung you twenty times today.'

'Thirteen, it seems.'

'Where were you?'

'Scott stayed over. We went out for a walk this afternoon.'

'Oh my God! You had sex, didn't you?'

'Yes.'

'How many times?'

'Four.'

'FOUR! Ivy, that's marvellous.'

'I'm trying not to get too excited. But yes, it's fucking marvellous.'

'Did you use protection?'

'Of course, I always do.'

'Because you know what they say, "the bigger the dick, the closer to the egg".'

'I don't think they do say that, Mia.'

'I want to hug you. I feel like I haven't seen you in ages.'

'I know, I'm sorry. I can't keep up.'

'You're doing much better than you think.'

'Maybe.'

'Are you going to tell the sexy teacher about Scott?'

'Mr Reid? No, he's his uncle. Did I tell you he was sexy? You can't tell anyone I said that.'

'I'm glad you're alive and all shagged out.'

'I am. Thanks for checking up on me.'

'We're doing brunch next Sunday, aren't we?'

I laughed.

'Why are you laughing?'

'Scott doesn't do brunch. It's cute, isn't it?'

'Cute? God, it's started already. You're going to be unbearable.'

24

Mr Reid knew that I was seeing Scott, but we never discussed it. Even though I thought about Scott almost every minute of the day, I wanted to show Mr Reid that I was one hundred per cent focused on my job, and nothing was going to get in the way of that.

We were expected to spend every evening planning, reflecting and preparing. But expectations versus reality are always different, and instead of doing all those things, I was thinking about Scott, or seeing Scott, or worrying about whether I was good enough for Scott. Had I got away with wearing my period pants for another date? Had he spotted the mounting pile of dirty clothes in the corner of my room, or the reams of paperwork I'd stuffed under the bed? Did he notice that sometimes when we were out, I went to the bathroom for a five-minute power nap?

We found out more about each other in those first few weeks than I'd got from a year of dating Jamie. He admitted that he disliked ice cream (too cold) just as much as brunch and quizzes. He also felt passionately about watermelon (too watery to be classified as a food) and apples ('Why does the crunch have to be so loud?'). He took an obscene amount of time to shower – his preferred place to 'brainstorm', apparently. At first, I thought this was a euphemism for wanking, but then I heard him talking to himself, and saw that he'd put his iPhone in a waterproof jacket beside the shower so that he could record all his ideas. He ironed everything. His flat was like a showroom – everything was stark and white and looked like it had never been touched. The first time I went around I opened the fridge to find a single bottle of Peroni alongside a tub of margarine – that was it. I worried for a day or so that he might be like Patrick Bateman from *American Psycho*, and I was going to end up in some real-life horror film, but I found myself warming to his OCD tendencies when I woke up to find him cleaning my oven. He had no idea how to turn on an oven, but he knew all too well how to deep-clean it, which worked out well for me.

He told me a date and a time, and I turned up. We kissed in the National Portrait Gallery, several cinemas, a cemetery, multiple restaurants and countless bars. We nearly had sex in the Zara off Tottenham Court Road, but just as I was unzipping Scott's trousers in the changing room, the security guard came in and chucked us out.

I showed him some of the drawings I used to do for Gramps, drawings I have only ever kept for myself. When I told him that one of my problems last year was that I wasn't feeding my soul with anything creative, he said, 'What are you doing to me?', and then went down on me. I'd never had so many orgasms in such a short space of time – my vagina couldn't believe the turn of events.

I saw Scott the night before I went home to Wales for half term. We'd been to the cinema, one of those plush ones with deep, comfortable sofas to *cwtch* up on. I'd fallen asleep halfway through the film, but he hadn't seemed to notice, which I was pleased about – I was worried he might think I was narcoleptic. We'd come back to mine and he asked me to play a game.

'You've got to say the first word that comes to your mind,' he said.

This disappointed me; I thought it was going to be a sexy game. But then he had just noticed that his shoulder was wet from my dribble, so he probably wasn't feeling all that erotic.

'I'll start with an easy one,' he said. 'Cheese.'

'Wine.'

'Classic Ivy Edwards. Animal.'

'Blankets.'

'What?' he said.

'As in pigs in blankets. You said to say the first thing that came into my head!'

'Happiness.'

'The sea.'

'Bed.'

'Sex.'

He smiled.

'And the City,' I continued.

'I will try not to judge you for that,' he said. 'Home.'

'Wales.'

'Wales? Not London?'

'It's not the same. I love London but . . . Wales calls to me.'

'It calls to you?'

'Yes, when I step off the train or we pass over the Severn Bridge, I can hear the cry of the seagulls and the Welsh lilt, and I know I'm home.'

'I'd best get myself to Wales then, see what all the fuss is about.'

I kissed him. 'I'd love that.'

'I think of Mum's in Crouch End as more of a home than my flat in Pimlico,' he said.

'That's because it's not lived in, and your housemate is travelling the world as a secret agent.'

'Foreign diplomat.'

'Have you ever thought about living anywhere else?' I asked.

'I love the States. I used to be obsessed with American culture, mainly Elvis. I'd try for hours to perfect his quiff.'

'I can imagine that would suit you.'

'It didn't, trust me. There's something so nostalgic about America, though – fifties rock 'n' roll music, African-American blues. Don't you think?'

'Honestly? No.'

He laughed.

'I love New York. I visited Mia a couple of times when she was out there on Broadway. We always said we'd go to LA together, too.'

'I spent a summer touring California, with my dad. Just me, him and a classic Chevy convertible. I toyed with the idea of moving there, but . . . ' he tailed off.

'What stopped you?'

'Life gets in the way, doesn't it? Parents become people. Dads leave.'

His facial expression changed, and he looked a bit lost. He didn't speak for some time. I kissed him on the lips and told him I wanted to eat him up. I should have said something more reassuring, but I had food on the brain as I'd spent my lunchbreak comforting Primrose after Mabel told her that Spotty the Horse from Mr Tumble wasn't a real horse, and I hadn't had time to eat.

'Where would you go?' he asked. 'If you could live outside of London?'

'I don't mind, as long as it's by the sea. I wanted to go travelling before my teacher training, I had this vision of me idling my time away on a beach.'

'You could always go away once you're qualified?'

'I wouldn't have the money. And even if I did, I don't think

I'd want to. It's taken me so long to realise what I want to do with my life; now that I'm here, I just want to get on with it.'

'OK, so somewhere by the sea, and – anything else?' he asked.

'Somewhere to run, a decent pub, a Turkish corner shop—'

'Why does it have to be Turkish?'

'Because Selim in my local corner shop is Turkish, and it's the best corner shop ever.'

'That seems fair.'

'And it's got to be within a three-hour train, bus or car ride to my family.'

'Speaking of family . . . when can I meet your sister?'

'Soon.'

'I'll be well behaved.'

'It's not you I'm worried about. Anna's so on edge these days, I don't know how to be with her.'

'Have you talked to her about it?'

'No. I don't want to cause her more stress.'

'Why don't you take her to a neutral place when you're back in Wales, get it all out? You'll feel much better for it.'

'Maybe. Anyway, what about you – where would you live?'

'I don't have much criteria.'

'What about your mum? You want to be close to her, right?'

'And you. Close to Mum, and you. That's it.'

I smiled.

'Don't take it too seriously,' he said. 'I'm only trying to get into your pants again.'

I got under the covers, whipped my knickers off and held them up to show him.

'Pants are off!' I cried.

He hurled my knickers across the room and we both dove under the covers.

25

'Ivy? Hello?' Anna said.

We were outside Anna and Mark's, piling our bags into the car, ready for the trip back home to Wales.

'What?'

'My jeans . . . '

I stared at her. 'I don't get it?'

'Ivy! For Christ's sake. These are my size-twelve jeans. Size twelve, Ivy! It's been months since these bad boys have been out on the town.'

'I'm very happy for you, you look great.'

Mark gave me a sympathetic look and rushed into the driver's seat. I went to check that Eleanor's car seat was in the correct position. The night before I'd dreamt that I hadn't strapped her in properly; we crashed on the motorway and she was thrown out the window onto the hard shoulder at lightning speed. Some might say I was stressed about a six-hour car journey with my sister. They'd be right.

'You know how many Green & Black's I had to refuse to get into these?' Anna said.

'I thought it was prawn and mayonnaise sandwiches?'

There it was again, the vein.

'We seem to be taking a whole lot of stuff back home with us,' I said.

'There's about a hundred bottles in there.'

'Why?'

'I thought I told you? Eleanor started taking the bottle.'

'That's amazing. Well done, Eleanor.'

'Now Mark can do some feeds, which he's thrilled about.'

'You don't need to be sarcastic, Anna,' Mark said.

'I'm not being sarcastic. It will be nice to get some help. You know, like when you took two days off work and instead of taking Eleanor out so that I could nap, you decided to fix the car radio.'

'I did not spend two days fixing the car radio. You're the one who asked me to fix it before we drove to Wales. I did as I was told. Like I always do.'

I got into the back seat with Eleanor. Anna got in the passenger seat in front of me and slammed the door. I kissed Eleanor and whispered into her ear that I loved her. We'd not been driving for ten minutes before she fell fast asleep, her precious little hand gripping my finger. I followed her lead and closed my eyes, too.

I was drifting in and out of sleep when I heard Mark and Anna whispering.

'I know Mags can be difficult, but can you please try to not let her bother you this week?'

'You have no idea, Mark.'

'Either you have a proper conversation with her about how much she's upsetting you, or you learn to let it go.'

'Whatever.'

'You're always teetering on the edge of full-blown rage.'

'I am not.'

'You're doing it now! Breathe, Anna. Remember what they told us in hypnobirthing.'

'I'm using the same tools to manage my mother as I did to manage childbirth. Fancy that.'

Mark put his hand on her thigh.

'Stop flirting and start revving,' she said. 'It'll be November by the time we're home with you at the wheel.'

I was about to drift off again when Anna mentioned my name.

'Do you think Ivy's OK? She's not said much about this Scott guy . . . it's unlike her.'

'Anna, don't meddle.'

She lowered her voice even more and turned around to check I was still asleep.

'I'm not meddling. But she's spending so much time with him and we barely know anything about him.'

'She's only been seeing him a few weeks. Leave her be, she's happy.'

'What if she isn't happy? What if she's feeling trapped and controlled?'

'You're steamrolling.'

'I'm not!'

'Darling, I love you, but stop it.'

'If she gets kidnapped and we find her locked up in his basement, you'll be sorry.'

I coughed, and Anna looked around to the back seat.

'He's from Crouch End, he lives in Pimlico with his brother, but he's never there and I think it's because he's a spy. His last relationship was earlier this year, but they were more friends than partners. His parents are divorced. It sounds messy, but he's not gone into much detail. Oh, and he was conceived in Wales. Anything else?'

'How long have you been awake for?'

'I'm not withholding information from you. It's new and nice and—'

'Ivy, you don't have to explain yourself,' Mark said. 'I'd like to remind your sister of when we started dating.'

'And, what of it?' Anna said.

I watched her through the rear-view mirror; the vein on her forehead was in overdrive now.

'You didn't leave my flat for the first three days,' Mark said. 'And you'd practically moved in by week two.'

'I remember that,' I said. 'We didn't hear from you for two weeks. Mam went ape-shit.'

'I can't believe you're making this about me.'

'Anna—'

'After everything that happened last year, is it not OK for me to worry about my little sister?'

'Anna—'

'I'm being penalised because I care.'

'Anna?'

'What?'

'Stop acting like Mam.'

She sank back into the passenger seat and looked out the window.

'You two are always ganging up on me!'

I was about to tell her that that was a direct quote from our mother, when Eleanor let out a loud, wet fart. I looked over at her, and soon enough we were all laughing. Then came the smell, and I saw that her last meal had gone all the way up her back and into her neck. The laughter stopped soon after that.

We had to stop off at two garages – one to clean the poo off Eleanor, and another for when she peed, and it leaked all over the car seat. That was my fault, apparently, because I hadn't put the nappy on correctly. I offered to take the next change, promising to do it right this time. After patting myself on the back for finally mastering how to change a nappy, I noticed a smear of poo on my corduroy dungarees. Did I get a thank you for trying to help? No, all I got was some mutterings about what a nuisance I was. I should've stayed in London.

Mam came running down the driveaway as we unpacked the car.

'*Dewch i mewn!*' she said. 'I just asked you to come in, though I think I might have used the formal expression. Never mind, it's not like you have a clue what I'm on about.'

'How's Welsh going?' Mark asked.

'I came top of the class in this week's test.'

'*Da iawn!*'

Mam noticed Anna's outfit and squealed, 'Your size-twelve jeans!'

'At last,' Anna said. 'Someone who appreciates this momentous occasion.'

Mam watched me struggle to get Eleanor out of the car seat.

'What's all that for?' she said, pointing at an oversized tote on the ground.

'They're my paints.'

'You've got paints here, darling.'

'These are for Eleanor; they're finger ones, that she can eat.'

'I knew it,' she said, throwing her arms in the air. 'I've just had Olga come to clean and you're going to mess everything up.'

'They're washable.'

'Olga's very busy, you know, she can't pop round willy nilly.'

'We'll paint in the garden, Mam. Can you hold Eleanor now, please?'

'Let me change out of this shirt first. This is my "arrival" outfit. I'll get into my lounge wear and then I'll be all over my baby lamb.'

Mam stood there watching us unload the car; she had her hand on her hip and was exhaling loudly.

'I thought you were going to change?' I said.

'Why has nobody commented on how fabulous my shirt is?'

'It's fabulous.'

'It's made from renewable energy.'

'Circular fashion.'

'What on earth is circular, darling?'

'It's what you're wearing.'

'Whatever it is, I look phenomenal.'

She walked back up the drive and into the house.

'I need a drink,' I said, looking at Mark.

'If there isn't a cold beer in my hand in two minutes, I'm leaving.'

When you have a child, you must travel with the entire contents of your house. Mam was picking things up and putting them in different places, a trick she liked to play to make us think she was being helpful. She kept saying how much effort she'd put into our stay. 'Look how full the fridge is'; 'I've bought this wine specially'; 'Have you noticed the canapés I've made?'

'Very impressive, Mam. They look very similar to the ones they sell in M&S.'

She was taking her plight to help the environment to a new level, so in addition to her new wardrobe of obscure Scandinavian brands that nobody had ever heard of, everything in the fridge was local, organic and sustainable.

I was getting some food out when Dad walked into the kitchen.

'Sorry I'm late, darling,' he said, coming towards me with open arms. 'The golf club was packed today, took us ages to get around the course.'

'It's doing you good, Dad,' I said, patting him on the stomach. 'You look very trim.'

'It's this diet your mother's forced on me.'

'Is this the plant thing?'

'I'm allowed to eat meat now, but only if the animals could run around and eat like kings when they were alive. We had to give up vegetarianism, Ives. Your mother's gas was out of control.'

'You don't need to go into it.'

'We had Linda and Marv over for dinner. Your mother and I spent hours making a nut roast, had some sprouts with chestnuts too—'

'Dad, you know you can't eat sprouts.'

'I only had a couple. But your mother, Christ, she couldn't stop; we tried to ignore it, but it was unbearable. We sent a bottle of wine over to apologise.'

'Times are tough in the Gower, aren't they?'

'I was at the club last week. I'd made this butternut squash dish for lunch, done three ways, with some chilli and yoghurt sauce—'

'Check you out.'

'I had to run off the course, my bowels moved so fast, *mun*. Thank God we were near the clubhouse.'

'Well, sounds like the worst is over with now.'

'It was a trying couple of weeks. But, you're here now, and that's the main thing.'

I hugged him again. 'It's good to be home, Dad.'

26

I woke from an eleven-hour sleep to find Mam on the ab-cruncher, an apparatus that none of us had seen since 1993. She had Linda on speakerphone.

'Listen, now . . . No, no, it's my turn . . . I've already got the ingredients . . . Tony's been perfecting his recipe for weeks.'

She spotted me at the door. 'Hang on, Linda. Ivy's just walked in.'

Linda's voice belted out of Mam's phone. 'Hi, Ivy! How are things, love?'

'Good, thanks, Linda. How are you?'

'Oh, you know, can't complain. Your mother tells me you have a new man.'

I looked at Mam, who was putting her hands up in defence.

'Yes, Linda. I'm seeing someone.'

'I was saying to your mother this summer, I wish our Ivy would find someone. It's been a heck of a while since Jamie, hasn't it?'

'It's been a year and a half—'

'And some!' Mam interjected.

I shot her a look and she retreated to her ab-cruncher.

'Was there anything else, Linda?' I asked.

'No, just take care of yourself. Lay off the booze and fags.'

'Sure. Great talking to you, as always.'

I was about to walk out the door when Mam called me.

'Stay here, please; we need to ask you about the tequila.'

'What tequila?'

'For the party?'

'Whose party?'

'Mine!' Linda shouted down the phone.

'Why are you going to be drinking tequila?'

'We wanted a Spanish theme this year,' Mam said, panting away as she continued with her sit-ups.

'Tequila isn't Spanish,' I said. 'It's Mexican.'

'It's pretty much the same though, isn't it?'

'Yes, you're right – Spain and Mexico are pretty much the same.'

'How many bottles do you think we need for fifteen people?' Mam asked me.

'I don't know, four?'

'Four! Linda, can you hear that! Four!'

I could hear Linda chuckling.

'Oh, Ivy, don't make us laugh; I've already done my ab workout this morning!' Mam said.

I walked out of the room and left them to it.

Anna was in the kitchen with the papers splayed out in front of her, eating a greasy-looking full English. Gramps used to get funny about calling it a 'full English'; he'd insist we add laverbread to the plate and thus pronounce it, 'A full Welsh'.

'Bloody hell, what time do you call this?' she said.

'Hang on, I'm up every morning at six—'

'Try four.'

'It's not a competition. I've not been able to sleep like this in ages. I don't get to bed till late because of the lesson prep and coursework I have to do.'

'Ivy, you're fooling no one. You're up all night shagging Scott.'

Dad came into the kitchen and faked a cough.

'I was going to take the bikes out and get some fresh air,' Anna said. 'Fancy coming with?'

'Where's Eleanor going to go?' I asked.

'Mark's taking her. I told you, she's taking the bottle now. Good to see you were listening.'

'Me not listening?'

'Don't look at me like that. Are you in?'

'Yes, I'm in.'

We high-fived each other as Mam came into the kitchen, holding 1kg weights in each hand.

'In for what?' she asked.

'The girls are going for a cycle,' Dad said. 'Fancy it, Mags?'

She was lunging around the kitchen, doing bicep curls.

'It's a no from me,' she said. 'I've already done thirty-two sit-ups this morning.'

She stood in the middle of the kitchen and started doing squats.

'I can't tell you how good this healthy living is making me feel,' she said. 'It's about having a well-balanced lifestyle. Everything in moderation. You girls should try it.'

The timer went off on the cooker. 'Oh, my wine's ready!' she said.

She walked over to the freezer and took a bottle out.

'Thirty minutes in the freezer and it's the perfect temperature,' she said.

Anna, Dad and I stood watching her.

'I'm so excited about Linda's Spanish Soirée.'

'Mexican,' I said.

'We're having seafood paella – sustainable fish, of course. We were going to go veggie but, after last time, we're staying clear of pulses. I just need to get fifteen bottles of tequila—'

'I thought you said there were fifteen people going?'

'Exactly.'

Dad held his head in his hands.

'Everything in moderation, right, Mam?' Anna said, smiling.

I went to kiss her on the cheek, as I bit my tongue and reminded myself that I was trying to be kinder. 'Never change,' I told her.

Anna called after me as I was walking up the stairs.

'You know we're only cycling to the pub, right? I want to sit on the wall and get tipsy.'

'Sounds perfect,' I said.

The cycle to the Anchor took longer than expected after I spotted a boy I'd had a fleeting love affair with one summer, after our first year at university. He used to go around with his dad's Leica camera, taking pictures of us all – we thought he was a real creep. But then he came back that summer having secured an internship with famed photographer David LaChapelle, and suddenly he was the coolest boy around. He told me he had assisted on a shoot with Britney Spears and I knew I had to have him; he felt me up around the back of All Bar One in Swansea that very night. I didn't think it best to approach him when he was with his mother and toddler, so I grabbed Anna and we hid behind the ice-cream truck until they were out of sight.

At the Anchor, I found a spot on the edge of the wall, overlooking the bay. The owner of the pub and Mam's good friend, Liz, came out to see us.

'This reminds me of the good old days,' she said. 'You two sneaking out of the house, cycling over here for cheeky pints of cider.'

'You probably shouldn't have been giving cider to children,' I said.

'Yes, good point; don't tell your mother.'

'I think she already knows.'

Anna took a sip of her drink and coughed.

'Christ, Liz. How much gin did you put in this?'

'I don't know, love. I lose count these days.'

Liz walked back inside, and Anna toasted to an afternoon of freedom.

'I really needed this,' she said.

'It doesn't bode well that we've only been home for twenty-four hours, and we're already looking for escape routes.'

We sat in silence, listening to the waves crash against the rocks below. Liz came out to give us a blanket, another round of drinks, and offer some snacks, but otherwise it was just the two of us, as I'd hoped.

'I miss this,' Anna said.

'I know. Coming here always makes me think of Gramps.'

'Last time we were here—'

'The funeral. I remember hitting Mark after Jamie texted me.'

'You were a nightmare.'

'Be kind.'

'You were. I can say what I want on the wall.'

'What – because you're pissed every time you're on it and you can't control what comes out of your mouth.'

She smiled at me.

'I was the worst version of myself back then,' I said.

'And now?'

'I'm doing all right. What do you think?'

'Out of ten, I'd say you're a six and a half.'

'I'll take that. What about you?'

'If I didn't miss work, I'd be a nine. No – an eight. I'm really bored of getting up seven times a night.'

'Do you miss it?'

'Work? Yes, but I don't have the brain capacity to think about it now.'

'When do you go back? Will you go back?'

'God, yes. Don't get me wrong, I love being a mother, but that's just the problem, right now it's like all I am is Eleanor's mother. I'm not Anna, the successful lawyer who bulldozes through court rooms.'

'I still think you're a bulldozer.'

'It can't go back to how it was – me taking work home every night.'

'You've got time to figure that out, set yourself some boundaries.'

Anna looked at me deeply. 'When I said earlier that I missed this, I meant us – me and you – hanging out together.'

'Me too.'

'I'm sorry I've not been there for you these past few months.'

'It's not that you haven't been there for me . . . ' I paused, trying to find the right words. 'I never used to worry about saying the wrong thing around you, but now all I seem to do is upset you.'

'You don't upset me.'

'It seems like I do. You snap at me – a lot.'

Anna looked out to the sea.

'Mark said the same thing to me last week,' she said.

'Do you agree with us?'

'You have no idea what it's like. Even Mark has no idea what it's like. It's not your fault; I had no idea what it was going to be like either.'

'You used to open up to me about stuff whereas now I just seem to irritate you. I miss our long chats and our walks together and making fun of Mam with you.'

'We still do that.'

'Not really. I knew things would change when you had a baby, but I didn't think they'd change between us.'

She finished off the last of her gin.

'It's really hard being a milk machine, and a bad one at that.'

'You're an amazing mother, Anna.'

'I was so one-track-minded about having a baby, and obviously Eleanor is our entire world but, Christ, it's hard. They tell you that breastfeeding is the most natural thing in the world, but they don't tell you that it's fucking excruciating. I don't know why I persisted when I should've held my hands up and said "enough". Why do I need to set myself these standards all the time?'

'You've always been a perfectionist; it's who you are.'

'Now I feel guilty because she's not on my boob as much, but she's happy, and I have some freedom back, so I should be happy too. It's this never-ending cycle of guilt and anxiety and worry that I'm not doing enough.'

A tear rolled down her cheek. I moved closer to her and put my arm around her.

'I wish you'd talk to me about this stuff,' I said.

'I don't want to bore you with this; this is what my NCT friends are for.'

'I'd love to be bored with it.'

'Thank you,' she said, wiping the tears away. 'You're happy, aren't you, Ivy?'

'Yes, I'm happy.'

'And it's not just because of Scott.'

'No, it's not.'

'Good, I want to be sure you're OK for you, before anyone else comes into your life.'

'I think Dilys has taken leave.'

'Have you fired her, or is she on sabbatical?'

'I'm not sure yet.'

She covered my shoulders with the blanket and we stared out to the sea.

'Do you think I've become boring?' I asked.

'Where's this come from?'

'I don't know, I used to be much livelier.'

'You mean drunk?'

'No, I don't mean drunk.'

'Sorry. You've grown up so much the past year, Ives. Your priorities have shifted . . . where there was once vodka—'

'Anna!'

'You know what I mean. You care about what you do now and you're working hard for it. You can't go out till six in the morning and then teach a classroom of four-year-olds.'

'I know. I just want Scott to think I'm cool.'

'You've never been that cool though, have you?'

She had a point.

'Tell me about him,' she asked.

'I like him . . . very much.'

'And he likes you?'

'Yes. He doesn't just say it, he makes me feel it. Every time I'm with him, I know.'

'Why haven't you let us meet him yet?'

'It's only been six weeks. He hasn't met Mia yet, either.'

'If you introduced him to her before me, I'd go ballistic.'

'I want to keep him all to myself. I feel like I'm making up for lost time with him.'

'I get all that, but I want an actual date. Mark and I have no plans. Aside from breakfast with our NCT group at nine a.m. on a Saturday, but I don't think that would clash with your schedule anyway?'

'Promise to be chill, and not bite my head off in front of him.'

'I'll be chill.'

'OK then, it's a date.'

She jumped off the wall in excitement.

'Calm down,' I said, laughing.

*

We got home to find Mark asleep on the sofa, with Mam and Dad sitting beside him.

Mam paused the film and gave us a disapproving look.

'You left Mark with Eleanor all afternoon whilst you were at the Anchor! You don't know you're born, Anna.'

Anna looked sheepish as she downed her bottle of water.

'Why are you watching *Lake Placid*?' I asked.

'You know your mother loves Bill Pullman,' Dad said.

'Don't change the subject,' Mam said. 'Don't you even want to know where your daughter is?'

'Mark called, she's having a late nap.'

'When I had you, did I get any help? No, of course I didn't. I had to do everything myself,' Mam said.

Dad tried to interject but she was having none of it.

'And here you are gallivanting around with your sister, when your poor husband is left to look after your child—'

I saw Anna's chest rise and fall, and realised she was practising her hypnobirthing techniques.

'Ivy said I can meet Scott,' Anna said.

'What! When can I meet him?' Mam said. 'If I at least knew what he looked like, I wouldn't mind so much.'

'Mags, give it a rest,' Dad said.

'I sent you a screenshot of his LinkedIn profile,' I said.

'It was blurry.'

'It wasn't blurry. And you've not met him because you've not been up to London.'

'Why didn't you invite him down here for the week?'

'We only started dating last month. Even you can appreciate that's a bit much.'

'If he had to be an actor in a film, who would it be?' Anna asked.

'Oh, I like this game,' Mam said.

Mark had since woken up, but hadn't said anything, knowing better than to get involved.

I contemplated this for a long time, so long that they started another conversation between themselves.

'OK, I have it,' I said.

'Well, spit it out,' Mam said.

'Don't laugh, but it's Jude Law in *The Holiday* ... though, maybe in a less obvious way.'

Mam groaned.

'*Ych-a-fi*, I detest that film,' she said.

'*The Holiday*?' I said. 'What's wrong with it?'

'Cameron Diaz, for one.'

'What's wrong with Cameron Diaz?'

'Nobody should look that good at her age; it's disturbing.'

Dad pretended to strangle her, and we carried on with the film.

27

Mia insisted I meet her as soon as I got back to London. She'd been to her eleventh wedding of the year and was being needier than usual. I expected the worst. Mia loves a wedding, but they don't agree with her. Something about someone else being the centre of attention.

'It's my last wedding of the year, thank God,' she said. 'I don't know why I'm invited to so many.'

She tipped the bottle of wine upside down to check that it was empty, then went back to playing the piano.

'I was on my best behaviour,' she said. 'I didn't say anything about the food. Even though they tried to serve roast beef for ninety people. Half our table's dinner was overdone, the other half raw.'

'I thought you weren't eating meat?'

'I didn't put vegan on the RSVP; what with that and my gluten intolerance I thought it might be a bit too much for them.'

'I thought it was lactose now?'

'Gluten, lactose, they're all the same. The whole affair made me question my own wedding.'

I said nothing.

'Don't pull that face at me, Ivy Edwards.'

'Your feverish mind needs no encouragement,' I said, hold ing my hands up.

She finished the song and came to stand over me.

'You've not mentioned Scott the whole time you've been here,' she said. 'Why are you being so coy?'

'I'm not.'

'You are. You're being smug and coy.'

'How can you be both smug and coy?'

'I don't know, you tell me?'

'It's just . . . I really like him.'

'I don't see what the problem is.'

'Well, what if, somewhere down the line, he thinks I'm . . . '

'Spit it out.'

'Well, crap.'

'Crap?'

'Yeah. What if everything I learnt last year goes out the window? What if I unravel again?'

She held out her hand for me and guided me to the piano.

'Don't let your past fuck up your future, Ivy.'

I rested my head on her shoulder as she started to play.

'You can't look back, you've got to keep moving forward. Every time I go into an audition, I have to pretend that I haven't just been rejected for five other things that morning. I've got to pick myself up and show them that I am this confident, supremely talented woman who is the only person for the job, when I know that right outside the door, there are twenty other women who look just like me, who are all as equally, if not more, equipped to do the part.'

'I don't know how you can pick yourself back up like that every day.'

'Forget what everyone else is doing or saying – it's about you,' she said. 'Trust yourself, Ives. Follow your gut – it's all there. In every moment of uncertainty, we have to look inwards.'

'Have you been watching *Oprah*?'

'*Oprah* is such old news, darling. I need to introduce you to my fearless friend Glennon.'

'Who?'

'Doyle! Seriously, Ivy. Sometimes I despair of you.'

'Scott told me this week that I'm the most interesting person he's ever met, and that he believes in me. He tells me how he feels all the time.'

'What sort of person tells you how they feel? What sort of game is that?'

'That's the thing, I don't think it is a game.'

She mulled this over whilst playing the theme tune to *Sex and the City*.

'Thank you for coming over,' she said. 'I miss our Saturdays like this.'

'We still have Saturdays like this.'

'Not as often.'

'It's not my fault, you're always rehearsing.'

'And you're always either working or snogging Scott.'

'I'm being an adult.'

'I know you are. You've stepped into your power and you're playing big.'

'Stepped into my power, I like that.'

I got up to find my phone. 'I need to text him to say what time he should come over tomorrow . . . '

'Text? Nobody texts, Ivy. Use WhatsApp so you can track when he was last online.'

'What can I say, he's a traditional man at heart.'

'If you're really lucky, sometime soon he'll share his live location.'

'Well, that's something to look forward to, isn't it?'

She nodded enthusiastically. She really thought it was.

'How are you feeling about tomorrow?' she asked.

'It's only lunch.'

'Lunch with your sister, your best friend, and your new boyfriend.'

I put my head in my hands. 'Why am I doing this again?'

'I spent two hours today deliberating my outfit. I want Scott to think I'm sophisticated, clever, fantastically witty, and super classy.'

'So what outfit have you chosen?'

'I'm going to wear this black tulle dress that's got a corset with ties up the back, with my new lace-up biker boots. And I have this tiny transparent handbag that only fits one lipstick in it. Oh, and of course Noah's dead aunt's mink coat.'

'Good to see you're keeping things low-key.'

'What about you? What are you wearing?'

'Jeans and a T-shirt.'

'You cannot be serious?'

'I haven't been shopping for ages! The last thing I treated myself to was a coffee from EAT.'

'What about your birthday money?'

'It went on rent.'

'Christ, that's dull.'

'Also, to manage your expectations, it's not going to be a boozy affair. I'm back in school on Monday.'

'Oh, Ivy. Stop being such a bore and start living.'

'Can you try not to call me a bore every time you see me, please?'

'Do I do that?'

'Yes, stop it – please.'

*

On Sunday morning, I opened the door to find Scott, armed with a bunch of flowers, a bottle of wine and a packed tote bag. There was an image of Dr Strangelove on it and a half-eaten breakfast baguette on top

'I panicked with dessert,' he said, clearly flustered. 'I spent three hours in Borough Market yesterday. There's too much choice. I ate two raclettes then thought, sod it, everyone likes cheese, so here we are.'

He handed me the bag and I looked inside. There were about eight different varieties.

'I know it's a lot, but I didn't know what everyone liked and so I told the woman to cover all bases.'

'I've missed you,' I said.

'You have no idea.'

I led him inside and we had sex – twice – before we got started on lunch.

Scott bragged that he was an excellent sous chef, though he had no idea how to peel an onion, and his version of crudities was to cut up monster chunks of carrot that could barely fit into one's mouth. He was also very distracting.

'Look, I don't mean to sound controlling, but can you sit down, please?' I said.

He started to kiss me.

'No, Scott, stop it. I've not cooked a roast for this many people in ages. Sit down.'

'I like this side of you,' he said.

'You're not meant to see this side of me yet.'

He laughed. 'OK, I won't move. I'll just watch you, instead.'

'Yeah, because that's not off-putting at all.'

He poured us both a glass of wine and swigged his back, before pouring himself another.

'I know you think I'm nervous,' he said, 'but I'm not.'

'Oh, really?'

'Yes.'

I liked seeing him on edge like this. It showed that lunch with my family and best friend meant something, and it meant something because I meant something.

*

Anna and Mark arrived bang on time, with Eleanor in tow. Eleanor had a gorgeous red velvet dress on, with a white Peter Pan collar; Mark was wearing his Burberry mac, which only ever comes out on very special occasions, and Anna, after messaging me seven times that morning to tell me how much she hated her wardrobe, was in black velour leggings and silver boots, with a hot-pink silk shirt that showed off her slim arms and killer cleavage.

'Wow, you guys look amazing,' I said.

'Shush,' Anna said, 'I don't want Scott to think we're trying too hard.'

'But you are trying too hard.'

'Shut up and take Eleanor.'

I went to unbuckle Eleanor from the pram when Scott appeared in the hallway.

'Hi, everyone.'

'Scott!' Mark, Anna and I said in unison.

Anna went straight in for a hug.

'I've been so excited to meet you,' she said.

I could feel the heat come off Scott's face.

'Me too,' he said. 'Thanks so much for coming over for lunch.'

Anna caught my eye. I knew what she was thinking. He said it like they were at our flat, mine and Scott's. I imagined us as home owners, welcoming them into our palatial manor in Primrose Hill. If there was ever a place that said 'I've made it', having a three-storey townhouse in Primrose Hill would be it. Pity I could barely afford a bedsit in London's poorest borough.

'And this is my niece, Eleanor,' I said, holding her in my arms.

He took Eleanor's hand in his. 'Aren't you cute?' he said.

Once Scott's back was turned, Anna started nodding her head like a madwoman, giving me a big thumbs up.

'Shut up and sit down,' I said, through gritted teeth.

'I made dip,' Scott announced. He said it very proudly, and I very nearly told him that I loved him. Mark and Anna didn't hear him speak, and Scott looked a bit crushed.

'Scott made dip,' I said, trying to get their attention. He put the dip on the table and Anna dove right in.

'I think I've nailed this,' he whispered to me.

'I call it "crack dip",' he said, 'because you want to keep coming back for more.'

'Interesting choice of words,' Anna said.

Everyone got stuck into the dip, whilst Scott played with Eleanor on the floor.

The dip was hotter than the sun. It was like he'd put a hundred chillis into a bowl, added a kilo of salt, and said, voila.

'Mmm, tasty,' Anna said, her eyes watering.

Scott beamed in ignorance.

'Oh, before I forget,' he said, 'I brought these over.'

He went into his bag and pulled out several coloured chiffon scarves, and laid them down beside Eleanor.

'I was at my mum's yesterday. She said they use these in those . . . what do you call them . . . sensory classes?'

'You brought these over for Eleanor?' Anna said.

'Yes. They're OK, aren't they?'

Anna hugged him.

'Thank you,' she said. 'This makes up for the dip.'

'What's wrong with the dip?' he asked. 'Is it bad? I didn't taste it.'

He got a spoon from the drawer, heaped sauce onto it and put it into his mouth.

'Oh my fucking God,' he said. 'That's disgusting.'

'It's the worst thing I've ever tasted,' I said.

'What exactly did you put in there?' Anna asked.

'I thought I did it right . . . but I might have got distracted. I was watching *Tidying Up with Marie Kondo* at the time.'

We were all laughing now.

'Jesus, that's really hot,' he said, fanning his mouth as he ran to the bathroom.

'I love him,' Anna said, as soon as he was out of earshot.

I looked over at Eleanor, who was giggling and clapping her hands.

'Look,' Mark said, 'even Eleanor approves.'

28

Despite everyone having to spoon yoghurt into their mouths for the next hour to get rid of the unbearable heat from Scott's dip, the afternoon was a roaring success. Scott shared horror stories from Serendipity, most recently about the time he went on a date with a girl who kept a photo of her dead pet goldfish, Bertie, as her screensaver. Mark asked Scott a hundred and one questions about what it was like to grow up in North London, and, in a desperate attempt to stay sober in preparation for school the next day, I devoured most of the cheese.

As expected, Mia was late. The front door was open, so she let herself in, threw her mink coat on the sofa and started hugging everyone, Scott included.

'I'm so sorry. He completely ran over.'

'Who ran over?' I asked.

'The acupuncturist,' she said, picking Eleanor up. 'Did I tell you he used to do Meghan Markle?'

'You're three hours late.'

'You said come for three?'

'I said come for one.'

Her face wrinkled as she tried to do the maths.

'He's ever so busy, Ivy. It was a nightmare getting in today.' She poured herself a large glass of wine.

'He told me I needed to reduce my alcohol intake, but fuck that,' she said, raising her glass, 'it's practically Christmas.'

'It's the first of November,' said Mark.

I looked at Scott, who was staring at her in wonder. She looked ever so beguiling, if not a touch deranged.

'Scott! Sorry, how rude of me. I'm Mia.'

She held her hand out regally for Scott to take it.

'We'll have to get going soon,' Anna said, looking to Mark.

'We can't leave now,' he said. 'Mia's only just got here.'

He took Anna's hand from across the table – his not-so-subtle way of asking her if it was OK for him to have another glass of wine.

'I guess it'll be me on duty tonight,' Anna said.

Mia shoved a roast potato in her mouth and smiled.

'Modern parenting at its finest,' she said. 'Here, a toast, to co-parents, here and everywhere.'

She sank what was left of her glass and went to refill it.

'So, Scott,' she said, 'you're from London, aren't you? I love a good London boy. It's so very glam.'

'Crouch End isn't glam. Though we do have a Gail's now, which makes it officially middle-class.'

Mia liked this comment. She pretends to hate chains, but I know full well that she spends a fortune in Starbucks every month. She only goes there because the barista fancies her and tells her she looks like a young Meryl Streep, which she does – and she knows it.

Mia turned her chair so that she was directly facing Scott. She rested her chin on her palm and fluttered her lashes.

'Tell us, Scott: what was your childhood like?'

Anna laughed. 'Yes, Scott, how was your childhood?'

I put my hand on his knee for reassurance.

'We were your typical, middle-class family. My dad worked hard—'

'Ivy said your parents are divorced,' Mia said, 'that must be tough?'

'It could be worse.'

'Could it?'

Mark cleared his throat, but Mia took no notice.

'It's much better now than when they were married.'

'I see,' Mia said, nodding.

'Mum is happy, which is the main thing.'

'So, family is important to you, then?'

'It is, yes.'

'And do you want children?'

'Mia!' I said.

Scott laughed. 'It's fine.'

'Let's stop with the interrogations,' I said.

She mimed zipping her mouth up.

'Mia, how's Noah?' Anna asked.

'He's good. Busy working, as always.'

'It's great you guys have so much work on,' Mark said.

'Yes, I guess. I still don't have a diamond, though.'

I was about to say something when I saw her hand go to Scott's hair.

'Ivy was right,' she said. 'You do have the most enchanting locks.'

Anna cracked up.

'Mia, come to my bedroom with me,' I said.

'Why?' she asked.

'I want to show you my new dress.'

'You don't have a new dress.'

'I do.'

'I want to sit here and talk to Scott.'

'And I want to show you the dress.'

In my bedroom, she fell onto the bed.

'Do you have any paracetamol?' she asked. 'I have a little headache.'

'I knew it! You're pissed.'

'I'm not pissed.'

'I thought you said your appointment ran over?'

'It did! But . . . I met my producer for a little Prosecco after.'

'You are unbelievable.'

'Ivy! He was nearby! You know I love fizz on a Sunday.'

'We have fizz here.'

'Yes, I brought some too, as promised. I'm good like that.'

'Pull yourself together. You're going a million miles an hour.'

'Sorry. I really like Scott. He has such great hair.'

'I know, thank you.'

'And he's handsome. More handsome than in the photos.'

'Thank you.'

'Is it bad that I have to stop myself from calling him Jamie?'

'Yes.'

'Do you still think about Jamie?'

'Are you having a neurological breakdown?'

She fluffed up her hair and walked back into the living room.

'Right, Scott, one last thing. Jennifer Aniston or Angelina Jolie?'

'Mia, what did I just say?' I said.

'Ivy, this is serious. Scott, answer the question, please.'

I willed for him to say Jen.

'Jen,' he said. 'Obviously.'

She grabbed his face and smacked her lips on his cheek.

'Yes! Welcome to the family, Scott.'

She proceeded to ask Scott about his last relationship, whether his brother was a spy, and what he thought of the Spice Girls. When it was Scott's turn to ask the questions, he did his best to cross-examine Mia. He asked about her childhood, how she manages rejection, was she aware that the cheese she was shoving in her mouth was neither lactose-free nor vegan.

Foolishly, we moved on to port. Mia announced to the group that she thought I should ask Scott to marry me, and Anna admitted that she was morphing into Mam. We raised a glass to Margaret Edwards, argued over whether we should feel sympathy for the Royal Family and Mia did a rendition of 'Don't Cry for Me Argentina' on the balcony, for all my neighbours to hear. After that, I sent everyone home. It was almost eight, I hadn't yet looked over tomorrow's lesson plan, and – despite every good intention – I was drunk.

We said our goodbyes at the door, and Scott rushed right back to the kitchen. There were red wine stains on the table, and gravy drippings on the floor. He got out a cloth and spray and started cleaning up.

'You are so like your uncle,' I said.

'I won't be able to sleep knowing your kitchen looks like this.'

'Scott, it's my kitchen, leave it.'

He put the cloth down. 'Sorry,' he said.

'You're not allowed to wake up in the middle of the night and clean it.'

'I'll try my best.'

I walked over to him and wrapped my arms around him.

'I'd forgotten how lovely it is to have a house full of people.'

'I had so much fun, Ivy. They're great.'

The room began to spin a little. I moved away from him and poured myself a glass of water.

'Are you drunk, Miss Edwards?'

'No . . . Maybe. You were meant to tell me to stop drinking at five.'

'Was I?'

'I'm sure I asked you to . . . '

'You didn't, and anyway, I could never say that to you. You'd punch me in the face.'

'I would, you're right.'

I drank another glass of water. He came up behind me as I was by the sink.

'Will you dance with me?' he asked.

'Now?'

'Yes, now.'

'What do you want to dance to?'

'Anything you like.'

I went over to my phone, knowing exactly what to play.

'I used to dance with my grandfather to this,' I said.

I put my hand in his and we slow danced in the kitchen to Frank Sinatra's 'I've Got You Under My Skin'. I could feel his heart beating against my chest and I tried not to get emotional. At the end of the song, he started kissing me, the gentlest kisses all over my face. I laughed, but he just kissed me harder, and when I moved away from him, our eyes met, and I knew right there and then that I was in love with him.

Gramps used to read me lots of Roald Dahl as a child, and there's a line in *The Twits* that I've always loved:

'If you have good thoughts they will shine out of your face like sunbeams and you will always look lovely.'

Lying in bed with Scott that night, I felt like all my happiness was shining out of me, and it took everything in me not to cry.

29

Social and emotional developmental milestones in four-year-olds:

Learning to express feelings.

Demonstrates more independence and seeks new experiences.

Finding balance can be challenging.

Struggles to navigate change.

Social and emotional developmental milestones in thirty-three year-olds:

See above.

*

It was time for my first formal observation, also known as an opportunity for me to get over my deep-rooted desire for everyone to love me and learn to accept feedback rationally. I looked for the handbook: How to unlearn thirty-three years of hard work; I was devastated to find that there was none.

My tutor Dawn always stressed the importance of finding balance as a teacher. In almost every session we had together, she asked us what we did that week to centre ourselves and relax. 'How do we marry instinct with technique?' I felt like I never had the right answer. She said there were no right answers, but I knew that was something teachers say to students when they're trying to be sympathetic and inclusive. Dawn had a terrible poker face, and I was very much aware that she thought I was a blubbering idiot. I thought the impulse for seeking new information was a positive human attribute, but I realised early on in those lectures that there's a difference between asking questions every two minutes and being curious: one means you're disruptive; the other means you're eager to learn. Unfortunately, I fell into the former camp.

Mr Reid put a lot of emphasis on preparing myself physically – how would I stand, what would my voice sound like. So, the week before the observation, I took Mia onto Hackney Marshes to practise projecting. I got used to standing on two feet, squarely, instead of shifting on my right leg. I worked on enunciation and breathing and what on earth I was going to do with my hands. I beat myself up about what could go wrong and lost sleep worrying about whether Mr Reid would find fundamental flaws in my approach – which of course he would; that's what first observations are all about.

The night before the observation, Scott arrived at my flat at 7 p.m., armed with ingredients for a risotto, which apparently he thought was just rice.

'I thought we could make dinner together tonight,' he said, walking into the kitchen.

I tried not to let my frustration show. 'By make dinner, you mean I make dinner, and you sit around playing on your phone?'

'Yeah, sound good?'

'You know you can't make a risotto with basmati rice, right?'

He laughed; I didn't.

'I've got to prepare for tomorrow. I told you, I have my first observation.'

'I know, I thought you could do with a break, though.'

'I had a break last night, when we went out for dinner.'

'Sorry, I thought . . . I don't know what I thought.'

'I can't get distracted tonight.'

'OK . . . Do you want me to leave?'

'I'm sorry, but yes.'

He looked wounded.

'You could've said that before I came over with dinner.'

'I told you last night that I wanted to get an early night tonight.'

'But you didn't emphasise that you'd want to do that alone.'

'I thought it was obvious.'

'I'm not a mind reader.'

'I never said you were.'

He picked up his bag from the floor. I moved towards him and gave him a hug.

'I'll see you tomorrow night, OK?' I said.

He made his way to the front door. We kissed, but it felt nothing like our usual kisses. It was rushed and without meaning.

I closed the door behind him and sat on my bed, where I went back to reading a blog on formal lesson observations titled, 'There is no failure. Only feedback'.

I didn't believe that for a second.

I didn't hear from Scott again that night. It was the first night we'd spent apart where he didn't message to say goodnight. I thought it was immature, but then again, I didn't message him either – but that's because I *am* immature.

*

'Today, we're going to learn about the importance of inner peace,' I said. 'And we're going to think of some tools we can use to help us find peace inside ourselves.'

'Ivy—'

I turned to Mr Reid, who was pointing to the back of the room. One of the chairs was empty.

I walked over and saw Amit lying on the floor in corpse position.

'Amit, would you please sit back on your chair?' I asked.

He didn't answer. Some of the children started to laugh. I asked them to be quiet. The laughter got louder. I tried again, with the same result. Mr Reid told them to be quiet, and they promptly shut up.

I crouched down to the floor and asked Amit if everything was all right. He remained motionless, his eyes clamped shut.

I touched his arm and he started screaming. I moved a step back, and he stopped.

'Amit, is everything OK?'

He said nothing. I could hear his breathing, rapid and short.

'Amit, we're going to be learning about peace today. I'd love for you to join in with us.'

He didn't move. I looked to Mr Reid then back to Amit. I asked him what I could do to help but he started doing scissor kicks with his arms and legs and I almost got whacked in the face.

Mr Reid got up and walked over to us. He crouched down to Amit and whispered something in his ear. Amit's eyes flicked open and he grunted loudly, before getting up and sitting on his chair. It was that simple.

I mouthed 'Sorry' to Mr Reid, and he half-smiled in a way that conveyed to me that the past ten minutes had been a complete and utter failure. I summoned all the confidence I had inside me and started the lesson again.

Using the markers, coloured pencils and crayons on their tables, I asked the children to draw an image of something that made them feel peaceful. I showed one I drew earlier, of a beach, with two people sitting down on the sand, sharing an ice cream.

'Is that your boyfriend?' Horatio asked.

'No, that's my grandfather,' I said.

I saw Nancy's face light up and I felt myself relax a little.

I told them to pick up a rock from their table, clasp it in their hands and breathe deeply into it.

'This will fill the rock with peace,' I said.

Sammy started to distract Jamar. I asked him to be quiet. He ignored me.

I thought of Gramps telling me and Anna off that time we got drunk at the rugby and embarrassed him by singing the Welsh national anthem in the wrong key. I channelled him, putting on a firm, confident, 'make one more sound and I will destroy you' voice.

'I'm not going to say this again,' I said. 'Please be quiet.'

I finally had his attention.

'Thank you,' I said. 'Now, let's start decorating our rocks.'

After I gave the initial instructions about how to decorate the rock, I asked for ten minutes of quiet time. They were meant to use the opportunity to lose themselves in their art, but, instead, two of the children needed the toilet, which then made everyone else think they needed to go, too. As I was telling them they could go after class, Sammy went over to the bookshelf and started pulling individual books out onto the floor. Mr Reid took him outside, where I hoped he would stay for the remainder of the year.

At this point, I had forgotten what my original objectives were. I wanted to stamp my feet and scream. I was a fraud, a four-year-old in a thirty-three-year-old's body.

The bell was finally called, and it was the end of the day. Mr Reid put a consolatory hand on my shoulder and said I did a good job. He didn't say great, he said good. He saw the disappointment in my eyes.

'There is no such thing as a perfect lesson, Ivy. Especially not your first. There's always more work to do.'

'It was a car crash.'

'It's important to have perspective.'

'I lost focus.'

'Don't get despondent,' he said. 'I'll give you thorough formal feedback once I've had time to reflect on my notes, OK?'

I excused myself to go to the bathroom, looked in the mirror and exhaled. I was about to crumble.

I ran into the toilet cubicle and slammed the door shut. I thought I was getting better. I had no idea how I'd gotten it so wrong.

I saw Amit's nanny, Kate, by the see-saw. She was eyeing everyone up and gossiping with the other nannies about the mothers – as she always did at pick-up. Whilst I was still fuming over Amit's display of rebellion that afternoon, I liked Kate – she had a naughty glint in her eye and a wicked sense of humour. Last week I overheard her tell one of the other nannies that Leopold and Tarquin's parents liked to wife swap.

I walked over to her and asked her for a quiet word.

'How's Amit doing?' I asked her.

'Why, did something happen?'

'He demonstrated some fine planking this afternoon.'

'He likes to lie in corpse pose and scream at the top of his lungs.'

'Is this a new thing?'

'Not really, he enjoys the attention.'

'Well, he certainly achieved that. Is everything OK at home?'

'His mum's got a new boyfriend, but I don't think that's anything to go by; everyone's playing happy families.'

'I didn't realise Amit's father didn't live at home.'

'It's all very amicable.'

'OK, well, it's good to know everything's all right. Thanks, Kate.'

I walked away, but not so far that I was out of earshot. I knew the minute I left Primrose's nanny Susie would be back and that's when the truth would come out.

As predicted, Susie moved back towards Kate.

'What's the new man like then?' Susie asked.

'He's closer in age to Amit than he is his mother.'

'No! Really?'

'Only just turned thirty.'

'How old is Rakhee?'

'Mid-forties. Not that she'd ever admit it.'

'What's he like?'

'He's filthy rich. His parents have this ginormous estate up north; you know, like, proper old-school English toffs.'

'Jesus. Well done, Rakhee! Does he work?'

'He works for his dad, but I heard they don't get along.'

Just turned thirty, estate up north, family drama. I felt my throat close. It couldn't be?

'Is he fit?' Susie asked.

'He's so fit. They have sex all the time. The cleaner found a cock ring by the bed last week.'

'Shut up!'

'I know! If Rakhee gets bored with him, I might just jump in. You never know, I could be the future Mrs Langdon.'

They carried on talking, but all I could hear was Langdon. Jamie – my ex-fiancé who left me on a whim last year – Langdon.

I walked quickly back inside to the same bathroom, where I closed the same door and promptly threw up.

If there was ever a time to find inner peace, this was it.

30

I had thought about what it would be like to bump into Jamie. I'd pictured myself walking arm-in-arm with Scott; I'd be in some stylish new outfit – probably paid for by my mother – and we'd be laughing uncontrollably. I'd see Jamie on the other side of the street, and I'd calmly walk over and smile. We'd make polite conversation, he would shake Scott's hand, then he'd tell me he'd recently purchased a one-way ticket to Mongolia.

But he wasn't moving to Mongolia; he was very much in London. And I wasn't calm; I was radioactive.

After sitting on the toilet seat contemplating how on earth it was possible that my ex-fiancé was having casual sex with my pupil's mother, I messaged Scott to cancel dinner. I told him that Mia had asked me to help her prepare a scene for a TV audition she had the next day. Scott asked why Noah couldn't help. I said that he was away shooting a TV advert for hair loss in Manchester. I don't know why I made the lie so specific. He called me right away.

'I wanted to see you,' he said. 'I felt distant from you last night.'

'I know, I'm sorry.'

'I haven't heard from you today.'

'You know I can't message in school. I'll see you tomorrow.'

'How did it go today then? Did you smash it?'

'Not quite. I'll talk to you about it tomorrow.'

After getting off the phone with Scott I messaged Dan and Mia. 'This is an emergency. I need to see you both tonight. Involves Jamie.'

'It's bad, isn't it?' I said to them.

We were sitting in Mia's kitchen, two bottles of wine down.

'I think we need to move on to spirits,' Dan said.

Mia went into the freezer and got out a bottle of vodka. She slammed it down on the table, got three shot glasses out from the drinks cabinet, and poured us each a double measure.

'So, he's having sex with the mother. It's fine. You're with Scott! You're happy. You're fine,' Dan said.

'I'm far from fine.'

'You're right. I think we need to go "out out".'

'No, I have class tomorrow with Dawn. She has it in for me already.'

'It's clearly just a fling. It's not like he's going to be doing the school run, is he?'

'Fuck,' I said. 'What if he starts doing the school run?'

'Ivy, don't be so ridiculous. This is Jamie we're talking about.'

'Why does he have to rear his perfectly chiselled face now?'

'I always said he was a cunt,' Dan said.

'I need more vodka – and cigarettes.'

I grabbed the pack on the table and went outside to the garden. I was kicking a plant pot when Anna called, asking how the observation had gone.

'It sounds like you did the best you could,' she said, after I'd told her everything.

'I ran away from the nanny and vomited in the bathroom.'

'Are you smoking?'

'How can you tell I'm smoking on the phone? What is wrong with you?'

'You shouldn't be smoking. Where are you?'

'I'm at Mia's with Dan.'

'Ivy, it's a school night.'

'Can you try to sympathise with me for just one second, please? This is Jamie we're talking about – the man I had planned my future with.'

'You can't get wasted and turn up late to class again.'

'That happened once when the Tube broke down!'

'Be an adult, Ivy.'

'Goodbye, Anna.'

I hung up the phone, finished off the cigarette, and went back inside.

Mia and Dan had moved to the living room, where they were putting on cleansing masks – a rejuvenating Juniper Berry made with love by Patricia, Mia's Professional Spell Caster and Experienced Spiritual Healer. It was meant to induce positive energy, so they lathered it all over my face and neck. She'd obviously been practising because it smelt far better than the last one, which was how I'd imagine the inside of a dead camel to smell. I let it dry as I *cwtched* Dan on the sofa while Mia sat beside us on an exercise ball, Martini in hand, doing the odd sit-up.

'Today was the hardest day of my entire life,' I said.

'Was it really?' Dan said.

'Harder than when Jamie broke up with you five minutes after you'd had sex?' Mia said.

'Harder than when you saw him snogging that really fit woman on the street a few weeks later?' Dan said.

'Can you both be quiet for five minutes, please?'

'It's important to keep perspective,' Dan said.

'Why does everyone keep saying that.'

After class the next day, Dawn asked me to stay behind to speak with her. She was wearing a T-shirt that read 'Big Uterus Energy' on the front. If I was wearing a T-shirt, the slogan would read: 'Is This It?'

'Take a seat,' she said.

She got out some liquid from her drawer and poured it into her vape, before taking a long inhale. I tried to suppress the urge to vomit. I got home at 2 a.m. and woke up five hours later with the curtains wide open and a wedge of cheddar cheese on the bedside table. I cursed myself as I ran into the shower. I told myself this was the last time. I wasn't going to let Jamie get to me. I was fine. I was happy. This positivity lasted all of three minutes before I had a meltdown on the bus watching a YouTube clip of John Legend performing at his dog's wedding ceremony.

'How are you doing, Ivy?' Dawn asked. 'You seem anxious.'

'It's been a long week.'

'Let's talk about it.'

She implored me to go on with her silent, deathly stare.

'I had my first observation yesterday.'

'I know, I've spoken with Mr Reid.'

My heart sank as I pictured them having animated discussions about how useless I was.

'She'd be an appalling teacher,' Mr Reid would say.

'Hideous,' Dawn would add.

'Have you taken the opportunity to reflect on some of the things that worked or didn't work?' Dawn asked me.

No, I thought to myself; I've been too busy reflecting on the fact that my ex fiancé is trying to ruin my life again.

'You know the most important thing during teacher

training is teaching and classroom progression. These observations are crucial in reviewing and monitoring progress.'

'I know.'

'They can be stressful.'

'It was – very.'

'Mr Reid said he thinks you might be struggling to find your own voice in the classroom. Would you agree with him?'

'Yes, of course I'd agree. He does so much by instinct. I don't know how to do that.'

'Be confident in yourself and your abilities, Ivy.'

'I was until Amit started planking.'

'Mr Reid said that you brought some great creative ideas of your own to the session. You should be proud of that.'

I picked at the skin around my thumb.

'Don't look so defeated,' she said.

'It's been a long week.'

'You said. Why don't you go home and get an early night?'

I got up from my seat and said goodbye.

'It gets easier,' she said.

Teacher training or life?

The tears came the moment I walked out the door. I put my head down and walked out of the building as fast as I could, all the way home.

When I got home, I ran a hot bath. I thought about confidence and self-belief and Jamie and Scott. There were sirens going off in my head and I didn't know how to stop them. Why had this hit me so hard? I was meant to be happy. I sank deeper into the bath, letting the water wash over me. When I resurfaced, I heard the doorbell go.

I got out of the bath and swathed myself in a warm towel. When I opened the door, Scott was smiling right at me. I said hello and leant in to kiss him.

'How are you feeling?' he said.

'Good,' I lied.

He followed me into the kitchen. I heard him mutter something, I asked him to repeat it. He started tidying up the papers on the kitchen table instead.

'Please don't do that,' I said.

'Where are we going to eat?' he asked.

'I'll tidy them up in a second. Let me do it, please.'

I went into the bedroom to put some clothes on. When I got back into the kitchen, he was wiping the table down.

'Scott, what did I just ask you?'

'You said not to touch the papers, so I'm cleaning the surfaces.'

'Why do you need to clean anything at all? It's not dirty.'

'It's messy.'

'Yes, but it's my mess.'

'Why are you being so defensive?'

'Because every time you come over you start cleaning up. It's like being in the classroom with Mr Reid. It's doing my head in.'

'I'm trying to be helpful. I know you hate tidying.'

'You like living in your show home. I like living in my organised mess.'

'What's wrong? Why are you so angry?'

'I'm not angry. I find it a bit controlling, that's all.'

'Is everything OK?'

'I'm tired.'

'Yeah, because you drank too much wine with Mia last night.'

'No, I'm tired because my job has taken over my life.'

He didn't say anything.

'I've got enough on my plate without your sarcastic comments about my flat and my drinking.'

'Sarcastic comments? Wow, OK.'

'And whilst we're at it, stop trying to plan everything. You never ask me what I want to do.'

'What?'

'The other day, with the risotto. I didn't want a risotto.'

'Well, aren't I an arsehole?'

'You're not an arsehole. I want to have a say sometimes, that's all.'

'I try to plan things so that you don't have to – because you're too tired to.'

'Fine, whatever.'

'Why are you being like this?'

'I'm not being like anything.'

'You clearly don't want me here.'

I sat down on the sofa and looked down at the floor.

'I knew you were going to fuck this up,' Dilys said. 'You're not ready for a relationship. It's too much, you can't handle it.'

I looked at Scott.

'This is too much,' I said.

'What do you mean?'

'I can't do it.'

'Can't do what?'

'Maybe we shouldn't see each other any more.'

'Are you being serious?'

'We've both got a lot on and the timing's not right.'

He looked like he was about to lose it. I opened my mouth, but nothing came out. He stormed out of the room.

'This is bullshit,' he said, grabbing his coat. 'Call me when you grow up.'

I heard the front door slam. I crumpled down to the floor and let the tears come.

'Should've placed a bet on that,' Dilys said.

31

When I was in my first year of university, Anna came to stay for the night. It was Mother's Day that weekend, so the plan was to go out on Saturday and drive home for Sunday lunch the next day. Anna was doing an internship at a child protection lawyers and needed to blow off some steam, so we went to Sweet Escapes: an airless, grimy club where the dregs of society went after midnight. It was a stalwart on the Bristol club scene, and a superb night out. We shared a pill and spent the night glued to each other on the dance floor, sweating profusely as we necked bottles of water to keep ourselves hydrated. When we got back to halls, Luke was up, smoking a joint. I went to bed, but Anna stayed up with him, sharing a spliff and drinking cheap vodka. We missed our alarms the next morning, and when I finally woke just before noon, Anna was nowhere to be seen. I found her asleep on the bathroom floor. She'd vomited in the bath.

We were four hours late for lunch. We had to stop on the motorway for Anna to be sick again. When we arrived home, Mam opened the door and burst into tears, before fleeing upstairs. We walked into the kitchen to find Gramps, sitting with his arms crossed.

'What time do you call this?' he said.

'Sorry.'

'You're sorry, are you?'

'I don't know what else to say.'

Anna ran over to the sink and splashed herself with cold water.

'You're a fucking disgrace,' he said.

We hung our heads low, as we awaited his wrath.

'Your mother doesn't have a mother. She can't take hers out today and remind her how special and loved she is. But you've got a mother, don't you? You could tell her how wonderful she is, how much you love her.'

'Gramps—'

'All you had to do was turn up on time, maybe buy some flowers, or a card. You couldn't even do that.'

'We've said sorry.'

He got up and walked to the back door.

'Don't ever pull a stunt like this again, OK? You'll understand when you're mothers.'

Mam didn't speak to us that day. The next morning, we made brunch for her at home. We gave her a framed photo of the three of us with Gran, sitting on the beach when we were children. We apologised until we were blue in the face and told her it wouldn't happen again.

We were getting stuck into our Eggs Royale when Mam asked us to tell her the full story.

'There's nothing to tell,' Anna said.

'Come off it, I wasn't born yesterday.'

Anna and I looked down at our plates.

I started to laugh.

'What's so funny?' Anna said.

'I'm remembering finding you on the bathroom floor, clutching a pillow, with a pile of sick in the bath.'

'Ivy! You promised you wouldn't say anything!'

'I can't believe you, Anna,' Mam said. 'Did you at least kiss any boys?'

'Nah, too pissed.'

'You have zero class. The pair of you.'

After brunch, Gramps called.

'Sorry for being so cross yesterday, Ives. *Tamping*, I was.'

'You can't just make up words, Gramps.'

'Don't push it, Ivy. You're on thin ice as it is, *mun*. Listen, I'll be round later for a *cwtch*, then we can go for a walk and a Knickerbocker Glory, *joio*?'

I laughed. '*Joio*.'

*

I don't know what time I fell asleep, but I woke just after three in the morning, my pillow soaked with tears. I reached for my phone, expecting him to have messaged, knowing that he wouldn't have. I needed someone to tell me how to make it right. I needed Gramps to tell me how to make it right.

I walked to Anna's the next morning. I stopped off at the corner shop to say hello to Selim, who commented that I looked 'like a sad dog'. It wasn't the best start to the day.

'Sometimes, I feel like I've fallen down a bottomless pit,' I said to Anna, 'and I'm scratching at the walls, screaming for help, but nobody can hear me. Or maybe they can, but they don't want to help.'

'You need one of those bracelets,' Anna said, 'but instead of "What Would Jesus Do?", it would say, "What Would Gramps Do?".'

I took Eleanor's hand in mine and kissed it. She started giggling. I kissed her rosy pink cheeks and told her I loved her.

'I know that you're feeling overwhelmed,' Anna said, 'and maybe if you'd have met Scott a few months ago, it might be easier to manage things. But he came into your life at a point when you were open to loving someone else. That means something.'

'I can't be all these things to all these people.'

'If you're referring to Mia and Dan, tell them to start being more supportive, or fuck off.'

'I barely see you any more.'

'You see us every week.'

'It feels like less.'

'You have to take responsibility for this. You must forget about Jamie.'

'I have. I don't want to be with him. I can't believe I let him get into my head.'

'Is there a part of you that didn't want it to work with Scott?'

'No, not at all.'

'Can I be straight with you?'

'You always are.'

'You don't think you deserve good things in life, so you self-sabotage.'

I reflected on this for a moment. Anna watched me; then, like the shrewd lawyer she is, began to argue her case.

'What about that guy you met over summer? Even after he undermined your teaching career, you still had sex with him. Why?'

'Isn't it obvious? I want to stop feeling so afraid.'

'Yes, but not at the expense of your soul.'

'OK, I'm sorry.'

'Stop apologising. You can't let your darker impulses get to you. You've worked so hard to get here, and now you're pressing the self-destruct button all over again.'

'I'm not pressing it. I'm hovering over it.'

'Whatever you're doing, stop it. It's time to grow up, Ivy.'

'I hate it when you get like this.'

'I love it when I get like this.'

I didn't call Scott that day, or the next. Instead I sat by my phone, waiting for him to ring or text. He didn't.

On the way to school on Monday, Mam called.

'You're not getting any Christmas presents this year.'

'Mam, it's November.'

'I'm donating in everyone's name to a social enterprise in Iran.'

'I thought you were saving silkworms?'

'It's good to diversify. I messaged Leonardo DiCaprio on the Gram asking for tips on other ethical projects. He hasn't replied. Did I tell you I have five friends now? There's Anna, Mia, Dan—'

'Dan?'

'Darling, we're besties. Then there's Mia's acupuncturist, the one who used to do Meghan Markle, and some man named Terry.'

'Who's Terry?'

'He owns a car rental shop in Pontypridd. He keeps sending me a ping asking if I'd like to go for dinner.'

'You need to block him.'

'That's absurd, I'm loving the attention.'

'Does Dad know about this?'

'I saw Dan in a little pleather number last week,' Mam said, ignoring me. 'He had a little collar round his neck, too. What a fun evening that looked.'

'I bet.'

'Anna said you argued with Scott, what happened?'

'I don't want to go into it.'

'Have you misbehaved?'

'Yes.'

'Then what are you doing wasting your time on the phone with me? Go and get him, Ivy.'

I smiled. 'I love you, Mam.'

'In moments of doubt, Ivy, ask yourself, what would Gramps do?'

'That's exactly what Anna said.'

'She takes after her mother. You need to listen to me. I'm always right. It's one of my best qualities.'

Nancy was on the edge of a tantrum all morning. Much like myself, she was tearful and irritable, refusing to engage with anyone in class. When everyone went outside to play, she remained seated, staring at the green apple in her hands.

'Do you want to talk about it?' I said.

Her eyes were red and puffy. I wanted to scoop her up in my arms and have a cry right there with her.

'I made Hakim sad.'

'I'm sorry, Nancy. Why don't you tell me what happened, and we can work through it together?'

'I hid his lunchbox. He said that Horatio was his best friend but yesterday I was his best friend.'

'A lot can change in the space of a day,' I said.

She looked up at me and I realised that wasn't the wisdom she was after.

'How did you feel before you took Hakim's lunchbox?'

'I was sad.'

'And how did it make you feel hiding the lunchbox?'

'Sad.'

'So, what do you think you'll do next time?'

She thought long and hard. 'I won't take his lunchbox.'

'Well done, Nancy. Recognising our mistakes and learning from them is very brave – I'm proud of you. Why don't you take a special treat from the tin and give it to Hakim, I'm sure he'd like that.'

'He likes the gooey ones.'

'That's because they're the best.'

I told her to go ahead and look in the tin. Her eyes lit up as she rummaged around looking for the purple one. When she found it, she threw herself at me.

'Thanks, Miss Edwards!' she said, before running outside to the playground.

I was tidying up the classroom when I saw Mr Reid standing by the door.

'Well done, Ivy.'

'What for?'

'You're able to sympathise with the children and help them navigate themselves out of challenging situations. It's a great skill you have.'

I smiled and went back to sorting the books.

'The tin of treats has gone down a storm, I see.'

'It's basically a kilo of chocolate, so I can't take credit there.'

'Learn to take a compliment, Ivy.'

'Sorry. And thank you.'

He was about to leave the room when he turned back around again.

'I'm glad you chose us, Ivy. We're lucky to have you.'

'You don't know what that means to me.'

'I think I do.'

He walked out the door and I sat down on Nancy's red chair, wondering why whenever I felt like I was moving forward in one area of my life, I went backwards in another.

32

In the corner of the room Mabel was *cwtching* Primrose. We were having free play and both girls were dressed as bees. Mabel's bee had a tiara on its head and Primrose's had a feather boa around its neck. They'd drawn love hearts all over their arms and were telling each other how much they loved one another. Jamar, waving an enormous light sabre/wand over his head, ran over to them.

'I love you, Mabel,' he said. 'And I love you, Primrose.'

'I love you,' Primrose said.

'Do you love me?' Jamar asked Mabel.

She pondered this for a moment before nodding her head.

'Who do you love the most? Me or Mabel?' Primrose asked Jamar.

He jumped up and down before shouting, 'Harry Kane.'

He fell on the floor in hysterics as Mabel got out a green pen and started drawing love hearts on Jamar's face.

Primrose caught me looking at them.

'Miss Edwards, do you love me?' she asked.

'Yes,' I said, without hesitation.

'Mummy said you should always tell someone if you love them,' Jamar said.

'Someone's put you up to this, haven't they?'

Three expressionless faces stared back at me. Turns out they hadn't been put up to this, but at twenty-nine years my junior, they knew a hell of a lot more about love than I did.

I wanted to run to Scott like they do in romantic comedies; we'd be at an airport and I'd have made a huge banner, and a flash mob would emerge from the crowds and sing Frank Sinatra's 'I Love You Baby' and Scott would cry and I would cry and then we'd hug and everything would be perfect for the rest of our lives.

But instead of some romantic gesture in an open public space aka Heath Ledger in a 1990s teen romcom, there was me, on a two-week period, with a face full of spots and the emotional constitution of a toddler.

I went by his flat after school. I stood under the awning of the corner shop, chain-smoking, until 7 p.m., when I remembered that he played squash on Wednesdays. I went to a greasy spoon opposite the flat, ordered an omelette because it was the cheapest thing on the menu, and waited for him to get home. At nine thirty, I saw him. I hurriedly paid my bill and ran outside.

He paused in the middle of the road when he saw me, then started walking again.

When we were less than a metre apart, I said hello.

'I'm sorry to turn up like this unannounced.'

He didn't say anything.

'Can I come in?' I asked.

'OK.'

He moved his umbrella over me to shield me from the rain, and we walked to his flat.

I was surprised to see some papers and magazines scattered on the table, instead of in the neat pile they're always in, at the top right-hand corner of the table. He always has two cashmere blankets sat on the arm of the sofa, but one was thrown over the furnishings. I thought about the time he wrapped me up in it after we'd had sex on the kitchen floor. It wasn't quite the steamy encounter I'd fantasised about. I ended up smacking my face into the cutlery drawer and was unable to carry on with proceedings due to the intense ringing in my head.

'I didn't expect to see you,' he said, breaking the silence.

'I don't know why I've left it this long. I should have run after you on Friday.'

'Should you?'

'Yes.'

He poured himself a glass of red wine and offered me some. I asked for water.

'I don't know where to start,' I said.

'Why don't you start at the beginning.'

I thought about what Anna had said. It was as good a starting place as any.

'I have a tendency to self-destruct,' I said.

I watched him as he drank his wine. He didn't say anything, so I carried on talking.

'Being me has taken some time getting used to. I'm not a hundred per cent there yet, but I want to be. And I know it might not look like it, but I'm trying.'

He still wasn't making eye contact with me.

'My ex, Jamie . . . he's going out with the mother of one of my pupil's.'

He finally looked me in the eye.

'How did you find that out?'

'I overheard the nanny talking about it.'

'Is that why you've taken up smoking again?'

'No . . . yes. This is only temporary, I promise.'

'You don't have to promise me anything.'

'But I do. I want to be a better person for you, Scott. I don't have feelings for Jamie any more. But when I overheard the nanny, I was thrown.'

'Does she know you were engaged?'

'I don't think so. I'd be mortified if she did.'

He drank more wine. I waited for him to speak.

'You lied to me, didn't you, about Mia's audition that night?'

'I was afraid you'd think I was still in love with Jamie, or something.'

'But you're not? Because from where I'm sitting, it sort of looks like you are.'

'No, I'm not, but it felt like a lightning bolt hit me and I panicked.'

He poured himself more wine and sat down on the opposite end of the sofa to me.

'I behaved appallingly last year. A lot of people lost faith in me – I lost faith in me. And whilst I can stand here and tell you that I don't love Jamie any more, that doesn't mean that I'm OK with what happened. I'm not over it. I wish I was, but I'm not.'

He remained silent.

'I think that's why I tried to push you away – Dilys said I'd fuck this up anyway, so I'd better just get it over with.'

'Who's Dilys?'

'The voice in my head.'

'Right . . . Sorry, what?'

'It doesn't matter. What matters is that I've been a total tit, and I'm sorry.'

I moved my hand closer to his. I wanted more than anything for him to take it. But he didn't.

'The thing is, Scott, I love you. I've loved you for ages.'

I watched him process this, trying to find clues in his face. There were none.

'I asked you to be honest with me,' he said. 'But I don't think I was honest with you.'

I waited for him to speak again.

'I told you my dad moved out for a couple of years when I was younger. He got into some gambling debt and Mum kicked him out. Oliver wasn't much use; his idea of coping with things was to stay out all night drinking on Camden Lock.'

'I'm sorry, I had no idea.'

'I know I try to control things, but that's how it's been since he left. I had to step in, because nobody else did. Nobody else could get us back on track as a family.'

'Scott—'

'It's really fucking hard to hold it together when you're fifteen and you're in the middle of your exams.'

'It wasn't up to you; you were a child.'

'You said you're not a hundred per cent comfortable with yourself; well, neither am I. I'm fantastically self-critical. I can't stand to not be in control of everything, and up until two months ago, I was a massive workaholic.'

'What happened two months ago?'

'I got bored of being the last one in the office. I got bored of not having a life. I wanted to be happy.'

'I know how that feels.'

'I know your teacher training is the most important thing, and I'm not trying to compete, but it's about balance. You're always saying your tutor Dawn goes on about that, and I wish you would try to relax a bit because you're doing so well. Finn thinks you're exceptionally bright – he said you've come on leaps and bounds since you first started.'

'Did he say that?'

'Of course, more than once.'

I beamed inside. 'I'm so sorry I hurt you.'

'I'm sorry, too.'

He moved towards me and held my face in his hands.

'I love you, Ivy. I should've said it earlier too.'

He pressed his lips to mine, and, before I knew it, I was crying.

'I want to work at this with you,' I said. 'I think we're great together.'

'I do too.'

His hands were suddenly all over me.

'I can't,' I said. 'I'm on my period.'

'I don't care about that.'

'I know but . . .'

He closed his eyes as I unbuttoned his trousers. It shows how much I love him that I volunteered to give him a blow job. It shows how much he loves me that he let me do it on his pristine cream sofa.

I must have fallen asleep because I was woken by his fingers grazing my nipple. I opened my eyes and told him that I loved him.

'I'm sorry about last year,' he said. 'I don't know your sort of grief, but I know other sorts, and anytime you want to talk about it, I'm here.'

He began kissing every inch of my chest.

'I want you to meet my parents,' I said. 'When they come up for Christmas.'

'I'd love that.'

'They're going to love you. Not as much as I love you, of course. Actually, Mam will fancy you just as much as I fancy you.'

'I'm ready for your mother's wandering hands.'

'Please don't,' I said, laughing.

'So, they're definitely coming up to London then?'

'My sister's working on it. Sometimes you need to take a softly-softly approach with Margaret Edwards.'

'Wow, our first Christmas together.'

'I'm expecting lots of very expensive, high-end gifts.'

He kissed me. 'You can have whatever you want, Ivy.'

'I want you, that's all.'

'You've got me.'

'What will you do for Christmas?' I asked. 'How does it work with divorced parents?'

'That's just it, it doesn't work. I start worrying about it from around about the first of February. Oliver's never here, so it's up to me to schedule everything. I end up running around London, trying to make sure Mum and Dad see me in equal amounts.'

'That doesn't sound very merry.'

'No matter how much I plan it, someone always gets the short straw.'

'Do you think they'll ever be able to spend it together?'

'No, I don't.'

'I'm so sorry it's so stressful.'

'It's Christmas, isn't it? It's always stressful.'

'We'll do lots of lovely things together, like go see *Love Actually* on a rooftop cinema and go ice skating at Somerset House. Oh, and we can have sex outdoors, after we've picked out a Christmas tree.'

'Why after?'

'Because I figure we'll have an argument about it.'

'There's no way we're getting a real tree for my flat. Just the thought of all those pine needles falling on the floor is making me tense.'

'It's starting already.'

'You get a real one, I'll get a fake one. Which means that with Mum and Dad's separate ones, I'm getting four. Does that seem extravagant?'

'Not at all. It's Christmas.'

'See, first hurdle accomplished. We are so good at this.'

He got up and walked me to the bedroom, where we lay

in bed holding on to each other. I lay wide awake, listening to his snores, thinking about all the things we were going to do together.

I wanted to do everything with him. And I was going to make sure I did it right this time.

33

I was trying to explain to Scott how contentious Christmas in the Edwards family can be, whilst also being conscious of not revealing the true nature of their infantile behaviour. It was a fine balance. Despite a messy divorce, his family sounded grounded, calm, rational, whilst mine are dramatic, argumentative, borderline insane.

This year was turning out to be more stressful than the last. Mam was outraged at Anna for suggesting we spend the holidays in London and Anna was outraged at Mam for how controlling and condescending she'd been since Anna had fallen pregnant. I tried to stay out of things – opting instead to spend my time having better than average, often mind-blowing regular sex, but it was no use. Whether I liked it or not, I was going to have to pick a side.

Don't you just love Christmas?

They'd not spoken to each other in over a week, which, considering they usually FaceTime up to four times a day, was a big deal. Mam had never spent Christmas outside of South Wales; she kept making snide remarks that Londoners don't know how to do Christmas like the Welsh, but it was clear what she really meant: Anna couldn't do Christmas like her. I knew from school that behaviour in the classroom can make or break your lesson. I also knew that Mam's behaviour could make or break Christmas. I caved, and stepped in.

'This is your home,' Mam said. 'You should all be home for the holidays.'

We were on the phone one day after school. I had an essay to finish, a paper to read and an evaluation to complete, but no, Mam needed to air some more grievances about Jesus's birthday party, so that's what we did. Before the call I wrote down a list of the techniques I use on the children to help settle them.

'Try to come at this from a place of compassion, Mam.'

'I knew you wouldn't be on my side.'

'Anna and Mark have their own family now. They need to set their own traditions.'

'Anna said I was being selfish. Me? Selfish? I don't have a selfish bone in me.'

'Why don't we make a plan?'

'Where are we going to get the champagne? We always have champagne on Christmas.'

'Why don't you go for a walk down the beach, get some fresh air. You love the beach this time of year.'

'I know you have a Sainsbury's down the road but what if they've run out and, God forbid, we have to have Cava?'

'Maybe tonight we can do some gentle yoga together, over FaceTime?'

'You think I'm being difficult but I'm not.'

Last year we didn't have a discussion about it; it was the first Christmas without Gramps, and of course it would be at home in Wales. Mam pulled out all the stops, to keep busy as much as anything, knowing the whole affair would be cloaked in heartache. It was memorable and touching, if not a little intense.

There was one unfortunate incident, which nobody has dared mention since. Things unfolded when Anna unwrapped a pair of size-eighteen pyjamas from Mam. I watched Anna's shoulders shudder as she looked at the size. Mam said she knew how much Anna was struggling to keep her weight down, what with all her pregnancy cravings. Anna went quiet, got up, and walked out of the room. Mam followed her and thus began a screaming match. Anna called Mam unsupportive, shallow and toxic. Mam called Anna oversensitive, uptight and lacking in sense of humour. In the hour they argued, Dad, Mark and I ate all the mince pies and went through a bottle of the fancy white. As is tradition, all was well – and all were drunk – by the afternoon.

'I'm looking forward to finally meeting Scott,' she said. 'I hope he likes me. Jamie loved me.'

'That right there. You can't say things like that.'

'I can't say anything these days without upsetting you – or your sister.'

'All I'm saying is, try to remember his name, OK? You can do whatever you like, but please, for the love of God, remember his name. It's Scott. Not Jamie. Scott.'

'I prefer the name Jamie.'

'Mam—'

'I'm aware his name is Scott, stop banging on about it.'

I got off the phone with her and rang Anna.

'I think I've persuaded her to come here for Christmas,' I said.

'She's not staying at my house.'

'They'll stay in the same hotel they did when they were last down.'

'Mam didn't like it there; she said the towels weren't soft enough, and the shampoo had parabens in it.'

'She can bring her own towels – and shampoo.'

'Where will we eat?'

'We can eat at yours or – at mine, I don't mind. If we do it at mine you'll have to bring the travel cot, but it's up to you. I'm happy to cook; you won't need to do anything.'

'Thank you, Ivy. You're by far my favourite these days.'

'I know she can be a pain in the arse, but you've got to remember this is only her second Christmas without Gramps. She's still grieving.'

'That doesn't explain why she's being such a bitch to me.'

'Please don't call her a bitch, Anna.'

'Sorry, I didn't mean that.'

'It's my turn to give you some advice now.'

'Christ, if you must.'

'Have a proper, frank conversation with her about the cutting comments and the biting remarks. Tell her how they make you feel, instead of skirting around the subject.'

'It's easier not to say anything.'

'Oh yeah, this has been really easy.'

'No need for that tone.'

'Do it for me, please? I want Christmas to be special this year. I want Scott to spend some time with you all and the last thing I want is for everyone to be arguing in front of him.'

'We won't argue.'

'It's all you've done so far this year.'

'OK, you have a point.'

'I'm going to go now. I need to run home and do some work.'

'You've not been running for ages.'

'I know, I've put on forty pounds. I need to start smoking again.'

'You are smoking again.'

'I've stopped, actually.'

'How's it going?'

'Fine. I'm eating a lot of cakes. I came second on *Bake Off* last week.'

'I meant the workload, you tit.'

'It's better; I'm learning to find balance.'

'Aren't we all.'

'Do you prefer the name Jamie or Scott?'

'Scott. Jamie is a shit name. Plus, he's a twat.'

'I knew I loved you. Now will you please ring Mam?'

'Yes. Fuck off the phone then and I'll ring her.'

I stared at the curvature of his neck as he spoke on the phone to his mother. There are three perfectly positioned moles at the base. I couldn't take my eyes off them. I imagined taking his clothes off and running my fingers over his soft skin. He turned around and clocked me staring at him. He mouthed, 'Are you OK?' and I nodded.

'I think we'll be there about two,' he said on the phone.

He looked at me for confirmation. I didn't say anything, I just started taking off my clothes.

'Mum, I'm going to have to ring you back, someone's at the door. Yup, see you this afternoon. We're looking forward to it.'

I unclipped my bra and let it drop to the floor. I pulled my knickers down and stepped away from them.

'Ivy . . . '

I walked to the sofa and kissed him. His mouth moved to my chest and he bit my nipple. I took his top off and pushed him back on the sofa as I took off his jeans and boxers. He was already hard. I climbed on top of him. His hand gripped my back as we moved in unison.

'Where did you come from?' he asked.

'Same place you did.'

We met his mother in Muswell Hill. We were both nervous and she was a lot quieter than Scott had let on. I started talking a million miles an hour to fill the silence and for some reason felt it appropriate to tell her about the time I photocopied my boobs in the Art faculty staff room in Year 12.

'It was quite rebellious of me,' I said. 'Not that I was a rebellious teenager, I wasn't – I'm not. But a boy I fancied told me to do it, so I did. Not that I do everything everyone tells me to do – I don't. We plastered them all over the school, too. I regret that. I really liked him. He had a pool in his house. And a games room. Come to think of it, they were quite wealthy. Not that wealth is important – it's not. I did like the pool though. And there was always a good selection of snacks. Crisps. Salted nuts.'

Nobody spoke. I gripped Scott's hand under the table. I was about to start talking about the variety of soft drinks in the mini fridge, when his mother started to speak.

'I've never told you about the time me and your aunt Debby took LSD in your grandfather's shed, have I?'

'Sorry, what?' Scott said. 'You? You barely drink, you don't smoke.'

'People can surprise you.'

Scott was speechless.

'I worshipped Debbie, she was so effortlessly cool. Do you know Marianne Faithfull, Ivy?'

'Yes, my mum has her records.'

'Well, my sister used to look like her. Can you imagine having a sister who looked like that?'

'That doesn't explain the LSD. Did Grandad catch you?' Scott said. 'My grandfather was a God-fearing man, Ivy. He drew faint pen lines on all his bottles of spirits, so he'd know if anyone had drunk from them.'

'That's the summer we went to Glastonbury,' his mother said. 'We couldn't get tickets, but we ran away to Worthy Farm anyway. Debbie paid a guy a fiver to build a tunnel under the fence for us to climb under. Well, I paid him a fiver, Debbie paid him in other ways . . .'

'Please, stop,' Scott said.

'We got back home three days later. Your grandfather didn't speak to us for a week.'

'I cannot believe this,' Scott said.

'And you thought photocopying your breasts was bad, Ivy.'

I thought about the last conversation I'd had with Jamie's mother, Cressida. She'd asked me if I wanted to come with her to watch Alan Titchmarsh's keynote at *Gardener's World* Live. I'd lied and said I was spending the weekend with Gramps. I hadn't wanted to learn how to transform my outdoor space . . . especially as I didn't even have an outdoor space.

What I did want was to go back in time to 1979 and take hallucinogenics in a shed with Scott's mother.

34

Later that afternoon, we went to meet Dan, Mia and Noah in a pub in Kensal Green. It was festive drag bingo, and Dan's alter ego, Lady Von-Titz Valley, was due to make an appearance. In classic Daniel fashion, however, he'd organised a stag at an underground rave the night before and had turned up to rehearsal that morning gurning his face off after taking too much ecstasy. The director said that his jaw was all the way in Birmingham and refused to let him perform.

I had warned Scott about Dan. He'd just broken up with Alejandro again, which, along with the E, meant that his mood would be even more unpredictable than usual. He grabbed a chair and sidled up to Scott.

'I'm so sorry you're not going to see Lady Von-Titz tonight,' Dan told him. 'But on the positive side for me, at least I'm not going to wake up with an arsehole full of sequins.'

It was an education for Scott, at the very least.

'What's everyone's vision for tonight?' Dan asked.

'Vision?' Scott said.

'He means what time do you want to stay out to,' I said.

'Oh, maybe one?' Scott said.

'One? No, Scott. That is not the vision.'

Dan scarpered to the bar and Mia leant over me to check

that Scott was OK. She was still doing her best to make up for her special appearance at Sunday lunch.

'You let me know if you need anything,' she said, squeezing Scott's knee.

'I'm good,' he said. 'Thanks, Mia.'

'A whisky, cigarette, someone to run their fingers through your hair . . . I'm here for you.'

'Get a grip,' I said to her.

Dan came back with shots of tequila for us all, terrified that unless he topped up on last night's escapades, he would fall into an unending shame-hole.

'They've put fucking Goldilocks on as my replacement,' he said, banging the tray down on the table. 'They know I hate that bitch.'

'Dan, you turned up to rehearsal wasted at eleven this morning. What were they supposed to do?' Noah said.

'It wasn't my fault!'

'Someone forced the pills down you? Did they?' I said.

'When did you get on your high horse?'

Dan was livid now, much to Scott's amusement.

'You don't know the pressure you come under as groomsman, and I was having an awful hair day.'

'Christ, not this again—'

'One of the groomsmen, and I won't name names because his housemate is probably lurking around here somewhere, suggested we play crazy golf. Golf! On a Friday night. Who are these people?'

'Crazy golf is quite fun,' Scott said.

'Fun? Ivy, I know he's hot, but who is this guy?'

I gave Dan the finger.

'I know he's teetotal and all but that doesn't mean we've got to do some shit activity just because he can't hold his booze,' Dan said.

'He's allergic to alcohol,' Noah said. 'He gets hives.'

'It's like being vegan,' Dan said. 'I'm fine with a person choosing to be vegan, but don't keep banging on about that weird cartoon film you watched with Scarlett Johansson befriending the cow, like I'm supposed to give a shit.'

It took us a minute.

'You mean the film with Tilda Swinton, and the pig?' Scott said.

'Whatever, I don't care. I had no choice but to get on it.'

'I think we should get on it tonight,' Mia said.

Dan's face lit up. 'Yes! Mia, this is why I love you.'

'Are you guys in, Ivy? Scott?' she asked.

'I've got an essay to write tomorrow, sorry.'

'Me and Ivy will stick to hard liquor,' Scott said. 'And by hard liquor, I mean I'll be in bed after five pints.'

'Well, these two are useless,' Dan said. 'Noah, you in?'

'I guess it is nearly Christmas,' he said.

Dan flew out of his seat and went to ring his dealer.

I'd never seen a drag show like it. After the first, relatively conservative dance number, a man came on stage and pretended to masturbate on the EU flag. Then, after a sensational choral rendition of Bing Crosby and David Bowie's 'The Little Drummer Boy', a one-legged woman appeared from the wings, stark naked aside from nipples tassels, and started to sing 'God Save the Queen'.

'This is the most shocking thing I've ever seen,' I said.

'It's irony, darling,' Dan said. 'I can't believe how much they've watered this down. I was expecting something much more political.'

After the final act, a choir came on stage, surprising the audience with a moving rendition of 'Over the Rainbow'. For the first time that night, the crowd was quiet.

Scott put his arm around me and whispered into my ear. 'Thank you for inviting me. I love your friends.'

'Even Dan?' I joked.

'Even Dan. Though, don't leave me alone with him for too long.'

I got shivers as he kissed my neck.

'Have I told you that I love you today, Miss Edwards?'

'Just the once.'

'Well, I love you. I love you more than anything in this world.'

I looked at the sparkling green in his eyes and I knew. This was it.

'I love you too, Scott.'

I closed my eyes and let him kiss every part of my face.

Dan came between us.

'Get a fucking room,' he said.

We danced until the early hours of the morning, to the cheesiest of Christmas hits, and told each other that this was the greatest night of our lives. At 3 a,m. Alejandro came flying through the doors, declaring his undying love for Dan, and they ran off together into the night.

Scott and I never left the dance floor. We just stood in amongst the ravers, grinning from ear to ear.

*

Mr Reid marched out of the room mumbling something about a broken sewing kit. Nancy didn't like the star on her head, Primrose didn't want to be a sheep, and Horatio was fuming about being a donkey. In my defence, I thought he was perfectly cast – his hair brought a pizazz to the role and his bushy eyebrows added a level of authenticity that was previously missing.

'Miss!' shouted Kitty, pointing to the cake. 'Why's Elsa's hair all funny?'

'I thought that's how you wanted her hair to look?'

'I wanted sea lions,' Tarquin said.

'Didn't we agree that we would have a lion, not a sea lion?'

'But I like sea lions. We have one in the garden.'

I saw Sammy put his finger in the icing of one of the cakes.

'Sammy, please don't do that,' I said.

He looked right at me as he put his finger in his mouth.

'It tastes like poo.'

'I'd really appreciate it if you could stop making references to poo. You are well equipped to use other, more meaningful comparative examples.'

'Miss, my wings keep falling off. They're too big!'

My head was about to explode.

'Please, can you all sit down – quietly – and get ready for assembly. There's lots left to do, and we don't want to be late for the nativity.'

Much to my surprise, the children sat down.

'Thank you for listening,' I said.

Mr Reid came back in the room, needle and thread in hand.

'Gosh, you're all sitting nicely. How lovely.'

'Yup, all under control.'

I hadn't quite appreciated the preparation that goes into a primary school nativity. There were hours of debate and discussions – should we include interpretive dance; how many narrators should we have; who's in charge of music?

And then there were the parents: 'Why is my son playing a pig, and not even the lead pig?'; 'Why isn't my little darling playing Mary? Surely, with her quiet maternal nature, she should've been picked for the role'; 'Do you know how much we splashed out on extra singing lessons, and you're telling me he's a goat? This is ridiculous!'

No, this is a primary school nativity; what's ridiculous is

that I stayed up until 1 a.m. last night making five different cakes because it appears that my overall sense of personal value is inextricably linked to the success of my baked goods. Hence me playing Mary Berry to a bunch of stoners in secondary school.

I was roped in at the last minute to assist with the dance routine. I had initially asked Mia to help me with some basic choreography, but I decided to do things on my own after she sent me a video of her dressed as a scantily clad chorus girl. It was simple, elegant and, most importantly, age appropriate.

Words were forgotten, stage directions were missed, and costumes fell apart. Jesus was thrown off stage, an angel's wing headbutted an audience member, and an entire song was sung in the wrong key. It was everything I expected it to be and more.

Afterwards, we had cake in the classroom with the parents. I watched Kitty's mother boast about their upcoming holiday to Antigua and listened to Primrose's father lament the fact that their second home in the Cotswolds had flooded. I was just thankful that my family had gone a whole twenty-four hours without having another row over what supermarket did the best Christmas canapé selection.

I surveyed the room as Nancy stood beside me, inhaling icing.

'What do you want for Christmas?' she asked me.

'I want a solid eight hours' sleep and a day with limited stress. What about you?'

'I want a magic forest and a puppy and lots of chocolate.'

I laughed. 'Anything else?'

'I want a baby sister.'

I squeezed her body close to me.

'Your mummy is very lucky to have you,' I said.

‘Do you think Santa will give us a baby?’

‘I don’t know, Nancy, but if he doesn’t, it will be OK. Your parents love you very much, that’s what matters.’

‘What else do you want for Christmas, Miss?’

I thought I might like a new pair of everyday earrings. Nothing too fancy. I was considering whether I might go for something a more upmarket, like rose gold, when I saw Jamie through the window, smoking by the fire exit. I’d recognise that cashmere coat from a mile off.

‘Nancy, I need to go outside for a minute. You stay in here with everyone, OK?’

She wasn’t listening; she was too busy wiping cake on her dress.

35

I crossed the playground and walked towards him. He flicked his cigarette onto the street.

'You're not supposed to smoke on school premises,' I said.

'I'm outside.'

'You're on school property.'

He moved outside the gates. 'Better now?'

'Yes.'

'Hello, Ivy.'

'Hello, Jamie.'

'It's nice to see you. You look great.'

'What are you doing here?'

'I came to support Amit.'

'He doesn't need support. He was a sheep.'

'It's important I'm here today. His father couldn't make it.'

'Do you seriously think this is appropriate?'

'I don't want to upset you.'

'Out of all the people in London, you chose Amit's mother.'

'I'm in love with her.'

'Come off it, Jamie.'

'I'm being serious.'

'Whatever. It doesn't matter. I'm in love now, too.'

It sounded much better in my head.

'So I hear,' Jamie said. 'I'm happy for you.'

'Are you?'

'Yes, I've always wanted the best for you.'

I walked away before turning back around again.

'This isn't about me,' I said. 'It's about a four-year-old boy. It's not a game – not when children are involved.'

'I know this isn't ideal, and I'm sorry. But I care about Amit; I'm trying to do the right thing. I'd like us to be friends, Ivy.'

'Friends? We can be civil, but I don't need your friendship.'

'His mother adores you. Everyone at the school does, it seems.'

'Thank you, Jamie. That's truly illuminating. I'm so grateful for such a thorough, in-depth report into my career progression.'

He got another cigarette out of his pocket. I wanted to grab the packet, throw it on the floor and stamp on it. But I didn't. I clenched my jaw, swore repeatedly in my head, and walked back inside.

My hands were trembling. I stopped off in the bathroom, locked myself in a cubicle and sat down on the toilet seat. I wasn't going to let myself fall apart. I closed my eyes and took several deep breaths.

Walking out, I caught my reflection in the mirror; there was a blob of icing on my forehead and a unicorn sticker in my hair.

'For fucking fuck's sake,' I said.

I splashed my face with water and went back to class.

Nancy was in the exact same position, picking the last of the icing off the cake. Her mother was standing near her, talking to Hakim's mother.

'I'm having some girlfriends over this weekend,' she said. 'I'm trying out some new Nadiya Hussain recipes.'

'Oh, I love Nadiya.'

'I might try to do my own condiments.'

'I love a condiment.'

'Me too. I love a good chutney.'

'I love an aioli.'

'You should come over, meet everyone.'

'I could bring an aioli!'

'You could bring an aioli!'

Nancy looked up at me.

'What's a condiment?' she asked.

'It's a sauce,' I said.

'Is a condom a sauce?'

'Where did you hear that?'

'Condom!' she said, louder this time.

'Nancy, please don't say that word.'

She almost said it again, but I held my hand to her mouth.

'You're not allowed to say that in class, OK?'

'It's funny.'

'It is not.'

'So why are you laughing?'

'I'm laughing because I'm remembering a joke Jamar told me earlier,' I lied.

I walked straight over to the cakes and shoved two frosted vanilla cupcakes in my mouth.

'Are you OK, Miss?' Mabel asked.

'Yes, I just saw my ex-fiancé but it's not a big deal. I'm over it.'

'OK!' she yelled and sprinted off.

After everyone had left, I walked around the room with a bin bag, clearing away the last of the paper plates.

'Leave that,' Mr Reid said. 'I'll do it later.'

As soon as I sat down on the fuchsia bean bag it hit me, and I couldn't stop myself from crying. I didn't know whether I was crying because I'd seen Jamie, or because I'd survived the first term. Either way, I was a mess.

'I'm so sorry,' I said. 'I wasn't supposed to cry today.'

'What were you supposed to do?'

'Remember a simple dance routine, not swear in front of the children.'

I'd also add, not bump into my ex-fiancé with cake on my face, but I kept that to myself.

'How will I cope without you next term?' I said.

'It's only six weeks, then you'll be back here with us. You'll enjoy the change of scenery.'

'The new teacher isn't going to be half as good as you.'

'It's very easy to judge other people's authority in the classroom, Ivy. I'd hate to think what you thought of me on your first day.'

'You scared the living daylights out of me.'

'Did I?'

'Yes! You came across all sweet in your grandad waistcoat, but you were terrifying.'

'Nobody's ever called me terrifying before; I quite like it.'

I smiled at him. Maybe it was because it was Christmas, but his beard was whiter than ever, and he had the beginnings of a paunch, like he was morphing into a sexy Santa Claus. I often pictured him as a young man, and, before I knew it, I was picturing him as Scott, which meant I was picturing him naked. I faked a cough as I tried to banish the thought from my mind.

'Here, I got you something,' he said.

He handed me a parcel with children's handprints painted all over the paper.

I opened it up to find two bookends – I and E – with the children's names written inside each one.

I flung my arms around him.

'Thank you,' I said.

'Well done, Ivy. For everything.'

'Was it the best nativity you've ever seen?'

He laughed. 'Yes, it was.'

I could feel his eyes on me as I read all the names on the bookends.

'Do you and Scott want to have a drink with Mel and me over Christmas? If it's awkward, because he's family and we work together, then I'll understand.'

'No, it's not awkward.'

'OK, great. Because I'd love to buy you a drink, several drinks in fact, to say thank you.'

'I'd love that, thank you, Finn.'

'Finn! My, times are a-changing.'

'You know what, it doesn't feel right. I think I'll stick with Mr Reid.'

He smiled.

'You should be very, very proud of yourself, Ivy.'

I'd never felt successful at work. I longed to come home from a day in the office feeling like I'd accomplished something. Despite the interaction with my ex-fiancé, and the fact that I looked like I'd been beaten up, I'd achieved a great deal. Some might say I'd achieved something remarkable.

'Do you ever feel like you're on the sidelines, watching everyone play?' I asked him.

'Ivy, you're not on the sidelines. You're captain of the game.'

'I got fired as captain of my netball team. My coach found me snogging his son before the semi-finals.'

'Maybe next year I'll teach you the importance of keeping things to yourself.'

Scott opened the front door and I jumped into his arms.

'I'm so happy to see you,' I said.

There were two sourdough pizzas on the kitchen counter, next to a bottle of champagne and a cherry-coloured poinsettia.

'I wanted to cook, but . . . ' he said.

'Best we stick to our strengths,' I said, kissing him.

'Congratulations on a cracking first term, Miss Edwards.'

'I can't believe I have to do this all over again – and at another school. Thank God there's the prospect of a well-paid job at the end of this. Oh no, wait.'

'Tell me everything. How was the nativity? Was everyone wowed by your world-class choreography?'

'Jamie was in the audience.'

'Jamie? As in your ex-fiancé Jamie?'

'I spoke to him in the playground.'

'Did you?'

'I think he's actually in love with Amit's mother.'

'Wow.'

He put his arm around me. 'I'm sorry, this must be really weird for you.'

'I actually believed him when he said he was trying to do the best by Amit.'

'Why does that surprise you?'

'He's got a fraught relationship with his father, amongst other things.'

'Oh, another one of us. I sense a theme here.'

He lifted the hair off my shoulders and started kissing me.

'I know what you're trying to do . . . ' I said.

'Is it that obvious?'

'Hang on, let me turn the oven on first.'

'I love it when you talk dirty.'

'Shut up, I'm starving!'

'Let me do it,' he said.

'Put it on one-eighty.'

'Fan or oven?'

'You're learning so fast, aren't you?'

That night, we sat under the soft cashmere blankets and talked about our best and worst Christmases. His was when his parents separated – it was so distressing that his brother and him got blackout drunk and ended up falling asleep against the fountain in Trafalgar Square. They woke to pigeons picking at their feet, their wallets and phones gone, and there was semen on both their trousers – and it wasn't their own. I told him my worst one was last year – the one after Gramps died.

'I can't talk about him today,' I said. 'I've cried enough as it is. Tell me about your favourite Christmas.'

'That's a no-brainer – when David Beckham bought me a pint in a pub in Fitzrovia.'

'Wow, David Beckham in the flesh.'

'I'd let you give David Beckham a hand job.'

'Why would I want to give David Beckham a hand job?'

'Because he's David Beckham.'

'But what's in it for me?'

'Who would you let me have sex with?'

'Wait, why do I have to give a hand job, but you can have sex?'

'I don't make up the rules.'

I mused over this for a few moments as he poured us more champagne.

'OK . . . J Lo,' I said.

'God, I'd ravage J Lo.'

'Stop it,' I laughed. 'You are disgusting.'

He leant in close to me. 'But you love me, right?'

'Yes, I do. I really do.'

*

I couldn't get Jamie off my mind that night. Yes, I would have preferred that he didn't show up at my school with such an attractive wintery glow and tell me that he was in love with Amit's mother. But I took some comfort in the fact that I'd seen him at my place of work, and the world hadn't ended. It had stopped moving for a bit, but it hadn't ended, and that's something.

I'd even argue that, aside from the cake and the sticker, I came across quite mature. Admittedly, I'd rather he be in Mongolia, but he's not. He's in London, trying to move on with his life, which is a sentiment I should empathise with.

36

Mam and Dad came up to London a couple of days before Christmas. Scott and I had arranged to meet them in Shadwell, so we could all watch Mr Reid and Mel's gig, the last one of the year. I thought having Mr Reid and Mel there would take the pressure off meeting Scott, but, if anything, it only made Mam more hyperactive.

They arrived late. Mam had spent the day organising eight hundred photos of Eleanor into albums, but she'd missed out a single photo from Eleanor's three-and-a-half-month photoshoot, and because everything needed to run in chronological order, she insisted on rearranging the entire collection. Four hours later, she arrived at the pub, frazzled, with Dad by her side with a face of pure exasperation on him.

She ran over and hugged Scott for an inappropriate length of time, then, without letting go of him, asked several questions in quick succession, ending with what he'd be getting for Christmas. The answer was knitted socks from his grandma – the same thing he got every year.

'Ivy tells me your paternal grandmother was Welsh?' she said to him.

'Yes, she was from Llandudno.'

Mam laughed. 'It's so cute when English people try to pronounce Welsh names.'

She put her hand on his thigh; I promptly moved it.

'Was she Welsh speaking?' Mam asked.

'She spoke Welsh when she was a child, but then they moved to Coventry, and I think she lost it after that.'

'Can't say she's Welsh then, can you?'

'Mam, stop it. You don't speak Welsh. None of us do.'

'I am learning, Ivy, and we're from South Wales – proper Wales – so we're exempt.'

Dad mouthed an apology to Scott.

'When will you come visit us in Wales?' Mam asked.

'I think we'll come down for half term in February,' Scott said.

Mam winked at me as Scott put his hand on my leg.

'I would love that,' she said. 'Hopefully we'll have the car back by then. It's still at Dai Cars. I don't know what he's doing with it. The man moves at the pace of a snail.'

'It's been nice . . . hasn't it, Mags?' Dad said. 'Going out for more walks, getting the heart rate going.'

'Heart rate? You're a slower walker than Gramps was, and that's saying something. Not having a car has been a terrible inconvenience.'

'You don't even drive, Mam.'

'Well, no. But your father likes to drive me everywhere, so I'm thinking of him, I am.'

Dad was silent. The car was a constant bone of contention between the two of them and it was best that nothing else was said on the matter.

'You see, Scott,' Mam said, 'they've changed the website.'

'Mags – please, not the website again,' Dad said.

Mam continued her ramblings.

'It's a nightmare, Scott, is what it is. Since the car's been out, I've been going with Tomos Taxi's, but he's been ill, bless him. So, then I went with Glyn's Global Cars but there's nothing global about them at all; they can barely speak English!'

'Mags—'

'So, with the car in the garage and the taxi services being completely incompetent, I've had to take the bus.' She paused for dramatic effect. 'And that, Scott, has been one hell of a palaver.'

'Mags, shall we give this a rest now, yeah?' Dad said.

'They changed the bus timetable, see. But the one on the website doesn't match the one in the station.' She looked directly at Scott. 'So, what am I supposed to do?'

He hesitated before answering. 'I don't know, Mrs Edwards.'

'Please, call me Margaret. Linda thinks we should start a petition, but I've already complained to the council and I used the last of my fancy stationery. I suppose we'll just have to see what happens. That's all we can do, isn't it?'

Scott was lost for words. I looked across to the bar, where a woman was setting up a fancy-dress box.

'Oh, Emma's back,' I said.

'Emma?' Mam asked.

'You can wear one of her outfits for the night, as long as you donate.'

'Who are we donating to?'

'It's a youth homelessness charity, for LGBTQ plus teenagers.'

'How marvellous. I love homosexuals.'

I tried to hide under the table as Mam got up from her seat and rushed over to Emma.

'I'd better go with her,' Dad said. 'In case, well ... you know.'

'Yes, please do,' I said.

'Really great to meet you,' Dad said to Scott.

'Thanks, you too, Tony.'

We watched Dad follow Mam to the bar.

'What do you think?' I said.

'I think we're going to get along very well,' Scott said.

*

'I loved last night so much,' Mam said. 'Scott is terrific. I cannot get enough of dimples.'

She was standing in the middle of Anna's living room, holding a plate of piping-hot crispy bacon.

'He had a great time,' I said.

'You're sure I wasn't too much?'

'You were exactly how I expected you to be.'

'It was so much fun. I feel so Christmassy today.'

'Well, it's Christmas Eve, and you did dress up as an elf last night and sing Wham! until two in the morning.'

'It was barely midnight.'

'It was two a.m.'

She ignored this and shoved another piece of bacon in her mouth.

I took a piece off her plate.

'Ivy, stop it,' she said, slapping my hand. 'I need this more than ever today.'

'This isn't exactly organic, is it?'

'I was only supposed to be eating lean South African game meat this holiday, but I can't find any ostrich. I thought London was meant to be cosmopolitan?'

I walked into the kitchen to see Anna. She was in a foul mood; her and Mark had clearly argued that morning and whilst Mark was doing his best to give off the impression that everything was fine, Anna was stomping around, exhaling loudly so everyone could hear.

'Why did you make so much food?' she moaned at me.

'I thought you'd appreciate it, with Mam and Dad here.'

'There's no space in the fridge as it is. Why are you here anyway? I thought you'd be with Scott today.'

'He's gone to see some Japanese horror film.'

'Whatever. Just make yourself useful.'

'I am. That's why I came over with the food. Are you OK?'

'Go out and entertain Mam and Dad,' she said, putting a can of coke in my hands and ushering me out of the kitchen.

'What's her problem?' I said to Mam.

'I don't know, but I heard a very hushed argument around seven this morning. She hasn't apologised for waking me up yet. She knows I need at least nine hours to function sufficiently.'

'You probably shouldn't have stayed out till two then.'

'You stayed out with me!'

'I am nothing if not my mother's daughter.'

I sat down on the sofa and *cwtched* up next to Dad.

'Tony, we need to fetch the hire car,' Mam said.

'Not now, Mags. My tendonitis is playing up, *mun*.'

'What does that have to do with it?'

'Can't I sit down for one minute?'

'Funny how it was fine for golf this week.'

'Where is the car?' I asked.

'It's at the pub,' Mam said.

Dad gave in, put his coat on and went out the door. I picked Eleanor up, and started singing 'Last Christmas' to her, which she seemed to love. I had an image of us dancing to George Michael together in a club. I took her into the kitchen to see Anna.

'Just think, me and Eleanor hitting the Big Smoke, dancing on the town, getting legless.'

Anna looked like she was about to explode. 'Don't you dare think about taking my daughter out.'

I was about to tell her to stop being so sensitive, when I remembered what happened last Christmas. I left the kitchen, closing the door behind me.

'Tony, what are you doing back so soon?' Mam said, seeing Dad walk back into the living room.

'The car's outside.'

I saw the horror on Mam's face.

'You drove home last night?' I said.

Mam looked at Dad, who was refusing to make eye contact.

He cleared his throat. 'I . . . I have no recollection of that.'

'Wow, talk about setting an example,' I said.

'We will never speak of this again,' he said, sitting down next to Mam.

'Do you remember doing the Irish jig with Mr Reid on stage?' I said to him.

Their faces went blank.

We heard a crash from the kitchen.

'Buggering shit fuck,' Anna cried.

I rushed in to find a broken jug on the floor and cranberry sauce everywhere.

'Look, I've had three hours' sleep,' she said. 'They got in at two a.m., woke Eleanor, who didn't go back to sleep till four. Then Mark had to get up because she was screaming again, having been woken by Dad, who walked into her room trying to find the bathroom.'

'I did tell you to book them into a hotel.'

'I was trying to be nice! I knew they'd want to wake up on Christmas morning with their grandchild.'

'Maybe we should go out for a walk?' I said. 'Leave you to it.'

'I asked you to take them out an hour ago,' Anna said.

'Do you want me to help you clean up first?'

'No, just go.'

I rallied Mam and Dad and we got our coats and left.

37

The park was full of exhausted parents, over-excited children and grandparents trying to keep the peace. We walked through the playground and Mam couldn't take her eyes off a little girl. She had a long French braid and metallic Converse trainers and was being pushed on the swing by her doting grandfather.

'I had quite the row with Gramps earlier,' she said. 'I feel all out of sorts.'

'Mam, you do know he's not with us, right?'

'Well, of course, that's what was most surprising.'

We carried on walking. I didn't know whether Mam was having a psychotic episode or was just very hung-over. I told her about the last row I had with him. He'd called me on the way to work one morning, shortly before he died. It wasn't a big deal that he rang me, because he did every day, and it wasn't a big deal that we rowed, because we rowed every other week.

'Can I ring you back?' I said to him. 'I'm just getting to work.'

'Listen, babes. No need to worry, but I've fallen down the stairs.'

'Oh my God, are you OK? Have you called an ambulance?'

'I don't need an ambulance. I need your mother, but I can't get hold of her, *mun*.'

'Let me call you an ambulance!'

'No! I just need some help getting up, that's all. Ring your mother and have her come over.'

'Where are you?'

'I'm at the bottom of the stairs. I'm OK though, don't fret, *bach*. Just ring your mother for me, will you?'

I got off the phone and rang Mam. I called the landline several times. I called her mobile too, then Dad's. Then I called Gramps' best friend Owen, who also didn't pick up. I called Gramps back.

'I can't get hold of anybody,' I said, panicking. 'What if you've broken something? I'm calling you an ambulance.'

He started to laugh.

'Why are you laughing? This isn't funny.'

'I was only joking, *mun*. Sitting on the sofa, I am.'

'You're sitting on the fucking sofa?'

'Don't use that language with me!'

'For fuck's sake.'

'Don't fucking swear at me, Ivy Edwards.'

'Don't ever do that to me again.'

'Come on, babes. I thought it would be funny.'

'How is this funny? You've not long come out of hospital! You can barely walk as it is.'

'OK, OK. Calm down. I'm sorry.'

'Christ, I almost had a heart attack.'

He started to laugh. I laughed.

'Why are you so annoying?' I asked.

'Everyone you love the most annoys you – me . . . your mother.'

'I'm going to go now, I'm late for work because of you.'

'You're always late for work, you lazy git.'

'Gramps!'

'How about you ring me tonight?' he said. 'We can watch *Sleepless in Seattle* together? Maybe after tea? *Joio*?'

'Yes, *joio*.'

'You know I love you, babes.'

'I love you too.'

Mam laughed when I told her.

'Sometimes I miss him so much I don't know what to do with myself,' I said.

'It won't be as hard as last year, and next year won't be as hard as this year. And you know, he's here, he's always here.'

Dad put his arms around her, and we carried on walking through the park.

'I'm sorry I was so reluctant to come to London,' she said.

'You don't have to apologise, I get it.'

'I knew you would.'

Back at Anna's, the lights were off, and their bedroom door was closed. We creeped into the living room, closed the door behind us, and turned the television on low. After a few minutes, Mam paused the show.

'What's that noise?' she asked.

'What noise?' I said.

It took a couple of minutes, but then I heard it – it was Anna and Mark, and they were having sex.

We thrust into action as we tried to find the baby monitor. We tossed everything onto the floor, we looked behind the sofa, outside in the garden, in Eleanor's play box. Dad was stretched out on the carpet trying to look further under the sofa as Mam paced the room. Throughout all the commotion, all we could hear in the background was the unmistakeable sound of two people having sex.

Dad finally found the monitor in the corner of the room, under a pile of nappies.

'Help me switch the damn thing off!' he said.

I ran over and turned it off. Nobody spoke as I put it back on the bookshelf.

'For the love of God can someone get me a wine,' Mam said.

I rushed to the kitchen and came back with a bottle.

We sat in silence as we drank. After a few minutes, Anna came in.

'Oh, you're here,' she said, opening the door to the living room.

She pointed to the bottle of wine on the floor. 'I was saving that for a special occasion.'

I struggled to think of something to say.

'You could've at least waited for me,' she said.

Nobody said anything.

'Why are you all being so quiet?'

'We're not,' I said.

'You're being weird. What's happened?'

'Nothing.'

She sat down on the armchair. 'Can someone press play on the TV, please?' she said.

The TV played and, after a few minutes, Anna looked over to the bookshelf, where the baby monitor was flashing. I saw her face register what had just happened. She went pale as she got out of her seat.

'Food, anyone?' she asked.

'I'll come help,' I said.

I followed her into the kitchen. She stood by the sink with her head low.

'You heard us, didn't you?'

'Yes.'

'You, Mam and Dad?'

'Yes.'

'How much?'

'Enough.'

She didn't say anything.

'Guess you guys have made up then?' I said.

She got a spoon and lobbed it at my head.

As is custom in our family, Anna and I spent Christmas Day in matching onesies, Mark kept himself busy in the kitchen, and Mam and Dad rowed. This year, it was because Mam had bought Eleanor seven potential outfits to wear for the day, one of which was £49.99. Sometimes I think she leaves the tags on just to annoy him.

She'd also spent a small fortune on personalised 'Eleanor's first Christmas' gifts; a bath towel, pyjamas, reindeer onesie and matching crockery set. When Dad pointed out that buying single-use products wasn't in line with Mam's eco-living ethos, she told him he was ruining Christmas. After a stroll in the park and a pint in the pub, things calmed down, and they spent the rest of the day *cwtching* on the sofa.

Eleanor was trying to crawl; she would move an inch and we'd clap and cheer like it was the most entertaining thing we'd ever seen. Anna and Mark bought everyone Eleanor-themed presents – there were photo frames, calendars, mugs, and – the *pièce de résistance* – a key ring. She was on solid foods now and there was mush everywhere. The banana was the most offensive; it got into every crevice. I took a photo and sent it to Scott, asking him if the mess made him anxious. He seemed genuinely excited that his mother had got him a whole new set of cleaning products, and said he'd be right over with the Marigolds. If it wasn't for the fact that it was Christmas Day, I think he would have.

He came over on Boxing Day to exchange presents. I bought him a book on minimalism, which promised him a stress-free decluttering journey, as well as a table book of rare photos of artists and authors of post-war America. He bought me a print by a Californian artist I'd never heard of. He told me he'd chosen it because her work explores loss and grief, and the importance of strong sisterly bonds. I cried when he gave it to me, I felt like he was seeing into my soul. But then again, I was hung-over and emotional.

That afternoon, as we walked through Hampstead Heath together, Dad and Scott got talking about Scott's parents, and how Scott feels the burden of their break-up. Sick of hearing Mam rant about the bus timetable, I edged towards Scott and took hold of his hand. I gave him a smile to say, I'm here, and I'm going to share the burden.

As contented as I was in that moment, walking through the park alongside my favourite people in the world, I couldn't help but think of Jamie. The last time Jamie and Dad had spoken, they'd had a heated discussion about the elitist nature of private schools. Dad argued that people from private schools had a disproportionate influence on society, and that an Etonian PM could never appreciate the challenges of the average working-class British family. Jamie said he couldn't help the situation he was born into, and that he shouldn't be made to feel guilty about his parent's wealth. This went on for some time until Dad eventually gave up and changed the subject. Dad was much more at ease with Scott, and I could tell Scott loved having someone Dad's age to talk to.

I don't know what it was about the day, but I thought about Jamie a lot. I thought about him sharing Christmas with Amit's mother, knowing he'd hate to spend another holiday at his parents' home in Hambleton. I thought about him exchanging presents with Amit, probably in matching knitwear, as he and Amit's mother shared a bottle of expensive wine from an exclusive vineyard. He almost broke me, and the thought of him sitting contentedly with another woman didn't quite sit right, but I did want him to be happy – because I was happy. Or maybe I just told myself that to make me feel better?

Later that night, we met Noah and Mia in Kentish Town. Mia walked in, her mink coat undone revealing an all-in-one glitter jumpsuit and gold sequin boots. She waved her arms in the air and screamed, 'I'M ENGAGED!'

Everyone in the pub turned to look at her as she ran towards me, almost knocking me over. She threw her coat onto the floor and held her hand out.

'Isn't it humongous!' she said.

Mam grabbed her hand as Scott and Dad congratulated Noah.

'Mia, this is stunning,' Mam said, putting Mia's hand right up to her face. 'Noah's got such good taste, such class. It's all down to parenting – I would know.'

Mia nodded enthusiastically but I could tell she wasn't listening; she was too busy gaping at her rock.

'Let me get a round of drinks in,' Dad said. 'Prosecco?'

'Tony, don't be so ridiculous,' Mam said. 'We're having champagne.'

'Isn't it the same thing?'

Mam looked at him, appalled and went back to Mia.

'Have you started planning the wedding?' she asked. 'Where will it be? Do you think Dorset or Hampshire?'

'So much to think about, Mags. I've already started on my binder.'

'Binder?' said Noah.

'I've spent a few hours on Pinterest, and I think I've got a theme,' she said to Mam.

'We've got a theme?' Noah said.

'Darling, don't worry. It's not like a "theme" theme, just a little theme.'

Dad came back with the champagne, muttering about the ridiculous price, and we toasted the happy couple.

Later that evening, Mia announced she was taking me outside for a cigarette. Mam gave me a disapproving look.

'Sorry,' I said. 'I don't do it half as much as I used to.'

'Yeah, only on special occasions,' Mia said.

Once outside, I told her how proud I was of her.

'Look at the year you've had,' I said. 'A leading role in the Royal Court and now this.'

She held up her hand to inspect the ring again.

'It really is exceptional, isn't it?' she said.

'It really is.'

I put my arm around her and we smoked in silence.

'Does it make you think about Jamie?' she asked. 'Is that weird? Sorry, it is weird, isn't it?'

'It's not weird . . . but yes.'

'You were thinking about him just then, weren't you? I've seen that face a thousand times.'

'I'm over the moon for you, you know that, don't you? This is your year, Mia.'

'I have aced this year.'

I laughed.

'But look at you,' she said, 'first term of school under your belt, and now Scott. We're killing it.'

We hugged again before she grabbed my face and kissed me forcefully on the lips.

'You know you're my maid of honour, right?'

I started to well up.

'Oh, for fuck's sake, don't, you're going to set me off again,' she said.

'It would be my honour and privilege,' I said. 'You are my queen and I will do everything in my power to serve and protect you.'

'I am basically the queen.'

'You fucking act like one.'

'Shall we get another bottle of champers?'

'Yeah, but you're paying for it this time. Dad's about to have a nervous breakdown.'

'I love you, you beautiful, Welsh goddess.'

'No, you're the goddess.'

'You're right, I am the goddess.'

38

Just like that, it was New Year's Eve, and, using this as an excuse to celebrate her engagement, Mia was throwing the party of the decade. Her vision: 'decadence on crack'. Hoping to channel Kate Moss circa 1993, she had borrowed a barely there vintage satin slip from her model friend and had embarked on a three-day juice detox to fit into it. As a result of her lack of energy and flailing blood-sugar levels, she'd been an absolute tyrant to be around and my patience with her was wearing thin.

I was sifting through her jewellery trying to find the right piece to match my outfit. I had bought a black velvet jumpsuit for the occasion, which I was going to wear with a black bralette. As Mam pointed out, a good bralette can hide a multitude of sins, and she'd bought me no less than four for Christmas.

Mia came up behind me and started putting all the pieces back in their boxes.

'What are you doing?' I said. 'You said it was OK for me to borrow something.'

'Let me choose for you; you'll take ages and it'll be all wrong for you anyway.'

'Mia, you need to eat something.'

'I had a rice cake with a quarter of an avocado.'

'Is that it?'

'Why are you being so unsupportive? Tonight must be perfect.'

'You know tonight's not your wedding, right?'

She gave me the finger.

'Does a Bloody Mary count?'

'Mia! Eat a proper meal – this is a marathon, not a sprint.'

'You're so full of wisdom. I'll go make some toast.'

She was leaving the room when I took my outfit out from my bag. She stopped and looked at it, making all the right noises.

'Go eat,' I told her.

She came back in with a marmite sandwich.

'What time is Scott getting here?' she asked.

'Not till later. His boss wants to take him out for drinks after work.'

'Must be nice to get some space from each other.'

'Not really.'

'Look at you, I can't mention his name without you acting like a loved-up teenager.'

'He's just . . .'

'I know.'

Of course she knew.

We put on our outfits and stood facing each other.

'How do I look?' Mia asked. 'Your candour is paramount.'

'You look like a million bucks,' I said. 'And me?'

'I'm glad you didn't go with the dress; you don't have the shoulders for it.'

'Mia!'

'Don't be stroppy, you know Mags would say the same.'

'You're a terrible person.'

'I'm only joking. You look like a fucking rock star.'

As is custom when I'm at one of Mia's parties, I spent most of the evening avoiding conversation with the older guests. This time around it was Sidney, a middle-aged philosopher who used to be a friend of Noah's dead aunt. Sidney's preferred topic of conversation was his cats – both of whom live in a drawer in his office at Goldsmiths – but after Mia told him I was a teacher trainee, he cornered me by the piano and started bombarding me with questions about the course: How was I nurturing the children's personal growth? Were they exposed to the right literature? Had I introduced philosophy?

'The thing is, Sidney,' I said, 'they're four. I don't think they're ready for Nietzsche.'

'Nietzsche? Don't feed them that nonsense. Inspire them with Plato, darling.'

'Plato? They prefer Peppa.'

'Who is Peppa?'

'It's a talking pig, Sidney.'

'Urgh, how vulgar.'

Every time he spoke, a crumb from his moustache fell into his mouth. He licked his lips and I felt my stomach turn.

'Barney, please don't do coke on the cabinet,' Mia said, speeding into the living room. 'We've only just had it polished.'

The dance floor parted as Mia charged towards Barney and stood right in his face. He looked like a rabbit caught in headlights and began whimpering as she ordered him to take his gear to another room or go home.

She walked up to me and Sidney and asked if I might be excused. Sidney tipped his hat and walked off.

'Sorry I left you,' she said. 'There were people having sex in the downstairs toilet.'

'Already?'

'Everyone's on heat.'

She grabbed the bottle of champagne and topped up our glasses, and we leant against the piano, eyeballing the room.

Dan walked over, looking bored.

'Why are all your friends so old?' he asked.

'They're mainly Noah's friends,' Mia said. 'You and Ivy are the only ones from my lot here.'

'Where is everyone?' I asked.

'They'll be here later. I'm expecting another sixty or so.'

'Sixty? Where will they all fit.'

'I don't know, in the bath?'

This was something that often happens at Mia's. She'll wake up the next day and there'll be a dozen people passed out in there. It takes until around the 5th of January for the last of the guests to leave.

'Until then, it's just us losers,' she said.

'And Davey,' I said, gesturing over to him.

'Don't talk to him, he's done too much MDMA and he's lost one side of his face.'

'Who's Davey?' Dan asked.

'You know, male model, super dull chat, fab bone structure.'

'Dammit, I was hoping he'd be my midnight kiss.'

'Not if he can't move his mouth.'

We scanned the room.

'What about him?' Dan asked Mia.

'Ricky? No, he has a girlfriend.'

'What about Matt? With the hair,' I said.

Matt heard his name and waved at us. We all made gestures about how gorgeous his hair was looking. It was so luxuriant and luminous and reached past his shoulders. He did a bow before going back to his conversation.

'You know he's moving to Manchester? He's helping his sister launch her new salon up there.'

Dan gasped. 'She can't leave London. Where am I going to get my hair done?'

'Tell me about it. I've not paid full price in years.'

Matt walked past us to get to the kitchen and we all air-kissed.

'Fucking selfish,' Dan said, as soon as he was out of earshot. 'To be fair, I still owe him for consulting on that Haggerston restaurant launch.'

'That was three months ago, Dan.'

'I know . . . Maybe it's best he does leave London.'

After saving Noah from Sidney, we all went up to the bathroom. Mia and I got into the bath as Noah made himself comfortable on the window ledge and Dan got out a bag of cocaine.

'What's everyone's New Year's resolutions,' Dan asked. 'Ivy, you go first.'

'To not fuck up the next six weeks at my new placement. And to make sure Scott never leaves me.'

'Definitely,' Dan said.

'Yes, good one,' Mia agreed.

'You three are ridiculous,' Noah said. 'He's not going to leave you, Ivy, and there's no way you can fuck this up.'

'Tomorrow's a new year, and who knows what could happen.'

'Are you still wearing sexy underwear?' Dan asked.

'No, I prioritised paying my rent. You need money to be sexy all the time.'

'He's met the whole family, hasn't he?'

'Yes.'

'And he's been in your flat? In that mess.'

'It's not a mess! Look, we balance each other out: he can't cook; I hate cleaning. It's the perfect partnership.'

Everyone looked at me.

'What?' I said.

'I think this bodes really well, Ives,' Mia said, after she'd inhaled a line.

'Yeah ... this is the most stable and mature I've ever seen you,' Dan said.

Noah came over and put his arm around me.

'What they're trying to say is, you are brilliant, and beautiful, and we are very happy for you.'

'Thank you, Noah,' I said, kissing him on the cheek.

'Hang on,' Dan said, 'this is the first time we've all been together since your engagement.'

'To Mia and Noah,' I said, raising a glass.

'To me!' Mia squealed, laying down in the bath and putting her legs up high in the air.

Dan and Noah jumped in the bath and we all tipped our drinks onto each other as we hugged. Dan kissed Noah on the lips and told him he was almost as attractive as Ryan Reynolds, if only he had more hair; Mia told me I was the greatest woman ever to walk the face of the earth, and Noah pointed out that we all needed to get a life.

After sitting in Noah's dead aunt's bath for an hour, we went back down to the party, where I spotted Scott in the kitchen, chatting to Davey. He ran over to me and picked me up by the waist.

'Look at you!' he said.

'I know, I splashed out.'

He hugged me again, harder this time.

'Scott, you're crushing me,' I said, pulling away. 'How were drinks?'

'Can we go somewhere, just the two of us?'

'We can later. Come outside, everyone's dying to see you.'

Scott followed me out to the garden, where Mia, Dan and Noah were sitting around the fire. The garden looked like a mini Glastonbury; there were brightly coloured lanterns everywhere, filled with flickering tealights, fairy lights hanging from the trees and a tepee erected at the back.

I grabbed a beer from the wheelbarrow and passed it to Scott, and we sat down on the blanket with the others.

More people started to arrive – much more than Mia's estimated sixty. It was a collection of London's most outlandish residents. I got cornered in the kitchen by a couple from university, ex-socialists who used to spend every waking minute protesting or lobbying. They'd since 'reformed' and now resided in Maida Vale with their two precious children – one of whom goes to private school with Princess Charlotte. They'd just been to see Cardi B in concert – in the VIP section, of course – and kept telling me how important it was to have a positive black female artist who wasn't afraid to talk politics. I stood there with a vacant expression on my face wondering how on earth we got on to this, when Scott came up behind me. I introduced him as my boyfriend, a phrase I relished saying.

'Can we find somewhere to talk?' he said.

'Is everything OK?'

'Everything's fine,' he said, kissing me.

We walked back out into the garden and sat down in the hammock.

'Christ,' I said, as Scott wrapped a blanket over me, 'it's freezing tonight.'

He tried to smile but his eyes told a different story.

'What is it?' I asked.

'My boss wanted to speak to me about something tonight – about a new job.'

'Did you get a promotion?'

'Yes.'

'I knew it!' I said, *cwtching* into him. 'You're amazing, Scott. Congratulations.'

He didn't move.

'Why aren't you happy?' I asked, registering his face.

'It's in LA.'

'LA? As in Los Angeles?'

'Yes.'

'Fuck.'

'I'm sorry to tell you like this. I wanted to leave it until tomorrow, but I can't sit here with all your friends and not say anything.'

'Wow. LA? Wow.'

'They want me to run the North America region.'

'Fuck. Wow. Congratulations.'

'It's a lot to take in.'

My heart was racing. I got up from the hammock and looked into the house to see if I could see Mia.

Scott was about to say something else when Dan ran over to tell us that the countdown was starting. He grabbed both our hands and dragged us into the living room, where everyone was huddled together, their glasses full and their eyes glued to the countdown on BBC.

We stood at the back of the room. I looked to Scott, unable to say anything.

'Five, four, three, two, one . . . HAPPY NEW YEAR!'

Scott told me that he loved me.

There were tears running down my face as I told him I loved him back.

39

I started my second placement in January. It was important for me to compare different approaches to teaching, so that I had a better understanding of the sort of teacher I wanted to become. It was also important for me to find a boyfriend who didn't harbour a desire to move halfway across the world, to a land of sun-kissed, plastic-chested women who lived off 500 calories a day. But I guess I missed the mark on that one.

They put me in a school in Holloway, North London. The building was a towering grey slab; cold and soulless, like it could have been a workhouse in a Charles Dickens novel. The infamous prison was down the road and I wondered whether they'd swapped the names on the door.

Mrs Bell, whose classroom I'd be in for the next six weeks, greeted me at the entrance. I'd first met her before Christmas on an induction day. She had a short weave bowl cut, and was wearing a long multicoloured, abstract print dress with leopardprint trainers, which were spotted with dots of paint. She carried all her weight on her stomach and walked with a bit of a waddle. Her voice was gentle, but she was strong and statuesque and commanded the utmost respect. I was immediately taken with her.

'There's been an outbreak of lice,' she said. 'We think we

know who it's from, but the mother's denying it. Don't be alarmed if the atmosphere at pick-up is hostile.'

'What's it usually like?'

'Hostile.'

I smiled.

'That wasn't a joke,' she said. 'But don't worry, all of this is excellent training. What do you think you do as a teacher, Ivy, except navigate small nits and self-affected parents?'

She beckoned for me to come inside, and I followed her through the front door.

The school was in desperate need of brightening up. The atmosphere was heavy, and dark, like the walls were caving in on you. It replicated the atmosphere I currently felt in my head, so I felt at home, at least.

Mrs Bell's classroom, however, was a different matter. It was an explosion of colour, with art products everywhere – boxes of pom poms, paint dispensers, soft dough, felt pens and paint brushes. Nothing seemed to be in the right place, but I got the impression that it was exactly how the room was supposed to look. I noticed some pink crystals on her desk and asked her what they were for.

'They're rose quartz. They carry a feminine energy,' she said. 'I'm trying to create an environment of compassion and peace, instead of chaos and rebellion.'

I think she was joking that time.

I was introduced to the headmaster, Mr Reynolds, who had a sort of superficial charm to him that you frequently find in serial killers, then to a few of the other teaching staff. Most were dismissive, bored of seeing yet another trainee come through their doors, but a couple were kind, asking me how I'd found my first term, and about job applications. Their thoughtful hospitality aside, I was not a particularly willing conversationalist. I tried so hard to be present and enthusiastic but all I could think about was Scott. And LA. And Scott in LA. I kept telling myself to get it together, but Dilys was back, and she had grown in confidence.

The first child I met was Layla, who came into the room with a mouthful of crayons.

Mrs Bell ran to take them off her and introduced us.

'Miss Edwards will be with us for a few weeks, isn't that great?' she said to Layla.

'This is Bunny,' she said, whilst rubbing a very un-clean-looking Bunny on her crotch. 'I washed her with my tuppence.'

I couldn't help but laugh. Layla began to laugh, too.

'Why don't we wash our hands and sit down nicely?' I said.

She bounced off, Bunny in hand.

'They've discovered their genitals,' Mrs Bell said. 'Don't stand too close.'

Carter came in next. I said hello to him and his response was, 'I don't want to speak to anyone today.'

You and me both, Carter.

Before long, we had a full class. Mrs Bell had warned me that the children had developed a keen interest in marriage – why some people were married, and some weren't. As if on autocue, Kobe, a boy with deep-brown eyes and hair as soft as a pillow, asked me if I was married.

'Can I marry you, Miss Edwards?' Kobe said.

'I'd love to marry you, Kobe. As long as you don't move to LA.'

'What's that?'

'It's a place very far away that pales in comparison to London.'

A girl asked me what I'd done for Christmas.

'Why don't you tell me what you did?' I said. 'Did you play any fun games with your family?'

'I dressed up as a princess and ate chocolate and saw Rudolph in the park.'

'That sounds terrific,' I said.

Finally, the sort of meaningless chat I was hoping for.

By lunch Kobe had said my name approximately seven hundred times. I was desperate for some personal space, which would be fine if we were living in a warmer climate – say West Coast America – because the children could play outside, and I could be left alone to stare into the empty void in contemplation. But the weather was apocalyptic, so I gave them some coloured origami paper, and we got started on our fish.

The children were content, admiring all their creases and sharing stories of their favourite presents from Santa. But then there was Kobe, who wanted to know whether I'd had too much to drink at New Year's, just like his mummy and daddy. I said no but what I really meant to say was yes, I drank everything I could get my hands on, then sobbed on my boyfriend into the early hours of the morning.

I caught Layla's eye. Her smile was so broad that I could see the insides of her little mouth, all pink gums and milk teeth.

'Daddy and I do origami on Saturdays after football and we have crumpets and he does my hair in a plait and then we go to the duck pond and then we go to the pub and he has a pint and I have orange juice.'

She finally stopped for breath. Her face shone, and my heart felt full again.

'Your daddy sounds so cool,' I said. 'I wish my daddy lived in London so we could do fun things like that together.'

I looked to the clock: five hours till home time. Five hours till I had to leave the solace of the classroom. Five hours till I had to face Scott.

'Thank you for today,' I said to Mrs Bell, as we tidied the worksheets away from the last lesson. 'You've created such a wonderful space for the children, they clearly adore you.'

'When you come to this school, you expect the children to behave a certain way. But they thrive off compassion and kindness, and I encourage that through creativity. Creativity is food for the soul.'

I wanted to hug her and tell her that she was my spirit animal, but I didn't, because I was so close to the edge that one touch would have sent me spiralling. It was a new year, and one of my resolutions was to avoid public tears. I wasn't prepared to fail four days in.

'Your goal for the next six weeks is to learn about different teaching styles,' she said. 'It's important for you to figure out how you want to move forward.'

'Bring it on,' I said, with a surprising amount of confidence.

'Excellent. I love it when fresh blood comes in.'

I got home that night to find Scott standing by the entrance to my building, reading a book.

'What are you reading?' I asked, as I approached him.

'A history of the feminist revolution in Central America.'

He got up and kissed me. It had been three days since I last saw him and all I'd wanted to do in that time was kiss him and tell him not to leave.

'You've been avoiding me,' he said.

'You know I'm not allowed to use my phone during the day.'

'I've missed you.'

'I've missed you, too.'

'How was your first day?'

'I was a little distracted.'

He sighed. 'We need to talk about LA, Ivy.'

'I know.'

'I'll attempt to make dinner,' he said. 'I bought fresh pasta from the market, and some tomato sauce from that Italian shop you like down the road.'

'Thank you,' I said.

I tried to act normal, but I didn't know what normal was in these circumstances. I put some music on and poured us both a drink. As I was stirring the tomato sauce, Scott asked me to dance with him. I lasted all of ten seconds before I had to stop.

I walked away from him, back to the hob.

'Please stop shutting me out,' he said. 'I've been trying to talk to you since New Year's Eve. You need to remember that this is just as much of a shock to me as it is to you.'

I wondered if this was true. He said he'd always wanted to live in LA.

'What do you want to do?' I asked. 'Do you want to go?'

'I don't want to mess this – us – up.'

'That's not what I asked.'

'They want me to go out next week,' he said. 'It would only be a trial run.'

'Next week?'

'I was thinking you could come out with me, to suss it out? You said you've always wanted to go.'

'I'm in school. How could I?'

'You could take leave?'

'Not in the middle of term I can't. I'm only in Holloway for six weeks.'

My stomach was in knots. This wasn't how I saw this going.

'You said you were a workaholic until you met me,' I said. 'Is this what you were working towards – a new life, in America?'

'No . . . my boss mentioned an opportunity a few months back, but nothing more was said.'

'You never mentioned that to me. Why?'

'There wasn't anything to say.'

'What happens if you go next week?' I asked.

'I don't know . . . I'd meet the team, get to know some of the clients. See if it's the right fit, I guess.'

'How long will you be gone for?'

'Three weeks.'

'Sorry, what are you saying? That you want to go out for three weeks, or for good?'

'I think I need to go out for three weeks. Then we can look at our options. We can make this work.'

'What are our options, though?' I asked him. 'Our options are you moving there, me staying here. Those are our options.'

'Don't say it like that.'

'But that's it, isn't it? Options are whether I want a starter or dessert. Do I pay three quid for a posh coffee or have instant? Those are options, Scott. This? This is bullshit.'

40

I allowed myself to be angry for all of forty-eight hours, then I stood in front of the mirror and told myself to get it together. It was only three weeks. I would relish my new-found independence. I'd focus on school because that's what I was in control of. I'd make lists and feel immense satisfaction from crossing off completed tasks. I'd finish my job applications for September placements, organise the reference list for my latest essay, meet Dawn for a one-to-one, go see Maude in the care home, take Eleanor to music class, eat less meat, drink less alcohol, go running. I definitely wouldn't take up smoking again. It would be a time for great personal growth and reflection.

On the other hand, I could use the time to temporarily revert to the me I was trying to keep hidden from Scott. I could lounge about in my period pants, sleep through several alarms, stand in front of the mirror naked and inspect every detail of my body, eat marmite out of the jar, eat Haribo for breakfast. I'd be back to the good old single Ivy, only without the loneliness, desperation and wine bloat.

We devised a plan. When Scott was in LA, he would ring me on his lunch break, or before he went to bed. If we timed it right, we could even speak before I went to work. It was only three weeks. We could do this.

*

'We'll never have to miss a date night,' he said, on the morning of his flight. 'I can FaceTime you and we can eat together. It'll be just like I'm here.'

'Don't worry about me. You should be going out, having fun.'

If he didn't ring me every day, I'd be fuming.

'I'll try not to return to my old bachelor ways, but I can't promise anything.'

'Bachelor ways?'

'You know – slobbing out in front of the TV with a takeaway, some porn and a six-pack of Bud.'

'Scott, who are you kidding? You'll be on your hands and knees every night doing a deep-clean with a bottle of bleach.'

'I'm going to miss you, Ivy.'

'It's only three weeks; if anything, I could use the time away from you.'

'You've changed your tune.'

'I'm seeing this as an opportunity.'

'To live your life without me?'

'Don't take this the wrong way, but sometimes I feel guilty that I spend so much time with you and not enough in the library. Even when I am in the library, I'm thinking about having sex with you, or kissing you, so not seeing you for three weeks might do me some good. I'll have so much free time, I won't know what to do with it. Actually, I do, I'll be in the library. I'll be so busy that I won't have a second spare to miss you.'

'I'll be busy too, so maybe I won't miss you.'

'If this were a competition for who was busiest, I would win.'

'I love it when you're sparky,' he said, pushing me onto the bed.

He took his shirt off and crawled on top of me.

I squeezed him as hard as I could. If I squeezed him until

his ribs broke, he wouldn't be able to go to LA. I wanted to feel him inside me. I held him and put him in, and I gripped his back as we moved together, slowly. He told me over again that he loved me. I kept telling him that I loved him, too.

We held each other for a while afterwards, until we realised the time, and he had to go to the airport. He put on his clothes, picked up his bag, and I walked him to the door.

'See you in three weeks, my Welsh beauty.'

I grabbed his hair as we kissed, and then he was gone.

The first thing I thought was: I need a cigarette.

I met Mia for brunch that morning at a Greek café in Highgate. She was preparing for a new role as the ill-fated lover of a disgraced shipping heir and thought that a Mediterranean diet would help get her into the right mindset. So far, the diet seemed to consist of her drinking a lot of red wine and eating an inordinate number of sardines. I didn't have the energy to question her.

Like my mother, Mia likes to share every detail of her life with everyone she meets, regardless of whether they requested the information or not, and after telling the waitress all about her new health regime, she asked me how I was.

'I'm good,' I said.

She touched my hand. I moved it away from her.

'Sorry,' she said. 'I will try not to touch you . . . or look at you . . . or show any sympathy whatsoever.'

'Stop acting like someone's died, Mia.'

'Have you done something to your skin?'

'Anna treated me to a facial.'

'You look sensational. You're like that diamond the old lady threw into the ocean at the end of *Titanic*. Cast-off. Ruined.'

'Why am I ruined?'

'Ruin is a gift, Ivy. Elizabeth Gilbert said so.'

'I don't care what Elizabeth Gilbert says.'

'You should, she's basically God.'

'He's only going for three weeks.'

'And we're sure he's going? It's just . . . remember that bloke I was seeing before Noah? He said that he was moving to Dubai, but he only moved to Putney. He lied about the whole emigration thing to get away from me.'

'I wonder why.'

'Listen, why don't you come to the farm with me next weekend?'

'I don't have seven hundred pounds to spend on a night in a barn.'

'What about the money from your grandfather?'

'It's for food, rent and my course. Some of us pay our own rent, Mia.'

'They give you a fancy juice blender on departure.'

'I thought you were saving for the wedding?'

'I am. But it's important to get out of London and find the space to re-connect with myself before becoming a married woman.'

I poked the egg with my fork and watched the yolk run out onto the plate.

'What are you doing this week?' she asked. 'Why don't we do something fun?'

'I can't, I have too much work on.'

'Ivy, live a little.'

'I am living.'

'But we haven't been out in ages.'

'What about Christmas, and New Year's? That was only a couple of weeks ago.'

'You're always working these days, it's so boring.'

I put the fork down and got my stuff. 'I'm going to go,' I said.

'You've not even finished your food.'

'I need to go before I say something I'll regret.'

'Ivy, I'm sorry. Please – sit down.'

'I need to see Anna.'

'I didn't mean to upset you.'

'I'll call you later,' I said.

She got out of her seat to stop me, but I walked right past her and out of the café.

The next weekend, I woke up early and punished myself with a ten-miler in the wind and hail. I hadn't run in weeks, and my lungs were on fire due to all the smoking, so when I say a ten-miler, what I mean is that I ran for two, before I gave up and chain-smoked for the other eight. I would stop smoking tomorrow.

On the bus to see Maude, I composed a message to Scott.

'I can't help but feel upset with you. It's the second night in a row where you haven't called.'

I stopped typing and deleted the message.

'Hi Scott. I don't understand why it's so hard to send a text message. I know you're busy, but you can text when you're on the toilet.'

I deleted that one, too.

'Hi Scott. STOP HAVING FUN AND CALL YOUR FUCKING GIRLFRIEND.'

I pictured him in a glamorous bar, the sort that has table service and leggy blondes as waitresses. Californian women are so intimidating; they're so effortlessly attractive and chipper. I put my phone away and got out my reflective journal. Today's entry read: This is the pits.

I found Maude sitting by the window, knitting yet another cardigan for one of her friend's great-grandchildren. I handed her a bouquet of orange roses, and some tea and biscuits from the Fortnum & Mason hamper that Nancy's mother Sharon had bought me for Christmas. I knew there was a reason I went into teaching: luxury gifts.

'Happy New Year, Maude.'

'My darling, thank you.'

She eyed the cake beside me.

'You can't keep on baking us cakes, Ivy. Bill's put on two stone since he met you.'

'It's not my fault he eats ten scotch eggs a day. Someone needs to project manage that man's diet.'

She put the cardigan down and reached under her wheelchair, where she took out a parcel wrapped in *The Snowman* Christmas paper.

'What's this?' I asked.

'It's for Eleanor. I've knitted her a little jumper. Does she wear green? It's more of a jade green. I hope she likes it.'

I gave her a *cwtch*.

'You are the kindest woman, Maude. Thank you so much. Anna will love it.'

'Do you have any new photos of Eleanor you can show me?'

'I've got something better than that,' I said.

I turned around and waved at Anna, who was standing by the entrance of the living room. She picked Eleanor up from the pram and walked over to us. Maude could barely contain herself.

'It's so good to finally meet you,' Anna said.

Maude took Anna's hand in hers and kissed it. 'I can't believe it. You've made my day.'

We all sat down, and Anna asked Maude if she wanted to hold Eleanor.

'She's quite the flirt,' Anna said, 'but watch out for your necklace; it'll be in her mouth within seconds.'

'I can't remember the last time I held a baby,' she said. 'She's so precious, isn't she, Ivy?'

'She has the face of an angel,' Anna said.

Maude laughed, unable to take her eyes off Eleanor. I caught Anna's eye and knew what she was thinking – she was thinking about Gramps. I took her hand in mine and we both watched Maude stroke Eleanor's plump cheeks.

'Right, tell me,' Maude said, getting comfortable, 'what's been going on with you?'

'Scott's gone to LA.'

'I loathe California,' she said.

I laughed. 'You can't loathe the whole of California, Maude.'

'There are no pavements. Everyone drives.'

'They've got the most famous pavement in the world – Hollywood Boulevard.'

'He'll be gone for three weeks,' Anna said.

'What's the fuss about?'

'There's no fuss,' I said.

Anna made a face.

'OK, there's some fuss,' I said.

'Three weeks is no time at all,' Maude said. 'I once went two and a half years without seeing Martin when he was in New Zealand. A letter every three months kept us going.'

'He's been offered a job over there,' I said.

'She's worried he'll take it,' Anna said to Maude.

'What's wrong with his job here?' she asked.

'Nothing.'

'Sometimes I think you overcomplicate things, Ivy.'

'I admit I have allowed Dilys to creep back in, but I'm over that now. I'm using this as an opportunity.'

Anna laughed. 'If you use that word one more time . . .'

'Sometimes when I feel anxious and Dilys is on me, I think, what would Gramps do,' I said to Maude.

'He'd tell you straight, Ivy. Sometimes you need to be told.'

'That's a direct quote from him.'

'He sounds like my type of person.'

'He was everyone's type of person,' Anna said. 'No, that's a lie. Lots of people thought he was intolerable.'

'Have you told Scott what you want?' Maude asked.

'He knows.'

Anna made another face.

'OK, OK,' I said, 'I'll make it crystal clear when he comes back.'

'Good,' Maude said. 'So we can stop making a mountain out of a molehill?'

'I like you, Maude,' Anna said.

Before I could respond, Bill approached us. He was wearing a train conductor's outfit, with a wooden whistle in one hand and a pocket watch in the other. Maude was right, he had put on a substantial amount of weight.

'Ivy, you're late.' He looked at Anna. 'And who is this?'

'This is my sister, Anna,' I said, 'and her daughter, Eleanor.'

Bill cast a critical eye over Anna. 'I don't have a ticket for Anna,' he said.

'A ticket for what?'

'The train! It's leaving in seven minutes, we must hurry.'

'Why don't you sit down?' Maude said. 'We can get the next train.'

'I suppose we could catch the three forty-two,' he said, looking at his pocket watch.

'Bill, I've got something for you,' I said.

I got out the gift bag and handed it to him.

'What on earth is this?' he asked.

'It's a tea towel, and that's Princess Diana.'

'I know full well who she is, but why on earth do you have this on your person?'

'Maude said you were a fan. I thought you'd like it.'

'Fan! I'm absolutely nothing of the sort. I was always on Camilla's side.'

Maude looked at me and begged me to leave it.

'I'm sorry, Bill,' I said. 'I must have gotten the wrong end of the stick.'

He held the tea towel close to his chest.

'I suppose the gesture is rather kind,' he said. 'And it would look good in my collection. Fine. I'll take it.'

He took off his hat, bowed and started walking backwards into the kitchen.

'Where are the scones?' he shouted. 'For goodness' sakes, people, this is meant to be a tea party!'

Anna and I looked at Maude and we all laughed as Eleanor tried to eat Maude's necklace. For a moment, I forgot what we were talking about.

41

I walked into Dawn's office at UCL. There were all sorts of gym paraphernalia lying around the room, and she was drinking a vanilla-coloured protein shake.

'What's all this?' I asked.

'The weights? I'm fifty this year, Ivy, everything's about to sag.'

I read today's slogan tee: 'When others quit, I get going'.

'What are you doing for the big five-O?' I asked, sitting down.

'Me and the girls are going to Vegas.'

'Wow, you are full of surprises, Dawn.'

'Do you lift?'

'Lift what?'

'These,' she said, lifting a dumbbell above her head.

'No. I haven't been to the gym in decades.'

'You came in wearing your joggers last week?'

'I'd run out of clean clothes.'

She shook her head at me.

'Bad joke,' I said. 'So, Vegas?'

'This isn't about me. How is school? You've only got a couple of weeks left of this placement.'

'I think I'm in love with Mrs Bell. Do you know she knows all the words to every children's book and song ever written? I'm in awe of her.'

'I knew you'd like her.'

'I do – very much.'

'Have you finished your application yet?'

'Almost. I took your feedback on board, for the personal statement. I made it a bit more . . . personal.'

She looked right at me as she inhaled on her vape.

'How are you feeling about it all?' she asked.

'You know what? I've done everything I can possibly do. I'm at peace with it now.'

'That's a healthy attitude.'

'If I don't get accepted for my NQT placement in September I will have a calamitous emotional breakdown, similar to, but not as bad as, the one I had two years ago. But we'll cross that bridge when we come to it.'

She smiled at me. 'Another joke, Ivy?'

'Sorry. I'll stop now.'

'Do you remember back in November, when we talked about the importance of finding your voice in the classroom?' she said.

I nodded.

'What do you think of that now?' she asked.

I sat back and reflected on the question for a moment.

'I've worked really hard at building relationships with the children,' I said. 'I think I've got better at recognising the warning signs.'

'Where do you think that's come from?'

'Watching Mr Reid and Mrs Bell, reading a million and one books. Learning to listen, instead of reacting when they're stressed or frustrated.'

'I think, at the start of this, your problem wasn't a desire to learn. It was confidence.'

'That sounds about right.'

'What I admire about you, Ivy, is that you've taken control

of your self-confidence. You've taken actions to improve it and look where you are now.'

'Where am I?'

'You're a person who is worthy of respect. You have an inner self-belief, a quiet confidence that makes the children feel safe in your presence.'

'Thank you.'

'This is a gift, Ivy. Now you've got that confidence, don't lose it. Listen to that inner voice, let it guide you in the pursuit of happiness.'

'I feel like I'm in therapy.'

'Maybe you should be in therapy.'

It wasn't such a bad idea.

She got up from her seat. 'Right, it's almost time for my PT session.'

'Thank you, for what you said.'

She shook my hand. 'Never be anything less than magnificent, Ivy.'

As soon as I was out of the room, I found a bin and threw my cigarettes in. Then I got my phone out and called Mia.

'I'm sorry I've not seen you since brunch,' I said.

'I'm sorry for being so selfish.'

'I need you to be more respectful of where I am in my life. Sometimes you make me feel like I've chosen my job – and Scott – over you.'

'God, I'm sorry.'

'I know things are different but that's a good thing, in my eyes.'

'It is good. I'm needy and spoilt, and you know I hate change. I'm sorry, Ivy.'

'No, I'm sorry. I should've told you this ages ago. I'm trying to be more honest.'

'I'm all for that. You know I always want you to tell me when I'm being a dickhead.'

'OK. Well, you've been a bit of a dickhead.'

'We're growing up, aren't we?'

'We are.'

'Did you like the Mariah Carey gifs I sent you?'

'They were inspired.'

'What are you doing tonight?'

'That's why I called. Do you fancy going to an art class with me?'

'I'll do anything you want me to do, Ivy.'

'Good, it starts at seven, I'll send you the address.'

'Can't wait.'

'Just so you know, Mia, we're not going "out out".'

'Wouldn't dream of it.'

'And don't offer me any cigarettes.'

'Noted.'

'I love you, Mia.'

'I love you, too.'

*

I got out of bed at 6 a.m., shaved all the areas that hadn't seen the light of day for three weeks, and tried to do an hour of mindfulness. I lasted two minutes before I gave up and put on *Friends*. There's only so much self-improvement I can handle in one week.

When I heard the knock on the door, I leapt up from the sofa and ran to let him in. Despite the ten-hour flight, his face was glowing from the Californian sunshine. He looked like he'd been on one of those luxury fitness retreats, whereas I looked like I'd been driving an open-top car in gale-force winds. Mam had tried to get me to buy a specific shampoo for my hair type, but I'd argued that it was reasonable for someone to just buy regular shampoo, not shampoo for dry hair that's flyaway and often victimised by split ends. She said I was deluded, and as that morning demonstrated, she was right.

'You've never looked better,' I said.

'I've missed you so much.'

'Me too. You must be shattered; did you get any sleep on the plane?'

'Not really. I feel a bit out of it.'

'Do you want to have a nap?'

'Not just yet.'

He led me to the bedroom and we did what I'd been longing to do for the past three weeks.

Afterwards, I left him in bed whilst I got started on our roast dinner. I went back in two hours later to find him awake, on his phone. He didn't even look up when I walked in.

'I'm making roast lamb,' I said, sitting beside him on the bed. 'With duck fat potatoes, your favourite.'

He didn't say anything.

'Are you coming next door?' I asked.

'In a minute. I need to finish this message.'

I couldn't shake the feeling that something wasn't right. I walked into the other room and poured myself a glass of wine. I drank it quickly and poured another.

Scott came up behind me. 'Can I get one of those too, please?'

It seemed we both needed a little something to take the edge off.

'That was my boss on the phone,' he said.

'Is everything OK?'

'She wants me to come in early tomorrow morning to chat about the trip.'

I looked at his face, and I knew.

'You loved it over there, didn't you?' I said.

'It's incredible, Ivy. The beaches, the food – the weather. It's better than I remembered. It's perfect.'

Perfect? How is being six thousand miles away from your family and your girlfriend perfect? I wanted to hit something.

'You lied to me,' I said.

'What? How?'

'You said we had options – that was a lie. I said I was fine with you going to LA – that was also a lie.'

'We do have options. I want us to go there together.'

'What?'

'They want me out there as soon as possible.'

'Are you serious? What about my job? I haven't even finished my first year of training.'

'You could finish your training, then you could move out to LA, in the summer. I've started looking at teacher programmes for you.'

I'd been telling Scott how proud I was of myself for how far I'd come. How I finally belonged somewhere, somewhere where I had a purpose. How had that translated into, 'I want to move to another continent?'

'When did you do that?' I asked.

'When they offered me the job. You said you didn't feel at home in London; well, I want you to build a new home, with me.'

He was looking at me with such hope in his eyes, but a fire had ignited inside me, and there was no way of controlling it.

'What about my interviews for next year's placement?'

'You might not get accepted. Who knows what could happen?'

I tried not to be offended by this. He should have said, 'Of course you'll pass your first year of training. Of course you'll get accepted for next year's placement. You can do anything because you're amazing and I believe in you.' But he didn't, and I stood there struggling to shake the feeling that he hadn't considered my future in any of this.

'You can apply for training schemes in LA. We could live on a beach – you've always wanted to live on a beach.'

'Yeah, but ideally somewhere a bit closer to home.'

'It would be a perfect place to raise a family.'

When had he turned into Jamie?

'We've never even discussed where we'd want to raise a family,' I said.

'I'm discussing it with you now. You've said more than once that you don't feel at home here.'

'But that was before … What about my life? I can't pack it all in.'

'I want you to think about it, please. That's all I'm asking. I said before I went that we could look at our options together. I want to do this together.'

Nothing about this conversation felt very 'together'.

42

I was standing by the entrance to school, inhaling a bag of jelly babies, with Mam on the other end of the phone.

'I called you four times last night,' she said. 'Where were you?'

'I was with Scott.'

'How is he? Did he miss me? How was *Unol Daleithiau America*?'

'I take it that means America?'

'Darling, did you pay any attention in school? This is God's language, *mun*.'

'You're morphing into Gramps.'

'I miss him very much this week. I had a little row with Linda yesterday. I'll never know why he had it in for her, but then again, he was a fattist.'

'What did you do this time?'

'You know her son, Lewis? With the overweight fiancée? Well, she's got herself pregnant, so now Linda is organising the baby shower and the wedding. I said I would help, but she said I steamroll. I said me, steamroll? You're the one who wanted to put bows on the chairs at the Alien Hand Syndrome gala. I mean really, Ivy. What sort of person puts bows on chairs?'

She started off again before I could muster a suitable response.

'To cut a long story short, I ended up calling her cheap, and now she's refusing to speak to me.'

'Do you want me to teach you some of the conflict resolution strategies I'm working on with the children?'

'If she's not speaking to me by next weekend, you might have to. Anyway, tell me about Scott. It must be lovely having him home.'

'It's fine. It's good.'

'Can you diversify your vocabulary, please? You're meant to be inspiring the next generation.'

'Sorry, I couldn't sleep last night so I made Layla a blanket for her bunny. I was up till two a.m. sewing the bloody thing.'

'My darling, you're such a visionary.'

'It looks like a homeless person's handkerchief, but at least I tried.'

'All you can do is try. Back to Scott. I hope you put on some fancy underwear and new lippy for his arrival.'

'I'm hanging up now, Mam. Love you.'

'See you on Saturday, darling. I can't wait.'

That morning, we went to the Roald Dahl exhibition at the British Library. I thought having a conversation with Scott about the future of our relationship was going to be the hardest thing I did that week. I was wrong.

It took over an hour to get everyone onto the bus, during which time I got kneed in the stomach and pushed into the sandpit. Questions on the journey included, but weren't exclusive to:

'Why can't I eat soil?'

'What do boobies look like on the inside?'

'Why do you pee from your bum?'

When I asked Kobe to stop jumping on his seat, he told me to, 'Have a biscuit and calm down.'

If only it were that simple.

I sat down beside Layla and put on my most convincing fake smile. I had fake-smiled so many times that week that my face felt like it had severe windburn.

The children were euphoric as we walked into the exhibition hall. It reminded me of that feeling you get when you first hit the dance floor on a night out, minus the illegal stimulants. There was a giant beanstalk erected in the centre of the room, with a gigantic puppet of Jack hanging from the top. Mrs Bell and I sat the children down with their snacks and a man dressed as the BFG came out and started to read to the room. The children were mesmerised as they gathered around the front of the stage, lying on their stomachs with their chins on their fists. Mrs Bell joined them on the floor and I watched her mouth move as she silently recited all the words. For the next half hour, they were blissfully quiet.

I took a seat at the back of the hall and googled: 'Are children in LA well-behaved?' The first thing that came up was an article about underfunding and overcrowding. I then googled El Matador State Beach, in LA. Scott said he wanted to take me there; it had breathtaking views of the ocean and the sunset was meant to be the best on the West Coast. I scrolled through all the photos of Rhossili Bay on my phone, to compare them, but it was pouring with rain in every single one of them. Come to think of it, every day on the Gower is pouring with rain. I then googled rainfall in South Wales versus California but all I got were complicated graphs of precipitation weather trends. I ate the last of the jelly babies, by which time the show had finished, and it was time to put on my fake smile again.

I got home and opened my laptop, ready to get started on my next essay. After two minutes I went on Google and searched,

'What happens if the love of your life wants to move to LA, and you don't?' One hit read, 'I moved to LA and I hate it!' I slammed the laptop shut, vowed to never ask Google anything ever again, and lay face down on the bed. I grabbed the pillow beside me, put it over my head and screamed into it. Then I got up and poured myself a glass of wine.

By the time I got to bed that night, I'd finished the bottle. The 'self-medicating without alcohol' thing was going well.

Scott came over the next morning.

'We need to talk about LA before we see your family today.'

I sat beside him at the kitchen table.

'This is the happiest I've been in years,' I said.

'Me too. I love you so much, Ivy.'

'I know, which is why I'm a bit blindsided by this. We're happy here – in London. We have a great life together.'

'But you said you didn't feel attached to London.'

'I never said that. I said I didn't think of it as my proper home.'

'Exactly.'

'But that's only because Wales is my home.'

'You've not lived in Wales for years.'

'That's not the point.'

'What is the point? This massive opportunity has come along, and you won't even consider it.'

'You keep saying massive opportunity, but what does that even mean? It's more money and a nice relocation package, but is that it?'

'It would be an adventure for us.'

'I don't want an adventure, I want to keep my life here. My family are here—'

'Your family do your head in.'

'Everyone's family does their head in!'

It was unfathomable to me that he didn't get this. How

could I leave my mother when she'd only just lost Gramps? What would I do without Anna? I'd miss so many milestones with Eleanor, and all because my boyfriend liked white sand and cucumber juices. He might have wanted this, but what about what I wanted? What about the life I was trying to build for myself in London? Didn't that matter?

'You keep thinking about the negatives,' he said. 'You need to open your mind to how great it could be.'

There was a low-level river of rage running through me. I thought I was articulating myself, so how come it felt like we were on different planets?

'Can we keep up appearances in front of my parents, please? I haven't told them about LA, and I don't want to bring it up on Anna's birthday.'

'Whatever you want, Ivy.'

Mam and Dad had arrived that morning and decorated Anna's house with balloons, bunting and banners. At least on this occasion, there was actual reason to celebrate.

'Why is Eleanor refusing to nap?' Anna said. 'Doesn't she know it's my big day?'

'Anna, she's a baby. You can't control her,' Mam said.

'Last week you were telling me I needed more of a routine.'

'Was I?'

Anna raised an eyebrow.

'I am sorry for interfering,' Mam said. 'You do whatever's best for you, darling.'

'She's lucky she's so cute,' Anna said, putting Eleanor in the Jumperoo. 'She's much prettier than any of the other babies in our NCT group.'

'Don't hold back,' I said.

'Ivy, you have no idea. Some people have such unfortunate-looking children,' Mam said.

'So, we've been talking more about Center Parcs,' Anna said. 'I'm keen to get it booked.'

'I won't say this again,' Mam said. 'Over my dead body am I going to Center Parcs.'

'Listen to this review,' Anna said, grabbing a copy of the *Guardian*.

Mam had walked into the house before Anna could even open her mouth.

'You'll never win her over,' I said.

Mam came back out with a bottle of champagne.

'Tony, help me open this, please?'

'Mags, is there an occasion that doesn't require champagne?'

'It's Anna's birthday!'

'Don't worry,' Mark said, 'I bought this one.'

'Tony, I was thinking we should go to LA,' Mam said. 'We could do a little road trip. We could rent one of those cars they had in *Thelma and Louise*. Oh my God, imagine if we met Brad Pitt!'

I picked Eleanor up, and she giggled as I kissed her dimpled hands.

'She hates it when I do that,' Anna said.

'That's because I'm her favourite,' I said.

'I think you are. Mark's worried her first word is going to be Ivy.'

Mark pulled a face and I laughed. I felt Scott's eyes on me.

'Darlings, when are you coming to Wales?' Mam asked.

'I'm back at Clerkenwell next week, but hopefully half term?' I said.

'I'll do an itinerary. We'll show you the true Cymru, Scott. The Gower is full of English people these days, but don't you worry, I know where all the Welsh hide out.'

Scott smiled, an expression I'd not seen on him since before New Year's. I got up and kissed him. When our lips parted,

I sat down on his lap, and we both held on to each other for dear life.

Later that afternoon, Mia arrived. She ran in wearing denim hot pants and a green crochet top that left little to the imagination. She was wearing Noah's dead aunt's cowboy boots – the ones she'd tried to pawn off on me for my first date with Scott.

'Anna! *Penblwydd hapus*!' she said, sashaying into the room.

'Terrific pronunciation,' Mam said, as she fawned over her outfit.

'Aren't you cold?' I asked.

'It's spring.'

'It's February.'

'How's your birthday been, Anna? Did Mark spoil you?' Mia asked.

'Well, Mark took Eleanor this morning, so I went back to bed and slept till nine, which was the dream. Then Mam arrived, and I lost the will to live.'

'How's wedding planning?' Mam asked Mia.

'I'm glad you brought it up. I've been thinking about my hen.'

'Oh, God. What now?' I said.

'Why don't we go to Ibiza?'

'No.'

'No?'

'Way too expensive. We've already decided on a budget.'

'But it's my big day. What about what I want?'

'Do you want to plan your own hen do? Because you're doing my head in.'

'Ivy, darling, don't be like that.'

'Mia, it would be a privilege to plan your hen,' Mam said.

'Don't listen to her,' I said to Mia. 'Listen to me, I'm going to be honest with you, OK?'

'Of course, transparency is the cornerstone to every good relationship.'

'You're being spoilt, demanding and ungrateful.'

'I don't see what the problem is. I just need you to re-create Glastonbury, in Ibiza, on a budget.'

Everyone laughed as Mia stood there looking exasperated.

I looked to Scott, who was doing his best to smile. I wonder if he felt like he had windburn, too.

43

We walked home from Anna's in silence. It wasn't until we were inside the flat that I spoke.

'I can't come to LA with you.'

His face went grey.

'I'm not prepared to lose you,' he said.

'Good, because neither am I.'

I knew that our only option was long distance – something I told myself I'd never do. I'd tried it once with a boy at university; there was only sixty miles between us and we still couldn't make it work. That was probably down to the fact that he spent most of his weekends with the University Viking Society, re-enacting traditional Viking games whilst clad in armour. To think he'd been one of the good ones.

'If you don't go to LA now, you will always wonder what if. And if you stay, you'll blame me.'

'I could never blame you.'

'I don't want to argue about this.'

He looked me dead in the eye, and I knew what was coming.

'I want us to try long distance,' he said.

I knew he believed we could make it work. I'm not sure what desire was greater – taking up a new opportunity on the West

Coast of America, or being with me – but it didn't matter. Or maybe it did, and I didn't want to face up to it.

'I can't have you ringing me every morning drunk. We need to have proper conversations – sober.'

'We will. I'm sorry I was so crap when I was out there, I was overwhelmed with the job and the new schedule and I wasn't thinking straight. It won't be like that this time. I've got flight allowance as part of the package, so I'll come back before summer, then again once school's finished.'

'Maybe I could come out and stay with you over summer?'

'I'd love that, Ivy. That would be perfect.'

I wanted to ask what would happen after summer, but he was so excited that I kept my mouth shut. He'd been despondent for weeks, but now there was a plan, and I owed it to him to give it my all.

*

There were several times over the next couple of weeks where I almost called the whole thing off. I'd be sitting in the classroom, looking at Google maps on my phone, and there'd be a sharp pain in my chest. I thought Wales was far, but California is a different ballgame, and I had no idea how we were going to make it work.

We had lunch with Anna, Mark and Eleanor; took his mum to the theatre; drank too much at Mr Reid and Mel's gig and almost fell into the canal walking home. We took the train to Margate and ate dozens of oysters; we scored weed off an elderly Scouser in Brixton and got stoned watching *Singin' in the Rain*. We walked for hours across Richmond Park; we pretended we were house-hunting in West Hampstead, stopping locals in the street and asking whether the neighbourhood was safe enough to raise a young family. We had countless arguments, followed by a lot of angry sex. It was the best fortnight of my life.

I was woken by Scott's alarm.

'I'm not going,' he said.

'Who said anything about going? I'm going to get up, put the kettle on, and try not to think about smoking any cigarettes.'

'You've already bought a new packet, haven't you? You couldn't even wait until I was on my way to the airport.'

'I won't touch them until after lunch, which I should be given credit for, given the circumstances.'

He kissed me. Everything felt heavy.

'You're the most beautiful woman in the world, Miss Edwards.'

'Where did you come from?'

'Same place you did.'

Half an hour later, the taxi driver arrived.

'We'll be together again in no time,' he said.

'I know we will.'

We kissed goodbye. I couldn't let go of him.

*

The tingling sensation on my lip had morphed into the world's largest cold sore, which had since taken over my face, and I was at breaking point. I called Dan on FaceTime for a crisis summit.

'The trouble is, every time you talk, it bleeds. Can you do your interview without speaking?'

'No, Daniel. Verbal communication is a key part of the process.'

'That's unfortunate.'

I took a sip from my orange squash and winced. I had to drink through a straw because it throbbed every time the glass touched my lip.

'It's like you had a spot,' Dan said, 'and that spot made ten new friends, and all the friends had babies at the exact same time, and then they moved into a house together, and that house is your face.'

'Fuck. Of all the fucking days. I've got to go, I need to do final prep for tomorrow.'

'Before you go, have you given any more thought to Barcelona?' he said. 'We'll take a box of wine for the trip; it'll be just like the good old days.'

'Those weren't the good old days, and I thought you were broke?'

'I'm saving money by getting the coach.'

'Dan, it's three hours to Dover, two hours on the ferry across the channel, three hours to Paris, a seven-hour stopover then fifteen hours to Barcelona. That's not an appealing journey.'

'Who's going to come with me? I can't take Alejandro.'

'Just break up with him for good.'

'I can't. He's four minorities rolled into one.'

'Do you know what "minority" means?'

'Yes, he's Venezuelan, he's gay, he's got that lisp thing going on and he lives in South London.'

'Can you hear yourself speak?'

'Also, your new vibrator will be arriving tomorrow.'

'Why did you buy me a vibrator?'

'Because you're miserable.'

'I'm not miserable – I'm readjusting. It's only been a month.'

'Has he booked his flight back yet?'

'He's not sure if he can come back for Easter.'

'That's bullshit, why?'

'It's only been a month – he's worried it'll look bad.'

Dan made a face.

'He's got to do what's right for him,' I said. 'It's important that he makes a good impression. He's only been there a month.'

'How many times are you going to mention the fact that it's been a month?'

'Stop it. I'm fine. I'm hopeful. I'm optimistic, I'm jazzy.'

'Jazzy? You're doing much better than last time at least, I'll give you that. But then again that's not anything to go by, is it?'

'What are you talking about? I've never been in a relationship with someone who lives on another continent!'

'I just meant with Jamie and the disastrous way you handled everything.'

'As ever, it's been an absolute delight talking to you.'

'Hang on, I need to say something.'

'Oh, God. What is it?'

'You know how Mia always goes on about warrior women? Well, I think you're a warrior. Not just a warrior, but a fucking warrior queen.'

'Wow, thank you.'

'I wish I could be more like you – you're strong and gutsy and your hair's in excellent condition these days.'

'Are you high?'

'Fuck off!'

'Thank you, Dan. I caved and bought that shampoo Mam was on about.'

'Mags always knows best. Now go take care of that calamity on your face.'

I put the phone down and went back to interview prep, but it only lasted a minute before I was back on my phone again, checking Scott's Instagram.

There was a photo of him from the night before, sitting on the edge of a rooftop pool. I'd looked at it approximately seventy times that day. Everything about the photo incensed me. Firstly, he was drinking a cocktail and he doesn't even like cocktails, he thinks they're too sugary. Secondly, he was wearing a baseball cap and I've never seen him wear a baseball cap, let alone backwards. Also, his new friend Wilder was beside him, wearing a kiwi-lime Ralph Lauren polo shirt, doing the hang loose sign. I hated Wilder and everything about his grotesque American aesthetic. I hated the view of the ocean behind them, I hated the sunset, and I hated the fact that Scott looked like he was having the time of his fucking life.

'He's practically forgotten about you,' Dilys said.

I turned my phone off and threw it across the room. Then I tucked into my emergency stash of cigarettes.

44

'Tell me, Ivy, what made you want to be a teacher?'

I was sitting across from the headteacher of Clerkenwell Primary, Ms Symonds. I opened my mouth to speak, and that's when the scab on my cold sore split open, and I felt blood trickle down my chin. I licked my lip to try to stop the bleeding, but it was so painful to touch that I shuddered.

'Why don't we pause things for a moment,' Ms Symonds said.

'I'm so sorry,' I said, holding my hand to my mouth.

'Take all the time you need.'

I muttered the F-word several times as I speed-walked to the bathroom.

Ten minutes later, I was back in her office, with a small piece of tissue over the sore.

'Are we OK to proceed?' she asked.

'Absolutely,' I said.

'Do you mind me saying that there's a piece of tissue on your lip?'

'I'm aware, Ms Symonds, thank you.'

'Righto then, let's get started.'

I was walking to Anna's when Scott called.

'Ivy! I'm so sorry I didn't ring you this morning. I know it's not an excuse, but I was up late doing a client briefing, and I lost track of time.'

'You could've texted, Scott.'

'If we're going to go down that route, you said you'd message me before bed last night.'

I couldn't face another passive aggressive conversation about how crap we both were at communicating.

'Shit, sorry, Ivy, the cleaner's just come in. Can I ring you back?'

'I wanted to—'

He'd already gone.

I went straight to his Instagram account. I don't know why; I knew it would send me apoplectic. He'd been tagged in a photo with several co-workers. They were in their plush, pretentious office, sitting in extortionate-looking meeting chairs that were probably made from reclaimed materials found in the Amazon rainforest. The girl beside Scott was ridiculously good-looking; doe-eyed with fabulous short hair like Gwyneth Paltrow's in *Sliding Doors*. Nobody can pull that haircut off. Her chair was far too close to Scott's. They were sharing a box of sushi. I wanted to scream.

We'd spent the first week apart in a suspended honeymoon state. We had phone sex every day, watched *When Harry Met Sally* together and sent each other cute videos to wake up to. I knew deep down it couldn't last.

I could barely function at school. All my energy was zapped from trying to work out the logistics of when Scott and I were going to speak, and on what medium and how long for.

I was made to believe the statistics of long-distance relationships were encouraging.

Where the fuck were those statistics now?

The door to Anna's was slightly ajar. I walked in to find her standing on a yoga mat, doing tree pose in her underwear, with Eleanor beside her, sitting in her nappy, playing with a toy parrot.

'This is quite the tableau,' I said.

Anna lost her balance. 'Ives! You're early.'

'Is that what you do all day on your own? Naked yoga?'

I walked over to Eleanor and kissed her chubby tummy. She grabbed a chunk of my hair and put it in her mouth.

'Don't laugh but Mia was telling me about her power yoga—'

'Yeah, I know – she does it naked in the garden; we've discussed this.'

'Have you tried it? It's so empowering, Ivy. It awakens every cell in you.'

'I can't say I had that reaction.'

'You're not as receptive as I am though, are you? You need to be open to the experience. Sometimes you can be too judgemental.'

'How has this turned into a character assassination?'

'Tell me about the interview!'

'I smashed it.'

Anna fist-pumped the air and ran over to hug me.

'This calls for champagne,' she said. 'I think we have a bottle left over from my birthday.'

I picked Eleanor up from the floor and sat down with her on the sofa. My heart was racing. I closed my eyes and tried to catch my breath.

'What's your face doing?' Anna asked. 'What's wrong?'

My voice was lost in my throat.

She came to sit down beside me.

'Ivy, what is it? You can tell me anything.'

'I'm not happy.'

'What? Why?'

'I keep reading blogs about how long distance makes your relationship better. But it's not making my relationship better, it's making it worse.'

'What's happened?'

'Every day I get up and I pretend this is what I want. But it's bullshit. I'm lying to myself.'

She went to get me a glass of water. 'Drink this,' she said.

'I came out of the interview today, confident I'd get the NQT position. I should've been elated, but all I could think about was my dying relationship.'

'But you've talked about the long-distance thing, right? About eventually living in the same place?'

'We've only discussed as far as summer.'

'Ah, I see. This doesn't feel like a champagne kind of conversation now.'

'But that's what annoys me – it is a champagne kind of conversation. This time last year I hadn't even sent off my application form yet – this is huge.'

'You're right, it is huge.'

My phone rang, it was Scott.

'I need to get this,' I said.

I handed Eleanor to her and went to sit in the kitchen.

'I'm sorry. You've got my full, undivided attention now, Ivy.'

'The interview went well.'

'I knew it would, I'm so proud of you.'

'Did you speak to your boss about when you might be able to come home?'

'It looks like I can't come back until half term.'

'In May?'

'I have to fly to San Diego for a meeting, so I'll come the weekend after.'

'But I'll be back in school then, we won't have any quality time together.'

'I know, it's shit. I don't have a choice.'

I heard Anna pop the champagne in the other room.

'I need to go,' I said. 'I'm at Anna's.'

'Oh, OK. That was quick. How's she doing? How's Eleanor?'

'They're great. They send their love.'

'I really miss you.'

'I really miss you, too.'

I walked back into the living room. I looked at Eleanor naked on the sofa, eating a Babybel, and at Anna pouring champagne in her underwear. There was no way I could ever leave them.

'Tell me what to do, Anna. I love him, but we cannot do long distance. I'm walking around like a fucking zombie every day, I can't focus, and I'm so anxious my bowels are in overdrive.'

'You know what we need to do,' she said. 'We need to make a list. You love a pros and cons list.'

She got a notepad and pen out from the drawer and handed it to me.

An hour later, and a bottle of champagne down, we had a list.

REASONS WHY THINGS ARE JOIO:

He's the best person I've ever met
I love him
He's got superb hair

REASONS WHY THIS IS ABOUT TO GO TITS UP:

He loves LA
I hate LA
We're shit at long distance

'This isn't my best work,' I said.

'Do you really hate LA?'
'No, but I can't move there.'
'You're sure of that?'
'I'm absolutely sure of that.'

45

I was in the shower, trying to wash the sand off me; I'd spent the morning building an obstacle course in the sandpit with Jamar, and it felt like it was in every crevice.

I hadn't spoken to Scott in three days. He'd rung to tell me that a new client of his had 'Baby I Need Your Loving' as their ringtone. We reminisced about our first night out together in Stoke Newington, about the dated working men's club, and the ludicrous amount of hairspray in Shelley's hair. Afterwards, I tried to watch *Bridget Jones: The Edge of Reason*, but the truth of the matter is that I'm not someone who can watch a Richard Curtis film unless I'm blissfully, smugly, unaware-of-everyone-around-me loved-up. And the truth is, I wasn't.

I was conditioning my hair when I heard the door go. I ignored it. When I eventually got out of the shower, I heard it go again.

'I'll be there in a minute now,' I said, grabbing my towel.

I walked out of the bathroom and, standing there in the corridor, was Scott. He was wearing a white cotton T-shirt that clung to his body, showing off his bronzed forearms.

'Surprise, Ivy.'

I dropped my towel and ran to him. His hands clung to my back as we held each other.

'I don't understand,' I said. 'How did you get here?'

'I needed to see you.'

I held his face in my hands and kissed him.

'Thank you,' I said.

I looked down at my pasty, naked body. I had an unruly pubic bush, and my legs were covered in bruises from the children clambering over me at school.

'Why don't you sit down,' I said. 'I'll get dressed.'

I put on a pair of leggings and Gramps' rugby union hoodie and made us both a cup of tea. He sat on the sofa, his eyes fixed on the floor. I asked if he wanted to put the TV on, but he didn't respond.

I passed him the mug of tea and sat down next to him.

He looked at me with a feeble half-smile, and I knew. I knew that he knew, and he knew that I knew.

'You're never moving to LA, are you?' he said.

'No. And you don't want to come back here, do you?'

'I thought if you came out in the summer, see what life's like out there, you'd change your mind.'

I would never change my mind.

'I've taken an enormous leap of faith to get where I am today. I'm finally happy, Scott. I can't give that up.'

'I know how much you love working with Finn, but you can get another class. There'll always be another class.'

'You know it's more than that. You talked about us raising a family together, but how could I do that six thousand miles away from my family?'

'We can come back all the time. You can FaceTime.'

'That's not enough. I need to be able to pop home for the weekend and argue with Mam over absolutely nothing. I need to sit on the beach with Anna and talk about Gramps—'

'You've never been open to the possibility of moving. You won't even try.'

It occurred to me in that moment that all of this was on me. All the questions were about my willingness to move to LA rather than his willingness to make a go of things in London. If he really loved me, why wasn't he willing to stay? Why wasn't I enough?

'What do you want, Scott? You need to be honest with me.'

He paused for a second, his eyes lowered. When he spoke, his voice was so cracked, I could barely hear him.

'I want to make something of myself. I have aspirations too, you know?'

'I understand that, Scott.'

'This job, the money – I can support Mum, she wouldn't have to worry.'

'So, this is about money?'

'We lost everything when Dad left. I can't let that happen to us again.'

'But it won't happen again. You're not responsible for your parents; it's not up to you to fix things.'

I could feel the tears start to come. I looked up at the ceiling and tried to compose myself, but it was no use. Whatever I said wouldn't have made a difference. His mind was made up.

'I can't do this any more,' I said.

'I don't want this to be it.'

'And you think I do?'

I was shaking now. He took hold of me and I dissolved into him.

'These past few months . . . '

'I know,' he said. 'I love you, Ivy.'

'I love you, too. I'm sorry it's not enough.'

I let go of him and stood up. My face was soaked; I could barely breathe.

He got up and tried to hug me again, but I took a step back.

'You should go,' I said.

'I'm sorry.'

He placed my keys on the kitchen table, walked out of the room, and out of the front door.

'I'm sorry, too,' I said.

You go your whole life, and nobody touches you. You think they do, but then you meet one person and your life is changed for ever. I knew when I met Scott that he was going to be that person. Yet there we were, breaking up.

46

Amit's mother was picking him up from school early. I walked him out to meet her and wondered at her graceful physique as she strutted down the pavement and into the playground. She was wearing gold block-heeled sandals and a kaleidoscopic kantha-embroidered silk saree, with a fixed tie to one side, showing off her delicate waist.

'Hello, Ivy,' she said.

'Hello, Mrs Chowdhury.'

'Please, call me Rakhee.'

She turned to Amit. 'Why don't you go play on the slide while I talk to Miss Edwards?'

Amit did as he was told and ran off.

'I wanted to thank you,' she said.

'Thank me?'

'For being such a wonderful teacher to Amit this year. And for being so gracious . . . about Jamie.'

'We don't need to do this, Mrs—'

'Rakhee.'

'Sorry, Rakhee.'

'It wasn't until things had progressed between us that I became aware of your history.'

There was a drain beside me. I wanted to crawl into it and drown in the sewage below.

'You don't need to explain,' I said. 'It was a long time ago.'

'I wanted to ask if you'd feel comfortable with Jamie picking Amit up from school sometime, or doing the drop-off? Our nanny Kate is taking some time off.'

This was exactly the conversation I wanted to be having before my final formal observation.

'If it's too much then I can get someone else to do it.'

What on earth was I supposed to say to this?

'It's not too much,' I said. 'We're all adults.'

'Thank you, I appreciate it.'

She called Amit back over. 'Say goodbye to Miss Edwards.'

'Bye, Miss Edwards.'

'See you tomorrow, Amit.'

I watched them walk away. Amit turned back around and called my name.

'Yes?' I said.

'You're my favourite person in the whole world.'

I choked. All I could do was give a feeble wave.

Back in the classroom, the observing tutor had taken her seat at the front of the class. Mr Reid walked over to me and asked if I was all right.

'You look like you've seen a dead body.'

I refused to let Jamie affect me in the classroom. This was my space, my time. He wasn't welcome here.

'Nothing,' I said. 'Can we get started, please?'

'Remember, Ivy – you're an outstanding trainee. Don't think of the tutor, look at the children and their faces – let them give you courage.'

Thirty minutes went by. Primrose was whining at Sammy for touching her pencil. Beside her was Hakim, using a ruler to measure his bum cheeks, and then there was Mabel, making fart noises with her mouth. I watched as the tutor made notes.

I wasn't going to let it rattle me. I placed my middle finger and ring finger on my thumb, before raising the pointer finger and pinkie finger to the air.

'Everybody, eyes and ears to me, please,' I said.

The room fell quiet as the children made their own 'Quiet Coyotes' and held them up in the air. I looked to Mr Reid whose smile was as big as his face, and I knew I'd done it.

I thanked the class for listening and visualised the pint of gin I was going to sink when this was all over.

'It's fantastic to see someone so consistent with their praise and sanctions,' the tutor said. 'That takes real skill. Bravo, Ivy.'

I was about to respond when I heard a scream from the back of the room. I turned around and saw Horatio bent over Jamar. Before I could process what was happening, I heard Horatio retch, and thus began an onslaught of vomit all over Jamar's hair. In a split second, Mr Reid had run over to them, his 'Cleaning Bee' basket in tow. Beside me stood the tutor, holding her bag up to her face, attempting to shield herself from any airborne vomit. It could have been so perfect. I was so close.

The children had since vacated the room, and Mr Reid and I were on our hands and knees, scrubbing the floor in a desperate attempt to get rid of the putrid smell.

'It was the beetroot chocolate brownies. I shouldn't have let them eat so much.'

He looked at me with a furrowed brow. 'It did bring a whole new meaning to "Purple Rain".'

He opened a new bottle of bleach and emptied it into the mop bucket.

'You are just like Scott,' I said.

He put the mop down.

'Have you heard from him?' he asked.

'No. It's easier for us both if we don't speak.'

'And how's that going?'

'Well, it's been sixty-six days since I last saw him, and forty-three since we last spoke and whilst I'm dying on the inside, I think I've mastered the art of outward composure.'

'Ivy, I'm so sorry.'

'It's fine.'

'Don't say fine; fine's half-dead.'

I smiled. 'You remind me of my sister. Have I ever told you that?'

'I hope that's a good thing?'

'It's the highest of compliments.'

'I won't mention him again, I can see it upsets you.'

'He was meant to be flying back next weekend. I'm either going to get blind drunk or sit in my bedroom and cry for forty-eight hours.'

'Please tell me that was a joke?'

'Yes, it was a joke. My sister's taking me for a spa day.'

'I hate the spa, I don't like people touching me.'

I laughed. 'You're rather odd, aren't you, Finn?'

'You're one to talk.'

He put the Stones on Spotify and turned the music up loud. I watched him as he danced, using the mop as a microphone. It says a lot about my romantic life that I was considerably aroused by his senior moves.

'Can we call it a day now?' I said. 'It's cleaner than before the vomit.'

'You go, I need to do the desks one last time.'

'The cleaner's due in tonight.'

'You and I both know he doesn't do a deep-clean, not to my standard anyway.'

I started to pack my stuff away.

'Before you go,' he said, running over to his desk, 'I wanted to give you this.' He reached into his drawer and got out an envelope.

'What is it?' I asked.

I read the first line.

Dear Miss Edwards,

I am pleased to inform you

'We can't officially offer you the role until today's observation is written up,' Mr Reid said, 'but it's safe to say you're going to meet the teaching standards, and, when you do, you'll have another letter, an official one, to say that we'd love to have you back with us in September, for your NQT year.'

I threw my arms around him.

'I can't believe it, thank you.'

'You belong in a classroom, and we're honoured you've chosen ours.'

'I needed this so much, thank you.'

'You did this, Ivy. Remember that.'

I phoned Mam on the way home to tell her the news.

'My darling Ivy is officially a successful professional,' Mam said.

'I'm not officially anything yet, Mam.'

'Stop it, you're ruining my speech.'

'You have inspired, motivated and challenged,' she said. 'You have set the highest standards in the classroom. You have created a safe place for children to learn and grow and develop into the first-class citizens of tomorrow. You are taken seriously, but you're also seriously fun. We are so proud of you. *Rwy'n dy garu di.*'

'I love you, too,' I said. 'And thank you for the speech, it was quite something.'

'I thought of it last week in the shower. It was only a matter of time before they told you the good news, and I wanted to be ready.'

'Thank you, Mam. You're a natural orator.'

'You're my clever, clever angel. How do you feel?'

'Overwhelmed.'

'Don't do anything stupid to mess this up.'

'Like what?'

'Remember the stunt you pulled in sixth form.'

'Fair point.'

I wanted to ring Scott. There were so many times over the past two months that I'd reached for my phone to contact him. But I couldn't, so I'd have to smoke a cigarette or eat a sickening amount of carbs instead.

I saw him everywhere. I saw him on the number 55 bus, in our café on the canal, and in the shower talking to himself. I saw him waiting for me at the school gates when I finished late, when Mrs Alan complained about her husband being an awful cook, and every day in Mr Reid's sympathetic glances.

I hadn't checked his Instagram for a while, but that evening I went on his profile. There was a photo of him and his dad, leaning against a crimson Chevy convertible, with the Californian coast behind them. It was the first photo he'd uploaded in a couple of weeks. He captioned it with 'Recreating summer of 2005 with Pops.' There was a love heart emoji next to it. They looked so relaxed together.

'Don't write anything,' Dilys said. 'You'll only look desperate.'

I ignored her and wrote, 'Have the best time together x'.

I turned my phone off and went into the kitchen to get started on dinner – a lavish blow-your-socks-off three-course Italian extravaganza for one. Shortly after my break-up with Jamie, there was a disastrous incident involving Nigella Lawson's squid spaghetti, but not this time around. This time,

I was prepped. There would be no more meltdowns in supermarkets, and, whatever happened, I could not, and would not, go back to 99p microwavable rice. I got out the Parma ham, figs and burrata, and got to work on the starter.

47

'What are you going to do this summer, Miss?' asked Mabel.

'I'm going to go to Wales, and somewhere else I haven't decided on yet.'

'Will you fight any dragons?'

'Yes – my mother.'

Nancy charged at me and fell into a heap on the ground.

'Remember to keep your journals and paintings for me to see next term, OK?' I said to her.

'Why can't you be our teacher next year?' Nancy said.

'Because you're going up a year, and I'm staying with Mr Reid. But I'll still be here, so we can see each other.'

Nancy asked me to come down to her level. I crouched down beside her, and she whispered into my ear, 'You're my best friend, Miss Edwards.'

She wrapped her arms around my neck and I told her I loved her.

Nancy spotted her mother walking towards us and started spinning in circles.

'Mummy's going to have a baby and it'll explode from her belly button like a big rocket ship,' she said, before running off to play with the others.

'She's so excited to have a baby brother,' I said to Sharon.

'She'd be more excited if it was a girl. She asked me last week if she could give him away.'

We looked out to the children and I wondered what on earth I was going to do without them all summer.

'I bet you can't wait to get to LA,' Sharon said. 'When do you fly?'

'We broke up,' I said, stumbling over my words. 'It was four months ago . . . '

'Oh, God. I'm so sorry – I didn't know.'

'It's OK. He wanted to be in LA, I couldn't leave . . . '

My voice trailed off.

'I hope you already know this, but the children adore you. Nancy has a photo of the two of you beside her bed, when you both dressed up as Tigger.'

'Jesus, Sharon, I'm trying to hold it together over here.'

She went in for a hug.

'Thank you so much,' I said.

'No, thank you, Ivy.'

We said our goodbyes, and I made my way back inside.

'Is that the last of them?' Mary asked.

'It is. I need a stiff drink. Are you coming to the pub?'

'Finally! I've been gagging for a pinot blush since noon.'

Back in the classroom, Amit was sitting with Mr Reid.

'What are you still doing here?' I asked him.

'His nanny's running late,' Mr Reid said.

At that moment, Mary came into the classroom.

'Your carriage awaits, Amit,' she said.

Amit jumped off his chair and ran down the corridor. I followed him, wanting to say hello to Kate. But it wasn't Kate waiting for him in the playground, it was Jamie. I'd not seen him since Christmas, but of course he'd make a guest appearance on the last day of term.

He tussled Amit's hair.

'I'm sorry I'm late. I was picking Dad up—'

'You need to be on time for pick-ups; it's not fair on Amit – or us.'

'From hospital, Ivy. He had heart surgery.'

'Oh my God, how is he?'

'You know how William is, offensively stubborn. He needs a total rehaul of his diet, which hasn't gone down so well.'

'I'm so sorry.'

'Don't be sorry. We talked about you last week; I told him you were a teacher now. He always liked you, you know.'

I laughed. 'No, he didn't.'

'He did; he has a funny way of showing it, that's all.'

'How has your mum been?'

'She's on the aperitifs from three every day now, instead of five, so supper is a lively affair.'

'Ah, Cressida Langdon, what a woman.'

'Can we go now, Jamie?' Amit asked.

'Yes. Say goodbye to Miss Edwards.'

'I miss you already,' he said, clutching my leg.

'I miss you too, Amit.'

Amit was talking to me, but I couldn't register what he was saying. There was a man walking across the playground towards us.

'Scott?'

He'd grown a beard and his hair was wild. He looked a bit gaunt, like he'd been living in a cabin in the woods for several months.

'Hello, Ivy.'

He looked to Jamie, then to me.

'Hi, I'm Jamie,' he said, holding his hand out to shake Scott's.

Scott was stunned. They shook hands. An unbearable silence followed before Amit burped.

'Let's get you home, kiddo,' Jamie said.

'Goodbye, Ivy. Good to finally meet you, Scott.'

'Give your dad my love,' I said.

I watched them walk away, hand in hand across the playground – one of my favourite pupils, and the ex-fiancé who broke my heart.

I turned to Scott.

'What are you doing here?' I asked.

'I came to see you. What was Jamie doing here?'

'He was picking Amit up.'

His gaze was fixed on me. I studied the colours in his beard, the same colours as Mr Reid's. I wanted to reach my hand out and stroke it, but I was paralysed.

'I wanted to give you these,' he said, handing me a parcel wrapped in brown paper. 'You don't have to open it now. You can take it away, read them later.'

'Read them?'

'I wrote you . . .'

I peeked inside. There must have been over a hundred postcards in there.

'The thing is, Ivy,' he said, 'LA isn't that great after all. I don't like surfing. I couldn't find Camden pale ale anywhere. I hate Pilates, and everyone's an actor. You know Mia and Noah are the only actors I've ever liked. But the main problem was you.'

'Me?'

'You weren't there. I saw you everywhere. But you weren't there.'

My chin trembled. I bit my lip. There were a million things I wanted to say, but all I could do was stare at the warm greys in his beard.

'My dad helped me figure a few things out,' he said.

'I saw the photo of you together on Instagram – you

looked so content. I wanted you to know I was thinking of you.'

'I was thinking of you, too.'

He cleared his throat.

'I owe you an apology. I thought if I made enough money to support them, then maybe we could go back to being us again, as a family. But the truth is, they were never happy together, and nothing I can do will change that.'

'Scott—'

'I'm sorry. I'm sorry it took me so long to realise that no job or amount of money is worth losing you.'

'What does this mean? Are you back in London?'

'Yes. I missed you. I missed London. I needed to come home.'

I reached my hand out and touched his face.

'I'll lose the beard, if that's what it comes down to.'

I laughed. There was no point denying it. I was utterly in love with him.

I kissed him so hard he fell backwards. He enveloped me in a gigantic hug and I lost myself in his arms. He smelt like airplane food and instant coffee. He smelt like home.

Mary interrupted us.

'I take it you're not coming to the pub?' she said, shouting across the playground.

'Fancy a drink with everyone?' I asked Scott.

'Yes, I'd love that.'

'We'll see you there, Mary,' I shouted back at her.

'Good, you owe me that pinot blush,' she called back. 'Lovely to see you again, Scott. Fabulous beard, very lumberjack-chic.'

'Tell me the truth,' he said. 'What do you think?'

'You look like Tom Hanks in *Castaway*, and I'm really into it.'

'I want to start over,' he said.

He took his hand out to shake mine. 'Hi, I'm Scott.'
There was only one thing to do.
'I'm Ivy,' I said. 'Nice to meet you.'

*

REASONS THAT EVERYTHING IS OUT-OF-THIS-WORLD EXPLOSIVE-KNOCK-YOUR-SOCKS-OFF PHENOMENAL:

Lack of back fat
Scott
I know what I want to be

REASONS TO BE MISERABLE:

None (for now)

Acknowledgements

When I started writing this book, I was blissfully unaware that a global pandemic was right around the corner. Our lives have been turned upside down, but as I write this, I am more hopeful than ever, and that is largely down to the following extraordinary people.

To the Warrior Women that make up Team Ivy –

My agent Hayley, for your unflagging encouragement and invaluable advice. You are the best in the business and your trust, guidance and friendship mean the absolute world to me.

Emma, Sarah, Anna, Beth and Brionee at Little, Brown, for investing so much time and energy into my work. Thank you for your dedication and vision. How anyone is able to publish a book without you is beyond me.

To Frankie and Lyndsey, for being so generous and feeding me such heart-warming, hilarious tales of what it's like to be a teacher. Your pupils are so very lucky to have you.

To the Faber Academy Class of '18, for reading early drafts, and for all the spot-on suggestions that have helped make this book what it is. Freya, Vanessa and Lissa, I am forever indebted to you.

To the lovely readers, bloggers and bookstagrammers, who continue to shout about Ivy. It's such a joy to be part of your community and I am eternally grateful for your kindness and support.

To Judith, for letting me write in your beautiful garden, and for supplying me with all the leftover wedding wine to get me through the brutal edits.

To my wonderful pals, for the laughs and the shoulders to cry on (albeit over Zoom). I can't wait to drink endless martinis with you again (definitely *not* over Zoom).

To my family, I wouldn't be able to do any of this without you. I'm sorry I swear too much and throw too many tantrums. I love you so much and can't wait to squeeze you tight when this is all over.

To Philip, where did you come from? Thank you for always dancing in the kitchen with me. You really are the greatest human around.

Glossary

Athrawes: Female teacher
Bach: Small (Can also be used affectionately to address a person you love i.e.'Hello, *bach*')
Cwtch: Cuddle or hug (pronounced 'kutch'and literally translates to, 'a safe place'. Can also be spelt, '*Cwtsh*')
Da iawn: Very good
Dewch i mewn: Come in
Diolch yn fawr: Thank you very much ('*diolch yn fawr iawn*' can be used, too)
Joio: Lovely. Grand. OK. (Used to emphasise that you're content with the situation)
Mae hi'n bwrw hen wragedd a ffyn: It's raining cats and dogs
Mun: A word that doesn't mean anything, used to add emphasis to whatever you're saying.
Penblwydd hapus: Happy birthday
Pob lwc: Good luck
Prynhawn da: Good afternoon
Rwy'n dy garu di: I love you
Tamping: Livid
Twmffat: Idiot

Twp: An affectionate way to describe someone who's acting silly.
Unol Daleithiau America: United States of America
Ych-a-fi: Yuck/Ew/Gross!

Hannah Tovey is from South Wales and grew up in Hong Kong. She graduated from the Faber Academy in 2018, where she finished her debut novel, *The Education of Ivy Edwards.* Hannah lives in East London where she misses Llanelli beach, her mother and cockles.

Visit Hannah on Twitter: @hannahctovey

Also by Hannah Tovey

The Education of Ivy Edwards